The
Heart
of
Summer

The Heart of Summer

A Novel

Felicity Hayes-McCoy

HARPER PERENNIAL

NEW YORK • LONDON • TORONTO • SYDNEY • NEW DELHI • AUCKLAND

HARPER ⬤ PERENNIAL

Originally published in Ireland in 2020 by Hachette Books Ireland.

FIRST US EDITION
FIRST HARPER PERENNIAL EDITION PUBLISHED 2022.

Library of Congress Cataloging-in-Publication Data has been applied for.

ISBN 978-0-06-288954-6 (pbk.)
ISBN 978-0-06-324622-5 (library edition)

22 23 24 25 26   LSC   10 9 8 7 6 5 4 3 2 1

for Brownie

~ Life is for living ~

Visitors to the west coast of Ireland won't find Finfarran.
The peninsula, its inhabitants, and the characters
Hanna encounters in London exist only
in the author's imagination.

Chapter One

Hanna Casey looked up from her computer and was briefly enchanted by dust motes dancing in sunlight. Lissbeg Library was housed in what had once been the town's convent school. The dark hall where generations of girls had giggled and yawned through assemblies now had large windows at roof level and had been extended to make exhibition space and a reading room. Glazed cases set into oak panelling contained musty books left by the nuns, while the public collection stood in parallel rows on open-access shelves. Today, on a golden day at the heart of an Irish summer, shafts of sunlight flooded the steel shelving and glinted on gilded leather-bound books behind their glass doors.

From Hanna's seat at the reception desk, she could see Conor transferring returned items from a trolley to the shelves, handling them as deftly as he dealt with farm animals and machinery, and the occasional idiosyncrasies of the library's computer system. As the paperbacks, CDs, and DVDs disappeared into their places, she could hear him whistling cheerfully under his breath.

Hanna's desk, at the front of the hall, stood with its back to a glass wall that divided the panelled library from the state-of-the-art exhibition space. At the other end of the library was the staff loo and, beside it, a slip of a kitchen where she and Conor made coffee and hung their coats. Logging out, she left her desk and went to wash her hands. Conor looked up as she passed him. 'I'm nearly done here, Miss Casey. D'you want me to man the desk?'

Everyone else addressed her as Hanna, but Conor, her assistant, had begun volunteering in the library as a teenager, when her elderly predecessor had insisted on proper respect. Though now in his early twenties, the habit had stuck and, while Hanna hadn't the heart to object, there were times when it made her wonder what age he thought she was. Probably he never thought about it at all. He wasn't given to introspection and, between the library, his recent marriage, and work on the family farm, he wouldn't have time.

'When you've finished there you can take the desk. The cruise-ship crowd are coming at four, but that won't keep me more than an hour. I'll deal with those emails from Head Office when I'm done.'

'Right, so.'

Conor's part-time job involved taking the mobile library around the peninsula as well as helping Hanna in Lissbeg. Where work was concerned, he was efficient and reliable, although, as Orla, his mother, had once remarked to Hanna, when it came to people he often missed what was as plain as the nose on your face. 'God knows you couldn't get anyone kinder or more sensitive, but he's the world's worst for trying to fix things before finding out what's gone wrong. There was a time I thought we'd never get him married to poor Aideen at all.'

Hanna had known what she meant. The whole Finfarran

peninsula agreed that Conor and Aideen were made for each other, yet Aideen's natural diffidence and Conor's instinct to problem-solve had made for an engagement fraught with misunderstandings. In the end, after months of planning a double wedding with his brother, he'd discovered Aideen had hated that idea from the start, so they'd sneaked off and made their vows in a cypress grove in Florence. There'd been a registry-office wedding later when they'd returned from Italy apologetic and exhilarated, and Aideen was now living on the farm. It had occurred to Hanna to wonder if newlyweds sharing a home with the groom's parents might produce tensions, but Aideen appeared to get on brilliantly with Orla and Paddy, and she and Conor seemed blissfully happy in their new life together.

Standing at the washbasin, Hanna inspected her reflection in the mirror. For a woman who wouldn't see fifty again, she reckoned she looked okay. Sooner or later, she expected, she'd take her stylish daughter's advice and get her hair cut and highlighted but, for now, she was happy to wear it in a single short plait. She'd never gone in for makeup when she was younger and, having retained the clear skin she'd inherited from her mother, still used no more than a touch of mascara. Smoothing her dark hair back from her forehead, she washed her hands, pulling a face as drops of water splashed onto her T-shirt. The library loo didn't rise to an automatic hand-dryer and blotting the marks with a paper towel wouldn't help; still, the day was so hot that they'd soon be gone. It was silly to feel one's appearance mattered when giving a short talk to a bunch of tourists, but the representative of the cruise line that had transported them to Ireland had banged on so much about its high-end brand that she almost felt she should be wearing Gucci. Which, she told herself cheerfully, was tough.

They'd get her in jeans and a *Live, Love, Read!* T-shirt, and if they didn't like it that was their problem, not hers.

The Finfarran peninsula on Ireland's rugged west coast was a dream destination, marketed to visitors as 'The Edge of the World'. Most of its tourism centred on Ballyfin, a former fishing village at its westernmost point, overlooking the turquoise Atlantic. It was reached by a road that divided the southern and northern halves of the narrow peninsula and was known locally as 'the motorway'. One side of the foothills of a mountain range had been blasted to accommodate the last few miles of road, and what had been a sleepy port now had jetsetters strolling its streets, a spa hotel above a marina, and a string of restaurants where champagne and oysters were permanently on ice. The rest of Finfarran offered stunning landscapes, deserted beaches, boat trips, and B&B accommodation, while Lissbeg, once a market town, had shops, a bank, a post office, and the Old Convent Centre, now owned by Finfarran's county council. As well as Hanna's library, the centre contained offices, low-rent studios and workshops, and a public space that had once been the nuns' garden, where the Garden Café was a favourite haunt of locals as well as tourists.

Ballyfin's marina was too shallow for ocean liners, but smaller cruise ships regularly moored there. They carried what the tour operators referred to as 'discerning groups of culturally curious travellers'. Often middle-aged, these were always wealthy, though that was never expressly stated in the shiny brochures. Initially, Ballyfin had offered no more than a stopover at the Spa Hotel and a coach trip to the county town of Carrick, for photos and shopping. Then a US cruise line called Your World Awaits had spotted the hidden potential in Lissbeg Library, where the exhibition space displayed a manuscript known as the Carrick Psalter. The psalter had been gifted by Charles Aukin, a retired American banker with family links to Finfarran, who had also paid for the library's renovations. This was gold dust for Your World Awaits. What could be more attractive to the culturally curious than a medieval treasure tucked away in a little local library? There was, however, one problem. The cruise line announced that its clients required exclusivity. They wouldn't wish to join the long summer queues for talks given by volunteers from the local history society. What was wanted was a private showing by the librarian.

Hanna hadn't been impressed. To her mind, private viewings were inappropriate in a public library, but the offer of a hefty fee had convinced the county council, so she'd had no choice in the matter. Today's talk would be the third she'd given to a group from Your World Awaits, and she'd had to admit that, for the most part, they'd been genuinely interested. The manuscript had been digitised and the exhibition had interactive screens that allowed visitors to zoom in on details and to access translations of the text in six languages. Normally, Hanna turned one page of the psalter a month, but a special page-turn per private showing had been part of the deal. Though this offended her further, it secretly delighted her as well. Turning the pages always sent a tingle down her spine, giving her a sense of being in touch with the skilled hands that had made it, and those that had kept it safe for a thousand years. She'd studied the manuscript and been part of its digitisation process, yet the moments when she handled it still felt magical, and always it revealed something new. A previously unseen bird or grotesque face would look out through fantastic foliage, a line of text would wander down a page, like the steps of a celestial staircase, or a city would appear within the curves of an illuminated letter.

With her latest group gathered around her, she opened the psalter's display case. About the size of a novel you'd buy in an airport, the book's Latin text had illuminated capitals in inks and paints that were still as bright as they had been on the day they'd been ground in the medieval scriptorium. Looking at the open double-page spread, Hanna smiled in recognition. The original psalmists had lived and worked a world away from Finfarran but the psalter's illustrators had been inspired by their own peninsula. Here was the mountain range she crossed when she drove the back roads to Ballyfin. The familiar peaks and passes appeared within the first capital letter, while spears of gold and green darted down both margins, shot from a rising sun and a crescent moon. Hanna stood back as the group craned to see. 'There'll be plenty of time for everyone to look at the text closely. Please remember, though, that it mustn't be touched.'

The culturally curious, most of whom were women, tutted, registering horror at the thought. Mentally noting the most outraged, who were also most likely to try to touch the book if she turned her back, Hanna explained about the interactive screens. 'And now I'm going to turn the page and reveal a new psalm.' She reached out and paused, anticipating a question, which came, as if on cue, from a tall man with a goatee and glasses. 'Surely you ought to be wearing white gloves.'

'That's a common misconception.' Not wanting to put him down, Hanna gave him a friendly smile. 'Wearing gloves actually increases the likelihood of damage. Plus they have a tendency to transfer dirt and dislodge inks and pigments. Using clean, dry hands is best practice.'

It was evident that he didn't believe her but she didn't wait to argue. Instead she turned the page, producing a mass intake of breath. One of the pleasures of the Carrick Psalter was its idiosyncrasies. The psalms appeared in random order and, in some cases, such as this, a single verse had inspired whole pages of detailed illustration. Hanna recognised it. 'It's psalm one, verse three. *"And he shall be like a tree planted by the rivers of water that bringeth forth his fruit in his season; his leaf also shall not wither, and whatsoever he doeth shall prosper."'*

Glowing between her hands was a series of little gem-like images, set in roundels. A gold-framed box enclosed the verse, around which the pages were covered with green, crimson, and ochre leaves, as if the viewer were looking down on a dense forest canopy. Among the leaves the roundels showed like little clearings in the forest, full of activity. Four monks, with their habits girded up, were felling trees and loading them onto a wagon. In another roundel a lady in dark robes and a wimple indicated to a servant in a blue jerkin where he should plant a tree. Elsewhere, boys lay on their backs eating apples from a basket, and in one clearing, where grain had been harvested, men wearing hoods and curly-toed boots were winnowing. The chaff had been rendered as tiny gold specks, and the men's hoods, like the servant's jerkin, were ultramarine, an intense blue, which, Hanna explained, was made of lapis lazuli.

'Where did it come from?'

'The mountains of Afghanistan.'

'Wow. How did it reach Ireland?'

'By sea. And before that by camel train across deserts. Ultramarine was one of the most expensive pigments you could get.'

'Do we know who the lady was?'

Hanna shook her head. 'We don't even know if she depicts a real person. It could be a portrait of an abbess, though. In some monasteries monks and nuns lived in separate buildings and shared a church, and we know that nuns, as well as monks, painted manuscripts. Scientists found flecks of ultramarine lodged in the teeth of a medieval nun who died in Germany. She would have licked the end of her paintbrush as she worked.'

There was a chorus of interest from most of the group and a dubious snort from the man with the goatee and glasses. Privately, Hanna wondered, for the first time, why whoever painted these pages had used such expensive pigment. Usually ultramarine was reserved for royalty, God, and saints, but here it appeared on labourers and a servant. Perhaps it was drawing the viewer's eye to the importance of the image expressed in the verse. The planters and the winnowers were the figures that mattered, not the lady giving the command. Bending closer, she noticed – again for the first time – that a gold thread, poured from a jug in the servant's hand, linked all the roundels, and as her eye followed it across the pages and down to the right-hand corner, she saw it was a stream of water running into a pool fringed with flowers. There was a starry sky above the pool and, dancing round it, a ring of forest creatures: squirrels, hares, deer, and rabbits, all with their heads thrown back, as if singing to the stars.

The tourists had spread out, some choosing to look at the screens before examining the psalter. Hanna drew back to give them space, knowing that after a while they'd want to ask questions. As she stood near the door, keeping a watchful eye on the display case, her mind had already turned to unanswered emails and to the dinner she planned to have that night with her daughter. Then a voice spoke behind her. 'Well, I said I wouldn't believe it till I saw you with my own eyes!' Hanna swung round. The woman who'd spoken was in her fifties, short, and expensively dressed. Stepping closer, she raised her neatly plucked eyebrows. 'So, Hanna Casey, this is where you've been hiding yourself all these years!'

Chapter Two

Half an hour later, back at her desk, Hanna was still flabbergasted. She could see Conor eyeing her, and decided she'd better compose herself before he thought something was wrong. Of course, she could simply mention what had just happened but, somehow, she felt she needed to process it first. It hadn't been earth shattering. All that had occurred was that she'd met someone she hadn't seen for years. No big deal and, actually, rather pleasant. Sitting down abruptly, Hanna bit her lip. The encounter had shaken her and she didn't quite know why.

Having sent Conor to tidy the kitchen, she looked at her list of emails, knowing she ought to clear them before the library closed at five thirty. Then she gave up. There was nothing in her inbox that couldn't wait till tomorrow and, right now, all she could think of was Amy. Despite the expensive clothes and the gamine haircut, Hanna had known her as soon as she'd seen her, though she'd never have recognised her from her voice. Thirty years ago, in the flat they'd shared with two other girls in London, Amy Costello's Wexford accent had been as thick as country butter. Now she sounded as cut-glass English as Hanna's ex-mother-in-law.

Closing her eyes, Hanna remembered the flat behind Paddington Station. It was on the fourth floor of a grubby Victorian terraced house, and had dark stairs covered with worn linoleum and a brick balcony outside the kitchen window. On summer weekends they'd sunbathed on the balcony, drinking Rioja from a box on a rickety table, while Diana Ross sang 'Endless Love' on a tinny transistor radio and the smells of the city reached them mixed with the scent of Ambre Solaire. Amy had been at secretarial school, Claire, from Cork, was training as a Norland nanny, and Lucy, who was English and older than the others, had worked as a sous-chef in an Italian restaurant. Hanna had come to London to take a course as an art librarian before fulfilling her dream of getting a job in a European gallery. The Louvre, perhaps, or the Rijksmuseum. Somewhere sexy and enviably exciting. Maybe not immediately, but ultimately. She'd been so certain of everything back then.

Her parents had been baffled by their only child's ambition, yet when she'd got her first job, in a local library in Dublin, Tom, her dad, had been proud as a dog with two tails. And, though she knew he'd hoped she'd come home and settle in Finfarran, he'd said he was delighted when she'd phoned with news of the offer of a place on the London course. Mary, her mother, had snatched the phone and told her she was daft. Hadn't her parents worked their fingers to the bone to build a solid business she could step into? Or was a post office and village shop not good enough for her ladyship? After what had sounded like a tussle, her mother had released the receiver, and Hanna had heard her father's gentle voice again. 'Don't be listening to your mam, pet. We're made up for you.' She'd known he was lying. She was an only child and, back then, people who relocated to London seldom returned home. It had saddened her to hurt him, but the truth was that no one could have stopped her. She was following a dream.

She'd been fourteen when her imagination was seized by a flyer for an art exhibition. Tucked into a library book she'd consulted for some school project, it showed a reproduction of an eighteenth-century oil painting. Standing at a horse's head, in front of a handsome manor house, was a young man in a tricorn hat, breeches, and an embroidered waistcoat, and in the open carriage to which the horse was harnessed, a woman in powdered curls and a quilted petticoat sat with a smiling toddler on her knee. For Hanna, raised by a querulous mother in a rural Irish village, it was a window into a world where people not much older than herself lived in gorgeous surroundings, apparently wrapped in domestic harmony. The colours and textures had mesmerised her, drawing her in as if she were listening to an exciting story. And, according to the flyer, you could go to places full of paintings like this.

That year, during the summer holidays, she cajoled her father into taking her to the National Gallery in Dublin, and by the time they emerged Hanna was hooked on art. Sister Benignus had already assured her she was useless with a paintbrush, but evidently people looked after this stuff, wrote the signs under the pictures, and created catalogues and leaflets, like the one she'd found in the book. She'd gone home with her mind in a whirl and later, when she discovered that big galleries had libraries, everything had fallen into place.

The London course was supposed to have been the last stepping stone to her dream. Lucy and Claire had been equally driven, full of plans for careers that would take them wherever they chose to go. Claire was determined to travel, while Lucy was focused on opening her own restaurant. But Amy had simply seen qualifications in terms of a decent pay packet. She'd planned to marry a man so rich and successful that she wouldn't have to bother with work at all. Though Hanna had liked her, she hadn't understood Amy's lack of ambition. Why look to a man to fulfil your dreams when you lived in the twentieth century and the whole world lay waiting at your feet?

Opening her eyes, she saw Conor hovering, wondering why she hadn't yet locked the door. It was past five thirty. As Hanna stood up, a woman approached, digging in her purse for her library card. Hanna swiped the books she carried and helped to stow them in her bag, smiling at a couple of browsers making their way to the door. As it closed behind them, Conor appeared, carrying his motorbike helmet. 'Is it okay if I hit the road, Miss Casey?'

'Of course. Go on, I'm sorry I've kept you late.'

'Not at all, you're grand.' He was twitching to leave but eager to show that he hadn't been inconvenienced. Hanna laughed and pushed him towards the door. 'Go on, go home to Aideen and put your feet up.'

'God, it's far from putting my feet up I'll be this evening. I've a rake of work to do on the farm while the weather stays fine. Chances are that Aideen will be asleep before I'm done.'

Ten minutes later, having set the alarm and locked up, Hanna edged her car into Broad Street, envying the ease with which Conor could weave through the traffic on his Vespa. He'd already be halfway home before she cleared the outskirts of Lissbeg. Idling behind the rush-hour cars and a battered red van, she found herself thinking again about Amy. They'd only had a moment to talk. Other members of the tour group had had questions, and almost before she'd replied they'd been chivvied off to their luxury coach, which would whisk them back to Ballyfin and an al fresco dinner. On the way to the exit Amy had caught Hanna's hand. 'What about lunch tomorrow? We're scheduled for a trip to Carrick but I could bunk off.' So that had been fixed.

Leaving Lissbeg and the motorway behind her, Hanna turned onto a country road, lowered her window, and drove at a steady speed, aware of the scent of summer drifting from the fields. Thirty years ago Amy had been ditzy. Now, though still petite and perky, she was full of languid assurance. Her deceptively simple linen shirt could have come from a boutique on Bond Street and, worn with leather espadrilles and scarlet tapered trousers, it went perfectly with the large straw bag she'd held under her arm. Her nails were buffed and her hair, a miracle of highlighting, had been blow-dried to support the sunglasses casually propped on her head. Instinctively, Hanna had glanced at the manicured left hand and observed a broad wedding ring and a stonking platinum-set marquise-cut diamond. Obviously, Amy had found her well-heeled man.

A farmer, who was wobbling along on a bicycle, emerged from a field driving a herd of cows. As she slowed to avoid spooking the animals, Hanna frowned at her mental use of the term 'well-heeled'. It was one she disliked and she'd no idea why it had sprung to mind. Then, as the cows' heavy hindquarters swayed down the road ahead, she remembered her mother using it. It was on the night of the call she'd made from a pay-phone in Paddington to tell her parents she'd got engaged. Mary had demanded the full story and, when it was told, had grunted and said that at least he was well-heeled. Tom had simply asked her if she was happy.

Hanna and the girls had met Malcolm Turner at Lucy's Italian restaurant, a place so posh that she'd never been there before. Claire and Amy had arranged the treat for her birthday, and Lucy, who'd been working, had wangled free *gelati* for their dessert. The platter, topped with sparklers, had been carried in by a waiter, and a couple of guys at a nearby table had clapped and sent them champagne. So, inevitably, the tables had joined up. That was the beginning. Within weeks Hanna had dropped her on/off boyfriend, was dating Malcolm exclusively, and had been invited to visit his parents in Kent. They drove down from London on a sunny Saturday morning. Louisa, his mother, met them in the large, square hallway where there was a fireplace with a carved overmantel and a bowl of scented lilies on the hearth. She'd taken Hanna to the morning room while Malcolm parked the car, and they'd sat in chintz-covered armchairs by an open French window. Hanna had liked Louisa at once. She was telling her about the fateful meeting in the restaurant when Malcolm came into the room and bent to kiss his mother's cheek. 'Fate? It was nothing of the sort. I saw her the moment she walked through the door and knew that I had to have her!'

That was Malcolm – arrogant, devastatingly attractive, and undeniably well-heeled. He'd proposed three months later and, helplessly in love, Hanna had accepted him. When she'd told the girls, Amy had announced that she might have to kill her. 'Honestly, Hanna, you're *such* a sneaky cow! Here's me, desperate to find a husband, and you, swanking around, all independent career woman. And you're only after bagging a bloody barrister for yourself! If you weren't one of my best friends, I'd swing for you.' They'd all fallen around laughing and Lucy had gone to open a bottle of wine. Hanna had followed, to carry the glasses, and stood by the open kitchen window from the noisy street. The hot air had made her choke and, for a moment, she'd felt faint.

The lowing cows ahead of Hanna's car ambled into their farmyard. After a mile or so, she turned down a side road that led towards the ocean. Her daughter had suggested they eat outdoors and, remembering the little tin table in the shade of a feathery ash tree, Hanna was looking forward to the meal. Time spent with Jazz hadn't always been easy. The spectacular breakup of her parents' marriage had angered and confused her in her teens, but she'd matured into a relaxed young woman, and Hanna had moved on from the shock that had ended her twenty-year marriage.

Jazz's present home had belonged to Hanna's great-aunt Maggie. Hanna, who'd inherited it, had lived there for several years after her divorce, and now it was providing a safe haven for yet another generation. Affordable rents were hard to find in Finfarran, and having a place of her own had made a huge difference to Jazz. Though, when Hanna had offered it to her, she'd been uncertain. 'Oh, Mum, are you sure?'

'Of course.'

'But you could let it. I mean, obviously I'd pay rent if I took it – but, with someone else, you could make an awful lot more than I can afford.'

'Most people willing to take a lease in the middle of nowhere would probably be eccentric or into growing funny tobacco. And tourists would only want it for a couple of nights at a time.'

It had proved to be an uncomplicated arrangement: Jazz paid a fair rent and, besides being happy to see her settled, Hanna was glad to have a tenant she could trust.

The house's clifftop setting above the Atlantic was idyllic and, as she parked by the familiar gate, she could feel her whole body relax. Then, as she opened the car door, she paused, suddenly realising why she'd been feeling edgy since Amy had turned up. Her hackles had risen when she'd been accused of hiding here in Finfarran, and that was because the joke was too near the truth. The fact was that, when things had gone wrong, she'd run home from London, feeling she'd every reason to hide her head. Because if she hadn't been fool enough to fall in love with Malcolm Turner, she wouldn't have walked away from her dream before it had even begun.

Chapter Three

There'd been a time when Hanna had wondered if Jazz would ever call Finfarran home. Born and raised in England, happy at school and with the life they'd led between their London house and a weekend cottage in Norfolk, Jazz had been freaked by her mother's abrupt return to Ireland, and had sulked for months when she'd found they weren't going back. And Malcolm, an arch-manipulator, had wrong-footed Hanna at every turn throughout the divorce. Having found him in bed with Tessa Carmichael, one of his colleagues, Hanna's first instinct had been to grab Jazz and leave; having nowhere else to go, she'd taken refuge in her widowed mother's cramped retirement bungalow. This had been a major tactical error. Though in the wrong, Malcolm had claimed the moral high ground and, when Hanna refused to return to him, had accused her of acting irresponsibly towards their daughter. To Hanna's horror, he'd also stolen a march by lying to Jazz. 'It's nobody's fault, sweetheart, just one of those things that happen. I guess you could say Mum and I fell out of love.'

If that hadn't been bad enough, Hanna had discovered, while

still in shock, that what she'd assumed was a fling was in fact a long-standing affair. So twenty years of her life had been revealed as no more than a sham. Lying awake in Mary's back room, she'd agonised about what to tell Jazz, who adored Malcolm, and, fearful of the effect of the truth on a volatile teenager, she'd decided not to contradict his version of events. Mary, who from the start had deplored Hanna's lack of strategic thinking, had announced over the kitchen table that she was stark, staring mad. 'One day that child will find out the kind of man her father is. And that's the day she'll discover her mother's a liar as well.'

It was true but, at the time, the course she'd chosen had seemed the lesser of two evils and, to Hanna's relief, things had worked themselves out. Though Jazz hadn't ceased to love Malcolm, she'd come to a shrewd awareness of her father's manipulation and, having uncovered what had actually happened, she'd realised he'd left Hanna stuck between a rock and a hard place. And with the unsentimental pragmatism that, ironically, she'd inherited from Malcolm, she'd dismissed Hanna's lingering sense of guilt. 'Truly, Mum, it's fine, you mustn't worry. What else could you have done? The bottom line is that you thought of me when Dad was only concerned to protect his own image. He couldn't bear his little daughter to see him as the bad guy. Which is totally pathetic, but that's how he is. He was the one who behaved irresponsibly. So let it go.'

But, for all her pragmatism, it hadn't been quite that simple. While the divorce had left Hanna prickly and wary of commitment, its effect on Jazz had been different. In her late teens, she'd vacillated between Lissbeg and London, constantly seeking stability and crashing in and out of a series of unhappy love affairs. But now she'd found a promising career in Finfarran and, living alone in Maggie's house, she was finally learning the pleasure of self-reliance.

As soon as Jazz had left school, Hanna had escaped from the bungalow to Maggie's house. At the time it was almost a ruin, with blind windows facing the ocean and a slate roof shattered by storms. It stood with its back to the one-track road that led to it, and its half-door opened directly onto a narrow field that sloped down to the cliff edge. In Maggie's day, the house had consisted of an earth-floored kitchen with a bedroom at one end, an open hearth at the other, and a sagging wash-house tacked on at the rear. Hanna and Fury O'Shea, her builder, had transformed it with a new roof and floors, a modern kitchen and a proper bathroom extension. She'd retained the open fire and kept the furniture simple, and Fury had refurbished Maggie's brass bedstead for her, then painted and restored the dresser that stood to one side of the chimney breast. So far, Jazz had made few changes, though Hanna had urged her to do whatever she liked. 'It's your home now, so put your mark on it.'

'What if you and Brian break up and you want to move back?'
'We won't.'

Hanna's certainty had made Jazz laugh. 'Oh, fair enough, Brian's a keeper. And any fool can see you're both wildly in love.'

That had been several months ago, when Hanna had moved in with Brian Morton, Finfarran's county architect. She could still scarcely believe her new-found happiness, or how deeply attached she'd become to the home they now shared. It was a house Brian had designed and built on the north side of the peninsula, in a river valley known as the Hag's Glen. At first Hanna had been unsure about committing to the move. It had been one thing to admit she was in love again and to know that their families and friends had accepted that she and Brian were a couple. Living together was far scarier. After years of being Malcolm Turner's wife and Jazz's mother, she'd rediscovered herself as Hanna Casey, and her little house on the cliff had been a symbol of her survival and proof that she could be happy on her own. So the thought of giving it up had felt colossal. The crunch had come when Brian had asked her to marry him and seen her shrink instinctively from his proposal. He'd stepped away, his face bleak with disappointment. Suddenly frightened of losing him, Hanna had grabbed his hand. 'I don't want to be married, I want to be happy. I want to be your love and live with you here in the Hag's Glen.' It was enough, she'd explained, to know that they'd be together. Marriage, which she associated with grief, guilt, and betrayal, belonged to a very different part of her life.

A gust of sea air hit Hanna as she came round the gable end of Maggie's house. Bracing herself against the wind, she threw back her head and breathed in deeply. Jazz, who'd heard the car approach, came to greet her. 'You look like a horse turned out to pasture!'

'That's pretty much how I feel after Lissbeg's traffic.'

'Oh, come on, Mum, it takes ten minutes to get through Lissbeg at rush-hour. Think of central London on a Friday afternoon.'

'True. Still, it's gorgeous to taste sea air again.'

'You've got a sea view from the Hag's Glen.'

'Only a glimpse from the roof, and we never get salt on the air. Well, only if there's a proper raging storm.'

'Shall we take a drink to the cliff and ease into our evening?'

The narrow field ran down to a wall, beyond which a grassy pathway followed the curve of the cliff: the path was only a few feet wide and the sheer drop to the waves below was breathtaking. On the far side of the stone wall there was a plank bench, its red paint blistered and worn by the force of the Atlantic gales. Carrying a bottle of wine and a couple of glasses, Hanna and Jazz made their way to the stile that spanned the wall.

'You've scythed a path.'

'It wasn't me. Fury sent a guy round to do it, and I didn't argue.'

Hanna smiled, thinking this was inevitable. If Fury O'Shea worked on a building he never quite lost a sense that it belonged to him. His proprietorial reach extended across the entire peninsula, from the medieval castle in Carrick, which had been the de Lancy stronghold, to two-roomed houses like Maggie's place, which, working for Hanna, he'd brought back to life.

On either side of the scythed path, the grass grew tall, starred with wildflowers. Hanna had used the field to grow vegetables, but Jazz was no gardener. She'd continued to tend the herbs Hanna had planted near the house, but the field was now a haven for bees and insects that droned among clover, cornflowers, and scarlet poppies. Here and there was a flash of orange, where marigolds Hanna had planted at the edges of her potato ridges had self-seeded among the waving grasses.

They climbed the stile and settled on the bench, nesting the bottle in a clump of wiry sea-pinks and placing the glasses between them on the plank. Hanna stroked the flaking paint affectionately. 'I was pretty sure this was one thing you'd change.'

'The bench?'

'The colour.' It was a strange cross between wine-red and terracotta. Hanna would never have chosen it, but Fury had applied it without consultation, announcing later that it was the original colour of the dresser by her fire. He'd also reapplied it to the dresser.

Jazz giggled. 'I did wonder why you put up with it. I mean, everything else in the house is cream or grey. You could have repainted after a decent interval.'

'I planned to. I even went out and sourced a tasteful alternative. But, I don't know, I suppose I just got used to things as they are.'

In fact, Hanna had grown fond of these jarring tokens of her great-aunt's former presence and, as time passed, she'd realised there was a whole lot more to Fury O'Shea than first met the eye. Though the bottom line was that he'd always do things his way. Never yours.

Jazz picked a flake of paint from the bench and flicked it towards the cliff edge. 'I might get my act together and do some decoration. But not for a while. I'm up to my ears in work.' She filled the glasses and they sat back, leaning against warm stone with their faces raised to the sky. In the distance, gulls were coasting on the wind and, where rocks pierced the waves, foam glittered on the breakers. Hanna kicked off her shoes and sipped the cold wine appreciatively. 'How was your day?'

'Busy, like I said. It's good to have this to come home to.' Lifting her glass Jazz watched the evening sunlight glint on the straw-gold wine. 'Just imagine if I'd listened to Dad and gone off to Oxford or Cambridge. I'd be faffing around with exams and stuff, and poncy college societies, with nothing ahead but an internship with one of his wealthy clients and a foot on the ladder in a boring City firm.'

Hanna shot her a sideways glance. 'You're sure it was the right decision? You didn't just make it to piss Dad off?'

'Well, that was a consideration.' Jazz met her eye and laughed. 'No, it wasn't. Not really. And I've told you a million times, Mum, I'm perfectly content, so you can stand down.'

'Mothers never do.'

'Well, maybe they should. I'm doing fine and you're happy with Brian. We've survived!'

Out on the horizon a boat wheeled like a gull, its sails flashing white against the blue ocean. Hanna wondered how Amy's dinner was going in Ballyfin. The group had three shore nights booked at the Spa Hotel, where an open-fronted veranda protected the al fresco diners, and tables laid with linen and silver faced the setting sun. Wriggling her bare toes against the cushion of sea-pinks, Hanna contrasted the thought of Amy's banquet with the prospect of the lazy meal she and Jazz were about to share. She'd nipped out at lunchtime and bought cream, meringues, and a punnet of juicy strawberries, and Jazz had told her on the phone that she planned to make an omelette flavoured with chives. 'There's masses growing in the herb bed. Actually, your herbs are all turning to triffids. I'll chuck together a potato salad with parsley, too, if you like.'

'Use marigold petals for decoration. They've a wonderfully peppery taste.'

'Okay, that's weird, but I guess you know what you're talking about.'

'Of course I do, I'm your mother. I'll bring wine.'

In winter, when the gales crashed in, thick mist could descend from the north making the little house feel like an island floating in fog. But at this time of year on the western seaboard, the sky remained streaked with silver until midnight, and the warm, salt-laden breeze was as mild as milk. Now, sitting on the peeling bench, Hanna felt a rush of contentment. Raising her glass, she smiled at Jazz. 'You know what? I don't think we've survived, I'd say we've triumphed. Here's to the two of us. I probably don't say it often enough but I'm proud of who you are and what you're doing. And look at me! I'm living the perfect life.'

'Are you sure, Mum? Don't you miss London at all?'

Hanna shook her head. 'Not one bit.' She smiled again and, reassured, Jazz returned to contemplating the mass of golden clouds on the horizon. But as Hanna sipped her wine she knew that what she'd just said wasn't the whole truth. Perfect though her new life might be, she did sometimes miss London yet, so far, she hadn't been able to face going back there. After Malcolm's betrayal it felt too much like reopening old wounds.

Chapter Four

Breakfast in the McCarthy household was more of a running buffet than a sit-down meal. Sometimes, in the pearly summer dawn, Aideen would get up and drink tea with Conor, who'd down a mugful, bolt some cereal, and disappear into the farmyard. Afterwards she'd go back to bed or potter around baking bread and laying the kitchen table, while the farm's two ginger cats lapped milk from a plate she'd set on the doorstep, and sunlight through the windows cast a grid of light onto the flagstone floor. Later Conor would be back for a proper fry-up, and throughout the morning pots of tea would be drunk between household tasks, or served with bread and jam when the vet or a contractor came by.

It was very different from life in the Lissbeg semi where Aideen had been raised. Instead of the laminate countertops she was used to, the kitchen work on the farm was done on a scrubbed table in the centre of the room. At home in St Finian's Close, the galley kitchen had looked out onto a tiny patch of grass and a brick wall. Here, one window faced the little paved yard outside the back door and another overlooked an orchard with apple trees and washing lines, and steep hills above it where sheep grazed in stone-walled fields. There was a sink under the first window and an oven under the second, and a couple of easy chairs by the range, where the bread was baked each day. The farmhouse was plain, grey, and unimpressive, as unlike a thatched, timbered picture on a calendar as you could imagine, but inside it held all the homely comfort that Aideen had grown up without.

Before Aideen and Conor were married, his mum, Orla, had always made soda bread first thing in the mornings. Now she and Aideen took turns. They'd got on like a house on fire from the day they'd met. Other brides might balk at the thought of sharing a home with their in-laws, but Aideen, the daughter of an unmarried teenage mum who'd died in childbirth, had been brought up by two elderly relatives, who, though kind, weren't convivial. They had died within months of each other during Aideen's last year at school, leaving her stunned. She was fond of her cousin Bríd, with whom she now owned and ran Lissbeg's delicatessen, and of Bríd's mum, who'd always been kind to her. But the closeness of the McCarthy family was new to her. And she loved it.

As she gathered utensils for her bread-making, she marvelled once again that this was her home. Conor, his brother, Joe, and their dad, Paddy, had struggled to make the farm yield a decent income, so she and Conor had agonised over the date of their wedding. With Paddy unable for heavy work after a farm accident, Conor's library assistant's income was important to the family, so how could he leave and set up a home of his own? And, although the deli was doing okay, she and Bríd had a business loan to pay off, so she had no savings. Then JohnJo Dawson, Joe's fiancée's father, had offered Joe an office job in Cork. This was a game-changer. Dawson's AgriProvision was the largest business of its kind on the west coast of Ireland, and Eileen, Joe's fiancée, was a go-getter like her dad. The double wedding, which was her idea, had only been the start. Arrangements were made to hire a man to take Joe's place when he left, and Eileen had persuaded her dad to offer to upgrade the McCarthys' farm machinery. Neither Conor nor Paddy had liked that, but it was kindly meant and the help was badly needed so, in the end, they'd accepted the offer as a loan. Joe had assured Conor that, as a gift, it would just be a tax write-off for old Dawson, but Conor had told Aideen that that wasn't the point. Accepting the cost of a labourer's wage from Joe made sense because he was family. Scrounging handouts from his in-laws was very different. Thinking it wasn't her place to comment, Aideen hadn't said much. But she agreed. She also knew that, although they hadn't said so, Conor and Paddy disliked the thought of any kind of fiddling. The tax write-off, if that was what it was, might be above board, but it belonged to a world the McCarthys weren't used to, and one that held no attraction for Conor, though Joe had reached out and grabbed it with both hands.

Aideen wasn't sure what she loved most about Conor: his honesty and dogged independence, or his unfailing optimism, which was so different from her own timidity. When she'd first known him, Lissbeg Library had been under threat of closure, and when they'd begun dating, she'd asked if he hadn't been frightened by the thought that he might lose his job. 'You must have been lying awake at night, panicking.'

Conor had just shrugged. 'There'd have been no point in that. Anyway, when the psalter got donated, everything worked out fine.'

No one seemed sure why the psalter donation had happened when it did, and when Aideen had asked, Conor had said he hadn't the faintest idea. 'Miss Casey told me she first heard the news from Fury.'

'Fury O'Shea? Why?'

'I think he was doing some work for yer man who donated it. Anyway, that's Fury. He always knows what's going on before anyone else. But the point is that if I'd lain awake, I'd have been losing my beauty sleep for nothing. That's the way things often are in life.'

Aideen wondered if you got that way when you came from a tight-knit family. Sure of yourself because there was always someone who had your back. Everything about her in-laws had been a revelation. It had never crossed her mind as a child that adults might be vulnerable, but while Conor joked with his parents in ways that her gran and elderly aunt would have called impertinent, he and Joe were also protective of them. And while Aideen had no special attachment to St Finian's Close, the McCarthys were fiercely devoted to the land their family had farmed for six generations – even Joe, who, according to Orla, had never really been suited to farm life. 'The Cork job is a godsend. He'll be happier there being bossed about by Eileen, and he'll always have his share in the place here if they want to come back.'

Sprinkling soda onto the flour she'd sieved into a bowl, Aideen was glad that Eileen was elated by the flat she'd found in Cork. If she'd fallen for a high-rise with a high-spec kitchen, they wouldn't be coming home to Finfarran any day soon. Though Eileen had a heart of gold, her bossiness was exhausting, and Aideen still cringed at the memory of the double-wedding debacle. Eileen had got carried away with plans for hordes of guests and mad designer dresses, and since Dawson was footing the bill and his loan was important to the farm, Aideen hadn't wanted to seem ungrateful. But, eventually, it had all got too much for her. She'd blushed as she'd tried to explain this to Orla on her return from Florence, where she and Conor had exchanged vows with no witnesses but the songbirds in the cypress grove. 'I know we shouldn't have gone off like that, without a word to anyone, but I didn't know what to say. Well, I wouldn't have got a word in edgeways anyway. When Eileen takes a notion you can't shut her up.'

'You mean notions like that orange strapless dress she fell for, with the spangled flounces? Or the silver sack she insisted was retro Versace?'

'And the dove release, and all that stuff about needing three days of rehearsal. I think I cracked when she dragged in the wedding planner, who kept sending me JPEGs of black bouquets. But, honestly, Orla, I'm sorry. I should have said.'

'It was Conor's fault, too, for not discussing it with you. Paddy and I just assumed you'd talked it through.'

That was typical, thought Aideen, cutting crosses on her cakes of bread and taking them to the range. Though Orla loved her family to bits, she could see their faults, and when she pointed them out nobody took offence. Aideen envied Conor's farm childhood. It must have been idyllic, she thought, as she began to set the breakfast table. He was always laughing and telling her that she saw farming through rose-tinted glasses, but what could be better than being raised on a farm with a family like his?

It was eight o'clock. Orla came in and began frying rashers and sausages. The smell mingled with the warm aroma of bread baking in the oven. Aideen laid places for five, knowing that Dermot, the new farm worker, would come in for breakfast with Conor. Paddy had gone up the garden to let out the hens. He returned with a bowl of eggs and gave them to Orla and, glancing at him, Aideen could see it was one of his good days. Having had a bad fall, Paddy lived with pain and suffered from clinical depression, and often found it hard to cope with what the doctor referred to as social contact. Sometimes this even extended to interaction at home, but today he was smiling and, as Aideen passed him, he reached out and ruffled her hair. 'How's the girl this morning?'

'Never better. Do you want tea or coffee?'

'I'm no university man. I'll stick to my mug of tea.'

The day Conor had hired Dermot he'd made the mistake of saying he was a guy with 'a proper agri degree from uni' and Paddy, who'd overheard, had teased him about it ever since. All the same, he'd said that Conor had made a good choice. Dermot was born and raised on a farm east of Carrick. His granddad still farmed and his dad was only in his sixties so, for the next while, he wanted to hire himself out. Paddy had said that the final decision was Conor's. 'Hire the man if you think he's a good fit. Whatever happens, we won't end up stuck with him. He has his own place to go off to in a few years' time and, meanwhile, we can take a view of what comes next for us here.'

Unlike Joe, who hadn't been keen on getting his hands dirty, Dermot's energy matched Conor's, and he was up for innovations, like supplying fresh produce for the deli. They'd even talked about looking into organic certification, which Aideen had suggested as a way forward. Squashed into the little room that was used as the farm office, they'd scrolled through government websites, discussing options with Bríd. Paddy had been iffy when Conor had put it to him, but Orla had told Aideen that he just needed time. 'He's not great with change, these days. Well, he never was, but things have got worse since he had his fall and went on the medication for his depression. If you don't rush your fences, he'll come round, love. It's just that there's been a lot of upheaval this year.'

Though Orla hadn't intended it to, the conversation had made Aideen feel rueful. She and Conor had been the cause of much of the upheaval. First the stupid wedding fuss, which she ought to have handled better, then the fact that she'd moved in, which had changed the dynamic of the household. Even though Paddy himself had said that having her around was twice as good as a tonic, she'd made a mental note that change wasn't good for him, and decided to persuade Conor to hold back on the plans they'd considered. Though she hadn't yet had a chance to discuss it with him, because most nights he came up to bed dead beat, and zonked out.

As she put her bread on a rack by the range, there was the sound of boots being scrubbed outside under the yard tap. Conor came in in his socks, with Dermot behind him. 'God, I could eat a horse. That fry smells massive!' He sat down and poured tea as Orla cracked eggs on the side of the frying pan. The rashers and sausages were piled onto a blue-rimmed platter, which Aideen carried across the kitchen with a plate of toast, stacked high, in her other hand. She set them on the table and Paddy nudged Conor. 'Now, there's a skill worth having!'

Aideen laughed. 'I've waited on plenty of tables in my time. When I was at school I'd a summer job in a café where they'd send you out with a plate in each hand and more balanced on your arms.'

Orla came to the table with the sizzling pan of eggs. 'Sounds like a proper apprenticeship for a farmer's wife. "Feed the brute" is a good starting point.'

'Is that a quotation?'

'I've no idea. I think it's just a saying.'

Conor spoke through a mouthful of buttered toast. 'It's from a book.'

'How d'you know?'

'It's called *Don'ts for Wives*. Written before the First World War by a woman called Blanche Ebbutt.'

'You're making that up!'

'Nope. Some old one came into the library asking about it the other day. She said her mam used to have a copy, and Miss Casey looked it up.'

'So what's it about?'

'It's a kind of how-to book. Social etiquette.'

Paddy said that at least the books Dermot stuck his head in had some use to them. Ignoring the well-worn tease, Conor sprinkled salt on his eggs. 'I didn't read it – we don't have a copy. There was a blog Miss Casey found online for your woman who came in asking. It had quotes and that was one.'

Aideen, who'd googled Blanche Ebbutt, looked up from her phone. 'She wrote a book called *Don'ts for Husbands* too. How about this, Orla? "Don't settle down into an old married man. Take your wife out and about, give parties and visit your friends."'

As Conor, Paddy, and Dermot snorted in unison, Orla winked across the table at Aideen. 'I bet Blanche Ebbutt didn't sell many copies to farmers. And don't hold your breath, love, the worst of the summer work has only started. If you and I want to party, we'll be doing it on our own.'

Chapter Five

Fury O'Shea had assured Brian that the Hag's Glen's name was barely two hundred years old. 'The place was abandoned, back in the time of the Famine, but one old crone refused to leave when her family did.'

'Why?'

'How the hell would I know? Do you want to hear the story or do you not?'

Suitably chastened, Brian had asked him to go on.

'So she stayed there, and lived till she died, and they called it "the Hag's Glen".'

'That's it?'

'That's the story.'

'I suppose it might be true. But the Hag's Glen is a common name. I mean, you find it elsewhere. So it could be a recent memory grafted onto something much older.'

Fury's sniff had contained all the scorn of the native's response to a blow-in, and Brian, who was a Wicklow man, had decided to leave it at that. Though Fury was well into his seventies and a byword for eccentricity, he was the best builder in the county, and the teams he could summon to a project were second to none.

Whatever the origin of its name might be, the Hag's Glen was stunning. Broad-based and with curving sides, it tapered to a rocky cleft at its head, where a peat-brown river fell as a slender waterfall before widening into a shallow river on the valley floor. A spur from a track to a farmhouse was the entrance to the valley, yet no dwelling or road could be seen from the site Brian had chosen to build on and, except for birdsong and falling water, there was no sound to be heard.

A scarecrow figure in a torn waxed jacket, Fury had been scathing when he'd first come to view the site. 'Do you know the cost of dragging the makings of a house all the way up here?'

'I do.'

'You're going to put in an access road, and sink a well, and generate your own power?'

'That's the plan.'

'And you've noticed there isn't a pint of milk to be had within six miles.'

'I have, yes.'

'Well, you're a fool. I'm telling you that from the start, so don't blame me later.'

Brian could find nothing to suggest that an entire village had left the glen en masse in the nineteenth century, but he knew that folk memory was often more reliable than Finfarran's incomplete county records. On the other hand, you couldn't believe a word Fury said. A beaky-nosed whirlwind, as temperamental as a diva, he had a theory that architects, like dogs, needed to be taught their proper place in a pack, so Brian was aware that his story of the name could have been an elaborate tease. There was no doubt, however, that the glen had been inhabited in the past. Tumbledown walls indicated the former presence of a small village with cultivated plots between little stone buildings. Wanting the house to refer to what was already there, Brian had designed a two-storey structure built of stone chosen to match the fieldstone used in the old dwellings. Its flat eco-roof, where he now sat at dusk among rustling grasses and flowers, had provoked an intense spasm of outrage from Fury. 'Holy God Almighty, man, why would you want a lawn growing over your head? Could you not use decent slates like anyone else? And did no one ever teach you that flat roofs are always disastrous?'

'They're not if they're properly built.'

Fury had stiffened dangerously. 'Do you tell me that? Well, let me tell you I was building roofs when you were pissing yer nappies. Have you any idea what the weather up here will do to your fancy membrane?'

'I took that into account. And planting typically extends the membrane's life by a factor of three.'

'You believe that, do you?'

Brian had told him he did. 'And, after all, I'm the eejit who'll be living with the result.'

Slightly mollified, Fury had grunted and stuffed the specification into his pocket. By the following week he'd mastered it so thoroughly that he'd given Brian a series of lectures on sustainable building methods, each of which had taken place in the open, in driving rain.

With his temper in check and his eye on the goal, Brian had doggedly worked his way through all the practical issues, though at night, in his rented flat in Carrick, he'd sometimes asked himself if he was mad. Hanna was showing no signs of wanting to live in the house when it was built, which wasn't too surprising since, for months, he'd lacked the nerve to broach the subject. But, in the end, everything had been worth it. The house was completed and Hanna, for whom he'd created it, had moved in and made his life complete.

Theirs was a slow wooing between two people whom life had taught to be wary. Months before their relationship had begun, they'd met in their professional capacities. Glimpsing her at council meetings, Brian had noticed her straight back and the uncompromising way she wore her hair and, seeing her across his desk, when she'd come to consult him about renovating Maggie's place, he'd liked her square, ringless hands and unpainted fingernails.

He disliked gossip, so it was weeks before he'd discovered she was divorced. When he did, they'd met for the odd dinner, or gone for a walk at weekends but, though he'd known she was attracted to him, her reticence matched his own, so the relationship had appeared to be going nowhere. Then, one sunny day, as they sat on a beach, Brian had dropped his guard and spoken about his late wife. 'It was cancer. Three months from diagnosis to death. We were both in our twenties and I'd just set up a firm with a friend – a bloke called Dom. I'd known him at school. Everything was taking off, but when Sandra died I locked my door and turned off my phone. Got into bed and stayed there for a week. Dom was outside the house, banging on the door like the antichrist. I don't know if I heard him or not, I just know I couldn't get up. We lost a major contract as a result.' He'd put the home he'd shared with Sandra into the hands of an auctioneer, priced to be sure of a quick sale. 'It was snapped up in a week. By then I'd already thrown a few books and clothes into the car and driven west.' Lying back on one elbow, he'd looked up at Hanna, shading his eyes from the sun. 'When the money came through from the house sale I sent it to Dom. I reckoned he was owed.'

They'd sat in silence until, biting her lip, Hanna had told him about her own marriage. When her story ended she'd scooped up a handful of sand and let it slip between her fingers. Her hand was shaking and Brian had found himself longing to hold her. Instead, he'd clasped his own hands round his knees, focusing his eyes on the horizon. 'It all sounds faintly ridiculous when it's said out loud. Doesn't it? I don't mean death or divorce or even betrayal. I mean how one reacts.'

'Why did you come to Finfarran?'

'I'd seen the county-council job advertised. Anyway, this was the edge of the world, the furthest I could get from the place I'd known before I lost Sandra.' There was another silence before he spoke again. 'Maybe the real reason was that I just couldn't face my partner. Not after losing us that contract.'

'You bolted. Like I did. But you said Dom was a friend. Surely he knew you were in shock.'

'Maybe he did. He was a good bloke. But that wasn't how I saw it. I just thought I'd done something unforgivably irresponsible.'

Another stream of sand had slipped from Hanna's folded fist. 'Malcolm called me irresponsible for uprooting Jazz.'

'Well, by the sound of it, Malcolm uses words as weapons. You should have more sense than to believe him. If you can see that I was in shock when I bolted, you must know that the same applied to you.'

Stars glimmered in the sky above the house in the Hag's Glen. Brian looked down at Hanna's face, drawn in charcoal on a sketchpad held on his knee. He was no portraitist, but the sketch he'd spent the evening making had captured what he'd once told Hanna was the beauty of her bones. It was one of several he'd done of her over the past few years, and made Sandra, as she existed in memory, seem impossibly young. She had been young, though, younger than he was, and he was four years younger than Hanna, a disparity that had bothered her at first. Having been the focus of Finfarran gossip as a woman with a broken marriage, she hadn't fancied the role of a divorcée who chased younger men. That, along with her sense of duty towards her troubled daughter, had been one of many obstacles Brian's patience had to surmount.

On their first night in the Hag's Glen house, Hanna had told him how much that hesitant conversation had meant to her. 'I was paralysed by guilt and grief. What you said on the beach that day brought me back to life.' Looking at his sketch with a wry smile, Brian smoothed the pencilled frown between the straight eyebrows. It had taken longer than he'd thought he could bear for Hanna to find closure, and she'd needed to know that Jazz was okay before embracing a new life with him. It hadn't mattered, though. None of the waiting or the uncertainty mattered, not now that things had come right.

There was a flurry of movement by Brian's chair and a border collie raised its head, cocking a pair of ragged piebald ears. It was a sign that Hanna's car had just turned off the farm track. Soon the headlights would appear in the grey distance and Brian, too, would hear the approaching engine. He was never sure it was sound that alerted the collie, whose awareness of Hanna was like a sixth sense. Scruffy and starving, the dog had first turned up when the glen was still a building site, and had hung around scrounging food from the men. Surprisingly, Fury's Jack Russell, known to all Finfarran as The Divil, had accepted her presence. As a rule, the little terrier brooked no intruders on a site run by Fury, yet when this limping stranger had wandered down from the hill, The Divil had barely growled and, a few days later, they could be seen curled up together in the shade of Fury's van. Brian had made enquiries but nobody came to claim the collie. She was old and, by the look of her, had been living rough on the mountain. Many of Finfarran's small hill farms were worked by elderly bachelors, so if she'd been a farm dog and her owner had died, it was likely there'd been no one to take her on. Certainly, her days of herding sheep and cattle were over, but you could see that she'd once been a handsome animal.

Hanna had fallen in love with her when she came to visit the site. The dog had pricked up her ears as her car had approached, and had thrust her nose into Hanna's hand as soon as she'd opened the door. Dropping to her knees, Hanna had exclaimed at the matted tags of hair on the creature's haunches and the pieces of furze tangled in her ruff. 'Oh, Brian, look at the state of her! Poor Jo.'

It wasn't clear why she'd decided that was the collie's name, but it had stuck. For the rest of Hanna's visit, Jo hadn't left her side, and by the time the house was built, she'd become a fixture. They'd taken her to the vet, where her coat was clipped and her leg taken care of, and, though she treated Brian with the respect she must have learned was due to a master, her heart and soul were wholly given to Hanna. Well-fed and exuding ownership, Jo had stood on the doorstep as The Divil had bounced away down the glen in the front seat of Fury's van. Thereafter, when Brian and Hanna were out, she lay stretched on the step with her back to the front door, supine but alert, like a she-wolf guarding her lair.

Jo was idiosyncratic. At night she took herself off to sleep among the tumbledown walls of the old village and, at first, she flatly refused to come into the house. After a great deal of encouragement, she overcame her misgivings and, still rolling anxious eyes as if expecting to be reproved, she found a window seat from which to view the glen during the day. The interior staircase leading to the roof had been the final frontier, but Hanna and Brian were up there so much that one night as Hanna sat alone, watching moths dance in the twilight, she'd felt the dog's cold nose nuzzling her hand.

Now Jo was standing by Brian's chair with her hindquarters quivering, uttering tiny whines of anticipation. There was a turn in the road at the foot of the glen where the lights of approaching cars showed like stars before disappearing between the high ditches that bordered the fields below. Laying aside his sketchbook, Brian stood up and gently pulled one of the collie's ears. 'You're absolutely right, Jo, she's on her way home to us. Will we go down and meet her at the door?'

Chapter Six

Hanna opened her eyes and squinted at the clock by her bed. Downstairs in the open-plan living space, mugs clinked as Brian made coffee. As he climbed the stairs with Jo at his heels, Hanna threw back the duvet and went to the bedroom window with its huge view of the glen. Brian strolled over and placed the mugs on the windowsill. 'It's another gorgeous day.'

'And there was I, still in bed when I'd all sorts of plans for this morning.'

'Well, you weren't home from Jazz's place till late. Anyway, what are weekends for if you can't chill out?'

Comfortably settled on the window seat, Hanna sipped her coffee. 'I can't today, though, can I? We're due at my mother's for lunch.'

'What had you planned for this morning?'

'Oh, I don't know. House stuff. Pottering.'

'Well, you can still do that.'

'Oh, stop being reasonable! I know I can, I'm just ratty because I'd rather not have to go.'

'And miss Mary's liver casserole?'

This was Mary Casey's signature dish, always served at family gatherings.

'Actually, I've got news for you.' Hanna put down her mug and fetched her phone. 'She texted last night. Check this out.'

LIVER~S THE WORST IN THE WORL>D THIS
WEATHER IM GOING FOR SOMETHING IN ASPIC

Brian grinned. 'Still doesn't do punctuation, I see.'

'And only uses capitals. It always feels like she's standing beside me shouting in my ear.'

Accustomed to Mary's texting habits, Brian looked for a second text, sent moments after the first. It was briefer.

BRING CREA£M I CAN WHIP

Hanna rolled her eyes. 'It's going to be the famous clove-studded apple tart.'

'Well, no one makes pastry like Mary.'

Scratching Jo's forehead, Hanna sighed. 'You're right. She's a star baker. And Jazz will be there. And Louisa.'

'So I'll take Mary, and you can hang out with Jazz and your ex-mother-in-law. If you and Jazz didn't talk yourselves to a standstill last night.'

'Never. She's great company.' Hanna smiled at him. 'You're a saint, Brian Morton, that's what you are.'

'No, I'm not. I think Mary's a hoot.'

'That's because she sets out to charm you. You know she does it to every man she sees.'

'I do know, bless her. Subtlety isn't Mary's middle name.'

Hanna laughed, finished her coffee, and went to take a shower. Her childhood relationship with her mother had been abrasive, and forced proximity as an adult had made matters worse. When she and Jazz had arrived at the bungalow without warning, Mary had welcomed them in and given Jazz the unstinting love and security she'd needed. But Hanna had had to negotiate a traumatic divorce while her mother gave unwelcome advice from the sidelines. Still shocked by the discovery that her marriage had been a sham, she'd rejected the thought of alimony and, in a furious row, had told Malcolm where he could stick his money. The satisfaction she'd got from the gesture had been immense but short-lived because Mary's indignation had known no bounds. In her view, a cheating husband ought to be taken for every cent he had. 'You're the two ends of an eejit, Hanna Casey! And your father and me after raising you to have a sound business head!'

Stressed out, and stabbed by a pang of longing for her dead father, Hanna had sobbed that he'd never failed to tell her to follow her heart. 'You're the one who was always counting every last penny! And you grudged every cent he ever spent on me!'

Mary's face had settled into a mask of injured innocence. 'So this is the thanks I get? For looking out for your interests when it's clear you've gone stone mad? What about Jazz? What's she supposed to do for money while you follow your heart?'

Choking on tears, Hanna had said that of course she'd considered Jazz. 'I'm not a complete fool, Mam, and Malcolm may be a cheat but he's not a monster. He adores Jazz and he'll always provide for her.'

Malcolm had indeed provided generously for his daughter, who hadn't realised until much later that Hanna had accepted nothing for herself, and because Jazz had found life with Mary cosy and loving, the thought that Hanna might find it oppressive hadn't occurred to her. Hanna had worked hard to maintain the illusion, determined that Jazz's teenage years would be easier than her own. In hindsight, and in secret, she'd questioned her decision about the alimony. Though she'd never regretted it. Telling Malcolm where to stick his money had given her confidence when it was badly needed. But the downside was that, for far too long, she'd had to depend on her mother's hospitality, and a sense of being beholden to Mary had made their relationship worse.

Yet things had worked out in the end. Having taken the Lissbeg Library job, she'd secured a loan against her salary and, with Fury's help, had made herself a home on the windswept cliff. Mary had dismissed it as a 'bockety old shed', but that was to be expected. Mary's idea of a proper house involved wall-to-wall carpets, nests of tables, and a floral three-piece suite. For Hanna, Maggie's bequest had been a healing refuge, not just a fortress against the power of Finfarran's winter storms but a place where she could lick her wounds in peace. She'd returned to Lissbeg feeling defensive and vulnerable, and being a local librarian had felt like a comedown after her dream of a high-flying career. But the sparse rhythms of her solitary life in Maggie's place had been soothing, the job and the local community had become a source of joy, and now, with the turbulent past behind her, her new home in the Hag's Glen seemed to hold all the mellow warmth of summer.

As she dried her hair after her shower, and pulled on jeans and a sweatshirt, she reminded herself of how far she'd come. There was no longer any need to struggle to placate her aggressive mother, or to justify choices about which she herself had been far from certain. Now she could see Mary through Brian's eyes, as a feisty, erratic old woman whose behaviour was entertaining; and since Mary was currently miles away, embedding things in aspic, it was dumb to allow the thought of her to impinge on a beautiful morning.

Opening the window, Hanna leaned out and drank in the air. Brian had discovered the Hag's Glen on a walk around Knockinver's northern shoulder. A steep scramble had taken him to a boulder above the waterfall from where he'd first looked down on the tranquil valley below. Later he'd brought Hanna to the same place. The view was breath-taking. Far below, on the floor of the valley, bracken, stone, and lichen merged in a grey-green blanket, touched here and there with outcrops of golden furze. A hawk above them had spiralled down at an angle, and suddenly swooped on some creature in the heather. Hanna had watched it rise with its prey in its talons and sheer off towards the rolling clouds massed on the mountain's peak. Beneath her feet she could feel the curve of the boulder's pitted surface, and off to her right, other grey rocks marked the point where the peat-brown river poured into the glen. Fearful of slipping, she'd edged gingerly towards them and reached down to dip her fingers in the water. 'I can see why you'd want to live there. There's an austerity about it. No, I don't mean that. Something essentially remote.'

'And you associate it with me? Personally?'

'I'm not complaining.'

'Am I remote? It's not intentional.'

'Actually, it's rather attractive.'

He'd burst out laughing and Hanna had made a face at him. 'Maybe I should have said reticence. I admire it as a quality, that's all.'

'Even after what you went through with Malcolm?'

'Malcolm wasn't reticent. He was a liar.' She'd reached up and touched Brian's cheek. 'You have no idea what it means to trust someone again. I thought I never would.'

The decision to leave her home for his was a measure of that trust, although Brian had hesitated when she'd agreed to move in with him. 'I want you here, of course I do, but, Hanna, have you thought this through?' They'd been walking by the river and he'd taken her hands in his. 'It's a big deal, sharing a home. I want you to have security.'

'I've told you before, I trust you. I know you love me.'

'I mean financial security, idiot. Look, if you won't marry me, let's get a lawyer and add your name to mine on the deeds of the house.'

'What? Don't be ridiculous.'

'Seriously, Hanna, have sense. What if I died in the morning? Or if I went gaga and some evil siren conned me into marriage?'

'How? By sneaking in the back door when I wasn't looking?'

'Say I was in a care home and she was a wily nurse.'

'You've been reading way too much Agatha Christie.'

'You need to think this through.'

'I promise you I have. I've a perfectly good job, so I don't need you, or anyone else, to look after me. And I own Maggie's place, so I'll never be homeless.'

'But Jazz . . . ?'

'Jazz will inherit Maggie's but she'll spread her wings one day. I can't see her spending the rest of her life there. And, for heaven's sake, Brian, you're younger than I am. By the time you're ancient and gaga enough to be conned by a wily nurse, Jazz will be off somewhere being a high-flying businesswoman. But here's the thing. Have you thought about Mike?'

Mike, Brian's son, was around the same age as Jazz. After his mother's death he'd been raised with young cousins in England and, though he and Brian got on well, they weren't close.

'What about him?'

'Isn't this house his inheritance? Okay, you hardly know him, but he's your son.'

'Well, but, if you and I were married, he wouldn't expect –' Brian had stopped abruptly, his face showing consternation.

'If I needed another reason not to marry you, it would be Mike. No, listen. You're not thick either. You must see what I mean. Neither of us will ever have all of the other. Too much has happened in our separate lives for that. I've got Jazz to think about. You've got Mike. We've both got memories of people we've loved and lost. I guess when you're our age it comes with the territory. Anyway, that's how it is. And I'm fine. I don't need to look to you for financial security, but one day your son might.'

She'd felt Brian's hands tighten painfully on hers. 'I didn't come into your life to bugger it up.'

'You haven't. And you won't. And if any wily nurse comes sniffing around I'll set Jo on her. How's that?'

She'd kissed him and they'd left it so and walked along by the river. And now here she was at her bedroom window, looking down on the same sparkling water, where Brian was skimming stones for Jo to fetch. Throwing her towel over the sill to dry in the morning sunshine, Hanna ran down to join them. As she crossed the little glen to the river, she smiled, glad her mother would never hear about that conversation. Mary, who adored Brian, was constantly dropping hints to her about marriage. 'Men are all the same, Hanna. You'll never get anything done unless you give them a bit of a kick.' When she'd heard that

Hanna was moving into the Hag's Glen house, she'd thrown up her hands. 'Ah, for God's sake, girl, do you not have a tither of wit at all? What pressure is on him now to put a ring on your finger?'

'Would you back off, Mam? This is between me and Brian.'

'Ah, Holy God Almighty, here we go again!'

Reaching Brian, Hanna caught his hand, and bent to pick up a stone to throw for Jo. To do her justice, she thought cheerfully, Mary was perfectly right. Despite everything life has taught me, and without a moment of regret, once again I've allowed myself to be ruled by my heart, not my head.

Chapter Seven

'So, you're telling me that your mam and your ex-mother-in-law are flatmates? What's that about?'

Hanna steered Amy across the nuns' garden, her eye on a vacant table by the fountain. 'I never said they were flatmates.'

'Okay, housemates. What's the story?'

They reached the table and began transferring cups and plates to its surface. Hanna took their trays and propped them against the wide basin where water spouted from carved flowers around the feet of a statue of St Francis. The fountain, which was the centre point of the garden, had herb beds radiating away from it in concentric circles, separated by box hedges and narrow gravelled paths. On two sides, the garden was enclosed by the stone and red-brick walls of the old convent buildings, on a third by a boundary wall, clad in crimson Virginia creeper, and on the fourth by the new entrance from Broad Street. The café had indoor seating, but on sunny days tables by the fountain were highly sought after. Amy sat down and dumped her bag on the basin's granite rim. After a moment's rummaging she produced cigarettes and a lighter.

'When did you take up smoking?'

'Ages ago. It's a foul habit but I can't break it, and at least it keeps me thin. So tell me about Louisa and your mam.'

'Nothing much to tell. They're both widowed and Louisa's got a flatlet in the bungalow. She needed a pied-à-terre over here, so it made practical sense.'

Amy exhaled a plume of smoke towards St Francis and tapped the tin table with a scarlet fingernail. 'Come off it, Hanna! There's practical and there's weird.'

'Okay, I admit that having the two of them living on top of me wasn't in my life plan. But, then, I hadn't planned to end up living here myself.'

Having taken no more than a couple of puffs, Amy stubbed out her cigarette and turned her attention to her plate. 'It's far from avocados and sundried tomatoes we were reared.'

'And we're not all still chewing boiled bacon and cabbage. How long is it since you were home?'

'Ah, the house in Cork is long sold and I've practically no family left over here. Whereas it sounds like you've been importing yours by the boatload.'

'No, I haven't. I told you. Jazz and I moved back when I broke up with Malcolm.'

'And what? You got his mum when things were divvied up?'

'No. Malcolm sold the London house.'

'Ah, shit. The one you put all that work into?'

'Yes, but that's irrelevant. The point is that, when she was up in London, Louisa always had it as a pied-à-terre. So, with that toehold gone, and the fact that the family home was far too big for her, she sold up in England and started a business here.'

'Why? Doing what?'

'Producing organic cosmetics. It's called Edge of the World Essentials and it's based here in the Old Convent Centre. Jazz is creative marketing director.'

'Nothing like having a rich gran to set you up with a job.'

The truth was that, having sold a large house, Louisa could have retired on the proceeds in comfort but, seeing Jazz unfocused and drifting, she'd set herself the task of giving her granddaughter a purpose in life. It was a duty as well as a pleasure, she'd told Hanna confidentially, crossing her ankles and folding her hands in her lap: Malcolm's disgusting behaviour had left Jazz rootless, and his late father would have wanted that put right. Hanna had been more grateful than she could say, and she'd felt that a double weight had been lifted when Louisa's move had also provided companionship for Mary. But she felt no inclination to go into all that now. Instead she shrugged. 'There was always more to Louisa than Pimm's and croquet on the lawn. It was she who laid the social foundations of Malcolm's stellar career. All those deceptively casual parties and networking weekends in Kent. None of that stuff is easy. I know because I was the mug who got stuck with it when we were married, dressing up as the perfect hostess and charming my way round the room.'

'Oh, come on! I was at one or two of those parties, remember? You loved being the belle of the ball.'

'Maybe I did when I thought I was part of a team. Not afterwards. Anyway, the point is that Malcolm would never have got where he did without Louisa and me to smooth the way.'

'Says the woman who's not at all bitter.'

Hanna laughed. 'Damn right I'm not. Malcolm's balding and lonely and I've made a new life.'

'Well, good for you!' Clinking her glass against Hanna's

coffee cup, Amy took a gulp of wine. Rolling it round in her mouth, she registered approval. 'It's far from Sauvignon we were raised too, but that's not bad.' Then she frowned. 'So as soon as her husband fell off the twig, Louisa emerged as a fully fledged businesswoman?' The little crease between her eyebrows and the slight thrust of her lower lip as she pursued a question hadn't changed over the years.

The interrogation was beginning to irritate Hanna. 'You could put it like that. She's sharp as a tack and she knows how to hire and fire.' Which was true as far as it went, she thought, and quite enough for Amy to be going on with.

Amy spread avocado on a crispbread. 'So where does Malcolm live now?'

'In a flat in a glass box near Tate Modern. We're not really in touch.'

That wasn't wholly true either because, for Jazz and Louisa's sake, a civil relationship had been restored. Applying herself to salad, Hanna wondered about her own instinct to edit the story for Amy. She was glad to have reconnected with her, and from the moment they'd met for lunch they'd found themselves chatting as if they were back on their London balcony, with exhaust fumes drifting from the street below and mixing with the scent of Ambre Solaire. Still, that had been a long time ago, and you couldn't be a librarian in a small town without learning the value of holding your tongue. 'That's enough about me. What about you?'

'Agency work in London to begin with. Then a stint in the States and another in Oz. Luckily I made a move before the bottom fell out of the market. I mean, who wants to pay a secretary when everyone's expected to run their own office from a laptop?'

'What did you do?'

'Met Clive.'

'Your husband?'

'Late husband. He died a couple of years ago.'

'Oh, Amy! I'm sorry.'

'So am I. He was a dote. Sort of bearlike and shy and terribly rich.'

Hanna managed to keep a straight face. 'How did you meet?'

'On a singles holiday. Well, I knew my shelf life was running out, so I thought I'd better do something fairly radical. There's always a gormless man or two on the average singles holiday and, usually, they're avoided like the plague. Most women go for the handsome, muscular type, though you'd think they'd have sense enough to see that those are only there for what they can get.'

'Oh, and you weren't?'

'I was looking for marriage, not sex.'

'And what was Clive looking for?'

'Heaven knows. I doubt if *he* did. He was totally out of his depth so I rescued him.' Amy speared a sundried tomato with a reminiscent smile. 'He truly was a dote, Hanna. And we made each other happy. Mind you, he had a roving eye – all men do, don't they? But nothing ever lasted long and each time he'd be guilt-stricken.' She fingered one of her pearl-set gold earrings. 'So I ended up with some really lovely gifts.'

'No children?'

'No, and that was sad. Still, it's left me free to gad about now he's gone.' She'd been going on lots of cruises, she explained.

'All for the culturally curious?'

'God, no, mostly to the Bahamas. This was an aberration. It's a fabulous cruise line and I fancied a quick look at Ireland.'

Her wink hadn't changed either. 'I bunk off the boring cultural stuff.'

'I'm not sure if that compliments or insults the Carrick Psalter.'

'Oh, I couldn't miss that. Not when I saw your name on the leaflet they handed out at breakfast.'

'Well, I'm glad you didn't.'

'Me too.' Amy gave her a warm smile and glanced around the garden. 'You know, this really is lovely. And right beside where you work.'

Although a high wall had been taken down to make the new entrance from Broad Street, the nuns' garden still retained a sense of cloistered calm: the sound of water falling from the carved flowers at St Francis's feet was soothing, and the creeper-clad wall was a haven for nesting birds. Each morning one of the volunteers who worked in the garden waded across to pour birdseed into the statue's extended hands. This ritual, begun by the nuns, had by now entered the birds' communal memory and, as Amy spoke, a flight of goldcrests swooped from the creeper to the fountain, snatching at the seed and whirling back to the wall. The flurry of gold and olive plumage echoed the colours of the stained-glass saints in the old convent's windows, which glowed like tall flowers between grey stone arches.

'Jazz has an office here too.' Hanna pointed to a third-floor window in the former school building. 'The company's leased several units up there, and some of the herbs they use in their products are grown here in the garden.'

'That sounds cosy, but doesn't it get claustrophobic?'

'How d'you mean?'

'Louisa and Mary shacked up together. You and Jazz working

within an ass's bawl of each other. Don't you all get on each other's nerves?'

'Now and again. But that's life, isn't it?'

'I suppose it is, if you end up stuck in the town where you were born.'

Unsure that she liked this turn in the conversation, Hanna asked if Amy had kept in touch with their other flatmates. Amy shook her head. 'Not really. Lucy opened her restaurant. But you'll know that?'

'Malcolm and I ate there a few times. We didn't see Lucy, though. She was off launching another branch. In Chelsea, I think.'

'That's been there for ages. Haven't you been to London since then?'

'Occasionally, but I do have a job, you know. Louisa goes back and forth a lot. I don't think she'd survive without her regular trips to John Lewis's.'

'You could do with a bit of town polish yourself.'

'Town polish! You sound like a bad imitation of Jane Austen.'

Amy giggled. 'If that's supposed to be an insult, it's gone straight over my head.'

Hanna's annoyance lasted only a moment. Amy had always been able to make her laugh. 'How about Claire, do you ever see her?'

'Not since you and Malcolm were married. I think she went nursing abroad.'

'You mean nannying.'

'Whatever.' Amy sipped her wine and cocked her head, her gold earrings catching the sun, like the goldcrests' flashing feathers. Her cut-glass English accent had begun to slip. 'You know something? The four of us ought to meet up again. A reunion. We could all go off on a cruise.'

'Did you miss the bit where I mentioned that I have a job?'

'I know, but you must get holidays.'

In fact, Hanna had some leave coming up. Amy saw the thought on her face and pounced. 'You do! Wouldn't it be fabulous? Just imagine! Three weeks in the Caribbean. We'd be ladies on loungers eating oysters and sipping chilled champagne.'

'It's *very* far from that you and I were reared.'

'Don't be a bore. What do you think?'

Hanna looked at her watch. 'I think it's time I got back to work.'

'I'll tell you something for free, Hanna Casey. You've stagnated.'

'Look, some of us don't get three weeks off to go swanning round on cruise ships. Not to mention what it would cost.'

'Well, how about a week in London? We could base ourselves in Windsor and swan up to town.'

Amy had shown Hanna photos of her detached house in Windsor, which had a garden running down to the River Thames. It looked beautiful and discreetly opulent, and had evoked memories of the Norfolk cottage that Hanna and Malcolm had bought as a weekend retreat. Hanna shook her head firmly. 'Honestly, Amy, this is all fantasy.'

'No, it's not. It's spontaneous living. Look at the great coincidence life has handed us! Who'd have thought we'd bump into each other after all these years?'

For a moment Hanna was swayed. Perhaps this was her chance to break the hex and revisit some of the good things in her old life. The restaurants she and Malcolm had gone to, the shopping trips and nights at the ballet with her girlfriends, and the very English pleasures of well-clipped lawns, tennis parties, and afternoon tea. After all, London was the city she'd called home for the greater part of her adult life. But, along with the rush of excitement came her old sense of revulsion. Every theatre, café, and art gallery was crowded with memories she felt she couldn't bear to revisit because, in the light of Malcolm's perfidy, most of them had turned out to be false. Still, she thought, that was all in the past. Now that time had intervened and the pain had receded, why not reclaim a place she'd loved before she'd ever loved Malcolm? It'd be great to see Lucy and Claire again, and fun to spend more time with Amy. The cruise ship was due to sail tomorrow, so it seemed a pity if this quick lunch was all the time they'd have to renew their friendship.

'Tell you what.' Amy pushed aside her plate and took her phone out of her bag. 'Give me your number and let's keep in touch. I'll see if I can track down the others and, when you've had time to think, we can take it from there.' She flashed her eyebrows. 'Unless, of course, this Brian guy is too hot to be left on his own.'

'Maybe you ought to start reading Jane Austen instead of watching the soaps.'

'Well, as it happens, I have read her. I was only messing before. And *EastEnders* is tame compared to some of the stuff in her books.'

Hanna drained her coffee cup. 'Name one novel Jane Austen wrote. There are six. Well, nine at a push, so you've plenty of choice.'

'Okay, maybe I haven't read the books, but I have seen the films.'

'You are *such* a bad liar.'

'And you *so* want to come to Windsor.' Amy returned her phone to her bag, stood up, and gave her a hug. 'Frankly, I can't see the problem. It's not like something bad will happen if you just take a holiday.'

Chapter Eight

An arched gateway led from the nuns' garden to the little paved courtyard outside the library. When Hanna was a child the garden was just a glimpse of flowers and greenery to pupils crossing the courtyard on their way to the school door. Now the side gate, always locked in the past, provided a rat-run for library users and people emerging from the old school building who fancied a cup of coffee by the fountain. Having kissed Amy goodbye, Hanna strolled back to work between hedges of flowering lavender, hearing the carefully raked gravel scrunch beneath her feet. As she reached the gate to the courtyard she saw Aideen emerge from the library putting a CD into her bag. 'Hi, Miss Casey. Conor'll be glad to see you back from lunch.'

'Is something wrong?'

'Not at all, he's coping, but I'd say he could do with somebody to distract the brigadier.'

The library had its share of cantankerous users but the brigadier, a retired army officer known for his martinet's manner, wasn't one of its regular patrons. Aideen grinned. 'Conor's always accusing me of dumping the brigadier on Bríd when he comes into the deli. Now he's finding out why!'

'How are things going for you and Bríd?'

'Grand. Business is building. I've cut back on my hours since I moved to the farm, but we've taken on a Polish guy to help Bríd for the summer.'

'And how's life on the farm?'

'Plenty to learn, I can tell you that! It's great, though.'

She looked tired, thought Hanna, but everyone was run off their feet at this stage of the summer. Aideen gave her a friendly smile and Hanna went into the library to find Conor dealing with a well-dressed man who had a ramrod-straight back.

'I've told you already I'm looking for the new Evelyn Waugh.'

'Er, right, I know, but which book specifically?'

'Are you deaf? I said the latest one.'

'Let me see. *Unconditional Surrender*?'

'Is that the latest? It's for my sister-in-law.'

'Was it the Sword of Honour trilogy?'

The brigadier clicked his tongue. 'Look, is the librarian here?'

Knowing the exchange would take a good deal longer if she introduced herself, Hanna shook her head at Conor behind the man's back. Conor chose his words carefully. 'Miss Casey took the early lunchbreak today, but I'm sure I can help you. The trilogy was published in 1965, so perhaps that's what your sister-in-law meant when she said the latest one.'

The man squared his tweed shoulders and leaned across the desk. 'I. Said. She. Wanted. The. Latest. Evelyn. Waugh. What part of "latest" do you not understand?'

From the far end of the room, where she'd gone to hang up her jacket in the kitchen, Hanna saw Conor looking agonised. He battled on bravely. 'Well, the thing is, sir, that we're talking about the late Evelyn Waugh.'

'What?'

'Waugh died in 1966.'

The man gobbled like a turkey cock. Conor lowered his voice discreetly, aware that two people who'd been browsing the shelves were hanging round, all ears. 'And the books in the Sword of Honour trilogy were written in the fifties and early sixties. So they would be the latest ones. Kind of.'

The brigadier was in a hole and, judging by his startled look, he was beginning to realise it but, as Hanna could have predicted, he kept digging. 'Look here to me, my sister-in-law has a first-class degree in English literature. So you'd better search again.'

Taking pity on the two of them, Hanna hurried to the desk. 'Everything okay, Conor? Anything I can help with?'

The brigadier swung round and glared at her, clearly deciding attack was his only possible form of defence. 'Are you the librarian? Because this fellow here seems to know nothing. My sister-in-law wants the new Evelyn Waugh novel.'

Hanna smiled at him blandly. 'I'm very sorry but I don't believe we have it in.'

As she'd known he would, he grasped at the chance of escape. 'Right, well, I can't see why I wasn't told that before. I dare say it's been well reviewed – these popular women writers always get screeds in the Sunday papers. I'll tell my sister-in-law there's been a run on it.'

Hanna avoided Conor's eye. 'And, another time, if she drops in herself, I'm sure we'll be able to help.'

'Yes, well, that would be good. She's twisted her ankle, you see, so she sent me along.'

'I'm sorry to hear that. I hope she'll be better soon.'

'Well, thank you.'

Pleased that she'd managed to defuse things without destroying his dignity, Hanna began to pilot him towards the door. He came willingly enough but, to her dismay, froze on the threshold. 'Just a minute. I expect a book like that has a huge waiting list?'

'Well . . . '

'Right, put her on it, will you? My sister-in-law. Got that? For the new Evelyn Waugh.'

He raised his hat and strode away, leaving Hanna to add the name of a woman she didn't know to a nonexistent waiting list for a new novel by a dead male author.

*

Conor was on his feet when she came back to the desk. 'Thanks, Miss Casey.'

'Just taking one for the team.'

'Is it okay if I shoot off now? We've the silage lads in today.'

The ways in which the outside world impinged on rural library life always delighted Hanna. Conor never gave less than a hundred percent of his mind to his job but, at this time of year, cutting grass to store for winter fodder was an urgent part of the work he did on the farm. Weather conditions were critical, so in fine weeks the silage contractors laboured from dawn till dusk and, sometimes, late into the night. Every farmer was anxious to book them for the optimum moment because mown grass lying on the ground could be spoiled by heavy rain. The sound of their huge machines rumbling at speed down the roads, and working in the fields, was part of the music of Finfarran's summer and, in his lunch-hour, Conor would rush home, change his clothes hurriedly, and scoot around the farm on his Vespa to check on the work.

'Will you have time to eat?'

'Mum gives the lads their dinner at one o'clock. She'll have kept something back.'

Orla and Aideen would have worked all morning to feed more than half a dozen men, each hungry enough to eat a horse, and Conor's share was likely to consist of a slab of ham off the joint, crammed into a roll. The meals cooked in farmhouse kitchens for contractors were immense. Huge stews or roast joints were served with mounds of potatoes and peas or cabbage and followed by fruit crumbles made with plenty of brown sugar and served with custard. Dermot and Paddy would have eaten with the contractors, but Conor would only have time for a bite on the run. As he'd done no more than sit at a desk since nine thirty that morning, he claimed he didn't need more than a hearty sandwich. All the same, he looked tired, having done several hours on the farm before coming to work at the library, and Hanna wished that, instead of going up to the fields, he could sit down and eat his lunch in peace. But there was no point in saying so, and Conor would only laugh at her if she did. The more grass a family managed to harvest from its own fields, the less money would have to be spent on buying in bales of silage during the winter. So, in terms of the family budget, the harder he needed to work the better.

Hanna watched him speed out of the door, swinging his

motorcycle helmet. Then she went to set up the Reading Room for the Monday Memories Club. Like Finfarran's other branch libraries, Lissbeg had a collection of reminiscence resources – books, pictures, jigsaws, and so on – which family members and carers often borrowed for older people with memory loss. A council day-care centre, housed in the old convent building, had access to them for people with dementia, and the local care home used the library's guidelines to help train staff. But the Monday Memories Club was something different. Ostensibly, it fostered informal discussion about the area's history, for which, as a starting point, Hanna provided books from the library's local studies collection. In fact, it was a chance for a group of elderly pensioners to set the world to rights over tea and cake.

There was a nominal charge for the tea, which the library provided, but the cake had been the members' own idea. They'd informed Hanna at the first meeting that no one could possibly drink tea with no bite to eat. Then, as she was about to say that the library might manage a packet of biscuits, they'd launched into lively debate about the merits of Madeira cake as opposed to Victoria sponge. Mary, who'd gotten a lift to the meeting from her next-door neighbour, had routed all suggestions that Madeira cake was the lighter. 'Holy God Almighty, are you all out of your minds? Look at the weight of the ground almonds you beat in with your regular flour! And the texture! If you haven't the sense you were born with, can't you slice it and see for yourself?'

A timid woman had announced in a doleful undertone that whipped cream could lie heavy on the stomach. 'And gooseberry jam can be woefully indigestible.'

Mary had drawn in her breath. 'Gooseberry? You wouldn't

have much chance on *Bake Off* ! A Victoria sponge is sandwiched with strawberry jam and topped with icing sugar. Only a savage would slather on whipped cream.'

The timid woman had subsided, but her neighbour, who'd driven her from Ballyfin, was made of sterner stuff. 'There's a Victoria sponge recipe in a book by Mary Berry that calls for whipped cream as well as jam. Hanna has it here in the library. You can check it yourself.'

Mary snorted. 'I thought you were rooting for Madeira cake.'

'I am. I think it's far better. But you can't argue with facts.'

Well aware that Mary could argue with facts till the cows came home, Hanna had said it would be very nice to have cake at the group's meetings. 'I'm afraid I can't provide it, but you're welcome to bring some along.'

Everyone had assured her that a roster could be arranged. A vote was taken on what should be brought and a motion to offer both a plain and a fancy option was carried unanimously, though, since Hanna's intervention had bereft her of her spotlight, Mary's input was noticeably half-hearted. The timid woman had agreed to kick things off with a batch of plain queen cakes and a cherry marzipan slice. Mary had sat in mulish silence for the rest of the discussion, which had hovered between recipes for cake and acid comments on the book Hanna had chosen for them to chat about. Called *Finfarran Fadó*, it had been written by a former parish priest. The woman from Ballyfin had been particularly disparaging. 'Sure, what the hell did Father Seoirse know about Finfarran? He was from Sligo.'

'Wasn't it Cavan?'

'Not at all, girl, that was the curate. A scutty little fellow with a hell of a Cavan accent.'

'And a desperate appetite.'

'God, he'd eat all around him. When he'd come to say the Rosary with your granny he'd always be edging towards the oven. Of course, the priest's housekeeper back then couldn't boil a decent egg. No, Father Seoirse was a Sligo man who'd been away on the missions.'

'Africa, was it?'

'It might have been, I don't know. It could've been Manchester. I'll tell you this, though. He wasn't in Finfarran more than ten minutes when the bishop had him moved somewhere else. So why he was writing books about us, God alone knows.'

A stout woman in a plastic mac had announced that the useless priest's housekeeper put chicory in her coffee cake.

'She didn't!'

'Well, coffee essence. It's the same thing.'

'Mind you, I'd put a drop of that into a rich chocolate cake.'

'You wouldn't!'

'I would.' The woman from Ballyfin had turned to Mary for support. 'So do you, don't you, Mary? That triple-tiered one you make for the summer fair? And that's gorgeous.'

Mary had graciously emerged from her sulk to accept the praise. She'd even softened enough to say that, while *Finfarran Fadó* was, for the most part, risible, Father Seoirse had got one thing right. 'That bit he has there about the price of sending parcels out to America at Christmas. I remember that because people were always coming into our post office, causing ructions about the cost of the stamps.'

In the end, the meeting had been a success and Mary had continued to attend the group. Hanna was glad. Like every woman with an ageing parent, she tried not to think too hard about her mother's future. Mary, who was easily bored, would probably drop out of the group eventually but, for now, it entertained her if Louisa wasn't around. It also provided structure and continuity, which Hanna welcomed because, recently, Mary's mind had developed a tendency to drift. At the weekend, when Hanna and Brian had gone for family lunch at the bungalow, they'd stopped on the way for cream, as instructed. But, despite her imperious text, Mary had demanded to know why they'd brought it along.

'Because you asked for it.'

'I did not.'

'You did, Mam. You sent me a text. You said you wanted cream.'

'I did no such thing. Why would you imagine I'd serve up cream with a cheese platter?'

'Are we not having apple tart?'

'Did I say we were?'

She hadn't, so Hanna had said no more, thinking she'd been mistaken while knowing that she hadn't. Later she'd checked her phone and found the text. It worried her, though Brian had laughed it off. 'Look at the size of the feast she prepared. She must have been up at cockcrow. I'm not surprised if something slipped her mind.'

As Hanna picked up the book she'd chosen for today's Monday Memories meeting, she reasoned that she'd probably overreacted at the weekend. Mary had been on her best form at lunch, chatting with Jazz, flirting with Brian, and telling genuinely amusing stories. And, as Brian said, the meal she'd served was gargantuan. So it was unsurprising if she'd been tired and the text had slipped her mind. And typical of her to bluster and deny that she'd ever sent it. Ruefully, Hanna told herself that the problem was probably hers, not her mother's. Perhaps she'd been anticipating what she secretly feared. Sooner or later, Mary was likely to need more care and companionship than Louisa's peripatetic presence provided, and if she became confused in her old age she might even need to be moved out of the bungalow. And that would cause problems because, whatever arrangements would have to be made, one thing was certain. Conor's family might have found the knack of intergenerational living, but Hanna knew she couldn't bear to share a home with her mother again.

Chapter Nine

Fury O'Shea stood with The Divil on the walls of Castle Lancy, surveying the world while he finished a cigarette. Carrick's only real point of historic interest was the castle, which reared dramatically above the ring road and the town's sprawling suburbs far below. Though built as a grimly fortified keep enclosed by high walls and a twin-towered gateway, it had changed with the fortunes of successive de Lancys, who by the 1800s had become successful spice merchants and established a London household. In Ireland, they'd replaced their gloomy keep with a charming red-brick manor, though the stone walls of the fortress still enclosed it like a fist. Then, in the late nineteenth century, a pioneering younger son had discovered a silver mine in Nevada, and the family had relocated to New York.

Lady Isobel, the last of the de Lancys, had come to Ireland on her honeymoon, back in the 1990s, and from the moment she'd seen her ancestral home it had become her hobby. Charles Aukin, her husband, now lived alone in Castle Lancy and, though the Victorian plumbing was teetering on its last legs, he refused to replace it, so Fury was repeatedly summoned to invent yet another way of cheating or coaxing it into staggering on.

Pinching out his cigarette, Fury placed the stub behind his ear and jerked his head at The Divil. 'I suppose we'd better go and find the lord of the manor. God alone knows what pipe has burst on him now.' It was a source of wonder to Fury's neighbours that he allowed himself to be treated like a handyman but, in an expansive moment, he'd admitted to Hanna that he simply felt sorry for Charles. 'He's only here because his wife is buried below in the family crypt. She wanted to sleep in the bosom of her ancestors, so here's her poor husband stuck in a daft castle that's nothing to him. I wouldn't mind but he's rich as Croesus, so he could buy and sell the lot of us and never know the difference.' Slurping his tea crossly, Fury had wiped his nose with the back of his bony hand. 'He's keeping that boiler in a constant state of jeopardy just so that, now and then, he can have a bit of a chat with a plumber. That's how lonely the poor man is.'

Hanna had said nothing, knowing that praise would insult him. Fury had grown up in a time when deals were done on a spit and a handshake, and neighbours had deemed it their business to keep an eye on each other's welfare. Not only that but, if he was to be believed, his family's presence on the peninsula predated the de Lancys by a thousand years or more. He was known to all, close to no one, and as touchy as he was arrogant, so that particular story was never questioned. What was certainly true was that generations of O'Sheas had owned and managed Finfarran's forest and, while his elder brother had had no feel for craft or interest in stewardship, Fury had grown up deeply imbued with both. Hanna had always taken care not to probe or ask personal questions but, in small communities, certain facts are common knowledge. Fury's childhood had been spent among trees, learning the pathways between them, the shapes of their limbs and their leaves, and the nature of the kinds of timber they yielded: hard or soft, straight or knotted, fit to make furniture, floorboards or joists, or delicate inlay. His knowledge of wood and skill in working with it was unrivalled, yet when his father died, the forest had gone to his feckless elder brother, with the exception of half an acre named as Fury's in the will.

Times were hard in Finfarran then, and work wasn't easy to come by. A few weeks after his sixteenth birthday, Fury had taken the boat to England, knowing he'd never go home until Paudie, his brother, died. Starting as an itinerant labourer, he'd had his share of tramping streets and sitting in public libraries to keep warm, but each job had taught him more about the building trade. As the years passed, lads from Finfarran would turn up in pubs in Hammersmith or Cricklewood with stories of how Paudie was selling off parcels of woodland for beer money. Then came the day when Fury heard that the whole forest was up for auction, and a few weeks later, he learned it was gone, sold to a wealthy Dublin man living out in Australia.

The man in Australia never came back to Ireland to check on his property, and by the time Paudie died, he'd drunk every penny he'd made from his inheritance, and the woodland once cared for by the O'Sheas had become a neglected wilderness. Finfarran had changed in the decades that Fury had spent in England, and life now moved to new and different rhythms. When he had first come home he thought he couldn't bear to live looking out at the untended forest and missing the world of his childhood with its different traditions and values. But in the

end, since it was all he had, he'd built himself a house on the
site his father had left him, set back from the narrow road and
closely surrounded by trees. He knew them all, from sapling to
giant oak and, after a while, simply behaved as if the land and
its timber belonged to him. But in this, as in everything else he
did, he was careful to keep a low profile, moving unobserved and
meeting questions with a blank stare. So, to an untrained eye,
the forest remained an unmanaged wilderness, though the signs
of attention were there to be read by anybody who understood
trees.

Having descended from the ramparts, Fury and The Divil
made a brief inspection of the boiler and, climbing the stairs,
proceeded along a corridor towards the castle's book room, the
scene of one of his discreet personal triumphs, which still gave
him pleasure whenever he called it to mind. A complex web of
lateral thinking and ruthless manipulation, it was a deal that
had worked in several dimensions, leaving nobody the wiser
and everyone better off. While working on Maggie's house, he'd
come to the castle in search of a kitchen sink. Hustling Hanna
into his van, he'd driven at speed to Carrick, propelled her upstairs to the Dickensian book room, where Charles was doing
a crossword, and slammed a newspaper parcel onto the leather-
topped desk. 'You know you've a class of a sink below in your
wash house?'

Charles had replied that he didn't even know he had a wash
house.

'Ah, for Christ's sake, man, if you don't know what you've got,
you shouldn't be left in charge of it. The sink's back there on a bit
of old slate shelf.'

Unwrapping the parcel, Fury had revealed an exquisitely

carved wooden lectern, which Charles received with a whistle of delight. Picking it up, he'd shown it to Hanna. 'Fury tells me it's probably sixteenth century.'

'Damn right it is. And it wasn't designed for propping up crosswords, or to bounce when some clumsy eejit knocked it over.'

'Well, you've done a stunning repair. What do I owe you?'

'Didn't I say when I took the job on that you couldn't afford my price? If you'd sent it to Sotheby's they'd be asking for thousands, and half the lads working there are cack-handed youngsters.'

'So break it to me gently.'

Fury, who despised modern kitchen fittings and could never resist the cut-and-thrust of barter, had planned the deal in advance with meticulous care. 'I'll tell you what I'll do for you. I'll take that old sink you've got in the wash house and we can call it quits.' Just as Fury had known she would, Hanna had protested, giving him a chance to suggest the slate shelf should be thrown in as well. 'God alone knows what use it'll be, but you'll have it off your hands.'

Charles had been quick to seal the deal with a handshake. Then he'd turned to Hanna, who was speechless in the knowledge that she'd just acquired a Victorian sink and a slate kitchen worktop. 'Care to see what that lectern was originally made to display?' He'd crossed the room and opened a shallow drawer in one of the bookcases, returning a moment later with an oblong cardboard box. Lifting the lid, he'd produced the Carrick Psalter. Fury had been gobsmacked, though he'd managed to conceal it, and Hanna had sat down abruptly. 'But the Carrick Psalter was destroyed by Viking invaders.'

'I know, I read that too. But apparently it survived and disappeared into another monastery and, eventually, my wife's Elizabethan ancestors got their hands on it. Paid good money too. I reckon the abbot lived high on the hog for the rest of his life.'

'You've got this on record?'

'I've even got the receipt.'

It was then that Fury had had his lightbulb moment. He'd seen how the deal, which was good in itself, could be made even better. Saying nothing to Hanna, he'd returned to the castle and cornered Charles again. 'Come here to me, do you have that psalter insured?'

'Insured? How could I? It's priceless.'

'And do you keep it displayed on the lectern that was made for it?'

'No, because –'

'Because you're scared that, if people know it's here, someone will break in and rob it.'

'Well . . .'

'Ah, will you hold your whisht, I'm no fool. I know why you pulled it out and showed it to us. You've been fretting about what to do with it.' He'd known by Charles's expression that he'd hit the nail on the head. 'So get rid. Give it away. Donate it to Lissbeg Library. You can tell them it's something you've had in mind for ages. Don't mention my name or they'll say I had some agenda of my own.'

A broad grin had spread across the retired banker's face. 'And that couldn't possibly be the case, could it?'

'All right, you're too cute for me. Here's the story. I've been working my fingers to the bone at Maggie's place, and I happen to know that Hanna's taken a loan to pay for the work.'

Thoughtfully, Charles had turned over the paper on which he'd been doing a crossword. It was the local *Inquirer* and the front-page headline read 'COUNCIL SHAKE-UP SEES FIN-FARRAN'S BRANCH LIBRARIES UNDER THREAT'. His eyes met Fury's. 'So if Miss Casey's library closes she might have trouble paying your bill.'

'But they won't close it down if it's home to a national treasure. Not if the donor says it has to be kept there in perpetuity. Not if he offers to pay for the state-of-the-art exhibition space.'

'All of which would be tax deductible, wouldn't it?'

'Bound to be.'

'Quite a project for a local builder too.'

They hadn't said any more but they'd understood one another, and what had been said would never be known beyond the book room's walls. From Fury's point of view, it had been the perfect deal. A load off Charles's mind when the man had been worried. The sink and the slate acquired without a penny changing hands, his own next building project set in motion, and Hanna's ability to pay for his work on Maggie's house ensured. And, best of all – though he had a shrewd idea that Hanna might have her suspicions – no one but The Divil would ever know the extent of what he'd achieved.

They reached the end of the long corridor leading to the book room, and The Divil's nails clattered as he bounded towards the door. As they came in, Charles greeted him fondly. 'Looks like this fellow's gotten a little less tubby.'

'Ay, well, the vet took him off his custard creams. And the Tayto. He wasn't happy.'

'No?'

'So she's trying another tack. Football.'

'He's joined a team?'

'Ah, for Christ's sake, man, what are you on about? Dogs can't play football. No, he goes to the matches and the training sessions and does laps round the field.' Fury sank into a chair and looked lugubriously at The Divil. 'The only thing was, it was making him dizzy. So now it's one way round for the first half, and the other for the second. He'd have a quick custard cream at half-time, mind. He couldn't be going cold turkey. I told the vet that could push him over the edge.'

Charles nodded and they sat in silence for the next few minutes. Then The Divil farted loudly and Charles looked at Fury. 'Have you been in the basement?'

'I have.'

'The boiler was making strange noises this morning.'

'Ah, would you not be making a fool of yourself, it's always making noises. That's not why you called me here at all.' Fury took the half-smoked cigarette from behind his ear. 'Go on, then, what's the story? Spit it out and let me hear the worst.'

Charles's eyes sparkled with enthusiasm. 'Well, as a matter of fact, I do have something to tell you. I had an interesting call the other day from a cruise-line guy. Fellow who works for this crowd Your World Awaits.'

Chapter Ten

It was another sunny day after a fine dry night and Aideen was in her bedroom deciding what to wear to town. She'd been up for hours helping in the kitchen and cleaning out the henhouse, and now, having shed her wellies, old jeans, and sweatshirt, she'd showered and put on a skirt and canvas lace-ups. The bedroom, which was low-ceilinged, had an en-suite bathroom and opened into an L-shaped sitting room. Together they made a little self-contained flat, which Paddy and Orla never entered without carefully knocking on the door. Plenty of heads had shaken in Finfarran when Aideen and Conor had moved in with his parents, and many subtle warnings had been given about the dangers of sharing a home with her in-laws, none of which had bothered her at all. She'd loved the farm from the first day Conor had brought her to tea there, and Orla now felt like the mother she'd never known. Humming, Aideen opened her wardrobe and selected an embroidered cheesecloth top she'd brought home from Florence. When Orla had first seen it she'd dug out a photo, taken on her own honeymoon, in which she was bare-legged and wearing a cheesecloth shift. 'See? The embroidery's practically identical. I got it in Greece.' Orla hadn't changed much in appearance, thought Aideen, despite being a farm wife and raising two children, having to cope with Paddy's health, and endless financial crises.

Because it depended on unpredictable prices and weather conditions, farming would never be anything but precarious. But things were looking up. Inch by inch the worst of the McCarthys' burden of stress was lifting. State-of-the-art machinery was making the work faster and safer, allowing Conor and Dermot to get more done. In a year or so, once things had settled, Conor's plan was to farm full time, and by then, with luck, the deli would be turning a decent profit.

Today Conor and Dermot were working on the out farm, in fields a couple of miles away from the house. Orla was going up in the jeep to take them their one o'clock dinner, bringing a few lambs, which, until now, had received special treatment at the farmhouse. With hand-feeding, they'd developed from weaklings into healthy specimens and the time had come to return them to the flock. Though Aideen had helped to give them their bottles and tuck them up in a warm corner by the range, she was glad no one had asked her to transport them to the field. With luck she might be able to herd them into the trailer but, so far, she hadn't plucked up the nerve to reverse the jeep with the trailer attached. Orla seemed to do it effortlessly and, even when the dogs were out with the men, she never had problems controlling skittish lambs. She'd assured Aideen that it all came with practice, and Conor had said so too. Aideen hoped they were right. Pulling her hair up into a scrunchie, she reminded herself that Paddy had said she'd a great touch with the bottle-feeding. She'd learned to stand in a gap, too, when livestock was moved. In fact, she hadn't needed to be taught that. On the first day she'd spent at the farm, she'd ridden on the back of Conor's Vespa when he'd fetched the cows for milking, and at the farm gate, she'd hopped off instinctively and stood in the road to turn them into the yard. So, she could pull her weight when needed and, even if she didn't know all that much about farming, her income from the deli might make a real difference to the family budget in future. Admittedly, there were still weeks, especially out of season, when she and Bríd barely made enough to take out a wage for each of them, but the important thing was to keep moving forward.

It was always hard to find parking in town in summer, and the little yard behind the deli was needed for delivery vans so, when she and Conor came home from Florence, she'd bought her own Vespa, which provided the nippiest way to travel in and out of Lissbeg. Whizzing happily along between flowering hedges, Aideen ran through a mental checklist of what she needed to do. She had a list of bits and pieces to pick up for Paddy, beginning with duct tape and printer ink and ending with a saw blade and a screwdriver, and, though it wasn't her day for working at the deli, she planned to drop in and say hi to Bríd.

Because the unit they'd rented in Broad Street had once been a haberdasher's shop, they'd named the deli Habber-Dashery. Aideen could remember the shop from her childhood, when it was run by two diminutive women always referred to as the Houlihan sisters. Gran had been no needlewoman but Aunt Bridge was an expert, and practically every week she and Aideen had walked from St Finian's Close to Houlihan's. The old-fashioned shop seemed to sell everything – threads, wools, and laces, cards of needles and buttons, and round boxes of pins. Crochet hooks hung in plastic sheaths on a revolving wire display stand, and dimpled steel thimbles could be tried on for size. Ribbons and tape were measured by eye and cut from spools that hung on rods set in slots between two wooden cabinets. There was a strict pecking order between the sisters, and only the elder used the large scissors. Once cut, the length would be checked against a brass rule screwed to the wooden counter. It was always correct and, when the small triumph had been silently acknowledged, the purchase was put into a brown paper bag. Everything about the haberdashery had seemed magical, especially the two gilt-framed mirrors that hung on opposite walls, facing each other. While Aunt Bridge matched yarn or selected broderie anglaise, Aideen would study the reflection of each mirror in the other, enchanted by glimpses of familiar things from unfamiliar angles. In the old glass everything appeared warped, as if seen through water, and the reflection of the brass ruler rippled like liquid gold.

When Aunt Bridge died she'd left Aideen the little house in St Finian's Close, which had been purchased from the council by dint of selfless scrimping and saving. The inheritance had provided seed-money for setting up the deli. By the time Aideen and Bríd were looking for premises, the old haberdashery had been stripped out and nothing remained of the Houlihan sisters' presence, but Aideen had never forgotten them and, for her, mirrors would always be linked with magic and romance. It was she who'd suggested the name HabberDashery and, when they planned the shop fittings, had persuaded Bríd that mirrored panels would make the space feel bigger. Having taken a stance on a childhood memory she'd been too shy to share, she'd worried she might have made a mistake, but when the panels went up they were perfect. She loved the flashes of colour when you turned with a bowl in your hand, and the multiple reflections of the flowers on the counter and of the jars of peppers and olives on the shelves.

Bríd continued to live in St Finian's Close, where the business was run from Aunt Bridge's sewing room, and Aideen's old bedroom was now occupied by a lodger. The cousins' partnership had the same dynamic as their friendship. Bríd, who was slightly older than Aideen, had always been the more confident of the two. While Aideen was still at school in Lissbeg, Bríd had been off doing a culinary-science course and, while Aideen's legacy had smoothed the way to a loan when they'd opened the deli, it was Bríd's qualification and drive that had brought the plan together.

Leaving the Vespa by the delicatessen's wheelie bins, Aideen went through the rear door and found Bríd behind the counter making coleslaw. The morning rush of workers snatching breakfast rolls was over, and the young mums wanting coffee and cakes had yet to arrive with their buggies. Aideen took off her helmet, shaking out her red-gold curls and pulling them back up into the scrunchie. Bríd, whose dark hair was hidden under a scarf that matched her green overall, nodded at the coffee pot and asked if she wanted a cup. Aideen poured for them both and they perched on a couple of high stools that stood at the customers' side of the counter.

'How's life?'

'Everything's grand. I'm a bit tired and I practically never see Conor, but I'm told we're making money. How's business here?'

'Masses of visitors looking for picnic food, as well as the regulars. Bartek's settling in and, I'm telling you, he's some worker.

He's been asking for extra shifts, too, which is great.' Bartek was the Polish student they'd employed when Aideen had cut back her hours. Bríd sipped her coffee. 'You're still okay to do Friday when I'm at the cash-and-carry, though?'

'No problem.'

The door opened and Aideen turned as Jazz Turner came in. Bríd put down her mug and went back around the counter. 'Don't rush, I just want a takeaway tea.' Jazz leaned against Bríd's vacated stool. She'd been a couple of years ahead of Aideen and Bríd at school and her easy sophistication always made Aideen feel young and gawky. Today she was carrying a large portfolio, and wearing leather trousers, a slouch jacket, and a tailored linen shirt. It wasn't the sort of outfit often seen in Finfarran, where most people's business suits were easy-care polyester and came from the branch of Marks & Spencer in Carrick.

Jazz sat on the stool and balanced the portfolio on her knee. 'I've just picked up our latest promotional images. What d'you think?' She displayed a series of large photos printed on thick card. 'It's our "Meet Our Growers" campaign. We wanted to use real people in our advertising. See?' She held up a photo of an old man standing in front of green fennel fronds and tall yellow flowers. He had brilliant blue eyes in a deeply seamed face, an old cap worn at a rakish angle, and a wide, gap-toothed smile. 'He's my nan's neighbour. I remember getting herbs from his garden for her when I was small.'

Carrying a takeaway mug of tea, Bríd came and peered over Jazz's shoulder. 'Oh, my God! It's Johnny Hennessy. Doesn't he look great?'

Jazz displayed the other photos. 'Obviously, it's way too early for us to source everything locally, but you'd be surprised how many people on the peninsula have organic herb gardens.' Bríd's eyes widened as she picked up a photo. 'Wow! Who's this and why don't I know him?'

Jazz grinned. 'Actually, he's the only one who's a model. We're going to run focus groups on which shots make the best impression on which demographic.'

'And my response was stereotypical, right?'

'Not to mention greedy. Your Dan Cafferky's pretty damn gorgeous.'

Bríd stiffened. She and Dan had been in an on-off relationship for years and lately they'd had a big breakup. In the past Aideen had found herself cast as peacemaker, a thankless role she disliked and tried to avoid. This time, though, Bríd had insisted the relationship was over and had even erased Dan's number from her phone. Evidently Jazz hadn't caught up on the news, so Aideen chipped in hastily. 'Bríd's a free agent now, she's allowed to be stereotypical.'

Bríd returned the photo to Jazz. 'The McCarthys are going to grow organic produce for the deli, aren't you, Aideen?'

Jazz looked at Aideen. 'Well, you ought to consider selling some organic herbs to us.'

Bríd nodded enthusiastically. 'That's a really good idea.'

Taken off guard, Aideen searched for words. 'Nothing's really been confirmed yet. I'd have to talk to Conor.'

Zipping up her portfolio, Jazz slipped off her stool. 'Of course. And you'll need to go through the process of getting organic certification. Let's keep in touch on it, though?' She'd paid for her tea and was out the door before Aideen could gather her thoughts.

Irritated, Aideen turned on Bríd, who registered surprise. 'What?'

'You could have checked with me before saying yes.'

'I didn't say yes.'

'You said it was a good idea.'

'Well, it is. Another buyer for your produce. You ought to be pleased.'

'What do you mean, I ought to be pleased? Don't tell me how I should feel!'

'Oh, chill out, Aideen, what's your problem?'

Aideen felt ashamed. She hadn't told Bríd what Orla had said about Paddy disliking upheaval, or her own decision not to precipitate more change at the farm, and now, when they were at odds, seemed a bad time to mention it. Nor had she found a chance yet to discuss the matter with Conor. Anyway, this was family stuff and none of Bríd's business. It was typical of her to rush in with a verdict but, at the end of the day, it wasn't her call to make. 'Look, things are different now that I'm married.'

Unused to Aideen standing up to her, Bríd stiffened again. 'Really? What kind of things?'

Aideen was already beginning to regret her stance. 'I know we're cousins, and you're my best friend . . .'

'But what?'

'But Conor's my family now and, well . . .' Aideen's voice tailed off lamely '. . . things are different.'

Bríd went back behind the counter and started to tidy up. 'Damn right they are. I'm here keeping this business running while you're dressed up in a frilly gingham pinny, playing house.'

'That is such crap!'

Bríd slammed a serving spoon into a tin bowl. 'Okay, I'm sorry, I shouldn't have said that.'

'No, you shouldn't, because it's not true and you know it. I'm not playing house!' Aideen's hands were shaking. 'Look, I'm sorry too. You and I will always be family. Of course we will. But I am married to Conor, Bríd, and that changes stuff. All sorts of stuff, which, as it happens, it's not always easy to get my head round. But that's how it is, and you're going to have to adjust as well.'

Bríd swept a chopping board clean and moved it to the sink. 'Fair enough.'

'Are we okay?'

'Of course we are. Don't be such an idiot.'

Biting her lip, Aideen said no more. It hadn't really occurred to her that her marriage might bring changes to her relationship with Bríd. I'm an eejit, she thought, looking at her cousin's rigid shoulders bent over the sink. I should have seen this coming and, of course, it's been made worse by the breakup. Here am I with all I've ever wanted, and there's Bríd pretending she's grand when she's really eating her heart out for Dan.

Chapter Eleven

As soon as you turned off the motorway, the road to the Hag's Glen appeared to lead to another world. Tonight it seemed composed of shadows and stars. Although it was several weeks since the summer solstice, Finfarran's sky remained light almost till midnight, and after work, in good weather, Hanna could look forward to hours on the roof or wandering by the river with Brian and Jo. A favourite walk took them to the head of the valley, where the little waterfall tumbled from the cluster of rocks above, and if they stayed at home, too relaxed to go out, the rooftop views across farmland and forest were enchanting. There was only a glimpse of the ocean beyond the forest, but the distant blue streak continued to shimmer long after dusk and dew had fallen in the glen.

The solstice brought public events involving bonfires and music, and 'pagan' festivities much enjoyed by holidaymakers who happily joined in modern rituals devised by the tourist board. Back in the hills, and out in the small villages, the peninsula's traditional St John's Eve celebrations had almost died out, but a few families kept up the old solstice rituals, which mixed reverence for the Christian saint with ancient fertility rites. Sitting on their roof on St John's Eve, with a bottle of wine on the low table between them, Hanna and Brian had watched small fires flicker on high rocks and field boundaries. In some places cattle were still moved to fields close to the fires so the bonfire's smoke would bless them, and glowing sods of turf were brought home to kindle fires on hearths around which neighbours would sing and play music. Although the Irish language hadn't been spoken in Finfarran for generations, many older people still pronounced 'bonfire' as 'bone fire', a direct translation of the Irish *tine cnáimh*, which had entered the language from the English term for St John's Eve fires. Brian had a theory that acrid smoke from burning bones might be good for killing parasites. 'That would explain the notion that cattle touched by the smoke were blessed.'

'But what if it's turf smoke?'

'Rituals change when materials can't be accessed. It's like thatching your roof if you can't afford to buy slates. You use what you've got.'

Hanna had looked at the scattered points of flame, thinking that one year she, Brian, and Jo should have a bonfire. 'We could light one up on the rocks above the waterfall.'

'Why there? Not that I want to be negative, but it's a hell of a distance to carry all those bones.'

'You know I didn't mean bones.'

'I thought we'd be going for authenticity. Leotards and face paint and lots of mystical chanting.'

'Oh, shut up!'

'I could brew some mead.'

'Shut *up*. You don't have to come. Jo and I will go up with a sack of turf and a flask of tea.'

'No smashed-up timber pallets? I bet Fury could find you one.'

'Well, maybe we'll invite him and The Divil to join us, and you can stay down here being a cynic.'

Suddenly Brian had reached out and taken Hanna's hand. 'Don't. It sounds brilliant. Let's go up, dragging our sack of turf, every year till we're old and grey.'

That night she'd woken in bed and found Brian looking down at her. Still half asleep, she'd begun to sit up, thinking something was wrong. Then he'd kissed her and she'd realised there was nothing the matter. Still, she'd asked the question anyway, wanting to hear his reply. 'What is it?'

'Nothing. Nothing at all. It's just nice that you're here.'

Tonight, as she turned off the motorway, she was tired after what had felt like a very long day at work. Three people had turned up late for a computer class and blamed her instead of their own failure to check the time. She'd completed a dozen online forms, then lost them when, uncharacteristically, she'd forgotten to hit Save. And a small boy had been sick in Kiddies' Corner. Added to the usual summer irritation of tourists blundering into the library in search of the psalter exhibition, this accumulation of pinpricks had made her feel unusually stressed.

Brian was home ahead of her and had changed out of the suit he'd worn for a meeting in Carrick. Hanna dumped her bag on a chair and joined him in the kitchen. In many ways the kitchen in the Hag's Glen echoed the spareness of the one Fury had built for her in Maggie's place, but Brian's sleek lines and restrained colours owed everything to choice and nothing to budget. Instead of her upcycled sink and worktop from Castle Lancy's wash house, he'd installed modern fittings by designers he admired;

and, if he'd had his way, every wall would have been a uniform white. But the first wall that met your eye inside the front door was blue. It had been the cause of a running battle in which Fury had insisted it would be a sin to waste a tin of cobalt paint he happened to have left over from a previous job. Unlike Hanna's craven response to the painting of Maggie's dresser, Brian had fought him tooth and nail and held out to the bitter end. Yet he'd come home one day to find the wall was blue in spite of him and, as he'd said later to Hanna, there'd been no point in demanding that Fury change it, or repainting it himself. 'If I did, he'd probably break in and do the damn thing again.' In fact, to their shared amusement, they'd agreed that they liked the vivid flash of colour. Fury's response to that had been to sniff. A home was supposed to look like a home, he'd told Brian dourly, not an art gallery or a church.

There were few artworks in the house yet it did feel a bit like a gallery, which was one reason Hanna loved it so much. She admired Brian's ability as an artist and, at first, had suggested he hang some of his sketches. 'Not the ones you keep doing of me. Something else.'

But he'd laughed. 'God, no. I just doodle in chalk and charcoal. If you think the place feels empty, we'll buy something good.'

'You're not bad.'

'I'm a decent architect and a mediocre artist. I don't want "not bad" on the walls of my good house.'

The cool emptiness of the kitchen charmed her as she came in with Jo, who'd met her at the door, padding at her heels. Brian held up a bottle of wine and a glass. 'I've just opened this. Want some?'

'I *so* do. Fill it up.' She took the glass to the window and asked how his day had been.

'Fairly irritating. Nothing major, just people being people. By which I mean self-centred idiots who insist I treat them as if they were frail flowers.'

'Snap. Never mind. Let's go for a walk before dinner. Up to the waterfall and back, and we won't bother cooking. There's plenty of stuff to pick at in the fridge.'

'Okay, but I'm starving. Let's have a starter.'

They sat at the table with Jo on the floor between them and ate hard-boiled eggs dipped in mayonnaise straight out of the jar. Afterwards Hanna changed out of the skirt she'd worn at work and they rambled down to the river, where midges were dancing in the dusk.

'We'll get eaten!'

'Not at all. The swallows are on the job.'

Flights of swallows were darting across the river scooping up midges, rising and then skimming back to descend on the insects again. Hanna pulled up the hood of her sweatshirt. 'Stray ones seem to find me all the same.'

'D'you want to go back indoors?'

'Of course not. Onwards and upwards.' She ran ahead and Jo followed, weaving to and fro. She always insisted on herding Brian and Hanna on their walks, circling behind them with her ears cocked, as if one of them might break away and make for a different path.

As they climbed towards the foot of the waterfall the wind picked up and there were fewer midges. Pushing back her hood, Hanna paused to regain her breath. 'Oof! I must be getting out of shape.'

'The trouble is that we both do sedentary jobs. Not enough exercise and too many meetings with idiots.'

'Do idiots affect muscle tone?'

Brian sat on a rock and pulled her down to join him. 'They seem to have banjaxed mine. I tell you something, I reckon we both need a holiday.'

Hanna looked at the slim cascade of amber-coloured water up ahead. 'What – from all this loveliness?'

'I meant from the idiots. Seriously, a break would do us good. Keeping cool at meetings is supposed to be my big strength, and lately I've been cantankerous. Not a good look.'

Hanna reflected that she hadn't been much better. Dealing calmly and efficiently with the public was central to her job, yet today she'd nearly snapped at the mother of the poor child who'd been sick. 'I do have leave coming up, and you must have some days due. You've been working flat-out. Will we see if we can co-ordinate and have a lazy week? No getting up until after ten and lots of picnic meals.'

'No, I mean a proper holiday. Let's fly to London, go to a show and see some exhibitions.'

Hanna remembered the conversation she'd had in the Garden Café with Amy. She'd been excited then by the thought of revisiting the good things in her old life and, surely, to do so with Brian would be wonderful. Yet she felt uncertain. The Hag's Glen was a paradise, so why would she want to leave it?

'But what about Jo?'

'We'll get someone to look after Jo, don't worry. And we won't be gone long. Think of it, Hanna. Room service, a West End show, and some great little galleries.'

'London is stifling in summer.'

'No, it's not. Anyway, think of Green Park. Or we could go up to Hampstead or out to Richmond. And it doesn't have to be London. We could fly to the Algarve.'

'Or a Greek island.'

'Or Tuscany.'

'We could just stick a pin in a map and see where we'd end up.'

'Now you're talking! We should do it.'

Sensing their excitement, Jo barked. Hanna hushed her. 'Maybe Fury and The Divil would look in on Jo. Mind you, leaving a key to Fury could be a mistake.'

Brian laughed. 'I don't care if we come back and find the place painted tartan. Let's go and find a map book and a pin.'

He pulled her to her feet and they began to retrace their footsteps down the glen. Above them the darkening sky was like a bowlful of silver pinpricks, and the shoulders of the hills were purple smudges against the gathering dusk. Hanna stepped carefully beside the gurgling river. Here, where there were no streetlights, and no visible dwellings besides their own, the stars shed a pale light that threw every rock and blade of grass into grey relief. As she was about to step from one foothold to another, she looked down and exclaimed aloud in delight. 'Look, a heart stone!' Crouching, she picked it up, and it fitted snugly in the palm of her hand. It was river rock, eroded and polished by water, left behind on the bank as the river continued to carve a narrower, deeper bed. Brian turned and came back to look, and Jo pushed her cold nose against Hanna's hand. Hanna held out the stone to Brian. 'See? It's a perfect heart. Do you think someone made it and lost it way up here?'

Brian squatted beside her. 'I'd say it's natural. There's a thing that happens when mountains are formed. You get a contact point between two slightly different rock types where a cleavage develops as the mountain responds to stress. Masses pressing and straining against each other, and things heaving up. Then the piece that breaks off at the cleavage gets washed down the river. Time and water erosion do the rest.'

'That's stress for you. Wears you down.' Standing up, Hanna slipped the stone into the pocket of her hoodie.

Brian laughed. 'Or else the two rocks just weren't meant to stay together. Time always tells.'

'Talk about stretching a metaphor. Come on, I'm getting chilly. Let's go and find that map.'

They'd left the door of the house unlocked, as always when they went for a walk in the evenings, knowing that no one ever approached the glen at that time of night. But as they strolled back between clumps of creamy heather, Jo began to bark and Hanna saw someone sitting on the doorstep. As they approached, the figure rose and, clicking her fingers, Hanna called Jo to heel. Then she recognised the slim young man with the tousled hair and the heavy backpack slung on one shoulder. It was Brian's son, Mike.

Chapter Twelve

Mary Casey assessed her kitchen judicially. Louisa, if prompted, would probably call it nice – possibly adding 'very' – but the English hadn't much of a way with words. Anyone with half an eye in her head would be hard pushed not to call it immaculate. In fact, Mary thought triumphantly, you could even go so far as to say it was perfect. There was no point in doing a job if you didn't do it properly. To be fair, though, Louisa couldn't be blamed for being English, and there was plenty else about her you couldn't fault. She was a decent, quiet, sensible woman, with no airs and graces, a real lady that you could trust to keep her bathroom clean and not to go burning the arse out of your saucepans. Not only that, but she adored Jazz. Admittedly, she was always talking Hanna up, too, but there was no accounting for taste. It was a strange thing, thought Mary, that the child you'd given birth to would annoy you, while your grandchild would be your pet from the day she was born. Actually, she'd got the impression that things might be much the same for Louisa. No mother would want a son like that cheating hound Malcolm, though you couldn't expect Louisa to say so out loud.

Finfarran had been astonished when Mary had divided the bungalow and given Louisa her own set of rooms. Hanna had gaped with the rest of them but Mary had taken no notice. The fact was that she'd felt a bit lost when Hanna and Jazz moved out, so the thought of someone sharing her home was welcome, and the great thing was that Louisa would never be breathing down her neck. Much of her time was spent on trips to London, which suited Mary. If nothing else, it demonstrated who owned the roof and who was only a lodger and, though that wasn't something you'd want to go making a big song and dance about, it never hurt to ensure that lines were unequivocally drawn.

Now and then, Mary had wondered if Louisa might have the measure of her. Sometimes that quiet English manner suggested amusement, but if that were so, it didn't trouble Mary overmuch. Tom, who had doted on her, had always found her amusing and it had never mattered to her so long as she got her own way. If you thwarted Mary she had no option but to bully you into submission, but if you had the sense not to cross her, things would be fine. It mystified her that Hanna had grown up unable to accept that basic, immutable fact. Pursing her lips, she thought, and not for the first time, that she didn't know why she found opposition so threatening. Probably, these days, there was some fancy psychological name for it and, no doubt, there were people out there dying to come and cure her. But, as she'd told Tom's photo only this morning, she'd no desire to go seeking them out at this time of her life.

The framed photo stood on her bedside table. Tom had been the best-looking lad on the peninsula when she'd married him and he'd kept his looks to the day he died. Though she prided herself on maintaining a good front before the neighbours, Mary had never recovered from his death. The idea that God would take Tom away offended her, especially since God was supposed to be omniscient and, therefore, should have known how much she depended on Tom. She'd always thought He'd have the sense to call her to Him first, with Tom holding her hand and Hanna in the background, far enough away not to annoy her but close enough to complete the picture of loving devotion and loss. She'd never imagined the horror of the day Tom had slumped to the kitchen floor, the paralysing fear she'd felt as she'd scrambled into the ambulance, or the violence with which the paramedics had slammed the hurtling trolley against the corridor doors. She knew well that everybody thought Tom had spoiled her, and maybe he had. But she knew, too, that he'd loved her from the moment he'd first seen her, and that, for all his charm and looks and personality, he'd needed her desperately, and that the day she'd agreed to marry him had been the happiest day of his life. That was the last thing he'd said to her in the cubicle in the hospital with the cow-faced doctor standing over him, claiming him for her own. Hanna had tried to ease Mary out but Mary had shaken her off. Tom had her hand in his and she was going nowhere, not if the heavens fell and the earth cracked beneath her two feet. She'd stood her ground against the lot of them, snarling at Hanna to get out of there and leave her with her husband. Then Tom had pulled her down to him and said that about their marriage. And the next thing he was gone.

Lately, Mary had wondered if she'd got that last bit wrong. Had the woman with the cow's face been the doctor or a nurse? And had Hanna really tried to stand between her and Tom at the end? Giving a quick flick of a cloth to a crumb she'd spotted on the table, Mary told herself that all that wasn't stuff you'd want to remember. And the trouble was you'd be hard put to forget it. People said grief receded with time but that was a lie, like the one about God being kind. No doubt God had had His reasons for stealing Tom from her, and she wasn't going to go losing her faith at this time of her life – that would be both undignified and daft – but she'd never again believe the old guff the nuns had taught in the convent. She might have known it was a lie from the way they'd laughed at girls whose mothers couldn't afford to buy them the proper uniform, and how they'd hit you when you couldn't do your sums. They weren't kind, and neither was God, with His bleeding heart and His big, sad eyes demanding sympathy. People lived and died, and that was the height of it, and no one, least of all the nuns, had any idea why.

It had struck her once or twice that God might have been wreaking vengeance. According to the sermons, He was very down on jealousy, and He'd have known how much she'd resented Tom's wasting time playing with Hanna. When she was small Tom was forever taking her out for walks and reading her stories and, though it shamed Mary to admit it, it had annoyed her more and more. You couldn't be punished for feelings, of course, because you couldn't help them, but God might have spotted the way she'd killed two birds with one stone. Tom used to always be slipping away to look after his aunt Maggie, a cross-grained old lady with a tongue like a rasp and no interest in the opinions of her neighbours. You wouldn't want to be seen to fail to care for an elderly relative but, at the same time, a man ought to spend his free time with his wife. So, as soon as Hanna was old enough, Mary had taken to sending her down to help Maggie round the house. It did the child no harm and it freed up Tom to get on with the hundred and one things that wanted doing at home. She had a shrewd suspicion that Tom had known exactly what she was at, and that he hadn't argued for the sake of peace and quiet, but in the end, thought Mary defensively, hadn't Maggie left Hanna her house? She'd died when Hanna was only twelve and no one had expected she'd leave the place to a child. Mind you, back then, Hanna had hardly understood it was hers. It was a bit of a dump, too, but land was land, and it never would have been Hanna's if she hadn't been sent down to dig Maggie's spuds. So how was it fair of God to go round wreaking vengeance? It made no sense, and that was a fact, thought Mary, so she'd best put it out of her mind and get the kettle on. Louisa was out in the garden, messing around with the hose and the secateurs, and she enjoyed a coffee before going to work.

The garden had never been Mary's province: foosthering with flowers had been Tom's pastime, not hers. A week or so after the funeral, Johnny next door had laid a new lawn for Mary and left a border of shrubs around her perimeter. Hanna had been married in London then, so no one could fault Mary for making the change. She couldn't be expected to manage all those roses and beds by herself. She'd kept Tom's pots of evening primroses and night-scented stocks on the patio, though. The scent made her cry if it caught her off guard, but Jazz had loved them since she was a toddler. So did Hanna, mind, to give her her due.

Louisa came into the kitchen and wiped her feet on the mat. 'What are you up to?'

'I've just been giving Hanna her due, which isn't like me.'

'Oh, come now! You're very fond of Hanna. In your own way.'

'Am I?'

'You took her in when she had nowhere to go.'

'And what would the neighbours have said if I'd slammed the door on her? Anyway, there was Jazz.'

'Well, you didn't throw Hanna out when Jazz flew the nest.'

'Throw her out? She couldn't wait to be rid of me. Off with her to Maggie's place when she could have stayed here in the back room and been comfortable! I tell you what it is, Louisa, a daughter's her mother's scourge.'

'You wanted her to be comfortable, though, didn't you?'

'Ay, well, no one would want their child living in a shed.'

'You worry about her too, but, you know, I don't think you need to. I'm glad she's found Brian. He's a good man.'

Comparison with Malcolm hovered in the air, so Mary whipped a tea-towel off a plate of sultana scones. 'Would we have one of these with our coffee?' It was, she felt, a suitably diplomatic intervention, one of the many little signals she repeatedly sent to assure Louisa that no blame was attached to being Malcolm's mother. Louisa gave her a warm smile and said a scone would be nice. Briefly, Mary wondered which of them actually needed assurance. Having liked Louisa from the first day they'd met, at Hanna's wedding, she'd been damned if she'd drop her just because Hanna hadn't been able to keep a husband in check. But, occasionally, she'd asked herself what Tom would think of Louisa being her lodger. Certainly, had he been alive when Malcolm's affair was revealed, he'd have got on a plane to London and confronted the cheating liar, even if he'd had to break down doors to get at him. Tom was the gentlest man on earth, but if he'd seen Hanna hurting, God alone knew what he'd have done. On the other hand, he'd never refused Mary anything, so he wouldn't want to see her bereft of Louisa, however he felt. Anyway, thought Mary crossly, as she brought the scones to the table, if Hanna, Tom's pet, wouldn't stay home and care for her mother, he couldn't complain if she looked out for herself.

Her scones had risen perfectly and the dash of vanilla she'd added when beating the eggs was just right. She was pleased Louisa noticed it. There was no point in baking if no one appreciated the work. Tom had always been a great one for sweet things, though you'd never have thought so since he never put on weight. Hanna had always been scrawny, too, thought Mary, who'd often told her she'd never catch a man. A chest like a board might be the fashion these days, but a proper bit of a bosom was what men liked. And, with the exception of Tom, who'd never strayed, or perhaps never had a chance to, men were all the same in Mary's book. Pouring the coffee, she sat down and confided in Louisa. 'Have you noticed that busty woman who works in the council planning office?'

'The planning office?' Louisa accepted her coffee and shook her head. 'I don't know that I've even been in there.'

'Oh, come on, Louisa. You know her. She lives in Carrick and shops in Aldi.'

'Well, that doesn't narrow the field.'

'Her name's Murphy. She's a widow. You do know her.'

'I thought you shopped at Tesco.'

'Ah, will you keep up! I do shop at Tesco. *She* shops at Aldi. I've seen her go in.'

'Honestly, Mary, I don't know her. Why do you ask?'

Mary picked a sultana out of her scone. 'Pauline Murphy, that's what she's called. Her mother was a Nolan from Crossarra. Maeve Nolan, she was at school with me. She had twins as soon as she married, both boys. They work in the Co-op. Pauline was an afterclap – she'd be about five years younger than Hanna. You know her, you do, Louisa. She goes prancing round on stilettos, and I'd say every stitch on her back was bought in Cork.'

'I'm sure I've never met her. Do you think you could get to the point?'

Mary looked at her darkly. 'I've told you the point. She works in the planning office.'

'I dare say I'm dense, but I don't follow.'

'Well, if you want it cut and dried, here it is. The apple never falls far from the tree.'

'Mary, I've a meeting to go to.'

'Would you hold your hour!' Mary poked her finger at Louisa across the table. 'I was born and reared with Maeve Nolan. She had a roving eye and that Pauline of hers is the same. You're right about Brian, he's a decent man and I'm glad Hanna found him, but she's a fool to herself for not getting him to put a ring on her finger.'

'Are you suggesting . . . ?'

'I'm not suggesting anything. I'm telling you. Pauline Murphy works in Carrick in the same building as Brian. She has her eye on him.'

'But that's ridiculous! He and Hanna are perfectly happy together.'

Mary snorted disparagingly. 'That won't make a pick of difference to Pauline. And when it comes to keeping an eye on her man, Hanna's useless. I mean, I'm sorry to have to mention it, Louisa, but look at what was going on with Malcolm all those years. As for Brian, you know yourself that I'm fond of him. But I'm telling you he won't have a chance if Pauline Murphy has him in her sights.'

Chapter Thirteen

Lissbeg's streets teemed with tourists in summer but the peninsula's back roads were seldom crowded. Driving the library van, Conor could daydream, and from his seat in the cab he could look out across his neighbours' fields. Silage was still being cut for farmers who, unlike the McCarthys, hadn't been first in the queue to book contractors, and cut land was being fertilised. Far in the distance a tractor turned and trundled down a hill field, almost lost from view in a silvery cloud of the lime its driver was spreading. Though there was a cooling breeze, it was another hot day and cattle clustered close to hedges and under trees, seeking shade. The field patterns of green, gold, and silver, bounded by walls and ditches, were lost on the foothills where there were no trees or boundaries, just miles of rough grass and heather and, above them, the black peaks of the mountain range. People from lowland farms grazed sheep among the unfenced heather, trusting to dogs to round them up when it came time to go to the mart.

Conor's mind was on his cattle. There was still a mart going strong in Lissbeg but most years brought rumours of closure and letters to the *Inquirer* from people like his dad. According to Paddy, the powers-that-be had no interest in agriculture. They'd kill farming with neglect if they could, just as they'd sat on their hands and done nothing while the fishing industry died. But, as Joe said, that was just Paddy grousing, and how could you blame him when he was stuck inside with online forms and paperwork, and dying to be out in the fields on a fine day like this? As Conor drove, he considered the future of the farm. Dermot was all for cutting back on livestock and growing more produce to supply the peninsula's restaurants, and even the supermarkets. Which was all very well if you could be sure the demand would continue to rise. But you couldn't. A little thing could knock the tourist trade sideways, and food fads were notorious. Kale or courgettes might be big one year and you'd hardly keep up with the orders. Then a celebrity chef would announce that kale was no more than pretentious cabbage, or a magazine would blame deep-fried courgette flowers for cellulite, and your deal with the supermarket would vanish, leaving your crop on your hands. Conor reckoned it made no sense to hitch your wagon to a single star, particularly a fashionable one. He didn't mind taking a look at certifying a few acres of land as organic, especially if he'd be growing for HabberDashery and a few local pubs and restaurants he knew. The farm might invest in polytunnels to get the produce out early. You could put your toe in the water that way and know you were unlikely to make a loss, and it could well be that organic stuff made sense. Though lately Aideen seemed to have gone cold about the idea. Which was odd, Conor told himself, because she was the one who'd come up with it in the first place. She'd been a bit moody on and off, too, though when he asked her she'd always tell him she was grand.

It was weird that he and Aideen had seen more of each other before they married than they'd managed lately. Conor remembered a family meeting when they'd still been planning the big double wedding. Jazz Turner had been there, as Eileen's chief bridesmaid, and suggested they ought to fix a date because wedding venues got booked up a good year in advance. Eileen had been all over the place, scrolling through lists of hotels and squeaking at photos of dresses, so they'd turned to Aideen, who'd looked across at him. Taking a gulp of tea, he'd said that they'd want to consider the date in terms of time off from the farm. But only a week or so afterwards he and Aideen had sneaked off to Florence at twelve hours' notice, so the issue of careful timing went by the board. And, back then, he'd been thinking of nothing but Eileen's huge shindig, which, according to her, was going to take three days. So his mind had been focused on small stuff, like who they could get in to cover the milking. It hadn't struck him that it might be best to be married in late summer, so he and Aideen could have some time as a married couple before the heavy farming months came round again. His mum was well used to it and, besides, she'd been raised on a farm, but it wasn't really fair on Aideen, who'd gone from dating to being a grass widow in only a few weeks. And, mostly, she was stuck at home when he was out and about.

Conor reckoned that the best part of his library job was the time he spent on the road. Today's route along the southern side of the peninsula had several official stops, scattered villages where he'd pull into a church car park, or by a little shop, and villagers and people from outlying farms would be waiting in groups by the road or sitting on walls. It was coming up to lunchtime when he approached a shop with a couple of houses behind it and a fingerpost on the seaward side indicating a slope leading down to a little pier. He pulled up in front of the shop, which was called Cafferky's of Couneen and had a sign in the window saying it was also an internet café.

Inside, there were three tables by the window, with shelves of supplies and a chiller cabinet beyond them. The middle-aged woman behind the counter smiled as Conor came in. 'There you are! Aideen said you were planning to stop here for lunch.'

Conor turned and saw Aideen sitting at a corner table. She looked up from the phone in her hand and waved. 'I was wondering if you'd got lost!'

'I'm behind schedule. There was a big crowd at Crossarra.' Conor went over and kissed her and she made room for him to sit down. There was a coffee cup in front of her. 'Do you want another of those? What are you doing here, anyway?'

'I've come to buy you lunch.'

'Cool. How did you know I'd be stopping here?'

'Mostly you do on this route, don't you? Orla said I should chance it.'

'I'll have a toasted special, so.' The woman had come to join them, tucking a tea-towel into the waistband of her apron. Conor sat on the bench beside Aideen. 'Plenty of mustard, Fidelma, and double onion.'

Fidelma looked at Aideen, who said she'd have the same. 'Hold back on the onion for me, though. Conor can have mine.'

'Ah, we won't need to ration it. Onions are about the only things we set this year that are coming. Dan's spuds are useless and the rabbits have got the lettuce.'

'He'd want to net them.'

'Ah, Conor, don't I know he would? I'm killed telling him.

But, you know Dan, he's no farmer and, to be fair to him, he's been working hard on the boat.'

Dan, who'd been at school with Conor, had always been mad about the sea. He'd had notions about running marine eco-tours from the little pier in the inlet below his parents' shop, but the business had sort of foundered, and he'd gone to Australia for a while. Nowadays, he kept going by taking tourists sea-angling. Though he'd never been what Conor would call reliable, you had to admire how he'd dust himself off when life gave him a knock.

As Fidelma went to make the toasted specials, Dan came in and lounged over to join Conor and Aideen. 'How's the old married couple?'

Aideen rolled her eyes. 'Kind of fed up with that old predictable line.'

'D'you want coffees with those specials?' He brought them from behind the counter, nicking an energy drink from a shelf for himself. Bríd had told Aideen he'd gone to Australia without the right papers and ended up having to work on the black. It was typical of Dan that he hadn't done it on purpose. He'd thought he'd be okay on a working-holiday visa and hadn't found out he was wrong until it was too late to get things fixed. Anyway, he wouldn't have known how to fix them, and he'd a chip on his shoulder a mile high about dealing with the authorities, so he wouldn't ask.

Fidelma brought the toasted specials, thick ham, cheese, and tomato sandwiches on white bread, with plenty of onion in Conor's case, and salad on the side. 'Can I get a book out while you're here, Conor? There's only me in the shop today so I won't get down to the village.'

Theoretically, Conor wasn't supposed to issue books other than at his designated stopping points, but he was allowed a measure of discretion and Fidelma Cafferky wouldn't boast about how she'd broken the rule. 'Of course you can. I'll open up when I've eaten. You'll have to be quick, though.'

'Ah, I know what I want. It's just something light to read when there's nothing on telly.'

'Well, I've a whole shelf of summer-holiday reads, so you ought to find something to suit.'

Fidelma put down the plates and laughed. 'If you ask me, I'm the type they write those holiday reads for – working women who never get time for a break!'

When she was gone, Conor asked Dan how the boat was.

'Good. I'm doing well on the fishing trips. It's not what I want but it pays me for the moment.' Dan glanced at Aideen. 'And, despite what some people think, I'll get the eco-tours started yet.'

Aideen held up her hands and leaned back. 'Don't look at me, I'm not my cousin's keeper.' The breakup had been about Dan's inability to get his life in order which, every so often, drove Bríd, who adored him, into walking away. This time, according to Bríd, it was permanent, though Aideen was sure she was missing him deeply.

Knowing how Aideen hated being cast in the role of go-between, Conor gave Dan a kick. 'You do realise you're interrupting a date?'

'I thought dating was over once you got married.'

'Yeah, well, that's where you're wrong, so you can feck off and give us a bit of space.'

Dan thumped him on the shoulder and went out whistling.

Aideen gave Conor a smile that made him wish they were at home. Sunlight through the window was touching her red curls with gold. He searched for the word. A nimbus. That's what it was. According to Miss Casey, artists all over the world had come up with the same idea. They'd put gold circles round the heads of people they painted when they wanted to show how glorious they were. It wasn't just halos round saints' heads or Jesus in stained-glass windows, you got it in paintings of queens and emperors, and the sun-god Helios, and Semiramis, the moon goddess. Actually, thought Conor, spreading mustard on red onion, Helios was Greek, and Semiramis, as far as he could remember, was Babylonian. But that was the point. Like Miss Casey said, artists everywhere all through the ages had had the same idea and, when he looked at Aideen, he could understand why. She was glorious. Back when she'd lived in her own place, where he used to stay overnight, there'd been a cut-glass bowl on her dressing-table, and the moving flames of the candles she'd lit made the glass gleam like the moon. When he lay there and she leaned down to kiss him, he could see her slim back reflected in the mirror. Sometimes, with her shining skin, and her hair shimmering above him, he'd thought she looked like a moon goddess herself. It wasn't a thing you'd say out loud, for fear you might be laughed at, but you could definitely see what all those artists had meant.

As he bit into his toasted special, he noticed that Aideen was wearing her crystal earrings. They were only glass but she'd fallen for them in Florence, though he'd wanted to splash out on something more pricey. She'd always been daft about crystal and mirrors and sparkly yokes. Even now as she sat here in Cafferky's, drinking cappuccino, it seemed to Conor that she shone like a goddess. Mind you, as Miss Casey said, you didn't just get nimbuses on goddesses and emperors. The psalter in the library had a whole margin full of little painted foxes, and each one was outlined with rays of gold.

Aideen leaned across the table and poked him. 'We're supposed to be on a date, you know. I could do with a bit of attention.'

'Sorry.'

'Tell me about your day.'

'Same old same old, really.'

'Anything new at the library?'

'No. Miss Casey's got a visitor at home. Brian Morton's son. He's called Mike.'

'Is he round for long?'

'Dunno. He's some kind of photographer. Or maybe it's videos. He goes round the world shooting stuff for travel sites.'

'Nice work if you can get it.'

'I suppose. He doesn't look like he's making a fortune, though. He was getting out of her car in Lissbeg when I went into work this morning.'

'What age?'

'Mid-twenties. Maybe more. Looks a bit like a student. Not my idea of somebody in films.'

Aideen grinned. 'Like you'd know what someone in films looks like.'

'True enough. And maybe frayed cut-offs and a scruffy sweatshirt are a look. Something Spike Lee would wear.'

'You're not saying this Mike works in Hollywood?'

'I've no notion. I'll tell you what, though. I'd say Miss Casey wouldn't mind if he fecked off back to wherever he came from.'

'Doesn't she like him?'

'Could be she doesn't. Or maybe it's two's company, three's a crowd.' Conor speared his last bit of onion with his fork and flicked it at Aideen. 'Like Dan Cafferky turning up when I'm out on a date with my wife.'

Chapter Fourteen

When Hanna came home from the library, Jo was prone in her usual place on the doorstep, ears pricked and head raised in expectation. Sinking her hands into the dog's shaggy ruff, she saw Fury's van parked by the house. Brian's car was nowhere to be seen, so apparently he was still at work, and since Jo had been guarding the door, it seemed that Mike wasn't home either. With that realisation came a flicker of relief, though Hanna suppressed it. Mike was charming and intelligent and occasionally looked touchingly like a juvenile version of Brian, so she had no reason to wish that, having now spent several nights sitting up chatting with his dad, he'd return his things to his scruffy backpack and move on. Yet she did, and it troubled her.

On the night Mike arrived, having exclaimed in surprise, Brian had shown him over the house while Hanna produced a proper meal from the freezer, instead of the bits and pieces they'd planned to graze on. When they joined her in the kitchen, the table was set, a beef casserole was ready to be taken from the oven, and she'd made a salad and assembled some cheeses and bread. It had made a welcoming spread along with a bottle of red wine, as well as the white Brian had already opened, and chocolates to have afterwards with their coffee. Brian had smiled at her warmly. 'Where did the chocolates come from?'

'They were a present from one of my regulars at the library. I had them stashed for a suitable occasion.'

Mike had picked up the box and whistled admiringly. 'Artisan, no less! And locally made. I'm honoured.' He'd been appreciative of the casserole, too, and spent most of the meal enthusing about the house. 'It's really cool, Dad. I didn't know you had it in you.'

'That's not surprising, since you've never seen anything I've done.'

'Well, but it's mostly municipal stuff, isn't it? Car parks and – I dunno – swimming pools? Isn't that what county architects do?'

'Absolutely. And, if we're terribly lucky, extensions to public libraries.'

Catching his eye, Mike had paused with a chocolate halfway to his mouth. 'That was a put-down, right? I just goofed?'

He hadn't seemed very apologetic and, though Brian had been amused, Hanna had found herself irritated. It was Brian who'd designed the glass space that housed the psalter exhibition, coping creatively with a tight and rigid footprint and turning the dark school hall into the welcoming library her workplace had become. So she was bothered by what she saw as Mike's dismissiveness, and annoyed by her own fussy protectiveness. Later, when Mike had splashed red wine from his glass as he'd sprawled on the sofa, she'd exclaimed and jumped up to find a cloth. From the armchair in which he'd been equally relaxed, Brian had reassured her. 'Don't panic, it's fine. No harm done.'

'It'll stain. Let me get it.'

'It won't. I'll deal with it later. Honestly, Hanna, leave it.'

If he was worried about how his son might feel, his concern had been misplaced. Mike hadn't seemed to notice either the spill or the moment of tension. Hanna had retreated, feeling she'd made a big deal out of nothing, and spent the next five minutes disturbed by the sight of the vivid red splash so close to the white leather sofa. Shortly afterwards, Brian, who'd gone to the kitchen for more coffee, brought a cloth and mopped up the spill efficiently. Yet Hanna had still felt tense. Deciding her presence wasn't helping, she'd said a cheerful goodnight and gone to bed, leaving them to it. Brian hadn't joined her till well after three a.m., when she'd been too drowsy to remember that they hadn't stuck the pin in the map to choose their holiday destination. They still hadn't done so now, almost a full week later.

The sound of a hammer on stone led her round to the rear of the house where The Divil was lying in the sun and Fury was working on a wall. As she approached he was bent double, squinting at a string he'd rigged to give him a straight horizontal. When the site for Brian's house was cleared, the ruins of a few small buildings had been retained. Back when the glen had sheltered a village, these had been little houses and sheds, and Brian had decided to restore one as a garage. It was a job he'd intended to tackle himself, but time had passed and he and Hanna had continued to leave their cars in the open.

Eventually, Fury had turned up and announced he was taking over. 'You're like everyone else. You reach a point when you run out of steam. God knows why you wouldn't spend the money and put up a decent prefab. You'd be parked in the dry by now if you'd had the sense to.' Before Brian could respond, Fury had pre-empted him. 'And don't talk to me about sympathetic con-struction. I'm not interested.' Then, having delivered himself of this massive lie, he'd set about restoring the building with ma-terials and methods carefully matched to the originals. Now he stood upright, saw Hanna, and jerked his head at a broken stretch of wall he hadn't yet reached. 'Look at that. Tidy work, the like of which you'd go far to find, these days. Why would anyone pay for blocks, and go knocking up sand and cement, when there's stone here and masses of good subsoil? Answer me that!'

As belligerence was Fury's default position at the start of most conversations, Hanna ignored it and asked after The Divil.

'He's missing his Tayto. Mind you, he's developed a fierce in-terest in the football. I've had to get tickets for the County Final and they cost me an arm and a leg.'

'Have you? My dad was a player when he was young, so I grew up going to matches.'

'I've no time for it myself. It's your man that's showing the interest.'

The County Final was played at the GAA's stadium in Car-rick, where the clubhouse was said to be better than any of sim-ilar size in Cork. Though she knew better than to say so, Hanna was fairly certain that dogs weren't allowed there. Hearing her unspoken thought, Fury fixed her with an eye. 'Oh, I've no doubt they'll try to keep him out of it, but they'll be on a hiding to nothing, I'm telling you that. I paid hard cash for two pre-mium tickets and I've every right to dispose of them as I choose. Ask any court in the land. And look at the way he's supported the lads right the way up the league. Not one local match has that fella missed, nor one training session, so if he wants to attend the final, there's no one can stop him.'

'I suppose not.' As Fury's blood pressure appeared to be shooting upwards, Hanna indicated the two dogs, who were lying in the shade of the wall, Jo on her side and The Divil against her back. 'That's a great relationship, isn't it?'

Fury wiped his nose with a grubby handkerchief. 'Well, you say that, but the fact is it's a matter of dynamic. When Jo turned up, this was The Divil's pitch. He was top dog. Fair enough, that was how things were, and they ran with it. But now that Jo has the ball, as you might say, the dynamic's shifted. And The Divil would have no problem with that. He's a team player, and he's one to play by the rules.' Fury came round the wall and considered it critically. Then he cocked his head at Hanna and nodded at Jo. 'What's the old girl going to do for a bed when I've this place done?'

Jo still slept in the old dwelling, protected from the weather by a piece of corrugated iron, the sole remains of a long-gone roof, which had fallen at an angle and formed a shelter. In her first few days of scavenging on the building site, she'd discovered a tattered anorak down by the river and dragged it up to make herself a bed. No amount of coaxing could make her change her mind and sleep in the house, and she'd eyed a dog-bed Hanna had bought for her with something close to panic, backing into her shelter until the threat was taken away. Looking at the bed's cheerful cover, patterned with paw prints and machine-washable at an eco-friendly temperature, Hanna had called herself a fool for thinking Jo would like it. Now she wondered what to do if, bereft of her shelter, the old dog decided to move indoors and insisted on bringing her anorak.

Fury looked at her reprovingly. 'Ay, you hadn't thought it through, had you? Of course not! You with your fancy plans for a two-car garage.'

'You were the one who said we ought to get on with it.'

'Oh, and this is the thanks I get?'

'No, but . . .'

'Haven't I carefully worked around her, awaiting instructions from the client?'

'You never said.'

'And why should I? She's your dog and it's up to you to make the position plain.' Having deftly put Hanna in the wrong, Fury sat down on a stone pile and took a half-smoked roll-up from behind his ear. 'Don't worry, you'll have time to come up with a strategy. There's a fair bit of work to get on with before we'll have to move her.' He struck a match and, sheltering the flame with his jacket, lit the cigarette and inhaled deeply. Then, without looking at Hanna, he blew a stream of smoke towards the house. 'I'd say you're a bit crowded up there these days.' Hanna opened her mouth but he interrupted. 'Ah, don't go trying to find something to say, for you won't fool me. I built that place, remember? It may have a guest bedroom with a no-holds-barred en-suite, but the fact is, it was designed for two.'

'Mike is family.' As soon as she'd spoken, Hanna wished she'd had more sense than to rise to Fury's bait. Triumphantly, he pursued his point, his eyes half closed and one hand scratching The Divil. 'And that's the problem, isn't it? You can't go pushing family out the door. Don't say you don't want to, because I won't believe it. From what I've seen of that fella, he's got a great welcome for himself, and I'd say he's one to spread himself about.'

In spite of herself, Hanna laughed. 'Well, I have occasionally wished that Brian had designed a bigger guest room.'

In fact she'd been secretly appalled by the amount of space Mike took up. For someone who'd arrived with no more luggage than a backpack, he'd managed to create an extraordinary amount of clutter all over the house. His books, clothing, and camera equipment seemed to cover every surface, including the window seats, so the only place she could comfortably sit with a coffee was in her bedroom. Even up on the roof there was evidence of Mike. The two seats by a low table where she and Brian sat in the evenings were now augmented by a third, placed where Jo normally lay. Its presence hadn't bothered Jo, who'd squeezed herself between Brian's and Hanna's chairs and seemed perfectly happy, and it certainly hadn't bothered Brian, who'd been in great form since his son had arrived. There was no denying that Mike was pleasant company, interesting to chat to and frequently coming home with a bottle of wine. Yet the fact was that she'd rather he wasn't there. It seemed such a churlish attitude that she'd done all she could to suppress it but, of course, Fury had detected it and, being Fury, was bent on making her see it for what it was.

'You hadn't expected to get the son thrown into the bargain, had you?'

'If you mean I hadn't expected this visit . . .'

'Ah, will you stop being prissy, it doesn't suit you. I mean it hadn't struck you that Brian's lumbered with family, the same as yourself.'

Acutely aware that she sounded pompous, Hanna replied that Brian wasn't lumbered at all. 'He has an adult son who's more than welcome to visit his father's house.'

'And, like I say, that's your problem. It's Brian's son in Brian's house, and you're wondering where you ought to put yourself. I'm not blaming you either, so you can take that puss off your face.'

'Oh, for feck's sake, Fury, would you mind your own business!'

Fury flicked ash from his cigarette and grinned. 'You see, that sounds much more like you.'

'Why don't you just build your bloody wall and let me get on with my life?'

'If I had a penny for every time somebody's said that to me, I wouldn't be building bloody walls at all.'

'Well, maybe you ought to take notice.'

'Oh, right, please yerself, I've said me spake.' Fury pulled on his cigarette and continued to look at her blandly. Crossly, Hanna turned to go, clicking her fingers at Jo, but, instead of leaping to follow her, the old dog thumped her tail on the ground and remained curled up with The Divil. Fury focused his gaze on a point in the middle distance. 'Of course, I could always rig up a bit of a roof for you there in the other corner. You could set up camp down here with herself if things get too tough in the house.'

Chapter Fifteen

The following morning Hanna called Jazz from the library. 'How are you fixed for lunch?'

'Nothing planned. Do you want to meet up?'

'Say the Garden Café at twelve thirty?'

'Okay. First one there grabs a table by the fountain.'

When Hanna arrived, Jazz was sitting on the top step of the terrace outside the café. 'Sorry, Mum, I'm a failure. The town's hopping with tourists and there isn't a table left. I got us a couple of sandwiches, though, and coffee.'

Her seat on the step was out of the way of the café's stream of customers and, with the tray between them, they began their lunch. Creasing her eyes against the sunlight, Jazz glanced at Hanna. 'You okay, Mum? You look tired.'

'Fine. I've just had a few late nights.'

'Partying with Mike?'

Hanna smiled. 'Nothing so exciting. He and Brian have been sitting up talking.'

Jazz had met Mike on the single occasion he'd visited Brian in

Finfarran, some years previously. 'I seem to remember Mike was the late-night type.'

'Well, they've plenty to catch up on.'

Jazz licked her coffee spoon. 'How come he ended up being raised in London by his aunt?'

Hanna hesitated. She wasn't sure how much Mike knew and, anyway, a direct reply would amount to breaking a confidence. She was the only person Brian had trusted with his story, and when he'd told it to her that day on the beach his pain had been almost palpable. She recalled the tension in his hunched shoulders, and how he'd spoken with his eyes on the horizon. 'Sandra was breastfeeding when we found out she had cancer. Mike needed to be weaned when they started the chemo, and Kate took him because, pretty soon, Sandra and I couldn't cope. We couldn't cope with anything. It was exactly like a nightmare. Kate didn't even bring Mike to visit. It distressed Sandra too much. Me too. I'd wanted a son desperately, and we'd been so happy. It didn't seem strange when he wasn't there, though. It just felt like part of the same nightmare. And when she died it somehow seemed right that he was gone as well.' He'd told her the story several times since, in almost the same words, usually when he'd had a bit more to drink than he was accustomed to. 'I didn't see Mike again until he was three. Kate and her husband made brilliant parents. You could tell he was happy, and they were happy to keep him, so we decided that they'd adopt him. It made sense in terms of lots of practical stuff. And what would have been the point of my uprooting him? They lived in London and he'd just settled down in a kindergarten. I had a stupid bachelor flat over here.'

Hanna could remember the flat, which was where he'd lived when she'd first met him. Though he'd rented it for years, the rooms had been oddly stark and unwelcoming, with books and portfolios stacked on the floor as if he'd yet to settle in. 'Did you visit Kate when Mike was growing up?'

'Sometimes. Just as a relation passing through. I stopped after a while, in case he got curious. Kate wanted to wait till he'd left school before she explained things. That was her choice and she had the right to make it. Anyway, she handled it brilliantly and everything ended up being straightforward. He's accepted that I'm just a figure on the periphery of his life.'

His resignation tore Hanna's heart whenever she heard the story, which was partly why she was so determined not to make Mike feel unwelcome. Now she spoke lightly to Jazz. 'Oh, I think the family decided on it when Mike's mum died. Brian was working, and in his twenties. He couldn't have taken care of a baby alone.'

'Makes sense, I suppose.'

'I know. And people do what they must. The thing is, pet, I think I should give them some space, so I wondered if you'd mind if I came over to Maggie's this evening?'

'You asked me to lunch to ask if I'd ask you to dinner?'

'Well, yes, if you put it like that.'

'Of course. I'll cook something for us. You don't have to pay for it in advance with an egg-salad sandwich.'

'You're the one who's paid. Let me give you my share.'

'Don't be daft!' Jazz flapped her hand as Hanna reached for her purse. 'I'm a filthy rich businesswoman. I can afford to treat my mum. Turn up whenever you want to this evening.'

'You're sure?'

'Oh, Mum! Stop being *soft*!' Suddenly, Jazz looked sharply at her. 'You're sure nothing's the matter?'

'Not a thing. Brian needs some time with his son and, frankly, I could do with an evening with my daughter. There's a bit of a blokey atmosphere up in the Hag's Glen.'

'Okay, come round and I'll show you our latest lipstick lines. We've a special one for middle-aged women. It's called Lascivious Lips.'

'It is not!'

'Okay, it isn't. That was just a suggestion from a focus group.'

'I bet Louisa vetoed it.'

'Actually, it was me. On feminist grounds, so I hope you're proud of your parenting.' Jazz drained her cup and got to her feet. 'We've plenty of time. Let's have another coffee. You enjoy the sun and I'll get them.'

*

Having decided to go straight from work to Maggie's place, Hanna called Brian as soon as she was back behind her desk. 'Am I disturbing you?'

'I'm just doing battle with a report. What's up?'

'I've made plans to have dinner with Jazz. Will you cook for Mike?'

'No problem.'

'There's a fish pie in the freezer, or you could pick up a couple of steaks.'

'I do know how to walk into a butcher's, and, actually, I made that pie.'

'I know. I'm sorry. I just want you guys to have a good evening.'

'Well, we will. And we won't spill wine or spit bones on the carpet.'

'Oh, Brian . . .'

'Stop it, idiot, I'm only teasing. We'll be fine and I hope you'll have a great evening with Jazz.'

As she drove out to Maggie's place, Hanna thought how lucky she'd been as a parent. Whatever mistakes she might have made, she'd been able to keep Jazz with her and, to do Malcolm justice, though he'd lied to Jazz, he'd never tried to claim her. But the cards had fallen differently for Brian. Fate hadn't just robbed him of Sandra, it had taken Mike too. What would they find to talk about tonight? Where his emotions were concerned, Brian tended to be tongue-tied. He'd poured his feelings for her, for example, into a house that, at first, she hadn't known was a labour of love.

According to Jazz, Mike took the view that family relationships weren't complicated. 'At least, he said they weren't if you didn't allow them to be.' On hearing the story, Hanna had blinked. 'And what did you say to that statement?'

'I said it was either admirable or unutterably selfish.'

And that, thought Hanna, parking her car outside Maggie's place, encapsulated her own view of Mike. Either he'd adjusted admirably to the fact that he'd grown up not knowing his father, or he'd no interest in anyone but himself.

Jazz came to greet her and they strolled to the door arm-in-arm. Now that evening had fallen it was shadowy inside the house. 'It's all looking very restful. I see you haven't repainted Maggie's dresser, though.'

'I'm getting used to it. Anyway, I like your idea that it's a reminder of Maggie. I sort of feel she's still here sometimes. Not in a spooky way, just as a benign presence.'

This was a strange remark from Jazz, who was famously pragmatic.

Hanna smiled. 'She wasn't very benign in her old age when I knew her. Acerbic would be nearer the mark. Your nan used to pack me off to help in the garden and the house, which was pretty boring work when I was a kid. Still, Maggie was content – she saw this as her fortress. I had much the same feeling when I lived here, so I'm glad you've settled.'

As she'd done a hundred times in the past, Hanna went and leaned on the half-door. She called back to Jazz, over her shoulder, 'Places seem to hold the memory of past generations, don't they? Everyone who's lived and loved and died there.'

'Oh, come on, Mum, that's taking things a bit far.'

'Well, just remember that this is a place for contentment. Someone will live here after you, someone who might feel your presence, so make sure it's benign.'

The scythed path was fast being lost in the surrounding meadow, where tasselled grasses were swinging in the breeze. Nasturtiums, which, with marigolds, had once edged Hanna's vegetable beds, straggled freely among the grass and rosebay willowherb. Here and there, umbelliferous flower heads swayed on branching stalks, three foot tall and fringed with delicate leaves. In London these cream-coloured beauties would be seen as exotic, and probably sold for several pounds apiece, yet they were no more than carrots gone to seed. Turning back into the room, Hanna saw that Jazz had several in a vase on the swept hearth. 'They look impressive.'

'It's far too hot for a fire, so I thought they'd fill the space.'

As Hanna's eyes reaccustomed themselves to the dim interior light, she noticed a framed photo on the mantelpiece. Moving closer, she exclaimed aloud in surprise: 'And this is wonderful!'

'I got it from Nan.'

'Really? I've never seen it before.'

Jazz lifted the frame down and carried it to the window. It was a photo of herself and her grandfather, taken when she was a child. 'It's the garden behind the bungalow, see? Before Nan got Johnny to turf over the flowerbeds.'

Hanna's throat tightened. Her father was sitting on a kitchen chair with Jazz, freckled and long-legged, perched on his knee. Behind them was a yellow rose bush in full bloom, one of dozens that Mary had had dug out when Tom died. The sight of the roses brought their scent back to Hanna, though she couldn't remember the occasion on which the photo had been taken.

'It was that summer I stayed with Nan and Grandpa and you went off for a weekend in Paris with Dad.'

Along with the remembered scent came a flood of memories of Paris in high summer followed by a stab of pain. Years after that ostensibly romantic weekend, she'd discovered Malcolm had planned to spend it with Tessa, who'd cried off, leaving him with unrefundable flights.

Jazz was still focused on the photo. 'Nan found it in a cupboard. Some group she's in at the library had made her remember it, so she went and dug it out the other day.' Unaware that the photo had shaken Hanna, Jazz smiled at her. 'Would you like a copy? I could get one made and you could hang it on a wall in the Hag's Glen.'

'Brian doesn't go in much for things hanging on walls. Not

even his own sketches. I suggested he put some of those up, but he wouldn't. He's sort of wedded to empty spaces and light.'

'Arty.'

'No, he's not.'

'Yes, he is, but he's a dote, so I forgive him. All the same, if you wanted to hang a copy I can't see why you shouldn't. It's your home.'

Unwilling to take this particular line of conversation further, Hanna was about to change the subject when, suddenly, Jazz frowned. 'You know what? I sometimes think Nan might be losing her marbles.'

'What? Why?'

'Well, she's taken to going off at weird tangents. Wait till you hear what she said out of nowhere the day she gave me the photo. "Never trust a man who wears terracotta trousers." Literally. That's what she said. I mean, what's that about?'

For a moment Hanna was troubled by this echo of her own fears about Mary's mental stability. Then her lip quivered. 'I'm pretty sure she was thinking about the Monday Memories Club.'

'I don't get it.'

'It's that library group your nan mentioned. Six elderly ladies and Mr Maguire, the retired school teacher.'

'That guy who wears smart-casual shirts with a row of biros clipped in the top pocket?'

'That's the one. Well, I think he must have spotted a bargain out shopping because he turned up wearing a most unlikely pair of red chinos.'

'Which upset Nan?'

'I imagine that even your nan would accept that a man had a right to choose his own trousers. No, what bothered her was the fact that he'd disrupted the cake roster. The arrangement was that she'd bake a Battenberg and arrowroot biscuits, but Mr Maguire muscled in with a fancy tart.'

'Seriously untrustworthy.'

'And embarrassing, because that's exactly how your nan put it, and Mr Maguire had brought a lady friend to join the group. Anyway, we've agreed that, from now on, I'll circulate the cake roster in writing before each meeting.'

'I suppose, if they're all ancient, it could have been a mistake.'

'They're not ancient, they're just getting on a bit, and it wasn't a mistake, it was a power-struggle. Trust me, things like that don't go away as people get older. Actually, I think they get worse.'

Chapter Sixteen

Brian had opted for the fish pie. It was defrosted and ready to go into the oven when Mike rambled in. His camera case was around his neck and he carried a six-pack of beer. Leaving the case on the table, he rummaged in a drawer for an opener and waved a bottle at Brian. 'Want one of these? They're cold.'

'There's wine in the fridge but, yeah, beer's good.'

Mike opened a couple of bottles and took his to the sofa, kicking off his shoes and slumping full-length. He swallowed a mouthful of beer and called across the room to Brian, 'Had a good day?'

'Busy and kind of boring. What did you do?'

'Got some great shots up on the cliffs. Couneen, is it? There's a little pier and a guy there who does boat trips.'

'Dan Cafferky. He's a nice lad. Bit of a rolling stone.'

Mike grinned. 'Like me.'

'What's your next port of call?' Having put the pie in the oven, Brian took his beer to an armchair. Jo, who'd been lying on the window seat, jumped down and flopped onto the floor beside him.

Mike shrugged. 'I haven't got any concrete plans.'

Brian looked at the figure comfortably stretched on the sofa, a lackadaisical version of himself at the same age. There was little of Sandra in Mike's appearance but, now and then, a fleeting expression recalled her, and the tilt of his head when he asked a question was hers. Brian wondered what she would have thought of their adult son. Here was Mike in his early twenties, a globetrotter with no responsibilities, when, at the same age, Sandra and he had been repaying a mortgage while he'd been struggling to build up his own practice. Still, Mike seemed to be doing well with his travel videos and, obviously, he needed to keep moving to find new locations for them. 'Are you planning to shoot some material here in Ireland?'

Mike threw him a glance that might have been wary or amused. 'Could do, if something turns up. The internet's saturated with Irish stuff, though. There's more chance of selling if it's somewhere less well known.'

Brian reapplied himself to his beer thinking that, though Mike seemed relaxed, he might justifiably resent questions from a father who, up to now, had appeared to take no interest in him. Though the appearance belied the facts. The arrangements Brian had made with his sister had included regular payments for Mike's upkeep and education, and the payments had only ceased when Mike had graduated from film school. It had never seemed appropriate to Brian to ask if Mike knew that. He believed that Kate and her husband ought to be free to make judgements about Mike's welfare, including the freedom to determine what they told him about his dad. This wasn't something he and Kate had discussed: though they were fond of each other, they'd never done much talking, having spent their teens at boarding schools while their father worked for a company based in the Gulf. Hanna, thought Brian wryly, would probably call them emotionally stunted. She disapproved deeply of boarding schools.

As the cool beer slipped down his throat, he reflected that, at the outset, he hadn't expected to see Mike again. At the time, he'd been frozen by the loss of Sandra and by what had happened to his practice. The only thing he'd felt certain of was that Kate would give Mike stability and that his own unpredictable presence would do more harm than good. He still felt that Mike had done better without him, and he'd wanted no gratitude, then or since, for the money he'd faithfully sent for his son's support.

Mike swung his feet to the floor and went to fetch some Doritos. He came back with a bowlful and threw one to Jo. 'Is Hanna not in this evening?'

'She's having dinner with Jazz.'

'How's Jazz doing?'

'Great. She's living at Maggie's. Hanna's place before she moved here.'

'That's over Lissbeg way, isn't it? I tripped over Jazz on the cliff path there when I was here before.'

'Literally?'

'Yeah. She was reading and I wasn't looking where I was going. I liked her. We got on okay.'

'Wasn't there vague talk of you meeting again?'

'We wondered about doing the Paris marathon. But, you know, stuff took over.' Looking thoughtful, Mike took a handful of tortilla chips. 'We ought to get together again. Have a family meal. I could cook.'

'You can cook?'

'Certainly I can. I used to work in a restaurant.' Mike picked up a fallen chip and flicked it across to Jo. 'Well, that's an over-statement. It was a burger place in the States. A few steps up from McDonald's but, essentially, I stood there flipping burgers. Then they moved me on to fries, so you could say I'm widely experi-enced.'

Brian laughed. 'Or we could cut out the middleman and just go to McDonald's.'

'I told you, this place was *much* classier. Our sauce was in bottles, not little sachets, and we didn't do paper cups.'

'Were you there long?'

'A few weeks. It lost its charms in the end. Actually, I was just filling in time before starting work in a film library.'

'Where was that?'

'California. They were updating their catalogue. Any fool could have done it, but they liked the fact that I was a film-school graduate. Especially one from London. It made them feel grand.'

'But you didn't stay.'

'No, it was just a contract thing. I rather enjoyed it, though. Plus it paid for a budget trip to Brazil. I shot some good stuff there and it sold well.'

Mike finished his beer and went to the fridge. Brian gestured with his bottle. 'I'm fine with this. I'm taking my time.'

They drank in companionable silence until Jo rolled onto her side and heaved a beatific sigh.

Mike grinned. 'Happy dog.'

'She's not used to comfort. Before she turned up here she must have hunted her food in the hills, and she's getting a bit too old for that class of thing. She still won't sleep indoors, though. She makes her own choices, does Jo.'

'That's pretty cool.'

Conversation subsided again and Brian didn't search for a new subject. It was enough to enjoy Mike's presence, and better still to feel that there was no need to fill the silence. Why rehash a past that couldn't be altered? Far better to live in the here and now. Anyhow, things couldn't have been done differently. If Hanna had been paralysed by guilt and grief when he met her, so had he, and for far longer, and if, as she'd said, she'd never dreamed she could trust someone again, he had never thought he'd recover from the horror of Sandra's death. It was his love for Hanna that had taken him to a place where he could see Mike as a person, not an element in a nightmare, and if he hadn't fallen in love with her he might never have had this chance to build a relationship with his son.

Hanging out, thought Brian, that's what will do it. Not soul-searching, or probing old wounds. Swigging the last of his beer, he got to his feet. 'So, do you fancy that fish pie?'

'Sure thing.' Mike wandered over to the table, followed by Jo, who settled beneath it. As he moved his camera case, he took out the camera to show Brian some shots. 'I got these at Couneen, see? This is Dan's boat.'

Brian came to look. 'These are good.'

'The light was brilliant. It's a cool boat.'

'Apparently Dan's doing good business taking tourists sea-angling.'

'Yeah? That's not what he said to me. It sounded like things were slow.'

'I suppose it depends on the weather as much as anything.' Brian took the pie from the oven and went to fetch plates. 'Where were you shooting before you came over here?'

'I did a bunch of videos in Spain. Look, here are some shots of boats I took in Galicia.'

Seated at either side of the table, they ate, drank more beer, and went through the photos, with Mike giving a commentary through mouthfuls of fish pie. His photographic skill delighted Brian. 'You really have an eye.'

'Glad you think so. Of course, it's still a case of having to do crap jobs on the side.'

'Burger flipping.'

'Burger flipping. House painting. Being a hospital porter. Nothing wrong with any of it. I'm seeing life.'

When they'd eaten they drifted back to the sofa, carrying the bottle of wine and still talking about Mike's photography. Brian went and fetched a portfolio of sketches. 'I've got one here I did of Couneen a few years ago.' Jo, who'd padded after them from the dinner table, pricked her ears and pushed insistently against Brian's legs. Shifting her gently, Brian laid the portfolio on the floor by the sofa. He hunkered down and opened it, looking up at Mike. 'Here, see? There used to be fishermen's cottages near the pier but they've been demolished. And here's another, from a different angle.'

As Mike reached down to pick up a sketch, several others drifted sideways over the floor and half under the sofa. At the same moment, the front door opened and Jo, who'd been whining impatiently, skittered across the room in delight. Hanna came in, wind-blown and cheerful, and Brian greeted her with a smile. 'I didn't hear the car.'

'You should see the sky out there tonight, the road was starlit all the way home!' Raising her head from Jo's ruff, Hanna saw the sketches on the floor. 'Were you showing Mike?' She moved towards them and bent to pick one up. 'Oh, no, Brian! Not these ones you keep doing of me. Show him something decent!'

Then she froze and Brian saw that the sketch in her hand was not of her, but of Sandra. It shouldn't have been embarrassing, but it was. Hanna dropped the sketch like a hot potato. Brian was pretty certain she hadn't recognised the sitter: he'd kept no photos of Sandra, and had thought he'd destroyed all the drawings he'd made of her when they were married. As he sought for words, he realised he had no idea whether or not Mike would know Sandra either, at least not from a half-glimpsed drawing. Hanna bent down and shuffled the sketches together, replacing them in the portfolio and lifting it off the floor. 'Honestly, I leave you alone for an evening, and look at the state of the place!'

No one who knew her would have been fooled for a moment, by either her voice or what she said. But, though slightly fuddled by beer and wine, Brian was fairly sure that Mike hadn't noticed anything wrong. Hanna gave them a bright smile and said she thought she'd go straight up to bed. 'I'll see you in the morning, Mike. Don't rush, Brian.'

But, of course, he did. After some desultory chat, and having finished his glass of wine, Brian let Jo out for the night and said he'd go to bed himself. He left Mike on the sofa, groping for the TV remote, and found Hanna in bed when he got upstairs. 'Darling, I'm sorry.'

'For what? You don't need to be.'

'Yes, but, you must have felt . . .' Brian stopped and dithered. Though he knew that she'd felt a fool, it seemed less than tactful to say so.

Seeing his expression, Hanna's slight frostiness vanished. 'Oh, Brian, don't. It's all right. Unless it bothered you.'

'Me? Of course it didn't.' Brian sat on the bed. 'I just don't want you upset.' Having hugged her tightly, he held her away from him. 'You know it was Sandra?'

'I didn't imagine it was your secret mistress.'

'And you don't mind?'

'Sweetheart, how could I mind? Don't be stupid. Were you talking to Mike about her?'

'God, no. I didn't even know that sketch was there. I was talking about the fishermen's cottages down by the pier in Couneen. They'd never have been demolished if I'd had my say.'

Hanna's lips twitched and, disconcerted, Brian frowned. 'What?'

'Nothing. Just I really love you.'

This made no sense to Brian, but the smile she gave him was enough. Despite the amount he'd had to drink, they made love as they hadn't since the night Mike had turned up and, afterwards, he plucked up the courage to broach a subject they'd both been avoiding. 'You know we talked about going over to London?'

'Or the Algarve, or some romantic Greek island.'

'Yes, I'm sorry. We were going to stick a pin in a map.'

'But Mike came.'

'Yes. And, here's the thing, I don't really feel . . .'

'. . . that you can go away while he's around. I understand.'

'We could take a break later in the summer.'

'Yes.'

'I'm not sure how long he'll be here. He doesn't have concrete plans.'

'Darling, really, it doesn't matter.'

He wasn't totally certain that she meant it because how could she? Still, she kissed him and they curled up back to back, ready to sleep. Then, just as he was drifting off, Hanna stirred. 'Brian?'

'Um.'

'I had a text from Amy on the way home tonight.'

'Amy who?'

'Amy who I used to live with in London. Ages ago. We had lunch. She was here on a cruise. I told you.' Hanna paused before she went on. 'She's been in touch with the others from the flat share.'

Deeply relaxed and already drifting off again, Brian rolled over and kissed the nape of her neck. 'That's nice.'

'No, but, listen, Brian, she's invited me over to London. To a reunion.' For a moment this didn't register, then Brian pushed himself up onto his elbow, fully awake and inexplicably frightened. Hanna looked up at him over her shoulder, a slight frown between her straight eyebrows. 'I think I'll go.'

Chapter Seventeen

Charles Aukin climbed the winding staircase of Castle Lancy's least dangerous tower, which was squat, three-storeyed, and crumbling. There was one on each side of the medieval gateway and, while this was comparatively safe, the entrance to the other had to be blocked up long ago. On his first visit to the castle, when his wife was still alive, Charles had been startled by his in-laws' casual attitude towards decay. Although far from risk-averse in his own dealings as a banker, he'd found their habit of literally closing doors on problems unnerving. Lady Isobel, though born in the States, had inherited her Anglo-Irish family gene. When throwing herself into restoration, she'd concentrated solely on the central Georgian building, leaving the walls and towers, which enclosed it, to the crows. And now, thought Charles, he wasn't much better himself. At least his late wife had bustled from basement to attic, ensuring that furniture was polished and floors swept. He couldn't remember when he'd last bothered to enter the rooms he didn't occupy, and he hadn't been up on the battlements for years.

Emerging onto a flat roof, he discovered a large buddleia

sprouting from the masonry. A Monarch butterfly was sunning itself on one of the purple flowers, its orange wings with their black, white-spotted markings looking like scalloped shards of stained glass. It was joined by a couple of Cabbage Whites. Observing that their spread wings shaded to grey at the edges, Charles wondered if the furniture in the rooms he seldom entered was covered with dust-sheets. Since Isobel's death he'd rather let things go. That, however, was now set to change.

There was a shrill bark from below and, edging warily to the parapet, he peered down and saw The Divil erupt from Fury's van. Fury descended from the battered cab more sedately and, leaning against the door, lit a cigarette. Charles waved and called from the tower and The Divil went berserk, bouncing on his back legs like a miniature kangaroo. Fury raised his voice above the barking. 'Name of God, what're you doing up there?'

'I'll be down in a minute.'

'You'll be down on your head if you don't keep back. Those stones are likely to fall.'

'Nonsense, it's safe as houses. Stay where you are.'

A few minutes later Charles appeared at the arched entrance to the tower. Wild with excitement, The Divil bounded over and worried his shoelaces. Fury clicked his tongue in reproof. 'You have his blood pressure up to ninety. He doesn't like people turning up in unexpected places.'

'He seems pretty pleased to see me.'

'Ay, that's because he knows he can get round you for a biscuit. Matters of health and safety mean nothing to you.'

'Let's go find him one.' Brushing lichen off his hands, Charles led the way into the house and upstairs to the book room.

Fury looked around suspiciously as they passed through the elegant hall. 'What's been going on here?'

'Nothing. I've just had the windows cleaned.'

'Have you, indeed? For the first time in a decade?'

'Can't let the old place go to rack and ruin.'

'You've been making a good job of doing that up to now.'

The Divil reached the book-room door and scratched it violently. Fury glared at him. 'What kind of way is that to behave in a gentleman's private residence? And where's your respect for the tradesman who varnished that door? Holy God Almighty, I'm ashamed of you. Have you learned nothing in all the years you've spent working with me?' Abashed, The Divil sat down on his tail, but Fury wasn't impressed. 'I'll tell you what, all this football is pumping you up like an athlete on steroids. Next thing I know you'll be going out nights, smashing windows and picking up women.'

Suitably chastened, The Divil stood back and followed them into the room. Deciding it was safer not to beg, he looked beseechingly at Charles, who'd gone to a table where he kept a kettle and a biscuit tin. Charles shook his head. 'No, sir, I don't think your master would approve.'

'Oh, go on, you might as well give him one. Maybe it's custard creams that keep him mannerly.' Fury eyed the little dog severely. 'But conduct yourself from now on, d'you hear me? Or there's no way we're going to the County Final.' Turning to Charles, he raised his eyebrows. 'And why do I get a feeling that you're running riot too?'

'You could say that I'm doing precisely the opposite.'

Fury grunted. 'I dare say *you* could, but I'm damn sure I wouldn't. You're still hell bent on this cruise-trippers thing, aren't you? You didn't listen to a word I said the last time we talked.'

'On the contrary, I was all ears.'

'I said you were a damn fool even to consider it.'

Charles handed him a cup of coffee. 'And your input was deeply appreciated. Guys as rich as I am are always plagued by crawlers and yes-men. I used to lose it in the boardroom when my people wouldn't get off the goddamn fence.'

'You're going to ignore my advice, though.'

'I never ignore your advice, Fury. It's just that sometimes I don't take it.'

Turning his eyes to heaven, Fury sank into a chair. 'So you're opening up your castle to a pack of snotty tourists.'

'The term is "culturally curious".'

'Culturally curious, me arse! Those cruise-trip fellas are just in it for the money.'

'I'm used to fellows being in it for the money. I own a bank.'

'Oh, right, well, if that's your attitude, there's nothing more to be said.'

Charles looked at him mildly. 'Really? Because I was rather hoping you'd help.' He reached for his spectacles and held up one of the cruise line's leaflets. 'I've had a pretty robust discussion with this guy from Your World Awaits. Seems people have been complaining about their Cultural Carrick Experience. Well, I don't blame them. Basically it comes down to half an hour in that place called the Georgian Tea Shoppe, and who's going to believe that Jonathan Swift ever popped in there for a dish of tea and a green fudge shamrock? Anyway, the bottom line is they need to find somewhere authentic to walk folks round and give them a photo break and, since they'll already have seen the psalter in Lissbeg Library, Castle Lancy's the obvious candidate.'

'I've told you already I think you're a fool. Why would I want to help you?'

With a disarming smile, Charles looked at him over his gold-rimmed spectacles. 'Because you're my friend.'

'And why would you want a pack of strangers traipsing all over your house?'

'Because, let's face it, you're pretty much my *only* friend, Fury. That's the point. I need a real reason to get out of bed in the morning, and a way to let you off a hook you've been wriggling on for years. And I'm not proposing to let them traipse all over the house. I have a plan.'

Fury scowled. 'I wouldn't come looking at your boiler if it didn't suit me.'

'I know that. Don't you want to hear my plan?'

'No, I don't. Go on, spit it out.'

'Okay.' Charles spread the leaflet on his desk. 'They only need half an hour or so to fit into their schedule. So it's pretty simple. Open up the basement so they can see a proper Victorian kitchen. Chances are there's some Georgian stuff down there too. We can scatter it about. Take 'em through the hall, up the stairs, and into one of the fancier reception rooms. Polished windows, red velvet ropes, smell of beeswax, fluttering drapes, cut-glass bowls brimming with old-fashioned roses.'

'You've got cut-glass rose bowls, have you?'

'Bound to have. Then on into the Prince of Wales's bedroom. The abdication guy, he stayed here with Mrs Simpson back in the 1930s. It was their secret love nest way before the story broke.'

'Highly cultural.'

'Then turn 'em round, herd 'em out, and let them take selfies by the tower. Say twenty minutes indoors, ten in the courtyard, done and dusted, they're gone.'

Fury eyed him suspiciously. 'Where do I come in?'

'I'll need someone to show them round.'

'What?'

Charles gave him a deadpan look. Then he chortled. 'Get a grip! Of course I won't. The cruise-line guy will do that. No, I need for you to get creative. Knock up the little stands for the red-velvet ropes. Paint tasteful signs.'

'I'm a builder. I don't paint signs.'

'Oh, come on! Where's your sense of theatre? Think of all those tourists getting an in-depth glimpse of the past.'

'For free?'

'Certainly not. The cruise guy tried for a tenner a head. I said fifty.'

Fury blinked. A four hundred percent mark-up was impressive, even to a builder. 'What did you settle for?'

'Fifty. I don't haggle. Never did.'

It was evident that, despite himself, Fury was impressed. Charles smiled. 'Believe me, I know what cruise ships charge their passengers. My wife never saw a liner she didn't love.'

'You're going to need insurance.'

'Sure. Public liability. I made enquiries.' Charles got to his feet. 'How about we go and check out Wallis and Eddy's secret love nest?'

'As a matter of fact, she called him David. The Divil and I watched a BBC documentary on them once.'

'Now you're talking! That's exactly the sort of thing you can put on the signs.'

Fury picked The Divil up and hitched him onto his hip. 'Go on, then, let's have a look. I'd better keep this man in check in case he'd go eating Mrs Simpson's hot-water bottle.'

The Prince of Wales's bedroom was one of the rooms Lady Isobel had restored. According to Charles, she'd been advised by an English expert from the National Trust. 'We met him at a reception over in London. Nice fellow. He stayed here on and off when she was working on the house. Knew all the right people to call and where to get things done. Look at this.'

He flung back a series of shutters and Fury looked. Revealed was a 1930s interior, correct in every detail except for a towering four-poster bed with damask hangings and plumes of Prince of Wales feathers. Charles sneezed. 'This is how we found it. One of Isobel's aunts had had it gussied up for the prince. I figure she thought Wallis would like the original Georgian bed. It all needs a bit of spit and polish, but it's pretty good, huh?'

'Well, no offence, but it's not. It's plain weird.'

'And that, my friend, is precisely the point! It is literally culturally curious.' Charles gave him a quizzical look. 'Oh, come on, Fury, this is going to be fun.'

'And that's why you're doing it?'

'I've told you why I'm doing it. It's a whole new chapter.'

Fury sat down on an art deco sofa and considered a dressing table fashioned in lacquered bamboo. 'You've been skittish ever since you gave that psalter to the library.'

'If that means I like being back in touch with a community, you're right. I do. I like wandering into town and dropping into the library and having a chat about whatever page Hanna's happened to turn. I never looked at the psalter when it was here in a drawer in the book room. Now it's got me energised. Plus it's giving pleasure to other people, which gives pleasure to me. Nothing wrong with that.'

'No.'

'I like the thought of a bit of life around here too. I mean, what am I going to do, Fury? Live till I die and they stick me down with Isobel? Don't get me wrong, I'm happy to be here. If this is where she chose to lie, that's fine with me. I'll lie right beside her. But I've been behaving like I've got one foot in the grave already. She wouldn't want that.'

'That's a fair point.'

'Damn right it is! I never laughed so much as in the years I was married to Isobel, and I'm not going to sit in silence till I join her in the family mausoleum.'

'Crypt.'

'What?'

'She's buried in the crypt under the chapel. A mausoleum is an independent above-ground structure.'

'Yeah? Well, you can paint that on a sign when you've helped me get the place shipshape.'

'Oh, now I'm humping furniture round and scrubbing floors, am I? No doubt you'll have me filling the rose bowls as well.'

'Wait till you see the reception room. That's going to knock your socks off. You won't be able to wait to get stuck in.' Throwing an arm round Fury's shoulders, Charles urged him through the door and back down the stairs. 'I told the cruise-line guy we'd be good to go next week. He's got a party of ten lined up.'

'I don't suppose there's any chance you'll plough the proceeds back into your plumbing?'

'Of course not. The boiler stays as it is. I wouldn't dream of spoiling your fun.'

'I didn't say I had fun with your damn boiler. I said I came around because it suited me.'

'That's not what you meant, though, was it? Not really. You meant that you love playing about with all those copper pipes.'

'I most certainly didn't.'

Delighted to have got a rise out of him, Charles gave a gleeful chuckle. 'Sure you did. I could tell by the tone of your voice, and you know why, Fury? Because I always listen carefully to everything you say.'

Chapter Eighteen

One of the first things to be dealt with each morning at the deli was a basin of hard-boiled eggs. They were put on to boil as soon as the kitchen opened and, once cooled, had to be hand-shelled. It was a job nobody liked so they always took it in turns, and whoever did it was absolved from having to mix the day's egg salad. On Aideen's arrival, Bríd announced it was her turn to shell. 'It was Bartek yesterday and me the day before so it's all yours this morning. Actually, it ought to be you whenever you're here, since you're in so seldom.'

'Several days a week doesn't count as seldom. Go on, though, I'll do it this morning, I don't mind.' Aideen put on her apron and tucked her red curls under her scarf. She went through to the back of the deli and tipped the pot of eggs into the orange plastic basin, calling over her shoulder to Bríd, who was shredding chicken at speed, 'It's not much worse than catering for contractors, though at least at the farm I don't have to wear plastic gloves. Is Bartek coming in?'

'No. I said you and I could cope. He's doing double shifts at the weekend.'

'Anything special happening today?'

'Edge of the World Essentials wants a sandwich platter for a lunch meeting, and someone's due to collect that birthday cake.'

The cake was on the side under a Perspex cover, a two-tier fantasy of lemon sponge, white icing, and yellow sugar roses. The deli's regular baking was done by Bríd, but special-occasion cakes like this were made to order by a retired professional baker, whose sugar work was famous.

Aideen had put on her gloves and was busily shelling eggs. 'Imagine still being at the top of your game when you're a pensioner!'

'Tell me about it! Sometimes I think I'm already over the hill.' Bríd went to wash her hands and paused to admire the cake. 'It's for Mary Casey.'

'Is it? What age is she?'

'Dunno. When Jazz ordered it she said it didn't need any greeting or candles.'

'I'm not sure I'd want my age flagged if I was ancient.'

'Me neither. I'd say she's probably in her seventies, maybe pushing eighty? She's no spring chicken anyway. I doubt if we could have got all the candles on.'

They were both giggling when, unexpectedly, Mary surged in through the open door. Praying she hadn't heard what they'd been saying, Bríd smiled at her. 'Morning, Mrs Casey, what can I do for you today?'

'You can give me one of your rye loaves and a slice or two of salami.' Mary leaned across the counter. 'Come here and let me look at you. You've a face as red as a turkey cock. Are you sure you've not got a temperature? If you have, you know, you shouldn't be touching food.'

'I'm grand. It's just hot in here.'

Sensing that something was going on, Mary rapped on the counter. 'Well, in that case, is there any chance of a little service?'

With great aplomb, Aideen slid out from the back and casually dropped a tea-towel over the Perspex cover. Since Jazz had ordered it, the chances were that the cake was intended to be a birthday surprise. Mary looked at her sharply. 'You're still working here, are you? I thought you were at the farm.'

'Conor and I are living there, yeah, and I'm still here on and off.'

'At your age, I was at home keeping an eye on a baby. But, sure, everyone's on the contraceptives now.'

Seeing Aideen go scarlet, Bríd intervened. 'Give her a chance now, Mrs Casey, she's only just got married.'

Mary snorted. 'As far as I can see, nobody waits till they've got their marriage lines, these days. If they marry at all, which, half the time, they don't seem to. Not that it's any business of mine, of course.'

Bríd whipped the rye loaf into a paper bag. 'Two slices of salami, is it?'

'Don't be daft, what would I do with two slices? Cut me six good thick ones there, none of your slivers of wind. It's for Louisa, not me. English people like it but, sure, they'd eat anything. Have you tasted that Branston Pickle stuff?' Thrusting the loaf into her shopping bag, Mary turned back to Aideen. 'I'll tell you what it is, you're looking peaky. I wouldn't be surprised if the both of you were coming down with a bug.' She stood back and inspected them. Bríd at this stage was pink with annoyance and Aideen, who hated being stared at, had turned her face away. Mary stepped farther back from the counter, her eyes narrowing.

'You get fierce flushed with a bug.' Turning to a customer who'd just come in, she announced that foodborne germs were the world's worst. 'And gastric attacks can be fatal.'

The woman, who worked at the pharmacy, winked at Aideen and Bríd. 'Very true, and if you want my considered opinion, you'd need to be careful at your age.'

'It's not my age at all, it's a matter of hygiene.'

'Oh, I don't know, now, Mary. Say what you like, but I've heard you've a big birthday coming.'

With massive dignity, Mary declared that, if she had, what she didn't need was the whole town talking about it. Then, feeling outnumbered, she took her package of salami and swept out.

Bríd dealt with the pharmacist and Aideen returned to the eggs. She came through from the back when she'd finished them and threw her gloves into the bin. 'Will I do the pasta salad?'

'Are you okay?'

'Of course, I'm grand, why wouldn't I be?'

'Well, Mary Casey's a cow on wheels. I thought she'd upset you.'

'I just hate it when oul ones think they've a God-given right to go round asking questions. I bet she thinks you're not really married if you don't have a huge church wedding.'

'Ah, that's just Mary.' Knowing how sensitive Aideen could be, Bríd changed the subject. 'Good for you for covering up the cake.'

'I could've thrown it at her.'

'Yeah, but then you'd only have had to clean it up.'

This produced a reluctant smile, and for the next half an hour they were busy prepping and serving. Then, in the gap between

the office workers and the young mums with buggies, Bríd asked
how things were at the farm.

'Madly busy. Still, I tracked down Conor the other day when
he was out on the mobile library run. We had lunch in Cafferky's
over in Couneen.' Rather than leave Dan's name floating in the
air, Aideen mentioned that she'd seen him. 'He made us coffee.'

'Did he?'

'And then Conor told him to bugger off because we were on
a date.'

'That's sweet.'

'How d'you mean "sweet"?'

'Well, it's cute, isn't it? Calling it a date when you're married.'

'Married people can go on dates.' Aideen heard herself sounding cross and wished she'd kept her mouth shut. Having lunch
with Conor like that had felt really romantic and she didn't want
Bríd talking about it as if it were cutesy and childish. If anyone
was childish it was Bríd, the way she and Dan were always either
fighting like cats or falling into bed. There was nothing mature
and superior about that.

An influx of customers interrupted Aideen's train of thought
but when they'd made and served several coffees and sandwiches, and sold three rounds of goat's cheese and a dozen cin-
namon buns, Bríd brought the conversation back to Dan. 'How's
he looking?'

'Good. He's taking visitors out sea-angling.'

'He ought to be getting a business plan for the eco-tours together.'

'Well, but it's his business, surely? I mean, what he does with
his business is his business.'

'Anyone with half a brain cell could see that he needs to get his act together. I said I'd help.'

Aideen pulled a face and, turning her shoulder, went on with what she was doing.

Bríd gave her a push. 'What?'

'Nothing, it's just, well, men can need careful handling.'

'What are you now, an agony aunt?'

'No, but it's true. Dan's all mouth and no self-confidence. He'd hate getting instructions from his girlfriend.'

'I think I know Dan Cafferky better than you do.'

'Suit yourself.'

But Bríd wouldn't leave it. 'Being married doesn't make you an expert on relationships.'

'I never said it did. But you can be really pushy sometimes. I should know. You've been giving me instructions all my life.' Bríd bristled and, immediately, Aideen felt bad. 'You always want to be helpful, and I'm grateful. It's only . . . I know how Dan feels.'

'You don't know Dan at all. He tries that big-eyed, little-lost-victim act on everyone.'

'He wasn't trying anything. I hardly exchanged two words with him, and I told him he could forget using me as a go-between.'

'But he tried to. Didn't he?'

'No. That's what I'm telling you. Conor told him to back off.'

'*Conor* did? You were all talking about me?'

'No, we *weren't*. Conor asked him how work was going and Dan said he was doing the sea-angling, and then he looked at me and said he'd get his eco-tours going despite what some people think.'

'And?'

'And I knew that "some people" meant you, and I said I'm not my damn cousin's keeper. Which I'm not, Bríd. I'm not getting involved.'

'Good. Because I don't want you to.'

'Good.'

Aideen wondered if being married made you ratty. She'd never had words with Bríd like this before. On the other hand, it was high time Bríd stopped treating her like she was seventeen so, despite her instinct to apologise, she decided to stick to her guns. She hadn't done anything wrong and it was Bríd who'd been aggressive. Well, maybe she'd overreacted a bit, but still.

At this point Bríd jogged her elbow. 'Where's Conor working today?'

'At the library.'

'Well, do you want to grab twenty minutes and go over? Say three o'clock, if he could take a coffee break?'

As well as being welcome, this was an olive branch, so Aideen said yes. They were worked off their feet from then till well after lunchtime but she managed to ping a text to Conor, who replied saying he'd expect her.

When she peered round the library door he was over by the computers. 'Hi. I'm just putting in new printer ink. Hang on till I wash my hands.'

Hanna was sitting at the desk and Aideen smiled at her. 'Sorry to come and steal him away.'

'Not at all. It's a lovely day, so he may as well take his break outdoors instead of sitting cooped up in the kitchen.'

As they crossed the courtyard and went into the garden,

Conor linked Aideen. 'Actually, I'm a bit coffeed-out. I had my first of many at six a.m. Will we just sit on a bench?'

They found one near the convent wall where the tall stained-glass windows glowed like flowers. It was made of silvery time-bleached timber, and a plaque fixed to its back rail was inscribed 'Sister Michael, born Sarah Cassidy, a Worker in this Garden'. Conor sat down and spread out his fingers. 'Between the ink and the muck, I need one of those hand-mask treatments.'

'What in God's name is a hand-mask?'

'You know. A deep-heat, seaweed-wrap, intensive-massage session.' He sprawled comfortably on the bench, his arms along the back rail. 'Or, better still, three weeks in Barbados. But, listen, a good thing's happened. Miss Casey's off to London.'

'On holiday?'

'I dunno. Some reunion. She's staying with a friend. We're getting a week's cover from the County Library, but I'm going to be doing some extra hours.'

'When? You work all the hours God sends already.'

'I know, but it's not a massive amount. Just a few here and there that the cover can't do. The thing is, it's a nice, unexpected little earner. I thought you and I could have it as a holiday fund.'

'Like we're ever going to take a holiday again.'

'Ah, don't be like that, of course we will. Just wait a few months.'

'Promise?'

'Totally. I mean, obviously, I *could* blow the extra earnings on man-pampering. But I reckon going back to Italy would be better.'

'Better than a seaweed wrap?'

'God, yeah. Seaweed's slimy.' Conor gave her a hug and then

pulled away. 'Hang on, I've got something for you.' Reaching into his jacket, he produced a book. It was written by an author called Lorna Sixsmith and called *How to Be a Perfect Farm Wife*. 'Remember Blanche Ebbutt? *Don'ts for Wives*?'

'Yeah, but what's this?'

'It came out a few years ago. Yer one who wrote it is Irish. You could have it as a manual.'

Aideen looked at the contents list, which included chapters called 'Desperate farm wives', 'How to avoid a divorce', and 'How to teach a calf to drink from a bucket'.

Conor pointed. 'Here, look, "How to run fast in wellies". It's gas. You'll enjoy it.'

The list of chapters included one called 'Isolation or blissful solitude?' and one on 'How to cope with stress', which didn't sound gas to Aideen. Then she noticed one called 'What does he really mean?' Feeling alarmed, she turned to Conor. 'Are you saying I need a manual?'

He'd closed his eyes and stretched his arms along the back of the bench again, the picture of relaxation with his muck-and-ink-stained hands and his sunburned face. 'Of course not. I just thought it might give you a laugh.'

Aideen saw a chapter about how to tell when a farmer was complimenting you. Maybe he didn't share her occasional suspicion that she was a useless farm wife. Maybe he thought she was doing a great job. So much so that he felt he could joke about it. She was about to ask, when she realised his breathing had slowed and deepened. Then, as he gave a gentle snore, she spotted a chapter on 'How to manage a sleepy husband when visiting friends'. Suppressing a giggle, she settled his lolling head against her shoulder. Here he was, fast asleep at ten past three in the afternoon, and planning to take on extra hours at work. The possibility of ever spending an evening with friends again appeared unlikely, and the prospect of having a holiday seemed too distant to contemplate. On the other hand, there were ten more minutes to be spent here on a sunny bench with the scents of flowers drifting from the herb beds. Leaning her cheek against Conor's hair, which smelt of new-mown grass and, very faintly, of the cowshed, Aideen decided that this would do her for now.

Chapter Nineteen

Mary's surprise birthday party was held in the Hag's Glen. Maggie's place was too small and, besides, Mary disliked it. To her mind, despite all Hanna's careful restoration, it was still no more than a bockety old shed. So, the agreed venue was Brian's house, with its big open-plan living space and long dining table, which could comfortably accommodate family and guests.

Jazz arrived early with the sumptuous cake at which Hanna exclaimed in delight. 'That's amazing!'

'Do you like it? I was inspired by the photo of Granddad's yellow roses.'

'It's perfect. He sneaked that rose bush into the garden as a birthday surprise for your nan.' Tom's birthday gestures had been lavish, and always included dinner and an overnight stay in Carrick's Royal Victoria Hotel. Hanna had worried that today's party would seem tame in comparison with that time-honoured ritual, though, in the years that followed Tom's death, Mary had rejected all suggestions of a birthday dinner or tea at the hotel. Nonetheless, the occasion required celebration, not least because it traditionally involved Mary making a visit to the Carrick Couturier for shoes, a handbag, and a new summer dress.

Hanna took the cake to the table and cleared a space between two small pottery bowls she'd filled with wildflowers. They were family heirlooms, presented by Mary to Hanna on her move to Maggie's place, an unspoken apology for the rows she'd provoked during the claustrophobic years of living together in the bungalow. Hanna had received the gift gratefully, but with no reference to what had prompted it. In those days, words, however carefully chosen, might easily have sparked another row.

She had brought little from Maggie's place to her home in the Hag's Glen, yet she'd packed the bowls – traditionally used for tea drinking – and a thick shawl made of beige wool with a fringe a hand-span deep. This, too, had been a gift from Mary. 'It was your granny's. My mam's. And her mother's before her. I don't suppose you're fool enough to wear it, like a hippie, but you might throw it on a bed or the back of a chair.' Coffee drunk from one of the bowls had become an integral part of Hanna's weekend mornings at Maggie's and, responding to Mary's suggestion, she'd hung the shawl on an upright chair by the hearth. The occasions on which she'd worn it were tightly woven into her memory. Nights at the fireside with it wrapped around her, feeling lonely, and certain that she could never trust a man again. Chilly evenings when she'd come home from work wishing someone was there to greet her. And the time she'd thrown it round her shoulders over her silk kimono and looked up to see Brian smiling in her bedroom doorway. 'Gold brocade chrysanthemums and creamy-brown homespun. It's very effective. You look like an exotic version of Peig Sayers.'

She'd laughed and said it was clear that he'd never been made to read Peig Sayers's classic autobiography at school.

'Well, I read it at some stage and thought it was rather wonderful. What's not to like about a memoir set on a wild, romantic island? I can see Peig with golden chrysanthemums peeking from under her shawl.'

'There's certainly a lot of nonsense talked about her generation. They weren't all rattling rosary beads and doing what they were told. Even the nuns.' As she spoke, Hanna had had a vision of Maggie, doggedly stumping down her field to dig spuds in her old age. 'She left Finfarran in her teens, you know, and stayed away for ages. Some priest had accused her of loose living. I don't know about that but she certainly was an original. My dad gave her a silk scarf one Christmas. A head square printed with abstract splashes of colour. I think she wore it every day from then to the day she died.'

'Summer and winter?'

'With an old sack thrown over it when she'd be digging spuds in the rain.'

'Hence the shawl and the kimono. What's bred in the bone will out in the blood.' With a look of ineffable tenderness, Brian had crossed the room to kneel beside her. 'You do know that I love you, don't you?'

'Yes, I do.'

It had been a turning point in their relationship, the moment at which she'd believed what he said with no reservation, and no fear that her trust would end in betrayal.

Setting the cake with its trailing sugar roses on a platter, Hanna smiled at the strangeness of life. Given how often her mother irritated her, it was strange to think that Mary had packed those gifts and brought them to the Hag's Glen. She could have left them at Maggie's for Jazz, particularly since they had no obvious place here. The shawl was folded away on a shelf, and she no longer drank from the glazed pottery bowls, wide enough to require two hands to grasp them and deep enough to allow her to dip a croissant into her coffee. Yet she'd wanted to have them with her, and today, rooting in a cupboard while preparing for the party, she'd admired the pattern of yellow flowers beneath the bowls' worn glaze and taken them out to decorate the table. They looked perfect on either side of the cake, and Mary might even appreciate the gesture. Though maybe that was a bit much to expect.

The table was laid and the presents wrapped, Brian was boiling a kettle, and Jazz was chatting to Mary's best friend, Pat Fitz, a bird-like woman who'd brought a vast pavlova, when Mary made her entrance with Louisa. She was wearing a flowered chiffon dress with a pearl necklace and what she called 'my little gold cocktail watch', and carried a smart clutch bag under her arm. Hanna kissed her and admired the impressive hairdo, which had taken the girl in the salon several hours to colour and style.

'Ah, she did her best but I'm not sure the cut really suits me.'

That was the cue for a chorus of denials and reassurances, which everyone else provided while Hanna moved off to greet Louisa. She'd never been able to stand her mother's unsubtle demands for compliments. As Louisa, elegant and quietly dressed as always, handed Hanna a bottle of champagne, Brian went gallantly to kiss Mary. 'Here you are looking beautiful, as always! Happy birthday!'

The door opened again to reveal Johnny Hennessy, his wife, and several members of the Monday Memories Club. Mary, who'd just taken in Pat Fitz's presence, swung round and saw them. 'What's going on?'

'It's a surprise party, Nan. Here's to the birthday girl!' Jazz raised a glass of wine and everyone cheered and clapped.

As Brian began filling and handing out glasses, Mary drew Hanna aside. 'I'm not going to have to put up with that Maguire fellow, am I?'

All the members of the Monday Memories Club had been invited, since Hanna had felt that omitting Mr Maguire would be rude and unkind. But fortunately he'd sent his regrets in a text, which began 'Dear Hanna', ended 'Yours sincerely', and explained at length that he had a prior engagement. Deciding not to mention this narrow escape, Hanna smiled. 'You needn't worry, he won't be here and we're going to have a great time. Look, Jazz brought this lovely cake for you.'

Since Jazz had brought it, Mary beamed at the cake, and since Brian had bowed deeply as he handed her a champagne glass, she inclined her head graciously in acceptance. 'Well, I must say this is very nice and most unexpected. I thought we were just dropping over for tea.'

Mike clattered down the stairs and wished her a happy birthday. Mary looked him up and down disparagingly. 'Oh, right, Mike, Brian's son, is that it? Aren't you the one who was supposed to be running races with our Jazz?'

'Well, we did talk about doing the Paris marathon.'

'Ay, so I heard. Never happened, though, did it?'

Jazz came to Mike's rescue. 'We were both too busy in the end, Nan. It's nice to see Mike here again, though, isn't it?'

'Is it? I dare say. In my day girls were less forgiving when lads let them down.'

Hanna saw Brian struggling to keep a straight face. Mike and Jazz didn't seem put out either, so she laughed and clapped her hands. 'If everyone has a glass of champagne, is it time to cut the cake? Come on, Mam, you do the honours and we'll all take photographs.'

Happy to be the centre of attention, Mary allowed herself to be brought to the table and given a knife. She cut the cake to applause and raised glasses while Mike, leaning against a wall, videoed the proceedings, and the guests broke into a ragged chorus of 'Happy Birthday to You'.

Later, when Brian had put on some background music, Hanna sat beside him on the window seat. 'It's going well.'

'Of course it is. Mary's in her element, and fair play to her. I hope I'm as feisty as that when I reach her age.'

Hanna looked across the room to where Mary was holding court among the guests. 'I'm trying to pluck up the courage to tell her I'm off to London tomorrow.'

'Why?'

'Oh, because she'll fuss and want to know why, and demand to know if I'm going to see Malcolm.'

'Are you?'

'I'm not planning to, no. Why do you ask?'

'I don't know. Green-eyed monster.'

Hanna gave a crow of laughter. 'No! Really? Honestly, Brian, that's daft. If I was planning to leave you for someone, I certainly wouldn't choose Malcolm. I've more sense.'

'Who, then?'

'Pierce Brosnan. Luke Skywalker. Possibly Caravaggio – though he did get done for murder.'

'You know, Freud would have had a field day with your sub-conscious mind.'

Hanna clinked her glass with his. 'I'll miss you.'

'You'll have a good time with the girls, though.'

'Yeah. And you can hang out with Mike.'

'That's not why you're going, is it?'

'No. Well, partly. But Amy's right, I have been stagnating. I mean, I fancy a trip to the bright lights. Maybe I'll buy a pair of stilettos like Mam's.'

On the far side of the room, with Johnny Hennessy as a be-mused partner, Mary was demonstrating dance steps to a record-ing of 'In a Sentimental Mood'. Other guests were beginning to dance around the kitchen table, under which Jo had retreated in dismay. Hanna called her and she came to sit on the window seat, squeezing between them and laying her head on Brian's thigh. In the midst of the slow-moving dancers, the red soles of Mary's sti-lettos flashed as she made an unexpected twirl. Hanna scratched Jo's ears. 'Mam and Dad were always going out dancing. I remem-ber her wearing those pearls. He gave her the famous cocktail watch for her birthday the year I was ten.'

'How long is it since he died?'

'Twelve, no, thirteen years. I was still in London. Still mar-ried to Malcolm. Still thinking I knew precisely the course my life would take. Nobody knows what's going to happen next, do they? Like I never imagined Mam having to cope without Dad.'

'But we can't control life, can we? We've just got to live it the best way we can.'

Hanna stood up and pulled him to his feet. 'Let's have a dance before I run off and leave you.'

'Don't.'

'Don't what?'

'Joke about it.'

She looked up at him in surprise. 'What's the matter?'

'Nothing. It must be the champagne at teatime. Makes me lose my sense of humour.'

He held her close and they drifted past Mary, who was now dancing with Pat. Mike was revolving with Jazz while holding his phone up to take a video. Johnny Hennessy and his wife were eating cake at the table with Louisa, and several members of the Monday Memories Club had annexed the sofa and a plate of ham sandwiches. The bowls of wildflowers had been pushed aside when Mary cut the birthday cake, and a wilting buttercup lay on the platter among scattered crumbs and broken sugar roses.

Fitting her head beneath Brian's chin, Hanna breathed in the scent of him. Though she'd felt excited when she'd booked her flight, the thought of leaving tomorrow was making her oddly lethargic. She felt unequal to the challenge, as if she were taking a momentous step that could never be reversed. Yet a quick hop over to London, a week in Windsor, and an evening out with her former flatmates wasn't exactly challenging, more like the boring sort of thing you might expect of a middle-aged librarian. Certainly not like sticking a pin in a map and flying off with your lover on a whim. The thought of that deferred plan brought a lump to Hanna's throat. Blinking away unexpected tears, she reminded herself of what Brian had said. The important thing was to live now, in the moment, which was something she'd never been good at. She always seemed to be looking back or worrying about the future. But there was no point in wishing this trip away or pining for another. The party was going well and, whatever fears she might have for her mother, Mary looked better than she had for ages. Drifting through the laughing, chattering dancers, Hanna forced herself to focus on well-clipped lawns, shopping trips, and Amy's brisk reassurance in the nuns' garden. Like Brian, she was probably just reacting to champagne at teatime. Nothing bad was going to happen if she just got away for a while.

Some of the dancers had spilled from the kitchen into the living area and, as the music changed to a track with upbeat vocals, the Monday Memories Club began to sing along. Brian kissed the top of Hanna's head, and Jazz, boogying past with Mike, reached out an arm and hugged her. Yet still Hanna felt strange and, as the music swelled, she pressed her face hard against Brian's shoulder, as if the warmth of his body could dispel a chill that had made her shiver and long to cancel her trip.

Chapter Twenty

Despite the previous day's misgivings, Hanna felt a rush of excitement when her plane touched down at Stansted. She'd left Brian and Mike to clear up after the party, gone to bed early, and got up at five. The rain-washed sky had been streaked with pink as she'd driven down the glen, and a single star had shone through the morning mist. Cobwebs trembling in the hedgerows had seemed to reflect the starlight, their dew-spangled threads lacing fuchsia blossoms to furze. When she'd turned at the mouth of the glen, she'd seen lights in the farm kitchen and heard the sound of machinery from the yard. Then, having driven along the back road by the forest, she'd reached the motorway and, before long, had cleared Carrick, crossed the county boundary, and was on her way to the airport in Cork.

In skirting the forest, she'd passed Fury's house. The shed at the rear had been shut, and no lights were on but, as she'd passed, Fury had appeared at the door. With the countryman's undisguised interest in every car that passed, he'd paused and scrutinised her as she'd approached. Then, when she'd pulled in to say good morning, he'd strolled over and leaned on the roof of her car. 'You're out early, then.'

'I am. I'm off to London.'

'For a holiday, is it?'

'That's right. Just a week.'

'I thought you might find a way to make yourself scarce.'

This time Hanna hadn't risen to his bait. There'd been no point in pretending she didn't know what he meant, or protesting that Amy's invitation had come before Mike's arrival. Instead she'd said that she'd best keep going or else she'd miss her plane.

'Fair enough.'

'Keep an eye on Brian for me.'

As she'd driven off she'd wondered why on earth she'd said that about Brian. It must have been because of a stupid conversation she'd had at the birthday party. The presents had been opened and exclaimed over, and the guests had moved on from champagne to coffee, when she'd found herself sitting alone in the kitchen with Mary. To her surprise, her birthday gift of a leather-bound pink notebook had gone down well. At a club meeting Mary had said she needed something convenient to jot things down in, and when Hanna had seen the little book she'd bought it in the hope it might be right. Finding presents for Mary was never easy: she was choosy and never scrupled to say if something didn't suit. But the notebook had been approved. 'Very nice and I like the colour. It'll fit in my new bag too.'

In the pause that followed, Hanna had straightened the wild-flowers in their bowls. 'Do you remember these?'

'I do, of course. I'm surprised to see you're using them.'

'I used them as breakfast coffee cups at Maggie's. Every weekend.'

'Well, I'd say Brian wouldn't have time for old things.'

'Not at all. I mean, I know this house is sleek and white . . .'

'Like a hospital ward.'

'No, it's not!'

'Don't go biting my head off. He's a good man, Hanna. I'm glad you've found him.'

Feeling touched, Hanna had smiled. 'I'm glad you like him. And you know he thinks you're great.'

It had all been going so well until Mary had lowered her voice conspiratorially. 'I hope to God you're going to have the sense you were born with this time.'

'What?'

'Well, don't get me wrong, but you know you were fooled before.'

Drawing back, Hanna had heard her own voice rising. 'For God's sake, Mam, what are you suggesting?'

'Suggesting? I'm far too old to beat around the bush. I'm *saying* that even the best of men can behave like a damned eejit. Especially round a woman who's marked him down as an easy catch.'

'What are you on about?'

'If you don't know, doesn't that prove my point? Sure, it's the talk of the seven parishes that Pauline Murphy inside in the council offices has her eye on him.'

'Pauline Murphy?' A vague memory of a pleasant woman she'd met at some council function had come back to Hanna. 'Brian hardly knows her.'

Mary had snorted. 'That won't bother Pauline. Come here to me, I knew her mother, we were at school together. Ask Pat Fitz, if you don't believe your own flesh and blood. Maeve Nolan always had a roving eye, and that Pauline of hers is the same.'

'Don't be daft.'

'Well, you'd best keep your eye on Brian, that's all. And I'll tell you this. You're a fool to yerself for not getting a wedding ring on your finger, because an unmarried man is fair game to the likes of Pauline Murphy. Mark that.'

Struggling to keep her temper, Hanna had tried to put a stop to things with a laugh. 'Well, I hope you're wrong because, as it happens, I'm off to London tomorrow.'

That wasn't how she'd intended to break the news of her trip to Mary, whose hands had instantly flown to her hips. 'Are you indeed? And when were you going to deign to tell your mother?'

'Oh, Mam! Calm down, it's only Sunday to Friday. It was a last-minute thing and of course I was going to tell you. It's just that the party's been great and I haven't had a chance.'

'And I'm supposed to believe that story, am I? Don't tell me! I'd have been lucky to get a postcard.' Mary tossed her head. 'And, with the way the post is these days, you'd have been back before I'd ever known you were gone.'

Goaded beyond control, Hanna had snapped that that wasn't likely. 'I've never known a week to pass without you demanding attention.' Then, shocked by what she'd said, she'd tried to take Mary's hand. 'I'm sorry, that was horrible. Truly, I didn't mean it. It's just – you shouldn't talk like that about Brian.'

Mary took a folded Kleenex from under the band of her watch.

This was an act Hanna had seen a thousand times before. 'Ah, for God's sake, don't start getting weepy.'

Thrusting the tissue into her bag, Mary had snapped it shut. 'I said nothing against Brian, so don't you go putting words into my mouth. What I *did* say was that I raised a fool for a daughter, and I'll say it again now if you haven't the sense to take a hint. Why would I open my beak if not to protect you? God knows it's little thanks I get for trying to help.'

'I don't need help and I don't need protecting. Because, I promise you, Mam, this is all in your head. I'm sure Pauline Murphy hasn't the least interest in Brian. Even if she had, it wouldn't matter. He and I are fine.'

'Oh, I can see there's no point in my pursuing the matter.' With a great show of dignity, Mary had risen and checked her watch. 'Good heavens, look at the time! I'm sure we ought to be getting along.'

'No, really, it's early, let me pour you another drink.'

But, having seen Mary stand up, Louisa had come over and, with Mary on her feet, the rest of the party had begun to disperse as well.

*

As Hanna stood in the arrivals hall, she hoped Jazz wasn't bothered by the way the party had ended. She comforted herself with the thought that everyone was used to Mary's knee-jerk decisions, which, in this instance, could have been put down to tiredness. Besides, Jazz was seldom troubled by her grandmother's sulks and tantrums, perhaps because she and Mary shared a strong, loving relationship. Whereas, Hanna thought sadly, I waste energy trying to knit up the ravelled ends of something that was always full of holes. It was a difficult admission and one she seldom articulated. In a way it was easier to think of

Mary as growing slightly bonkers than to face the fact that they'd been at odds for as long as she could remember; and bonkers felt like a safer, easier way to think of it when words like 'senile' and 'dementia' were too scary to confront.

There was no doubt that this latest idea of Mary's was off the wall. Retrieving her case from the carousel, Hanna smiled at the thought of Brian as the hero of a Regency romance, captivated by the wiles of a man-hunter, and only saved by a series of plot twists intended to keep the reader hooked till the very last page. The idea of Pauline Murphy flaunting an ivory-handled fan around the council building in Carrick entertained her until she boarded the London train. As soon as she'd settled herself and her luggage, she took out her phone to contact Amy and found two texts from Mary on her screen. Dreading the thought of a re-run of last night's conversation, Hanna took a deep breath before reading them. But the first simply said SAFE# JOURNEY, and the second MIND YOURSELF NOW MIND ME YOU WOULDNT B USED TO THE TRQAFFIC. Apparently Mary was still standing on her dignity, or else she'd been gripped by one of her maternal spasms of concern.

Having pinged back a text to say that she'd landed, Hanna tapped out another and sent it to Amy, who must have been waiting to hear from her, because she responded at once.

Hi. On Stansted Express.
Fab. Give me a shout when on your train
From W/Loo. Do you like capers?
Yes
OK. Salmon for lunch.
C U soon.

The layout of Waterloo station had changed since Hanna had last been there, but she found the Windsor and Eton Riverside train with no trouble and, once she'd stowed her case and let Amy know she'd boarded, she relaxed. It had been a long journey but this was the last leg, and it was good to know she'd be picked up at the station.

Amy was waiting when the train pulled in, petite and perky in an expensively faded denim bomber jacket, a white satin top, and lime-green palazzo pants. She hugged Hanna and wrinkled her nose at the hoodie and jeans she'd worn for comfort on the journey. 'You *so* need new clothes.'

Hanna dumped her suitcase on the platform. 'If you're going to be snarky, you can drag this.'

'I hope it's not full of more sad T-shirts and stretched hoodies.'

'I promise I'll scrub up beautifully if you're planning candle-light suppers.'

Amy's car was as shiny and new as her outfit. They drove through the steep streets of the town and turned into a leafy road of detached red-brick houses, most of which had alarm systems and electronic gates. Amy's was on a corner plot, a very English, 1950s Stockbroker Tudor home. Taking Hanna's case, she ushered her through a door from the garage to a utility room. Beyond it, a large kitchen looked like a display model in a showroom. 'Here we are. Feel free to nose around and make tea and coffee. That's a double oven, but I'm not sure I've opened it. I live on ready meals, so I just use the microwave.' Talking over her shoulder, Amy took the suitcase through to the hall. 'Clive grew up here, so when we were married the whole place reeked of his mother. Not a woman I'd have wanted to meet, and I bet she'd have hated me. A little one from Cork wouldn't have been her idea of marriage material. Fortunately, by the time I met Clive, she'd joined her husband pushing up the daisies, and I got carte blanche to redo the house.' They reached a square landing and Amy led Hanna down a corridor. 'Your room's down here, over-looking the back garden. There's a bathroom next door, with a decent shower, and the water's always hot. I've left towels and stuff, but shout if you need something.'

Hanna was reminded of Malcolm's parents' former home in Kent, though everything here was newer and more suburban. The bedroom was furnished from the chintzier end of Heal's de-partment store. There was a double bed, built-in wardrobes, and a blanket chest, and a button-back chair stood by a round table in the window. The curtains were patterned with daisies and pop-pies and there was a charming view of the River Thames, which flowed past the end of the garden.

'This is a lovely room.'

'Well, that's a compliment. You're the one who always said my taste was in my mouth.'

'God, did I really? I must have been a cow!'

'Not at all, you were right, I hadn't a clue. I probably still don't, but now I use a personal shopper for clothes. The house was done by a designer and I'd say she ripped me off big-time. Still, it suits me, and Clive liked it. He thought it was wildly trendy but I suspect it's just his mother's taste brought up to date.'

'Well, I think it's great, and I'm really grateful, Amy. I needed this holiday.'

Amy eyed her shrewdly. 'I've been wondering what hap-pened to change your mind about coming. You don't have to say, though you might find it cleansing. Like colonic irrigation.'

'Please tell me you don't go in for that.'

'I did once, in a salon on a cruise ship. Never again, though. I mean, who wants to watch mucoid plaque floating by through a hose stuck up your bum?'

'Shut *up*.'

Amy left her to settle in, saying she'd go downstairs and see to lunch. Hanna unpacked and freshened up, showering and changing into a shirt and chinos, finding a pair of FitFlops, then brushing out and replaiting her hair, which had come loose on the train.

Lunch was laid on a table in a conservatory off the living room. It was cold poached salmon with a lemon caper sauce, served with little dough balls and a frisée lettuce salad. The bifold doors were drawn back to let in the breeze from the garden, where insects hummed in neat herbaceous borders. After they'd eaten, they carried coffee down to a pair of cushioned loungers by the river, and lay with their cups and a cafetière on a low table between them. It was nothing like sitting with Jazz on the high cliff behind Maggie's place, with a wine bottle cushioned on sea-pinks and the waves pounding below. Here, the garden they'd strolled down was immaculate, the loungers were placed on a railed wooden deck, and the broad river drifted slowly between manicured banks. But it was beautiful. Damselflies with flashing wings skimmed over the surface, and geese and ducks paddled serenely by. Trees in heavy summer leaf grew close to the water, where trailing willows made islands of the twigs that floated on the current. Houses with long, well-tended gardens lined the far bank, many with decks like Amy's where small craft were tied up. Hanna exclaimed at a little boathouse opposite them, which had scalloped tiles and a gilded weathercock.

Amy yawned and admired her own painted toenails. 'That's the Morrisons' place and they're not nautical. I think they use the boathouse to store deckchairs. Clive had a dinghy and mooched around pretending to be butch. I sold it when he died.'

'So he wasn't actually butch?'

'God, no. I told you, he was a teddy bear.' Amy cocked her eye at Hanna. 'What about Brian?'

'He builds things. I don't mean with his bare hands.'

'Kind of half-butch, then.'

Hanna laughed. 'You'd like him.' She was about to issue an invitation to visit sometime when she stopped, wondering if Brian would get on with Amy. He wasn't wild about fashionable women who giggled and painted their nails. So, maybe an invitation would be an unwise hostage to fortune. Instead of speaking, she sipped Amy's excellent coffee and relaxed. This trip was supposed to be about living in the moment, and that was precisely what she intended to do.

Chapter Twenty-One

Conor was dealing with emails when Mike put his head round the library door, saying he wanted to see the Carrick Psalter. Accustomed to the fact that the public never seemed to read notices, Conor told him the entry times were posted on the exhibition's door. 'There's a guided tour each half-hour at this time of year.' More often than not, at this time of year, there were long queues as well but, for some reason, there were few visitors today.

Mike came in and sat casually on the edge of the desk, cradling the camera that hung round his neck. 'I know, I saw. But there seems to be no one to let me in and I don't want to hang about.'

Conor glanced over his shoulder at the glass wall that separated the library from the exhibition space. It was ten fifteen and, beyond the wall, Oliver, the volunteer guide on duty, was perched on a stool in a far corner, reading a book on his Kindle. 'You're Mike Morton, aren't you?'

'Does it make a difference?'

'No. But hang on, I'll give Oliver a shout.' Conor scooted his chair back and, rapping on the glass, caused Oliver to look up.

Then he propelled his chair back to the desk. 'If you go round to the door to the exhibition entry, he'll let you in.'

'Do I pay him or you?'

That information also appeared on the notice, but Conor refrained from saying so. 'If you haven't already booked online, Oliver has tickets.'

'Cool. Thanks.'

As Mike left, Conor called after him. 'You can't take photos inside in the exhibition. Not using a flash.'

'No problem. You're Conor, aren't you?'

'That's me.'

'Nice to meet you.'

As the library door closed, Conor reflected that Fury's widely shared summation of Mike had been right. He appeared to have a great welcome for himself.

Oliver, a stickler for procedure, issued Mike with a ticket before allowing him through the door. 'I shouldn't really let you in after the published time, and I can't offer the full tour at a quarter past the hour.'

'I know. It doesn't matter.'

Slightly shocked, Oliver positioned himself in the centre of the room. 'The Carrick Psalter, one of the lost jewels of Ireland's medieval heritage, is believed to have been compiled in the eighth century –'

Strolling across to the display case, Mike interrupted him. 'Really, I'm fine, I don't need that stuff.'

Oliver, who was short and wore round glasses, looked at him reprovingly. 'There's a great deal of detail, you know, which enhances the experience.'

'Sure. But I'm just here to see the latest page.'

Pursing his lips, Oliver returned to his Kindle, and Mike looked down at the little book in its low-lit glass case. Hanna had turned over a new page before leaving for London and, listening to her description of it during the birthday-party preparations, Mike's interest had been piqued. Now, looking down at the open book, he could see what she'd meant.

The image illustrated a verse from Psalm 104. It ran diagonally across two pages, from the top right-hand corner to the bottom left. There was only one line of text, which a screen on the wall translated as '*He waters the hills from His upper chambers. The earth is satisfied*'. There was a squiggle after 'satisfied', indicating that the verse continued on the following page. Looking at the riotous wealth of colour, Mike grinned appreciatively. Evidently, the single image of God at an upstairs window with a watering-can had given the illustrator quite enough to be going on with.

In the top corner, between two hills, a moated castle stood at the head of a valley. Star-strewn flags flew from its turrets and, from a golden urn poking through the topmost window, a stream of water arced across the moat, fell as a foaming waterfall, and became a river on the valley floor below. Where it curved to gush down the double-page spread, the water was spanned by a rainbow. Leaning closer, Mike could see that a shimmering effect had been produced by rows of tiny gold dots between the rainbow's colours. Slender blue and gold fish leaped through the waterfall, and birds flying above the river were painted in shades of indigo, violet, and red. Honeysuckle twined around the initial letter of the text and, determined to show the earth's satisfaction, the illustrator had filled the valley with green rushes, yellow irises, and trees bowed down by bright crimson apples.

Automatically, Mike reached for his camera, and Oliver, watching from behind his Kindle, immediately bounced off his stool. Mike laughed. 'It's okay. Just a reflex. I know the rules.'

'All the pages have been digitised to allow close inspection, and images can be bought as cards and posters in the gift shop. We ask visitors not to touch the display.' Oliver looked pointedly at the glass case, where Mike's hands had left faint marks when he'd leaned over the psalter.

'I'll pass on the posters, thanks. I could polish the case if you happen to have a duster.' Seeing Oliver's reaction, Mike laughed again. 'Sorry, just a joke. Not one of my best. It's a pretty stunning thing, the psalter, isn't it?'

'Have you seen all you've come for? I've a party of ten booked for my next slot.'

'Yeah, I'm done. Thank you.'

'You're very welcome. Enjoy the rest of your stay here in Finfarran. As we say in Ireland, *go néirí an bóthar leat*, may the road rise with you.' Having reverted to his official script, Oliver couldn't open the door fast enough, and the smile with which he ushered Mike out was a tribute to his training.

Outside, with time to kill, Mike wandered through to the nuns' garden. There was a vacant table by the fountain, but he'd got up late and recently had breakfast so he didn't want a coffee. Wandering aimlessly along a gravel path, he saw Jazz emerge from the Old Convent Centre. She was dressed for work and carrying an armful of papers. Pleased to see someone he knew, Mike went to meet her. 'Hi. Taking a break?'

'On my way home. I had a meeting with a crowd from Dublin at the crack of dawn and I spent all Sunday preparing for it, so I'm taking the rest of today off in lieu.'

'Nothing like being your own boss.'

'I'd probably have kept going till lunchtime, but it was a very successful meeting – entirely down to me, I may add – so when Louisa shooed me out, I didn't say no.'

'What're you going to do?'

Jazz shifted her papers from one arm to the other. 'Hang out at home. Go to the beach for a swim, maybe. Could be I'll do a sneaky bit of work on these if I get bored.'

'On a free day!'

'Might do. I've a really low boredom threshold.'

'Why don't I come along? I fancy a swim, and two's company. I'll stave off boredom by telling you traveller's tales.'

'You see, I was interested there for a minute until you said that.'

'Okay, no traveller's tales. I would love a swim, though. Can I tag along?'

'Sure, why not?'

He fell into step beside her and they made their way to the car park. Mike remembered their first chance encounter, on his previous trip to Finfarran. She seemed very different this time, far more cheerful and less tense. 'You're living out in the country now, aren't you?'

'Yup.' Jazz manoeuvred the car into Broad Street's mid-morning traffic and cut through Sheep Street as the quickest way out of town. 'I'm renting the house Mum had before moving in with your dad.'

'Can you swim nearby?'

'Not far. It's called Seal Beach. We used to go there when I came here on holidays as a kid. There's proper golden sand, and it's safe for bathing.'

'Proper seals too?'

'Masses of them. With pups at this time of year.'

'I might shoot some photos.'

They had reached a one-track road bordered by pasture and Jazz slowed the car to avoid a loping hare. 'There's plenty of wildlife round here, if that's what you like to photograph. Brian took some shots of seals on the beach. I've seen them. Did you get your love of photography from him?'

'Not unless it's genetic. I didn't see him much when I was a kid.'

Jazz shot him a glance. 'You told me once that families were only complex if people allowed them to be.'

'That's pretty profound.'

'Or really trite.'

'It needs context. I can't remember what we were talking about.'

'Me, I expect. I was kind of neurotic back then.' Jazz swung the wheel, pulled in by a gate, and reached to take her bag from the back seat. 'Welcome to Maggie's place.' She could remember their first meeting, on the cliff path, perfectly, and she suspected that Mike did too. She'd been curled in a patch of sunshine reading, and he'd rounded a corner, tripped over her feet, and sent the book flying. They'd chatted and later, when they met again, he'd invited her out for dinner in Ballyfin. Her boyfriend had just dumped her in the worst way possible, by moving out of her studio flat and leaving a note stuck to the wardrobe door. Hurt and humiliated, the last thing she'd wanted was a confidant and, to her relief, Mike hadn't pestered her with questions. Later, when the sun had gone down, and lights on yachts and fishing boats were reflected in the dusky water, they'd strolled out into the warm night. The marina wall was the perfect height to lean on, so Jazz had rested her elbows on it and propped her chin on her hands, watching the last of the daylight fade and stars beginning to appear in the ink-dark sky. 'Weird to think of the rest of the world out there in darkness.'

'Well, half of it's just getting up to a bright new day.'

'But that's what I mean. All those lives being led in other places, and we don't see them.'

Though he'd responded with a polite noise, the thought of other lives hadn't seemed to interest him, and when she'd talked about her family he'd said little about his own. Later, as they'd walked back to where her car was parked behind the restaurant, he'd made the remark about families not being complex unless you allowed them to be. Now Jazz wondered if that was how he approached all relationships. But it doesn't matter to me, she thought. He's here for a swim and a lazy day, nothing more.

His response when she led him into the house was gratifying. 'Wow. Cool place.'

'I love it.'

'I would too. It's pretty isolated, though. You don't get lonely?'

'Never. I'm enjoying my own company more and more.' Jazz glanced round the sunny room. 'This place is like a snail-shell. Small and cosy.'

'But not like the cardboard box you had before.'

'God, no. The walls here are two foot thick. And I've more

than one room. And a garden. *And* a clifftop bench with a breath-taking view. Talk about luxury! I'm not much of a gardener, though.' She looked at him speculatively. 'I don't suppose you know how to use a scythe?'

'Haven't a clue.'

'Me neither, and the path down to the cliff is becoming a jungle.'

'You can't just use a mower like everybody else? Or is it special Finfarran grass that only responds to a scythe?'

'Of course not. I just think it might have got too long for a mower. There's an old electric one in the shed but I can't set the blades high enough. The thing that moves them up and down is too stiff.'

'Well, there I might be able to help. Is there any oil in the shed?'

'Yup, and I've applied it. Still can't shift them.'

'Okay, last-ditch offer. Do you want me to try brute strength?'

'I don't suppose it could hurt.'

He didn't look particularly strong but, to her surprise, he moved the blades easily, setting them at the right height for mow-ing the long grass.

'Impressive.'

'It might have had something to do with the fact that the oil had had time to sink in.'

Jazz laughed. 'How about I make us lunch when I've done a bit of mowing?'

'How about you tackle the grass and I make the lunch?'

'Do you cook?'

'Only when showing off, and I'm fairly limited. Do you have a freezer?'

'Yes.'

'Does it contain burgers?'

'Probably.'

'Okay. You mow, I'll do something spectacular with a pack of frozen burgers, and, after a suitable pause for digestion, we can go for that swim.'

Chapter Twenty-Two

Hanna woke and automatically reached out for Brian. Realising he wasn't there, she sat up abruptly, thinking she must have overslept and that he'd already got up. At first, the unfamiliar surroundings confused her, then, remembering where she was, she pushed herself upright against her pillows and looked round the sunny room with its poppy-and-daisy-patterned curtains and highly polished furniture. Though her own London house had been in a Georgian terrace, she was reminded of it by elements of Amy's designer's chosen décor.

Back then, enchanted by the tall, neglected building she'd found for herself and Malcolm, Hanna had hired professionals for the structure and planned the entire interior herself. The bedrooms were hung with hand-printed paper, and she'd spent hours searching for amber-glass doorknobs, and sanding and polishing yards of mahogany banister. After months of searching, she'd found the perfect cream-enamelled vintage range for the basement kitchen, which the builders had extended under a glass roof to provide more light. In the garden she'd planted espaliered pear trees against the red-brick walls, and added a table and benches to turn it into an outdoor dining room. It had taken nearly a year for the house to be ready, and by the time they moved in she was deeply in love with it. On their first evening there, she and Malcolm had wandered about hand in hand. For the master bedroom, she'd chosen fabrics to complement the sage-green papered walls, and when she'd opened the door there'd been a bottle of champagne by the bed. Malcolm had laughed when she'd seen the silver wine cooler it stood in. 'What do you think? It's supposed to be exactly the right period.'

It had been so perfect that Hanna had almost burst into tears. As he poured the champagne he'd told her how much he loved her, and that night she'd told herself that here was the true fulfilment of her dream. Years afterwards she'd realised that when she'd been searching for doorknobs and choosing fabrics he had already begun his affair with Tessa.

But this was no time to be thinking of the past. Stretching luxuriously, Hanna rolled out of bed and went to the bathroom to take a shower. A fluffy white dressing-gown hung on a hook but, though Amy had provided a stack of towels and every possible Crabtree & Evelyn product, there was no shower cap. Making a turban out of a towel, she managed to shower without wetting her hair and, twenty minutes later, joined Amy downstairs for breakfast.

'Did you sleep?'

'Like a log. It's such a comfortable bed.'

'Claire's really excited about the reunion. Lucy *still* hasn't replied. Her assistant says she's on her way back from India.'

'Was she on holiday?'

'Sourcing spices or something. Anyway, she's been off-radar, but the assistant said she'd be sure to pin her down as soon as she can. She'd want to get a move on.'

Helping herself to fruit salad and muesli, Hanna said she might go for a wander round Windsor. 'Just to reorient myself, unless you've got something else planned. I'm going to pick up a shower cap for your bathroom.'

'Oh, Hanna, who needs a shower cap these days? Other than you? I mean, no one our age goes around with her hair hanging down her back.'

'It's not down my back, it barely touches my shoulder blades.'

'Whatever. And look at those greys!'

'I rather like having silver threads. I think of them as high-lights.'

'Well, I see them as greys. Don't you have decent hairdressers in Finfarran?'

'When did you turn into such a bully?'

But Amy had always been like that, outspoken to a fault and hard to fall out with. There was a look on her face now that made Hanna laugh. Amy raised her eyebrows. 'What?'

'You're appraising my outfit.' She was wearing beige chinos and a cream sweater and, anticipating a walk around the shop-ping streets, had paired them with dark brown tasselled loafers.

Amy shrugged. 'Actually, I was thinking that you're looking rather smart. You've certainly kept your figure, whereas I pile the pounds on whenever I try to stop smoking, and you can carry off that cool, classic look. You always could – it used to make me sick.' She poured more tea, put down the pot, and continued to appraise Hanna. 'Though you really ought to get yourself a haircut.'

Hanna spread butter and honey on a slice of toast. 'I'm grand as I am. I don't fancy having to maintain a haircut. I've better things to do. And how would you like it if I told you that you ought to change your appearance?'

Amy giggled. 'I'd love it! We could go up to town and hit the shops big-time. Have ourselves a couple of makeovers. Let's do it, Hanna. It'd be fun.'

'And knock the sight out of Claire's and Lucy's eyes?'

'Absolutely. Are you up for it?'

'No, eejit, of course I'm not. I told you, I'm happy as I am. Let me help you with this washing-up when we've eaten, then I'll go and find that shower cap.'

'I've a Mrs Barker who comes in and cleans. Leave this lot, she'll manage it.'

'Amy, what do you actually do all day?'

'Don't give me that po-faced look. I've masses to keep me busy.'

'Okay. It's none of my business anyway. Do you fancy showing me around Windsor this morning?'

'Not if you're going to faff about buying shower caps.' Amy got up from the table and gave her a hug. 'You have a mooch around and I'll see you later. Have a lie-down, though, if you come in feeling knackered. You must be tired after yesterday's flight.'

Hanna returned the hug and went upstairs to get ready. Checking her phone, which she'd switched off before going to bed, she found a text from Brian and two from Mary. Brian's simply said *Good morning*. Mary's read:

I CANT FIND THATNOT$BOIOK YOU GAVE ME
I FOUND IT IT WAS IN MY NEW BAG

Having responded to Brian with a kiss and a heart emoji, Hanna typed *Great* and pinged it off to Mary, hoping it wouldn't elicit a response. Then she brushed her teeth, gathered her bag and her sunglasses, went downstairs, and asked if she should pick up something for lunch. Amy, who was scrolling through shopping sites, looked up and shook her head. 'No need. I've an online account at Waitrose. I just order stuff up.'

'Will I get some flowers?'

'Masses in the garden. Not that I ever pick them. But, actually, yes, flowers would be nice. Not lilies, though. Clive always brought them and the scent made me sick, and I never had the heart to say so. It worked out in the end, though. They poisoned the neighbour's cat and Clive gave up buying them.'

'Poisoned it? How?'

'It licked the pollen. Fatal to cats, apparently. We didn't know. The neighbour came round the following day with the poor thing in a shoebox, wanting compensation.'

'So what happened?'

'Oh, Clive rolled over and forked out – he didn't do conflict. I bet Malcolm would've fought the case all the way to the High Court. Or threatened to sue the neighbour back for letting the cat trespass.'

'I bet you're right. He could never resist a challenge.'

'That must have been wearing.' Amy returned to Instagram, and Hanna left her sitting with her feet up on a footstool, a cigarette dangling between her fingers, and her eyes fixed on her phone.

The steep streets round Windsor Castle were crowded with groups and individuals eagerly consulting apps, eating ice-cream, and buying souvenirs. The press of tourists reminded Hanna forcibly of Lissbeg and, for a moment, she wondered if she ought to call and check that Conor was coping at the library. But common sense kicked in and, turning her back on the crowds with their corgi mugs and Harry and Meghan tea-towels, she found a department store in a mall, which sold her a shower cap patterned with daisies and poppies. Then, taking a half-remembered route to the river, she crossed the bridge to Eton, which was less crowded.

The last time she'd been there was with a friend whose thirteen-year-old son had been at school at Eton College. Grace had called her one evening in a panic. 'It's his second term – no, I must call it "half" – and I still haven't turned up to mingle.'

'God, do you have to? Who with?'

'Oh, there's this dreadful bit in the stuff they send you, about how the headmaster and his wife are "at home" after Chapel. Jonathan says he's too busy, and that it's always down to the mothers, and Charley says he's beginning to feel like an orphan, so I've got to go. It says "parents, their sons, and any other guests", Hanna, so will you come with me? I could introduce you as Charley's godmother. That should go down well.'

'Don't you get struck down for lying in Chapel?'

'I'll cross my fingers and get Jon to up our donation to the organ fund. Say you'll come.'

Jonathan had chambers next to Malcolm's, and Grace hadn't grown up expecting to send her offspring to Eton so, feeling sorry for her, Hanna had agreed. They'd turned up suitably dressed and wearing appropriate hats, and had been rewarded by Charley's look of relief as he greeted them. Hanna had wondered whether, if she'd had a son, Malcolm would have insisted he went to Harrow School, which he'd attended himself. As it was, Jazz had been sent to a co-educational day school close to home. Now, watching a group of Eton schoolboys pass in a tight, tribal group,

Hanna found herself thanking her lucky stars. It had taken time for Jazz to settle in her new school in Lissbeg, but at least she'd been spared the culture shock of removal from this kind of rarefied upper-class bubble, and the need to adjust to the company of boys as well as girls.

Yet, despite its smug air of privilege, the far end of the high street felt like a charming village and reminded Hanna of much that she'd missed about England. The beautiful, dignified school buildings, the well-kept grounds, and even the boys' daft tailcoats and waistcoats, stiff collars and pinstriped trousers spoke of a prosperous heritage Finfarran lacked. Any of these kids with their clear, high-pitched voices could be descendants of the young couple who'd posed for the eighteenth-century painting she'd found so captivating in her teens. Even then, she'd been aware that it radiated achievement. There was a groom somewhere in the background, wearing livery, but the hand on the horse's bridle was the master's and the swagger with which he presented his good fortune to the viewer was almost as touching as it was self-satisfied. Sometimes she'd wondered if she'd fallen for Malcolm simply because he'd exuded precisely the same air of vulnerable arrogance, though by the time she'd moved to London, she'd thought she'd ditched the notion that her dream required the presence of a man. She'd even faintly despised Amy's lack of independent ambition. The fact that, in reality, she'd ditched her dream for Malcolm still irked her in retrospect, and the memory of a friend's jokey engagement card saying "How Have the Mighty Fallen!!!" still made her wince. Yet how could she regret her marriage? Without Malcolm, she wouldn't have had Jazz.

As she dawdled down the high street past a shop where a tailor sat working in a window, Hanna's thoughts returned to the visit she'd made to Eton with Grace. Meeting the headmaster and his wife had been less formidable than they'd feared, and Charley had been sweetly grateful for their presence in Chapel, and for his large lunch afterwards in the Christopher Hotel. Yet on the train back to London, Grace had burst into tears. Gulping, she'd explained how much she'd hated the stoic look on her son's face when they'd left him, and the way he'd stepped back when she'd offered him a hug. There was nothing Hanna could do but produce Kleenex and reassurance, neither of which had stopped the flow of tears. Then, when she'd reached home, she'd found that ten-year-old Jazz had spent the afternoon baking. The kitchen door was open to the tiny town garden, where Malcolm, sitting on a bench, was holding a heavily iced bun and a glass of Gewürztraminer. Jazz had rushed to greet her, with none of Charley's painful, self-imposed repression, and Hanna's heart had ached at the thought of Grace's desolate face.

'I've made buns – it's a surprise. Do you like them? Taste them, Mum! They're chocolate. The icing is almond fondant. Dad says the sprinkles are very effective.' Releasing Hanna from a sticky hug, Jazz had danced away and returned with a glass. 'And I opened a bottle of wine, so you two could chill out under the pear trees. The label says "bosky notes", so it's right for the garden.'

Hanna had accepted a bun so sweet it had practically taken the enamel off her teeth, and was hustled out to join Malcolm on the bench. Biting heroically into his bun, Malcolm had raised his glass to her, pulling an eloquent face behind their excited daughter's back. It was a shared moment of amused love that Hanna had never forgotten and, even knowing what she now knew about her hollow marriage, she wouldn't have changed the memory for the world.

Chapter Twenty-Three

The Divil was partial to a saucer of tea and didn't care how hot it was. Fury had recently refused him his usual spoonful of sugar but he bore this patiently, lapping steadily till he reached the bottom of the saucer and sneezing when the dregs got up his nose. Tea and toast were his usual breakfast, followed by a trip to the yard to dig up his latest selection of bones. Having cleaned and sharpened his teeth, and aided digestion with grass, he was ready to join Fury for whatever the day might bring.

Today they were on the road to Castle Lancy when Fury slowed the van and pulled in. Mary Casey was standing on the verge with her hand raised, as if to halt a bus. Scooping The Divil up in one hand, Fury tipped him over the back of the seat and, opening the passenger door, called down to Mary, 'Is it Carrick?'

'It is.'

'Can you climb up, or will I come round and give you a bit of a hoosh?'

'I've not lost the use of me limbs yet.' Mary thrust an Orla Kiely shopping bag onto the seat and climbed up to join him. Having adjusted the seatbelt across her massive bosom, she sniffed loudly. 'Holy God, the stink of linseed oil that's in here! Is it Silvermints you're eating?'

Fury opened the glove compartment and offered her a tube of mints. There was an immediate burst of barking from The Divil, who was lying in the back on a tangle of tools and timber.

'You don't feed these yokes to him, do you?'

'Not at all, he's on a strict regime.' Raising his voice, he glanced threateningly over his shoulder. 'And there'll be no going to the County Final if he doesn't stick to it.'

Mary put a mint into her mouth and ran a suspicious finger over the dashboard. 'Do you never take a damp rag into this van?'

'I do not.'

'Easy seen.' Comfortably settled in the seat, and raising her voice above The Divil's indignant barking, Mary announced she was going to Aldi in Carrick. 'Louisa never has a minute to give me a lift into town, these days, and Hanna's off wandering in London.'

'You'd do well to wait for the bus.'

'Ah, the bus never runs when I want to be up and going.'

'Still and all, you wouldn't want to get into a car with a stranger.'

'Do you take me for a fool? Didn't I see who it was I was stopping? Anyway, these days a stranger wouldn't pull in for you.'

'God knows that's true. You'd do right to be careful at your age, though.'

'I'm a spring chicken compared to yourself. Don't be talking to me!'

'A matter of a couple of years, girl.'

'At least I've more sense than to rattle around in an old van, looking for trouble.'

'If you don't like the van, you can always step out.'

'Ah, don't be annoying me. Can I get you anything in Aldi?'

'Not unless they do a decent Battenberg. The Divil hates marzipan, so it's the only cake I can have in the house, these days.'

'No supermarket ever did a decent Battenberg.'

'True enough. I'm game ball, so.'

With the air of one who'd come out on top in a hard-fought war of words, Mary helped herself to another mint. 'Come here to me, Fury, do you ever find that you can't remember what you went looking for?'

'Is this philosophy or a trick question to make me admit that I'm staggering towards my dotage?'

The philosophy question was lost on Mary, whose mind seemed troubled. 'Well, if it's a symptom of dotage, I'm staggering that way meself. Half the time I'll stand in a room and I can't, for the life of me, work out why I went into it.'

'Ah, sure, that's a thing that happens to everyone.'

'Would you say?'

Fury looked across at her. 'Are you worried about it? Would you go to a doctor?'

'I am and I amn't. And, no, I wouldn't go near any doctor. They'd have you prepped for surgery down in Cork as soon as look at you.'

'What – because you're a small bit forgetful?'

'I take no risk when it comes to the medical profession. Any chance to experiment and they're reaching for the knife.' Mary studied the pattern on her bag. 'I'd say it's been happening more in the last few months, though.'

'Age comes to all of us, girl.'

'I read in a magazine that we need to keep active.'

'You mean rattle around in an old van, looking for trouble?'

She gave him a snort of appreciation. 'Is that your excuse?'

'I'm going to die with my boots on, I can tell you that for nothing. As long as I can be useful I'll be rattling round in the van.'

'But that's the thing, isn't it, though, Fury? You can go out and do a day's work. People, these days, can't give a big enough welcome to a builder. But what has an oul one like me got to offer, and who'd want it?'

'That's no way to talk. Haven't you family?'

'Isn't that my point? Jazz is up to her eyes with the business, and Hanna never had need of me. She was her father's pet from the start, and I was the one left in the ha'penny place. And don't mention Louisa because she doesn't need me either, with her appointments and her iPad and her little Chanel suits.'

They'd reached Carrick and Fury was steering through the back-streets towards Aldi. Mary folded her empty shopping bag over on her knee. 'God knows why I'm talking to you about any of this. Mind you don't go repeating it.'

'Do you think I would?'

'I suppose I don't or I wouldn't have opened my beak.'

He swung the wheel to avoid a tourist's hire-car. 'I'd say your man there is having trouble with his sat-nav. Come here, if I drop you behind the car park, can you walk through to the entrance?'

'I'm not on me feckin' walker yet. I can walk a few yards.'

'Will you be all right to get home?'

'Ah, there's a bus in an hour, I'll take that. Go on away from me.' Swinging sideways, Mary opened the door, then, balanced on the edge of the seat, she spoke with a sudden formal assumption of dignity. 'It was good of you to pick me up, and much appreciated. You must step in and let me give you tea the next time you're passing the bungalow.'

'There's no need for that, I don't want payment.'

Mary slid from the seat to the ground and, having smoothed her skirt down over her knees, she turned and glared up at him, her voice regaining the rhythms of their youth. 'Don't I know damn well that you don't want payment, and don't you know that that's not what I offered! I'm saying come by if you're passing because I could do with a bit of company. But don't worry if you can't fit me into your busy schedule. I might be out doing better things with my own valuable time.'

Fifteen minutes later, Fury drove into the cobbled yard behind Castle Lancy. He parked and strolled around to the front entrance where Charles was straightening a notice saying 'Private'. A series of arrows indicated the way to a side door, and a large sign at the blocked-up entrance of the gate tower read 'Danger of Falling Masonry. Keep Back.'

Charles beamed at Fury. 'What d'you think?'

'I still think this is a daft idea, but I suppose the Yanks that's going will go for anything.'

'Today's first group is Japanese.' Charles glanced around. 'Where's The Divil?'

'Wasting his time chasing your kitchen cat. And don't tell me you didn't know you had one. There's generations of them breeding behind the wash house.'

'I've been doing some research about the de Lancys online. There's a mass of records here in the castle too. Did you know that the family used to employ a rat-catcher?'

'They did, of course, and they probably gave him the rats to take home for his dinner. You don't get rich enough to build a castle without sweating the locals.'

Charles grasped him by the arm and hustled him indoors. 'Did you know that they kept visitors' books?' He threw open a chest in the hall, revealing stacks of leather-bound albums. 'Nineteenth century, most of them. Full of good stuff for the culturally curious.' He opened one at a page marked by a piece torn from a crossword. 'Check this out. *The splendour falling on your castle walls will remain with me for ever. Your affect. friend, Alfred Tennyson, August 1842.*' Before Fury could respond, he delved into the chest and opened another volume. 'And this. *Forgive me for feeding my greedy son all the figs at dinner! Jane (Speranza) Wilde. 11 October 1864.* See? The de Lancys hung out with everyone. Oscar Wilde's mom. Victorian poet laureates.'

'Poets laureate.'

'Really?'

'We had a schoolmaster beat that kind of stuff into us when I was young. Never taught us a thing that was useful, mind. Not when we were up to our knees in mud, digging trenches for gas pipes.'

'Look here. *Killarney's lakes take the lead, I think, of any one of our English lakes, but in Finfarran I perceive the finest landscape in these islands. My gratitude for your hospitality on our hasty visit, and for her ladyship's kind loan of a pair of excellent reading glasses.* Who do you think?'

'How would I know?'

'William Wordsworth, September 1829.'

'That's great altogether. Will the Japanese be wanting to wash their hands?'

'Oh, right, yes, the boiler. The water's running hot okay, it's just spitting out rusty bits.'

'I'd better go and wrestle my way through the rats, then.'

Charles's eyes were gleaming with enthusiasm. 'On your way down, check out the things I've scattered around in the kitchen. It's "*Downton Abbey*, eat your heart out". The Japanese are going to love it. And when you're done with the rats, bring The Divil up to the book room. We'll have an inaugural drink.'

Chapter Twenty-Four

There was a utility room at the farm equipped with a washing-machine heavy enough to deal with dirty overalls, and an equally robust spin-drier, but Aideen loved pegging laundry outdoors. On fine days things were dried on long lines in the orchard and if it rained, or the forecast was bad, they were hung in the big open-sided barn, where the roof gave shelter and wind blowing through aided the drying process. There had been a rotary clothesline in the cramped yard behind the terraced house in St Finian's Close, but Aunt Bridge had been fiercely proud of her high-speed washer-drier so, in Aideen's childhood, laundry had seldom been hung out to dry.

The orchard lines were stretched between poles in an open, grassy space, with enough height to take double sheets and duvets. Closer to the house, Paddy had strung a length of cord between two gnarled apple trees, on which kitchen cloths could be pegged out. It was handier than walking up to the proper washing lines and, as Orla said, a kitchen cloth could be rinsed and wrung easily if a bird up in the apple trees happened to shit on it. With the laundry basket against her hip, Aideen walked from the kitchen to the orchard and, setting the basket at her feet, began to peg out floor cloths, tea-towels, and dusters. It was a bright, breezy day with a faint suggestion of autumn in the air.

According to Orla, the oldest trees in the orchard had stood for three generations. 'Conor's gran told me her mum planted one when she married into the farm. It was still bearing fruit when Joe was a toddler, and for a good few years after, but it went in the storm we had the week Conor was born. I set a replacement down near the house when I brought him home from the hospital.' The tree she had planted was one of the two between which Paddy had strung his length of cord, and Aideen liked the idea that it was the same age as Conor. The apples it produced were Braeburns, which had firm flesh that kept its structure when chopped into chunks for a tart. Not like the Bramleys on the second tree, which collapsed into frothy foam when baked or boiled. Paddy always insisted that the proper filling in an Irish apple tart ought to be sugared purée, but Aideen, like Orla and Conor, enjoyed the Braeburns' melting, honey-sweetened chunks.

Although it was Bríd who had culinary qualifications, Aideen had always enjoyed home baking. She delighted in kneading soda bread while the cats lapped milk on the kitchen step in the mornings, and in picking and preparing fruit to make pies, jams, and tarts; and now that she lived at the farm she had an appreciative family, and plenty of passersby, to eat the results. Her aunt Bridge and her gran had enjoyed the latest cakes advertised on the telly, and the pastries Bríd made for the deli were uniformly delicious, but Aideen's approach required no such uniformity. It depended on whatever came to hand. Thin slices cut from windfall fruit made toppings for sponge cakes when thickly sprinkled with dark Barbados sugar. An excess of eggs when the farm hens had appeared to go into overdrive could yield a batch of ham or spinach quiches. Or a rich butterscotch pudding. Or Hot Milk Cake, which used four egg yolks, or Chocolate Profiteroles, which took six. Leftover pastry from pie-making could be pieced together and rolled out for little jam tartlets or twisted into long straws flavoured with cheese grated from rinds, which, otherwise, would be discarded. She loved the forethought and economy that went into such household baking, and to her the term 'cheese-paring' conjured up creativity, just as the sour taste of a raw Bramley apple produced visions of sweet puddings to come.

Moving from the short washing line to the first of the three long ones, Aideen began hanging out sheets and duvet covers. As they billowed in the wind, she began to peg clothes to the next line, catching glimpses of the apple trees and gooseberry bushes between fluttering shirts and flapping jeans. By this time of year, most of the orchard's trees were fruiting, and beneath their rustling canopies, windfalls were scattered in the grass. Lichen stippled the branches of one tree at the top of the orchard, which had thinning leaf cover and bore little fruit. When Aideen had first seen the grey and yellow lichen, she'd assumed it had caused the leaf loss, but Paddy, who'd left his desk for a break, had shaken his head when she'd said so. 'Not at all, girl, lichen's benign. It hardly absorbs a thing from the tree, barring a few minerals, and it won't do a pick of harm.'

'But it's only growing on the one where the leaves are thinnest.'

'Ah, trees get baldy on top for all sorts of reasons, but lichen's not one. It's there because that's where it thrives. See? The sunlight on the branches creates the right environment for it.'

Inspecting the frilled growth more closely, Aideen had been charmed. It looked as if layers of lace had been dipped in liquid silver and bronze and draped on the branches, where it had stiffened. The silvery sections had flat surfaces, which almost seemed to have been polished, yet, when touched, the lichen crumbled like dust in her hand. Some of the frills were coarse and some delicate, and the combinations of texture and colour were marvellous. 'So, why has this tree gone baldy?'

'It's had its time, love. That's an old fellow getting ready to die. Isn't it a grand thing, though, that it puts on a coloured cloak on its way out?'

Paddy's expansive moments always surprised her. He could go for days without saying a word beyond a request for tea or a gruff demand for a lost receipt, yet sometimes he'd tell Aideen things about the farm that she'd never heard from Conor. Once, when they were alone in the kitchen, he'd spoken about Old Dawson. 'He's a decent old skin, and it's not that I mind taking his money as a loan. You can't stagnate in farming. It never makes sense. But you can't be chasing all the new-fangled notions either, Aideen. Not without you give them a hard stare first. I've nothing against the stuff they teach them at uni, but you've got to understand your tools before you take them in hand.'

'How d'you mean?'

Paddy had frowned and then, to her surprise, launched into a lecture. 'Well, take the cameras they have, these days, in calving sheds. You have them installed and that saves you from staggering out twenty times in the night to see how she's doing. Fair enough. She's warm and dry inside and there's light, so you're not groping in the dark if something goes wrong. And I'm not saying a word against that. It makes sense. But I'll tell you this, now. My father wouldn't bring a cow down to calve in a shed if she'd found her own place in the field and wanted to stay there. I've seen him get up and go out with a torch as many times as it took to keep an eye on her, and he'd always keep downwind and stay back, the way she wouldn't be troubled by him. And that man never lost a cow.'

'But things do go wrong, don't they?'

'They do, of course, I'm not saying they don't. You have to take a view. And you'd have to know what you were looking at. My father could tell by looking whether things were normal or not, and I swear to God, she'd trust him and come below in advance if she was going to need help. Don't ask me how. I've seen it. It was the same with his father, too, and he was a mighty herdsman. And it's something Conor and Dermot will never see, because the cameras are up and the cows are down and that's the way of it now. When a new way of doing things comes in, there's always a gain that you can measure. But here's the point, girl. Something always gets lost as well, and once it's gone, it can't be measured, so there's no way to do a proper comparison. And it can't be got back. Mark that.'

Aideen never told Conor about these conversations. It would have felt like a betrayal of Paddy's confidence, though, for all she knew, he might have said the same sort of things to his sons. According to Conor, when he and Joe were growing up Paddy had been a great teacher. 'I don't really remember my granddad but Paddy was great for passing on stuff he learned from him. Joe never really listened but I was always sitting there with my two ears flapping.'

Joe's inability to listen had caused Paddy's accident, though the McCarthys seldom talked about that. Conor had told Aideen that

Joe had always been prone to kicking over the traces because, as his mam said, he'd never really been suited to farming. Sometimes he'd go on a batter, as if he'd just had enough. The accident had happened the day after he'd been out on a pub crawl and come home wrecked around four a.m. The following morning he'd only been half awake on the job, and when a pregnant cow in a pen had got aggressive she'd nearly trampled him. Quick action by his father had given him time to escape, but Paddy had had to roll over the rail at the last minute and had come down on his spine in the cobbled yard.

It was typical of Joe to have failed to attend to the safety rules Paddy had drummed into his sons since the day they'd begun to walk. His father had never blamed him for his accident but, as Conor had told Aideen, Joe had never got over the shock of it, and Aideen knew without being told that Orla was torn between anger with Joe and deep pity for them both. So Old Dawson's offer of a job in Cork had been a godsend in more ways than one, and the money Joe sent to pay Dermot's wages was, in a sense, reparation.

There was a further complication in that Paddy, too, carried a burden of guilt because, when it came to claiming his medical bills on the farm's insurance policy, it had turned out that the cover he'd taken wasn't nearly enough. Their financial worries were largely behind them now, which was making a difference, yet Paddy's dark mood swings still cast a shadow. He was in chronic pain because of the damage to his spine and, according to the doctor, much of his depression arose from the side effects of medication, which, in his case, apparently, was 'the least worst option'. Aideen was certain that it wasn't just about medication and side effects. For someone raised in a tradition of teaching by

206 / Felicity Hayes-McCoy

practical demonstration, the frustration of being unable to join in field work must be frightful. To her mind, it was no wonder that Paddy sometimes retreated into silence, and the times when he was forthcoming appeared too precious to jeopardise by talking about them. Even to Conor and Orla.

Swinging the empty basket, Aideen returned to the house. The McCarthys' hens had the run of a section of the orchard, where they scratched and sunned themselves between currant bushes. As she passed, she looked in and called, 'Chook, chook, chook.' A younger hen raised an interested head but the old biddies, ignoring Aideen's call, went on foraging. They knew that a pan of potato peelings was brought for them in the evenings before they scuttled up to the henhouse, and that nothing was likely to be on offer at this hour of the morning. So, for the time being, they were concentrating on insects and worms, juicy purslane, chickweed, and dandelions.

In the kitchen Orla was stringing beans with the radio on in the background, and as Aideen entered, Paddy looked in from the office. 'You might want to shut the hens in early this evening. I'd say we have a fox.'

'Ah, for God's sake! Are you sure?'

'A fox or a mink, maybe. Them devils are moving down from up the country.'

Orla rolled her eyes. 'Right. If you're shutting them in, Aideen, will you be careful?'

'Okay.' Aideen sat at the table and began to help with the beans. 'Why would mink be moving down?' The image had suggested an organised invasion, like the weasels and stoats in *The Wind in the Willows*, or the threatening march of the orcs in *The Lord of the Rings* film.

'Because some animal-rights eejits released them from a mink farm up north a couple of years back. They've been breeding like the bejaysus since, so they have to keep moving on, looking for hunting grounds.'

Orla interrupted Paddy soothingly. 'Ah, now, Paddy, it might just be the fox.'

'I've yet to meet a fox that could get through a two-inch fence link, the way some fella did that was digging around the hen-house last night. No fox ever shat the way he did either. I'd say it was a mink.'

'Will you set a trap?'

'We'll have to. Tell Dermot when he's in.' Paddy went back into the office and Orla smiled at Aideen. 'Don't look so worried, pet. If you have hens you'll always have predators.'

'Are mink very big?'

'You get them the size of a dog fox, and they're fierce. But they wouldn't attack unless they were cornered. Mostly you wouldn't even see them.'

'Were the ones that got released being farmed for fur?'

'Yes, and it's illegal now, which is why Paddy's annoyed. Letting them out, the way they'd spread and breed, was just bananas.'

It was dreadful to think of little animals raised in cages to be killed. Aunt Bridge had had a mink stole, which she'd worn to Mass on Sundays, and Aideen had always felt embarrassed by it. Everyone at school had been going round collecting for animal shelters and eco charities, and there was Aunt Bridge marching up to Communion with a little furry dead guy around her neck. On the other hand, here was Conor, raising lambs and calves for slaughter. Having cared for the weakling lambs and nursed them to health by the range, Aideen had tried not to think about what it had meant when Orla had brought them up to join the rest of the flock. It had actually made her feel queasy. From little patients, wrapped in crochet shawls and hand-fed from bottles, they'd reverted to being units on Paddy's spreadsheets. Because Conor had accused her of seeing farming through rose-tinted glasses, she hadn't wanted to talk about it, but now she wondered what Paddy would say if she raised the subject with him.

Chapter Twenty-Five

Brian had rearranged his workload in anticipation of a holiday with Hanna, so now he found himself free to spend time with Mike. Evenings relaxing over a meal and a few beers were all very well but spending entire days together was different, and Brian had a feeling that his son might not welcome quite as much of his company as was on offer. For someone in his twenties, Mike's self-containment was disconcerting. Looking at himself in the mirror as he was shaving, Brian remembered what Hanna had said about his own reticence. Perhaps the apple hadn't fallen too far from the tree. Indeed, he thought, reaching for a towel, reticence hadn't been Hanna's first choice of word. She'd begun by calling him remote.

Downstairs, Mike was sitting by an open window with his laptop on his knee. Brian opened the front door and whistled for Jo, who padded in and looked pointedly at the window seat. Relinquishing his place, Mike moved to the kitchen table with his laptop and Jo heaved herself into her usual position, nose on her extended forepaws, eyes fixed on the road that ran through the glen.

'This really is her kingdom, isn't it?'

'She's actually rather deferential. Knows her own mind, though.' Brian looked at Jo. 'I wish she hadn't chosen the window seat as her vantage point. She's getting a bit old and stiff to jump onto it.'

'Do you know what age she is?'

'The vet said she could be pushing seventeen.'

Mike considered the dog. 'So she was a pup when I was still at prep school.'

'Possibly. And when you were struggling with algebra she was probably herding cattle.'

'Algebra was one of the things I never struggled with.'

It was a casual remark but it reminded Brian of how little he knew his son. Though Mike's attention had returned to his screen and Brian hesitated to interrupt, a mixture of curiosity and a desire to redress the past overcame him. 'Did you enjoy school?'

Mike looked up politely. 'Yeah, I suppose I did. Maths was a big thing. Art not so much, till a new master set up a film club. Then Mum and Dad got me a camera for my birthday, and things took off.'

Brian remembered that camera. He had called his sister just before Mike's sixteenth birthday and told her he'd like to buy him a gift, instead of sending money to be spent on one, as he'd done each previous year. 'Don't make a thing of it, though. I mean, you needn't say it's from me.'

Kate had demurred. 'Are you sure, Bri? I've been wondering if we ought to have a talk with him about you.'

'I'm certain. Don't rock the boat. You said you'd explain things when he left school, so let's stick with that. I don't want to hijack his birthday, I'd just like him to have a camera.'

'I think he'd like that too. He's got really interested in a film club at school.'

'There you are, then. Let me buy it and send it to you. If that's okay? You can say it's from you and Bob.'

He'd been aware of continued uncertainty at Kate's end of the line and had felt bad about it. If the gift really would be so welcome to Mike, his giving it would, in a sense, hijack the birthday, for his sister and her husband if not for his son.

Mike's voice, newly animated, interrupted Brian's thoughts. 'It was a brilliant camera. Miles better than anyone else's I knew.'

'When I was a kid all I ever wanted was a proper toolkit. Sharp chisels and a hammer that would actually drive in a nail. Year after year I kept being given useless kiddy stuff – crap screwdrivers and saws that wouldn't cut butter. It drove me mad.'

'I can imagine.'

Brian wondered if he could. Getting to his feet, he went to switch on the kettle. 'Want a coffee?'

'What? No, I'm good.'

Mike had returned to his laptop but, since everyone of his age seemed to converse while staring at a screen, Brian persisted. 'How about the film school? Did you enjoy that?'

'It was cool.' Mike flipped his laptop closed and pushed back his chair.

Feeling dismissed, Brian took out his phone to see if he'd had a text message from Hanna. They'd already exchanged texts to say good morning and, before she'd left, they'd agreed not to behave like obsessive teenagers. Nevertheless he found himself checking more often than made sense.

There was nothing to see and, as he put away his phone,

Mike spoke from the window, where he'd wandered to scratch Jo's ears. 'Are you busy this morning?'

'Not particularly. Did you have something in mind?'

'I thought I'd walk up to the head of the glen and take some shots of the waterfall. How hard is it to get to the top where it spills over the edge?'

'Only a scramble. There's a fine walk above it, too, around the curve of the foothills.'

'Does it need boots?'

'Preferably. I've a spare pair, though. They might fit you.'

'Okay. Shall we give it a go?'

'Do you have something on this afternoon?'

'I've a lunch thing. We could start now, though. Would a few hours do it?'

Brian got to his feet. 'It's a matter of choice. We can pace ourselves and turn back when we need to.'

'Then let's go with the flow.'

They set off, leaving Jo lying on the doorstep, her eyes still on the road that led to the house. Striding out in his borrowed boots, Mike looked back over his shoulder. 'She's missing Hanna.'

'Um.' Brian had an absurd vision of himself stretched on the doorstep, like Jo, gazing intently at his phone, awaiting Hanna's next text. Deciding that Mike mightn't get the joke, he didn't share it. Instead he led the way between outcrops of heather and furze towards the river and began to head upstream along the bank. Mike fell into step beside him.

'How do the boots feel?'

'Fine. We've got the same size feet.'

Sandra's feet had been long and slender. Brian had thought of them as being like a ballerina's, though when he'd first said so she'd rolled onto her back with a shout of laughter. 'Easy seen you've never slept with a dancer!'

'Why? What's funny?'

'Ballet dancers have famously ugly feet. Well, not ugly, unless you happen to see them like that. Think bunions, scars, and overdeveloped arches. And engage your brain, for feck's sake. They get all those airy-fairy effects by balancing on little blocks of wood on the tips of their calloused toes. Usually bleeding buckets into their pink satin shoes.'

'Well, that's done wonders for my libido.'

They'd been lying on his rumpled bed, having made love for the first time. Her bright red lipstick had streaked the pillow and her skirt and shoes lay in a tangle on the floor. Still laughing, she'd stretched a slim, tanned leg into the air, grasped her toes, and flexed her extended foot. 'Really? You've had enough of me? Should I get dressed and go home?'

She'd never gone home again, except to pack and move into his cramped basement flat. A year later, when she'd finished a course in ceramics, they'd taken a mortgage on a house in Wicklow and got married. Far too soon, according to their parents, though Sandra's had been less censorious than Brian's, probably because her father had seen her qualification as useless. 'He only let me do the course because me and Mum ganged up on him. And, bless her, I think she regretted it when she found I wasn't going to be making dainty cups and saucers.' Brian had had a sneaky feeling her parents had been right, not because the pieces she'd made had been experimental to the point of perversity but because, as soon as they'd married, she'd simply lost interest and given the whole thing up. Utterly dedicated to his own work, Brian had found this unsettling, and part of the misery of losing her had been an underlying suspicion that one day, had she lived, she might have lost interest in him as well. On the morning Kate had come for Mike, Sandra had scarcely spoken to her and had smiled brightly as soon as she'd left with the baby in her arms. 'I'll say one thing for cancer, it means an end to cracked nipples and lost sleep. Otherwise I bet you and Mum would have forced me to breastfeed that poor little brat until he was drawing his old-age pension.' She hadn't taken easily to motherhood, and the black humour with which she'd faced her diagnosis had produced more than one such remark, each of which had tormented Brian in the empty years that followed.

Grass grew sparsely on the riverbank where, for the most part, the shallow water was bounded by pebbles and stones. The sun had released the warm scent of the furze flowers and captured it within the valley's walls, and, ahead of Brian, Mike's loose-jointed figure climbed steadily, his feet easily finding footholds among the unsteady rocks. It was just about here that Hanna had found the heart stone and, while everything then had been thrown into grey relief by starlight, today the glen glittered and shimmered in the heat. As Brian looked around, trying to pinpoint the place where the stone had been lying, his mind returned to the conversation he'd had with Hanna about the Hag's Glen. 'It's not particularly remote physically, though I suppose that depends on where you measure from. People lived and thrived here for hundreds of years before the poor hag and the Famine. Maybe even thousands. And not just farmers scratching a living. They'd have been prosperous.'

'How do you know?'

'We found a sluice box. It emerged when Fury was digging my foundations.'

'But what is it?'

'Basically a box made to filter water. It's filled with material to catch gold deposits washed down from the mountain. Gold is dense and the lighter stuff flushes through.'

Mike paused and lined up a photo. Catching up with him, Brian mentioned the sluice box.

'That's awesome.'

'There was lots of gold prospecting in ancient Ireland. They found a sluice box, thousands of years old, up in Woodenbridge in Wicklow, where I was born.'

It was where Mike had been born, too, but Brian didn't mention that.

'How old was the one you found here?'

'Never easy to be sure. You need to carbon-date them. You could tell by the nails that this one wasn't early, though. Probably late nineteenth century.'

'Did you keep it?'

'It fell apart when the digger brought it out.'

He had joked to Hanna that Fury's hag might have stayed behind when her neighbours left because there was gold in the glen. Now he said the same thing to Mike, who looked blank. It had never been much of a joke to begin with, but Brian found himself thrown on the defensive. 'Actually, if there was a folk memory of gold being washed down in the river, starving people might have made a desperate attempt to catch some. There probably wasn't much to be had by that stage. Well-known sources often got worked out.'

'No hope that I'm going to inherit a fortune, then.' It was an offhand comment, made as Mike had hunkered down to take another photo. Looking at his son's bent head, Brian remembered how Hanna had assumed that the house in the glen would come to Mike. In saying so, she'd taken Brian by surprise. He'd never grudged a penny of the money he'd sent Kate for Mike, yet somehow he'd never seen the glen, or the house he'd built there for Hanna, as having any connection with his son. Yet Hanna had seen the house as Mike's inheritance, and now it appeared that Mike took the same view. Why shouldn't he? There was no practical reason that Brian could think of. As Hanna had said, if he should die, she had Maggie's place to return to, a house into which she'd poured as much love as he had invested here. Biting the inside of his cheek, Brian took the argument further. Why should he view the Hag's Glen as his to control or claim? The stones he'd used to build his walls had been piled up into dwellings long before he was born or thought of and, no doubt, his house would fall, too, and be forgotten. So why try to project a purpose onto it or its setting? There was no point and surely he, as an architect, ought to know better.

As Mike rose to his feet and they continued to walk towards the waterfall, Brian felt unreasonably aggrieved. According to Hanna, neither he nor she could ever have all of the other because each of them had a past life, which impacted on the present. She'd presented this as an unassailable fact, a piece of logic, which, once grasped, he would be sure to accept. At the time he'd rejected it, though he hadn't said so aloud. Yet following his son's feet in their borrowed boots up the valley, he knew he'd never be able to share, or even unpick, the complex web of anger and love through which he and Sandra had struggled towards her death. It would continue to be tangled inside him forever. So, whether or not he was prepared to admit it, Hanna had been right.

Chapter Twenty-Six

Amy knocked on Hanna's door and shouted that Claire was due in twenty minutes – she was driving from her home in north London and had said she'd arrive in time for a proper catch-up before lunch. Hanna had offered to help prepare the meal but Amy had shaken her head. 'There's nothing to do, honestly. I've ordered lunch and dinner from Waitrose and Mrs B will put it on plates.'

'So what are we having?'

'Cottage pie and prawn paella.'

'Talk about carb overload!'

'Ah, but the potatoes are light and fluffy and the rice is saffron-infused.'

'You do realise that light and fluffy means whipped with cream and butter?'

'I thought we'd go all nostalgic. Remember the cottage pies we made in Paddington? Ninety percent buttery spuds and ten percent mince?'

'I remember Lucy making them and you wolfing them down. Nothing will convince me that we ever had paella, though.'

'Okay, we may not have risen to prawns, but there was lots of brown rice.'

'And the ends of baguettes that Lucy brought home from the restaurant. Do you remember that weekend we were all skint and lived on stale baguettes dipped in red wine?'

'I've ordered Rioja.'

'Amy, you didn't! I haven't tasted it for years.'

'In bottles, mind. Not the stuff in a box we used to get from that scary shop on the corner.'

'How many bottles do you think three middle-aged women can drink in a day?'

They'd been sitting chatting in the garden and Amy had turned and looked at Hanna severely. 'Christ, your spark really has gone out! That's the third time since you've been here that you've called us middle-aged.'

'Well, it's what we are.'

'No, it's how you define yourself.'

'I don't.'

'You *so* do.'

'What's wrong with being middle-aged, anyway?'

'Nothing, but you don't have to make a career of it. Or drag yourself around dressed for the part.'

'Give it a rest, Amy! There's nothing wrong with my clothes!' Amy's response had been deadpan and Hanna had glowered at her. 'What?'

'It's so easy to make you rise to a bait.'

The reminder of Fury in this most English of settings had made Hanna grin. Today, however, she'd decided to give Amy no ammunition so, having come back from an early saunter in Windsor Great Park, she'd gone to her room to dress with extra care. She brushed her hair, which had benefited from the products in Amy's bathroom, and pinned it smoothly on the back of her head. Then, sitting at the dressing-table, she decided to improve on her usual touch of mascara with a tinted moisturiser and a dusting of pressed powder. The outfit she'd chosen was one of a few she'd kept from her days with Malcolm, a fitted black shift with three-quarter-length sleeves, a boat neck, and a hem that just touched her knees. It was still in perfect condition and looked relaxed and chic with grey sandals and a fine gold chain. Revolving in front of the mirror, Hanna was pleased with the effect. Not only that, she thought rebelliously, but with earrings, a shawl, and a pair of heels, it's going to become a dinner dress at some point in this visit, and Amy can like it or lump it.

Claire arrived as Hanna came downstairs. There were shrieks of recognition in the hallway and, after an orgy of hugs, Amy swept them through to the garden, where champagne was cooling in an ice bucket down by the river. Claire shook her head at the sight of it. 'Amy! I'm driving!'

'Oh, for heaven's sake, we have to celebrate. One toast and we'll all go on to water until we eat. And if you're too smashed at the end of the day you can always stay the night.'

'Is Lucy not coming?'

'She's joining us for dinner. She only got home from India at midnight and she says there's a tottering pile of work on her desk.'

Hanna raised her glass to Claire. 'Here's to reunion! It's lovely to be here.'

'Aha!' Amy returned the champagne bottle to the bucket. 'I've given her a new taste for London. She'll be back!'

As Claire chattered about her globe-trotting career, and

the suburb she'd now retired to, Hanna considered this well-upholstered woman in sensible shoes and a navy blouse and skirt, trying to see the earnest girl she'd once shared a flat with. Is this, she wondered, Amy's view of me? Changed to such an extent by the years that all my youthful dynamism appears to have drained away? Admittedly, Claire had always been the responsible one of the four, as dedicated to her charges' welfare as to the high salary she could expect as a qualified Norland nanny. Still, thought Hanna, reprehensibly, if Amy thinks my spark has gone out, maybe she'll have a rethink after all these anecdotes of Freya, who married a Scottish grouse moor, and Topher and little Jolyon, who were doing so well in the City.

It was pleasant, though, to sit by the Thames in the sunshine, hearing Amy's raucous laugh and Claire's discreet giggles, and joining in reminiscences of the times they'd shared in the flat. A pair of swans drifted by, followed by a half-grown cygnet whose gold-grey plumage matched the autumnal tint of the willows. On the towpath opposite Amy's deck, a woman and a little girl were wheeling bicycles. The dark-haired child in a kilted skirt and a sweater reminded Hanna of Jazz in her school uniform. In the past, late-summer shopping trips in London had meant Marks & Spencer for socks and knickers, WHSmith for folders, and Liberty's for special items, bought with Jazz's carefully hoarded birthday money: she had inherited Hanna's love of stationery and, each year, had insisted on a beautiful notebook or pen to give solace in the classroom after the long weeks of freedom.

The previous day, Hanna had taken the train up to London and visited Liberty's, planning to buy Jazz a nostalgic gift, but as soon as she'd turned the corner from Regent Street and approached the iconic mock-Tudor building, she'd known she was really there for herself. Amy might accuse her of having lost all sense of fashion, but colour and design had never ceased to enchant her. Liberty's had much of what she missed at home in Finfarran, from the shop's dramatic interior, constructed of timber from decommissioned warships, to the sumptuous stock presented in intimate rooms and long galleries, like a cross between a souk and a Paris boutique.

Leaving the selection of Jazz's gift for later, she'd climbed the stairs to the third-floor fabric department, tempted by the riot of colours and patterns she knew she'd find on display. Even the staircase was wonderful. It had worn treads, and mullioned windows with painted panes salvaged from the ships' captains' quarters, and on each return there were flower displays and silk cushions set on the deep windowsills. As a small child, Jazz had loved the carvings on the oak rails and banisters: little polished figures of birds and monkeys, and an elephant sitting on its haunches. In Hanna's own childhood, they would have informed one of Tom's bedtime stories, but Jazz had been less enthralled by fantasy than by hard statistics, which she'd demanded each time they went to the shop. Yesterday, to her surprise, Hanna had recalled the statistics easily, and mentally recited them as she'd made her way up the stairs: constructed in 1924, at the height of the Tudor revival in design, the shop's interior had taken 24,000 cubic feet of ships' timbers from two vessels, HMS *Impregnable*, built from 3,040 hundred-year-old oaks from the New Forest, and HMS *Hindustan*, which had measured the length and height of the entire building.

Jazz's voice had come back to her from the past. 'A ship as big as the whole shop?'

'That's right. And the floors are made from the decks.'

'Who made the elephant?'

'Nobody knows. All the carvings were made for the shop, but no one remembers the names of the men who carved them.'

Sitting in Amy's garden with her eyes on the child on the far side of the river, Hanna could recall that conversation as if it had happened yesterday. Being in England seemed to be making time ripple, spewing memories of London, like molten lava, over the familiar landscape of her existence in Finfarran. And yesterday, to her confusion, Finfarran had invaded Liberty's, throwing images of her new life over scenes she'd half forgotten. Standing on the third-floor gallery, surrounded by floral- and paisley-patterned fabrics, she'd been riveted by the thought of a page in the Carrick Psalter, on which a meadow full of flowers, bees, and fantastic gauzy insects appeared within the curves of a capital letter. No one remembers the name of the monk or nun who made that either, she'd thought, or of the craftsman who, centuries later, carved a lectern to hold it. Fury's skill will be forgotten, too, all the craft and care he brought to restoring the broken lectern. And it doesn't matter. What matters is that someone saw insects, flowers, and bees and painted them at a high desk in a medieval scriptorium. Just as London craftsmen in the 1920s saw monkeys and birds in timber that had sailed oceans, and had once been sapwood and heartwood in a living forest, like Fury's.

The cottage pie was a huge success and, when it was eaten, Amy produced *gelati* from the freezer. Claire, who'd become excitable after the champagne, squeaked with enthusiasm. 'Oh, my God! Another blast from the past!'

'Chocolate, hazelnut, pistachio – and vanilla for wimps. What can I offer you, ladies?' Amy put the platter on the table and stood poised with a serving spoon in her hand.

Claire turned to Hanna. 'Do you remember that restaurant Lucy worked in? We had *gelati* when we went there on your birthday. She got the waiter to stick sparklers in them. That was a super evening!'

Hanna remembered it perfectly. The crowded little restaurant in Praed Street where Lucy had been a sous-chef, and the noisy group of guys at the next table who'd sent them champagne. And Malcolm slipping into the seat beside her, rumpled and handsome in an open-necked shirt.

Amy crossed her eyes at Claire and rapped on the table with the spoon. 'Not the best of recollections, eejit! That was the night Hanna met rat-fink Malcolm.'

Claire's neck flushed bright purple. 'Oh, Lord, Hanna, I'm dreadfully sorry.'

'Don't be. No need.'

'No, but, honestly, I'd completely forgotten.'

'Why should you remember? It was yonks ago. Water under the bridge.'

'I heard about the divorce.'

'Well, that was yonks ago, too, so let's not revisit it.'

'And she's got a gorgeous new guy in her life now, haven't you, Hanna? A toy boy, no less.'

Claire's eyes widened and Hanna tweaked the spoon from Amy's hand. 'I'm having pistachio. What do you fancy, Claire?'

'What? Oh – chocolate, I think. Or shall I be greedy and go for a taste of everything?'

'Why not?' Hanna briskly served the *gelati*, mentally daring

Amy to reopen the subject of Brian. Amy sat down, her eyes gleaming with mischief, but she demolished her dessert and said no more.

Their long lunch, at which they drank Rioja, slipped imperceptibly into teatime, for which they went into the garden again and lounged in striped deckchairs. Amy gave up tormenting Hanna and began to tell amusing stories about her own travels, and Hanna entertained with descriptions of Lissbeg's more eccentric characters. Boosted by alcohol and a sugar rush from honey-soaked crumpets, this mild disloyalty made her feel young and gleefully irresponsible. And this, she thought, was absolutely fine. The indiscretion was taking place in a foreign country, where nobody could be hurt by it. And she was living in the moment, which was exactly what she'd come on holiday for.

As the lazy hours passed, Hanna felt more and more relaxed. Lucy's arrival produced further hugs, reminiscences, and another champagne toast. Apparently as driven as ever by her hugely successful career, she nevertheless seemed genuinely elated by the reunion. 'I'm going to need intravenous coffee, but I wouldn't have missed this for anything!'

Claire had sobered up by then and at dinner they all stuck to mineral water and a single glass of wine with their paella. Afterwards Amy produced a photo album and they exclaimed over shots of their younger selves.

'Look at Lucy! What did you do with all that hair in the kitchen?'

'Don't you remember she was always threatening to cut it? But your boyfriend – what was his name? Stan? Steve? – kept making a fuss.'

'Oh, my God, your perm and the mad fringe, Hanna! What was that about?'

'I think I was being Alison Moyet. I haven't had a fringe for ages.'

Amy snickered. 'That's because she's rocking a Croydon facelift.'

'Amy! I am not!'

'Look at that forehead, girls. I bet it's not Botox, so it has to be the ponytail.'

Lucy emitted a hoot of laughter and Hanna gave Amy a push. 'I'll have you know that this is a very happening French pleat.'

Amy tugged back her own pixie curls, lifting the skin on her forehead and crossing her eyes even more hideously. The others shrieked and Hanna giggled as if she were twenty again.

As she undressed that night, she was sleepily content. Having brushed out her hair, she climbed into bed and, propping herself against the pillows, wondered if she ought to text Brian. There was a message on her phone, sent at ten thirty, wishing her goodnight, but now it was long past midnight, so she decided not to disturb him. Instead, she rummaged in her bag and took out the gift she'd bought for Jazz. It was a set of cards in Liberty's designs with cream envelopes lined in glowing colours. Possibly, like a cat or a child, Jazz might be more delighted by the packaging than the present: a purple box stamped with the Liberty crest in gold and floral tissue paper enclosing the ten notecards. Most of Jazz's communication was by email, but Hanna knew that, even so, the cards would be appreciated. While in the shop, she'd wandered about, wondering if she might find a gift for Brian. But nothing had presented itself. Now, slipping down under the duvet, she smiled, thinking of him asleep in the Hag's Glen. It was only an hour's flight away but it seemed like another world. As she settled herself to sleep, she wondered how Fury's work on the garage was going, and with the thought came a vision of Jo, shaggy in her dark shelter between the fallen stones and the sagging roof.

Chapter Twenty-Seven

Fury sat down and observed Conor swiftly unstacking chairs in the library's reading room. 'I see it takes muscle as well as brains to work in this place.'

'That's the way of it. I'm the brawn and Miss Casey's the brains.'

'How's her holiday going?'

'I haven't heard but I'd say she's having a whale of a time. Bit of a rest, bit of a break from this place.'

'The library or Lissbeg?'

'Both, maybe. You'd get tired this time of the year. I'm flattened myself, and Aideen's been wild ratty the last while.'

'Have you any plans to be going off somewhere?'

'I want to take her back to Florence. We were married there. Well, not married, because we had a registry office ceremony later, we just made vows to each other in a cypress grove. God, you should've seen her, Fury, she looked amazing. And afterwards we found a little trattoria, just a place halfway down the hill, with benches and a table outdoors and local people sitting round drinking wine. And Aideen was looking lovely, in a white minidress thing, with flowers and stuff, and they got excited and started bringing out bottles and plates of food. She ended up dancing on the table, and I was there with my mobile, taking photos, and an old guy was playing a squeezebox, and people were cheering and singing. It was deadly.'

'She's a grand little girl.'

'I know. I'm lucky. It's kind of good that Miss Casey's away, too, because I'm getting in extra hours to pay for the trip.'

'What's the crack today, then?'

'I've got volunteers who'll be working one-to-one with a couple of members. The rest are going to be sewing.'

'In a library?'

'God, Fury, you're fierce out of date.' The library's weekly Job Club ran sessions at which you could either work on a text with a mentor or join a group activity, which, while requiring reading ability, centred on skills people might feel more at home with. Conor explained it all briskly. 'So, with sewing, you'd need to read a pattern, say. Or some weeks we'd do singing and they'd have to read the words.'

Enlightened, Fury sniffed. 'I've known a fair few lads on building sites who can only tell what they're using by the colour of the tube. You get big surprises that way if the boss changes supplier.'

'Paddy says there was an oul fella used to work for my granddad who couldn't read a word of English but read books in Irish like a scholar.'

'Sure we're all at the mercy of whatever bastard stands up in front of the blackboard.'

'Only, these days, it's a whiteboard. Actually, sometimes it's digital and you use your finger as a mouse.'

Fury stood up. 'Any chance that you'd still have a few ordinary books round here? Paper pages? Cardboard covers? Smelling of printer's ink?'

'One or two. What were you looking for?'

'It's not for me, it's for Charles.'

Conor led the way to the desk. 'Where's The Divil?'

'Ah, Hanna has conniptions if I bring him in here.'

'True enough.'

'Don't tell me you're letting the rules go by the board while she's away.'

'Nope. I've just never known you to stick to them.' Sitting down, Conor looked at him expectantly. 'What does Mr Aukin want?'

'A Japanese phrase book.'

Conor blinked. 'Right. Well, I wouldn't say we'd have one here at the branch.' His fingers flicked across the keyboard and he scrolled through lists on the screen. 'Er, no. I could do you *Lafcadio Hearn's Japan*.'

'Is that a phrase book?'

'Nope. Travel writing. Hang on, *Japanese Fairy Tales and Others*, that's Hearn too.'

'Holy God, did you buy a job lot of him?'

'I'd say we have him in stock because he's Irish.'

'With a name like that?'

'His dad was from Offaly and his mam was Greek, from an island called Lefkada. He has a Japanese name too.' Conor wrinkled his nose at the screen. 'Er, Koizumi Yakumo – is that how you pronounce it?'

'Jesus Christ, man, I don't know. What's he doing with a Japanese name anyway? I thought you said he was Greek.'

'That was his mam. His dad was in the British Army.'

'Well, that's as clear as mud.'

'It is a bit weird, isn't it? Give me a minute.' There was a pause in which Fury looked bored while Conor made interested noises. 'Okay, so Lafcadio Hearn became a journalist for some American newspaper and he got sent to Japan as a correspondent. Then he married a Japanese woman, settled down, and kept writing books and stuff there till he died.'

'Did he write a bloody phrase book?'

'Not that I can see.'

'Then why am I standing here talking about him?'

'You don't want the fairy tales, so?'

'Lookit, Charles Aukin is back there in the castle with coaches turning up every five minutes.'

'Oh, right, I heard he'd opened the place up. So he needs to talk to his visitors?'

'No, he doesn't *need* to talk to them. That's supposed to be down to the feckin' tour guides. But that won't do Charles. Not at all. He's got interested now so he wants to communicate. And interact.'

'In Japanese?'

'Well, only with the Japanese ones, obviously. I mean, he's a Yank himself so he's got no problem talking to a crowd from the States. God, you couldn't stop him. He's leppin' around, all eyes and teeth, as soon as they're out of the coach.'

'That's kind of nice, though, isn't it?'

'Steerin' them round and handing out all sorts of guff about local history. Next thing you know, he'll be giving them cups of tea.' Fury scowled ferociously. 'I've told him it'll all end in tears.'

Carefully trained by Hanna to avoid local gossip, Conor

retreated to safer ground. 'I can order a Japanese phrase book, no problem. It'll take a couple of days to come in, though.'

'I suppose that'll have to do.'

'Are you sure you don't want one of Hearn's books to be getting on with? He's big in Japan.'

'Really?'

'There's an article here says that every Japanese schoolkid learns about him.'

'Fair enough, throw him out to me. I suppose if yer man can't talk to them, he can wave the book and they'll recognise the name.'

'Would they, though? They might know him as Koizumi Yakumo.'

'Well, that's Charles bloody Aukin's problem, isn't it? I'm only the gofer.'

When Conor fetched the book it turned out that Fury had no library card. 'Didn't Charles give you his?' Checking the system, he frowned. 'Actually, Mr Aukin isn't registered, so he can't really take a book out.'

'Well, he's not taking a book out, is he? I am.'

'Yes, but you're not registered either.'

Fury raised his eyes to Heaven and slapped his hand on the desk. 'Right, well, come here to me, tell me this. Do *you* have a library card?'

'I do.'

'Then, in the name of God, would you take the damn book out and give it here to me.'

'But people aren't supposed to lend library books.'

'Lending library books is literally your job description.'

'Yeah, but I'm not supposed to borrow the damn things first.'

Fury leaned in, lowered his voice, and locked eyes with Conor. 'Look, we're talking Charles Aukin here, right? The millionaire whose generous gift kept this library open. I'm not saying that's relevant, mind. I'm just saying it makes sense for you to hand over them fairy tales without any more argument. D'you follow me drift?'

*

Leaving the library with the book in his jacket pocket, Fury crossed the road to HabberDashery, where a queue of people was stretching out of the door. Sauntering past them, he went inside and perched on a high stool. Behind the counter, Bríd and Aideen were making and serving takeaway orders at speed. Aideen looked up and called to him. 'We'll be a while dealing with this lot, Fury.'

'Take your time, girl, I'm in no hurry. Did she make any Portuguese custard tarts today?'

Bríd handed an order across the counter. 'I did, yeah. Did you want some?'

'I'll take six when you've got a minute.'

Aideen was briskly slicing sourdough bread. 'When did you start eating custard tarts, Fury?'

'I'm just the errand boy. Charles Aukin has fierce high-class tastes.'

'Where's The Divil?'

'Back at the castle, trying to pull a fast one. I've put a strict embargo on his custard-cream biscuits, so he thinks that, if he butters Charles up, he'll be in with a chance on the tarts.'

As the queue moved forward, more customers joined it at the rear. Bríd called over her shoulder, 'Could you leave those dishes, Bartek, and give us a hand?'

With three people serving flat-out, all conversation from behind the counter stopped, but, as many of the customers were tourists who'd arrived on the bus from Carrick, there was a constant flow of chat as the girls explained the sandwich fillings and offered suggestions for suitable picnic places. A couple of tall Americans asked Aideen about hiring a boat. 'We want to get some sea-angling. Any idea where we can find a captain to take us out?'

Fury saw Aideen glance sideways at Bríd before she replied. 'You could ask in Cafferky's shop if you go out as far as Couneen. Dan Cafferky has a boat and he knows the best places for fishing.'

'Well, thanks, we'll try that.'

'No problem. Do you want a pot of salad to go with those pies?'

'No, we're good.'

As the young men departed with two large pork pies, Bríd shot a furious glare at Aideen. Nothing was said while Bartek remained at the counter but, as soon as the queue cleared and he had gone back into the kitchen, Bríd began to clatter cutlery crossly into a bowl. Aideen watched her for a moment before beginning to wipe a chopping board. Eventually she put a hand on her hip and broke the ominous silence. 'So, his name is taboo now, is it? No one can mention Dan without you getting into a strop?'

'I never said so.'

'No, but you're behaving like a wagon. Have sense, Bríd. You can't go getting upset because Dan's business isn't thriving and then make a fuss when I try to give it a boost.'

'Oh, right, and that's going to make a big difference. Giving his name to a couple of Yanks who probably won't even bother to go to Couneen?'

'It might give him a day's work anyway.'

'What are you now, his agent?'

'Ah, would you listen to yourself, you're sounding like an eejit.'

Fury leaned forward and coughed, and Bríd swung round and blushed. 'Sorry, Fury, I'd forgotten you. Six custard tarts, is it?'

'Make it seven and we'll give The Divil his due.'

'I thought he was on a regime.'

'He's not doing badly, though, and them things are organic.'

'I hear he's working towards the County Final.'

'He is. I've the tickets bought and we're all set.'

Bríd groaned. 'I'm so jealous. It's going to be a brilliant match and I couldn't get a ticket.'

'I snapped up two at the crack of dawn the first day they were on sale.'

Aideen passed Bríd a cellophane bag. 'Do they let dogs into the stadium, Fury?'

Fury dug in his back pocket and produced a roll of notes. 'I'd like to see them try to keep him out.' Looking at the price tag on the dish of tarts, he sniffed and peeled a twenty-euro note from the top of the roll. 'Jaysus, at that kind of money you'd want them to suck the fat right out of you.'

'Just because they're organic doesn't mean they're slimming.' Bríd's tongs hovered over the tarts and Fury shrugged.

'Ah, sure, I'm only the lackey. Throw the extra one in, print me out a receipt, and I'll bring it up to Charles.'

'Seriously, Fury, they'll have a lot more calories than a custard cream.'

'I'll mention that to The Divil, so, and leave it up to his conscience.'

With the fairy tales in one sagging pocket and seven custard tarts in the other, Fury returned to his van, which he'd parked by the library, and drove to Carrick whistling through his teeth.

Charles was standing in the castle gateway with The Divil in his arms, waving at a departing coachload of tourists. On seeing Fury, the little dog, who'd been licking Charles's chin, froze and attempted to look innocent. Charles strode across the courtyard. 'Did you get the book?'

'I got *a* book.' Fury addressed Charles while looking severely at The Divil. 'I got your custard tarts, too, and, by all accounts, they're loaded down with calories.'

'That's good to hear. Let's go and eat them.' Charles set The Divil on his feet and led the way into the house. Fury produced the book of fairy tales. 'Conor's ordering up your phrase book. This is just a stopgap.' As they climbed the stairs, he relayed what Conor had told him about the author. Charles beamed. 'But that's fantastic!'

Fury sniffed dourly. 'Culturally curious, yeah, I know. I thought you'd see it like that.'

In the book room, having switched on the kettle, Charles slid the tarts out of their cellophane wrapping. Aware of a coolness in the atmosphere, The Divil staunchly ignored them and sat down meekly on Fury's foot. Charles picked up the book and glanced at the foreword. 'I see this Hearn worked in Cincinnati and New Orleans. The de Lancys had property in Ohio. We might make something of that.'

'I wouldn't doubt you.'

'You've gotten really crabby lately, you know that?'

'And I'm usually such a little ray of sunshine.' Fury took a tart and lowered himself into a chair.

Charles looked at him mildly. 'Seriously, what's your problem?'

'I still think you're ridiculous.'

'And you've still to explain why.'

'You've got all sorts of nickable stuff scattered around like Smarties. I can't be all the time keeping an eye on the crowds you have traipsing about.'

'But I don't want you to. The whole point of this enterprise is to make me less dependent on you. Surely I've made that clear.'

'Oh, you've said it all right. That doesn't make it true.'

'Look, they're perfectly decent people. A bit naïve, some of them, maybe, and, okay, I joke about that. But most of them actually *are* fairly cultured. They turn up, go around with a guide, I chat a bit, and they take photos. I've told you before, they don't traipse about. For the most part, they stick to the route that's laid out for them.'

Fury stiffened. 'For the most part?'

Charles looked sheepish. 'Well, okay, the other day I found a guy in my bedroom.'

'What?'

'Don't shout. It was a young guy who'd taken a wrong turning, is all. I came out of the bathroom and there he was.'

'Holy God Almighty, this is exactly what I've been on about!'

'I said don't shout – you'll give The Divil a heart attack. Look, it's no big deal. He was flustered, and he apologised, and I took him back to his group. And that was that.'

Chapter Twenty-Eight

With only a few days of her holiday remaining, Hanna was eager to visit more of her old London haunts, and, as she explained to Amy, she still hadn't found a gift for Brian and wanted to get something for Mary and Louisa as well. Amy showed little interest but, as Hanna reminded herself, it must be a bit sad to spend much of your life on cruises and have no one to buy gifts for in the far-flung places you visited or to share in your traveller's tales when you came home. She'd wondered if Amy had any friends to spend time with when in England and was relieved to be told she was planning a dinner party.

'It's tonight. I've said seven for seven thirty.' The lack of notice was typical of Amy. 'Just us and Roger, who's an old friend of Clive's – and a sweetie – the Morrisons, who run the riverside watch committee, and Nicholas Armstrong.'

'Who's he?'

'Clive knew him from some board or other. He's a class of a do-gooder. I thought he'd do for you.'

'I'm not sure I'm in need of a do-gooder.'

'It's not about you, it's about symmetry.'

Amy had summoned what she called her 'usual caterers' and intended to spend the day on her appearance. 'I'm booked in for a beauty session. Hair, nails, massage. Then a facial and a makeup job.'

'Okay, I'll see you for dinner.'

'I probably should have mentioned it sooner.'

The belated misgiving was equally typical of Amy and, knowing it was only a nod to politeness, Hanna laughed. 'I'm not going to reassure you, so stop fishing.'

Amy chuckled. 'It's awfully nice to spend time with someone who sees straight through me.'

'Didn't Clive?'

'Probably more than I imagined. Old friends are the best, though.'

As Hanna went to her room, her phone buzzed and delivered a text. Seeing that it was from Mary, she sighed, sat down to read it, and discovered she'd missed two others, sent earlier.

LOUISAS OFF OUT AGAIN TODAY IM FALLING BAKXC ON JOHHNNY
YOUD QAWHNT IT **OD SENSE BUT** OF COURES YOU DPONT WANT ME SAYING SO
I THOUGHT YOU SAD BRIAN WAS TAKING TIME OFF WITH MIKE

It was evident from the first text that Mary was feeling neglected. The second was obscure, and the third was clearly intended to provoke a response. With a guilty sense that she could have kept in touch more conscientiously, Hanna hit Call.

Mary picked up immediately. 'So you've seen me texts.'

'Yes, sorry, my phone was off.'

'Anything could have happened to me.'

'Well, nothing has, has it?'

'No, but you didn't know that. I could've been stone dead.'

Restraining herself, Hanna asked if everyone was well.

'How would I know? I see nobody.'

'Oh, come on, you see Louisa every day.'

'I see the back of her and she whippin' out the door.'

'How's Johnny Hennessy?'

'Ah, the Hennessys are well enough, I don't want to be annoying them.'

'Have you seen Jazz?'

'Well, if you don't know the answer to that question, you must be neglecting her too.'

Hanna drew a deep breath but, before she could reply, Mary rushed on: 'I dare say you've no idea what Brian's been up to either?'

'What's that supposed to mean?'

'Don't you take that tone with me, my lady. I'm only saying I saw him inside in Carrick. Running up the steps of the council building. Mark that.'

'Mam, he works in the council building.'

'And he's supposed to be off work, isn't he? So why was he slipping in looking cagey?'

Breathing in again, Hanna contrived to control herself. 'You know what I'm doing today? Going up to town to buy you a present.'

Mary made a slightly mollified noise. 'Don't go spending your money on me.'

Aware that there'd be hell to pay if she came home empty-handed, Hanna smiled. 'What better way could I spend it?'

'You'd do well to keep it safe for a rainy day.' Having delivered herself of this in a voice full of portent, Mary announced that her kettle was boiling over. 'I'll have a flood on the counter if I don't go and catch it. Mind yourself now and, for the love of God, give that man of yours a call.'

She rang off, leaving Hanna faced with a ludicrous dilemma. Not having talked to Brian yesterday, because of the reunion, she'd intended to call him before setting off for her train. But to do so after what Mary had said felt weirdly like checking up on him. Evidently her mother was still wedded to her vision of Pauline Murphy as a siren and Brian as bewitched by her charms. Which, of course, was ridiculous. But, as far as Hanna knew, Brian had had no plans to go into the office while she was away so, in spite of herself, she felt thrown.

Irritated, she hit Brian's number, knowing that if she didn't she'd spend the day feeling foolish. As soon as she heard his hello everything slipped back into perspective, and the sound of a bark in the background made her heart leap. 'Is that Jo?'

'Well, good morning to you too.'

Hanna laughed. 'I'm sorry, it's just lovely to hear her.'

'How was yesterday?'

'Grand. It all went swimmingly.' Tucking her phone under her chin, Hanna collected her handbag and a sweater. 'It was great to see the girls and now I'm on my way up to London. What about you?' She was aware of a slightly false note in her voice as she asked the question, and immediately came clean because anything else felt insane. 'I spoke to Mam. She's convinced you're playing away behind my back.'

'I thought she was one of my fans.'

'It's not your fault, you're ensnared by a wily predator.'

'Am I? Who?'

'Pauline Murphy. You were spotted rushing into her arms the other day in Carrick.'

Brian gave a shout of laughter. 'Oh, my God! Bless your poor mother! She couldn't have hit on a less likely predator.'

Unable to stop herself, Hanna asked why he'd been in Carrick. There was a pause in which she wondered if he was cross. Then she heard him chuckle. 'Brian? Are you laughing at me?'

'Darling, yes. But really I'm awfully flattered.'

'Christ, I could kill my mother!'

'Ah, no, where's your gratitude? I see her as a lioness defending her fubsy cub.'

'I can think of other metaphors.'

She could hear a smile in Brian's reply. 'Have a wonderful day, sweetheart.'

'Same to you two.' She was about to end the call when curiosity overcame her. After all, he was supposed to be spending the week with Mike. 'Hang on. How come you went to the office?'

'Mary's got super-duper antennae. It actually was a bit hole-and-corner. I invented a meeting to get myself out of the house.'

'Why? What happened?'

'Nothing, it's fine. Mike and I have been doing a lot of talking. I think we ran out of steam, that's all. Just a temporary glitch.'

*

Having visited the Bridget Rileys at the Tate and spent an hour or two browsing in the National Portrait Gallery, Hanna took a tube to Sloane Square and wandered down the King's Road. She found a thank-you bottle of perfume for Amy, and saw possible gifts for Mary and Louisa, but nothing looked suitable for Brian, and by three o'clock she found herself hungry in Chelsea. It was three thirty by the time she'd chosen a café and eaten a sandwich and, stepping into the street again, she began to compute how long it would take to get back to Windsor. It appeared that the years she'd spent in Finfarran had blunted her sense of London distances, and she feared she wouldn't be home in time to get ready for dinner. Given the fact that it would be catered, and Amy's intention of spending the day in the beauty salon, rushing in at the last minute and running a brush through her hair wouldn't count as adequate preparation.

As she stood on the pavement, looking around for a bus stop, she noticed a hairdresser's on the opposite corner and, making a quick decision, crossed the road and went inside. It was an expensive little Chelsea place, the kind she'd known well during the years she'd been married to Malcolm, and the girl behind the desk looked like a model.

'Do you have an appointment?'

'I'm afraid not, but I just want a wash and blow-dry. Is anyone free?'

There were three customers' chairs, none of which was occupied, but the receptionist frowned at her computer screen before answering. 'Fabien has half an hour. Would you care to sit down?'

Hanna managed to avoid saying that a quarter of an hour would be better. She sat on one of the fashionably scuffed leather chairs and pulled her hair out of its plait as Fabien appeared from behind a screen. He was a short, tubby Frenchman and she could see his face in the mirror hanging in front of her. Ignoring his tortured eyebrows, she said she was in a rush.

'*Oui, Madame.*' Fabien cocked his head and ran his fingers through her hair. Twisting the long ends up at one side, he pulled a few loose strands forward to make a fringe. Then he gesticulated at the mirror. Hanna was amazed. On one side of her face her hair hung level with her jawline and, with the wispy fringe, the difference was remarkable. 'You see, Madame? The focus on the eyes. On the beautiful chin. The effect a little choppy. Some movement in the layers.'

'No, I really don't have time. I just want it clean.'

'But of course.' Fabien whizzed her chair backwards and tilted it, and there was a sudden gush of warm water through her hair. 'I will wash it myself. The cut, it takes no time.'

'Honestly.' Hanna found she'd been swathed in a silver cape. 'Just a wash and blow-dry.'

'Certainly.' Fabien was working up a lather with citrus-scented shampoo. 'Your appointment is when?'

'Seven for seven thirty, but I have to get home and get dressed.'

'And you go to?'

'Windsor.'

'Of course. From Waterloo station. Zoë will call you a taxi.'

The water gurgled smoothly away and Fabien began to massage Hanna's scalp before combing scented conditioner through her squeaky-clean hair. Moments later he had rinsed it, enfolded it in a towel, and whizzed her chair back to its place. With a bizarre sense that this was all happening to someone else, Hanna watched in the mirror as he moved to and fro behind her, silver scissors flying and an intense frown on his face. In no time the hair that he'd pinned up in sections was cut, being combed into place, and blow-dried. Then, he turned the chair to face him and, frowning ferociously, began to chop into the fringe. As a shower of feather-light strands fell on her lap Hanna panicked but, before she could speak, he swung her back to the mirror. 'So, you see? It takes no time at all, and what a result!'

In fact it had taken less than twenty-five minutes and, as he removed her silver cape, the taxi drew up at the door. Gaping at herself in the mirror, Hanna couldn't believe the transformation. He'd been right about the effect on her eyes, which now looked twice as large, and somehow the feathery bob seemed to elongate her neck. The cost made her blink but she swiped her credit card without a qualm. She had been in the hands of an artist, and who could put a price on that?

When she reached the house the caterers were busy in the kitchen and Amy was nowhere to be seen. Hanna got to her bedroom unnoticed and, shedding her clothes, hastened into the bathroom. Giving thanks for the shower cap, into which she carefully tucked her hair, she showered, wrapped herself in a towel, and went to stand before her dressing-table mirror. This was the test. She whipped off the cap and immediately chided herself for her moment of doubt. Her hair had tumbled triumphantly into place, looking just as good after the shower as when it had left Fabien's masterly hands.

With her new look, and after inventive work with an eyeliner, her old black dress exuded minimalist elegance. So, discarding the idea of adding a shawl, she settled for her small gold earrings, which glowed discreetly behind the feathery curves of her sleek hair. The eyeliner, flicked up at the sides, made her feel Parisian, so, buoyed up by a confidence she felt could withstand even a sly gibe from Amy, she rejected uncomfortable heels in favour of a pair of soft leather ballet flats, and floated downstairs with her chin well up.

One of the hired waiters had just opened the door to a couple who must be the Morrisons. Hanna smiled warmly at them, noting that he was shiny and evidently a drinker, while his wife, who was wearing beige sequins, seemed nice but vague. Through the open living-room door she could see Amy chatting to a man who, judging by his age, had to be Roger; he had a kind face and was wearing a spotted bow-tie. The waiter was about to close the door when another car pulled into the drive and a tall man got out. This, presumably, was Nicholas Armstrong, the do-gooder. He climbed the steps, his overcoat flapping, and as he came in, Hanna could see he was somewhere in his sixties, thin and tanned, with unremarkable features and a quiet, commanding presence. The waiter took his coat as he greeted the Morrisons, and as he held out his hand to Hanna, Amy came into the hall. Words of welcome and introduction froze on her lips, and she stopped in amazement. Meanwhile, Nicholas Armstrong grasped Hanna's hand and smiled into her eyes. Recovering herself abruptly, Amy descended on the group, scattering kisses. She crossed her eyes at Hanna covertly as she pecked her cheek and propelled her into the room. But, evidently, her persona tonight was to be *grande dame*, not tormentor. That, Hanna assumed, would come later.

Roger's voice proved to be as gentle as his appearance and, having been introduced to Hanna, he wandered off in pursuit of Amy and another gin and tonic. As Hanna sat down, Nicholas Armstrong approached her carrying two glasses of wine. Amy was gazing across the room in undisguised astonishment. The Morrisons, ensconced on the sofa, had accepted a bowl of olives, which the wife held on her lap while her husband shot admiring glances at Hanna. Having handed a glass to her, Nicholas drew a chair around and sat beside her. Hanna hadn't had this kind of effect since the years when she'd entertained Malcolm's colleagues and, remembering their conversation over lunch in the nuns' garden, she realised, to her amazement, that Amy had been right. She'd enjoyed being the belle of the ball at parties. Not only that, but she'd missed it.

Chapter Twenty-Nine

Aideen came into the farm kitchen and slumped on a chair at the table. Orla was on her knees in front of the range and, without looking round, she exclaimed aloud in disgust. 'Dammit, this thing always soots up after a service! Sometimes I wish we'd never gone over to oil.' Standing up, she wiped her hands on her apron and, seeing Aideen, her irritation changed to concern. 'What's the matter, love? Why are you home early? Is something wrong at the deli?'

'No, nothing's wrong. Everything's grand.'

'But it isn't. Look at the state of you, you've been crying.'

One of the ginger cats leaped from the chair by the range onto Aideen's knee, and she stroked it. 'It's nothing. I just – Bríd and I had a row.'

'Ah, love, I'm sorry. But that happens. Maybe you need to give each other a bit of time to cool off. Would you call her later on and patch things up?'

'Maybe.' Aideen bit her lip. 'She can be such a cow sometimes, Orla. Even when you're trying to help.'

'Ah, that's when people can be the world's worst. Do you want to talk about it?'

'No.' Aideen tickled the cat behind the ears and it settled into her lap. Orla sat down and said nothing. Aideen began to talk. 'There's times I wonder if she's just jealous about me being married. I know that sounds daft but, honestly, it's like she has to keep proving she's older and bigger and better than me. God knows why. I mean, she'll always be older and she's the one with the big qualifications. She's got nothing to prove.'

Orla reached out to pat the cat. 'I don't know why she should think she's better than you. Are you sure you've got that right?'

'Oh, I don't know! It's just the way it feels.' Aideen's voice wobbled. 'The awful thing is that I really lost my temper with her. She's not just my cousin, she's my best friend, Orla. She's always been the one who's looked out for me. At school, and then when Gran and Aunt Bridge died. She could have stayed up in Dublin after she finished her course, but she came back to Lissbeg so we could start up the business.'

'Well, I'm not saying a word against her, and that is one way of looking at it. Here's another, though. If you hadn't put your inheritance into the deli, she wouldn't be as well set up as she is.'

'Bríd could get work anywhere she wanted it.'

'There's a difference between having a job and being a partner in your own business.'

Tears began to roll down Aideen's face. 'I know. I know you're right, but I hate falling out with her.'

'Well, I bet she feels exactly the same way.' Orla came over and gave Aideen a hug. 'Give things a while to simmer down and you'll be back on good terms in no time.'

'You think so?'

'I do.'

As Aideen fetched a piece of kitchen roll to blow her nose, Conor walked in from the yard, having left his boots on the step. He was elated by the results of the farm's silage tests and was coming in to relay them to Paddy. 'God, Mum, he's going to be delighted. Our target feed-into-milk value is way up on last year, and all the rest of the figures are up too.'

'That's great. Go on in and tell him, love.'

Conor was about to walk through to the office when he caught sight of Aideen. 'Hey, what's the story? How come you're home at this hour?'

Aideen threw the scrunched-up kitchen roll into the compost bucket, turning her face away so he couldn't see it. 'Nothing. I just knocked off early.'

Orla tried to catch Conor's eye but he'd gone across to Aideen, who, having no option, looked round and gave him a watery smile. Conor's eyes widened. 'You've been crying. What is it? What's the matter?'

'Conor!' He glanced round and saw Orla shaking her head at him but, swinging back, he took Aideen by the hand. 'Ade, tell me. Are you all right?'

Without seeming to hurry, Orla reached him in seconds and steered him gently towards the office door. 'Go on and tell Paddy about the results. He'll be made up. Aideen's going to help me in the garden now she's home, aren't you, love? I need a hand tying up onions.'

Aideen went to the drawer where they kept the gardening gloves and string. 'Yeah, sure, I'll go out and make a start.'

She was gone before Conor could speak and Orla stopped

him following her. 'Let her be, love. She needs a bit of time by herself.'

'But what happened?'

'She and Bríd had a tiff. Leave it so. It'll be least said, soonest mended. Give her some space.'

Taking a pair of scissors, she followed Aideen into the garden, leaving Conor staring after her, his face puckered in concern.

*

Having given the test results to Paddy, Conor went out to put on his boots and, stamping his feet into them, with one hand on the doorframe, he looked across the garden and saw Aideen and his mum. It seemed at first that they were just tying up onions, but then he saw Aideen sit down on the edge of a ridge with her face in her hands. Orla stood looking down at her and, after a moment, squatted beside her and took her in her arms. Helpless rage rose up and choked Conor. His mum had said Aideen was fine and, clearly, she wasn't. She was sitting there bawling, and he'd been told to back off, like it was none of his business. Frowning, he watched the figures in the garden rocking to and fro. By the sound of it, this was all Bríd's fault, which made absolute sense because Bríd had always bossed Aideen around. Still in his muddy wellingtons, he marched round to the shed and took out the Vespa. Dermot was above in the field, expecting him to come back and help with a fence, but that was too bad. The thought of Aideen's miserable face and red eyes made him frantic, and if his mum was going to hold him off, and Aideen wouldn't talk to him, he'd damn well go and find Bríd and sort this out himself.

Twenty minutes later, having driven much too fast, he was scooting through the backstreets of Lissbeg. Bríd was alone in the deli when he burst in. The look on his face startled her. 'What is it? What's happened? Is something wrong?'

Conor had balanced his helmet on the top of his head when he'd got off the bike. Now he banged it down on the counter and glared across it at Bríd. 'You know fine well that there's something wrong.'

'No, I don't. Conor, what is it?' Suddenly Bríd relaxed. 'Oh, it's Aideen, right? She's sent you along to fight her battles for her.'

'No, she hasn't. She doesn't even know I'm here.'

'And, for feck's sake, could you not have left your filthy boots outside? This is a delicatessen, not a slurry pit.'

'Don't have a go at me, Bríd, I'm serious. What are you after saying to Aideen to send her home in tears?'

'What am I after saying to Aideen? Oh, that's rich. Did you ask her what she stood there and said to me?'

'No, I didn't.'

'Yeah, I bet you didn't. You don't even know what happened here, do you? You just leaped onto your high horse and came riding into town.' Stiff with anger, Bríd came round the counter and turned the sign on the deli door to Closed. 'Right so. Let's have this out.'

Conor sagged slightly under the force of her attack. Then he put his back against the counter and squared his shoulders. 'She's at home there at the farm, crying buckets.'

'Yeah, and I'm here still doing my job. Despite what she called me.' Bríd strode up and down the shop, like a lioness lashing her tail. 'She said I'm a controlling bitch and I don't have a pick of respect for her, and I told her to simmer down and not to be such an eejit. Then she threw a submarine roll at me and walked out the door.'

'She called you a bitch?'

'And that submarine roll was like a feckin' torpedo. The end of it got me on the jaw.'

There was indeed a red mark, and a suggestion of a bruise, on the side of her face.

Conor stared, the wind completely taken out of his sails. 'Aideen chucked it at you? I don't believe it.'

'Oh, right, fine. Call me a liar, why don't you?'

'No, wait, hang on.' Conor tried to muster his thoughts. 'I'm not calling you a liar but this isn't like Aideen. What were the two of you talking about?' Bríd scowled, and he hurried on, afraid he'd sounded judicial. 'I'm only trying to understand, honest.'

'Yeah, well, I'm sorry to sound aggressive. But, Jesus Christ, Conor. The bottom line is that I'm not going to have her talking to Dan about me.'

'What? Was she? Why?'

'Probably because he cornered her and gave her the poor mouth. He wants to get back in my good books and he's using her as a patsy.'

'But she hates him doing that.'

'Yeah? Well, she doesn't have to listen to him, does she? And she sure as hell needn't come and make his case for him. I told her in no uncertain terms to stop doing it.' Back in lioness mode, Bríd glowered at him pugnaciously. 'And if she can't take straight talk, she needs to get a bit of cop on.'

Conor got out the back way before a new row could start up, leaving Bríd to stump to the door and reopen the deli. As he put on his helmet and mounted the Vespa, he decided he'd go to Couneen. A word with Dan might help to straighten things out.

Probably he ought to go home and apologise to Dermot for walking off and leaving the fencing, but the thought of Aideen's tear-stained face still made him frantic. He couldn't bear to think that he couldn't fix things and make her smile again. That was his job, too, and if he could just get it right, surely the family would understand that he'd felt it should take priority over mending a fence with Dermot.

Dan was sitting outside his shed on Couneen pier, stripping down an engine. Conor parked the Vespa and came to sit beside him on an upturned fish box. 'Is she fighting back?'

'She failed when I was out with a couple of Yanks last evening. There was a lad out looking at lobster pots and he gave me a tow in.'

'Bit embarrassing.'

'You're telling me. And the bastards'll probably stick something up on TripAdvisor.'

'Were they leppin'?'

'Nah, they were cool enough, but you never know.'

Conor shifted his position on the fish box. 'I was just passing and I wanted a word.'

'Just passing at this time of the day in muddy wellingtons?'

'All right, so. I came on purpose. I've been talking to Bríd.'

Dan turned and looked at him. 'Oh, yeah?'

'Well, it's not really Bríd I'm here about, it's Aideen.'

'So why were you talking to Bríd?'

'No, you see, the thing is, Aideen came home in tears today. She and Bríd fell out. And, well, I just wanted to say, would you not be using her as a go-between? Don't be talking to her about Bríd.'

'Is that what Bríd says?'

'No.' Conor frowned. 'Well, yes, but she didn't ask me to come here. I mean, I'm not wanting to be a go-between either. I'm just saying Aideen's really upset.'

Dan stood up and wiped his hands on a rag. 'I'm not in the best of places meself, Conor. That engine's buggered.'

'Is it? God, that's crap.'

'And if it turns out I can't fix it, I haven't the savings to re-place it. So if Bríd told you I'm a lousy businessman, she was dead right.'

'She didn't. I wasn't talking to her about you.'

'That's not what you said just now.'

Conor tried to reassemble his thoughts. 'Lookit, I just know that Aideen's back at the farm in a state, and I'm asking you to leave her out of whatever's going on.'

'Well, as it happens, I didn't ask her to be a go-between. I met her in town and she announced that I was looking rough. Which is no great surprise, considering the way my life is. I never asked her to say a word to Bríd, because I knew she didn't want to, and, anyway, there wouldn't be any point. The fact is, I'm just as use-less as Bríd seems to think I am. She's well shot of me.'

'Ah, Dan!'

'Would you feck off home to your wife and not be annoying me? No offence, but I can do without this right now.'

Crestfallen, but feeling that, at least, he'd clarified things, Conor got onto the Vespa and went home. When he walked into the kitchen the entire household was there and they all turned and stared at him. Paddy was sitting at the table, Orla was stand-ing behind the easy chair by the range, where Aideen was sitting, and Dermot was in the background, looking as if he felt like an intruder. Aideen was clutching her phone to her chest and crying. Orla gave Conor a despairing look and took Aideen by the shoulders. 'Here's Conor now, love. I'm sure he meant no harm.'

Conor was baffled. What had he done? He went and dropped onto his knees in front of Aideen but when he tried to take her hand she shook him off. For a minute he thought she was going to throw her phone at him, as she'd hurled the roll at Bríd in the delicatessen. Instead she tried to shout through her sobs, which was worse. Unable to hear what the matter was, he turned to Orla, who seemed to be almost as cross as she was troubled. 'What's happened?'

Orla bent over Aideen. 'Stop it, Aideen. Do you hear me now? You'll make yourself sick.' Aideen gulped, put down her phone, and clasped her hands in her lap. Looking up, Orla spoke to Conor. 'She made a phone call to Bríd to smooth things over.'

'But that's good. I mean, I saw Bríd and, by the time I left, she was reasonable.'

'And then you went on to Couneen and saw Dan, didn't you?'

'Yes. He never asked Aideen to talk to Bríd. It was all a misunderstanding, wasn't it, Ade?'

Aideen gulped incoherently and Orla shook her head at Conor. 'Ah, Conor! What am I going to do with you? You're right, Dan didn't ask Aideen to talk to Bríd about him. It was Aideen's own idea.'

'Oh.'

'And Bríd knows that now because she's had a call from Dan.'

Conor faltered. 'Has she? What did he say?'

'He wanted to know why *she*'d been talking to *you* about him. He wasn't happy.' Aideen sobbed and Orla patted her. 'And

Bríd's now livid with the lot of you. So she didn't respond well when Aideen phoned her. Not well at all.'

'Oh, Christ.' Conor sat back on his heels in horror. 'I only wanted to make things better.'

'I dare say you did, love, but the fact is that you've made everything worse.'

Chapter Thirty

The morning after the dinner party Hanna slept late. She'd slipped up to her room the previous night during the final fare-wells, but Amy had followed her upstairs and sat on the end of her bed. 'Tell me all.'

Hanna was cleaning her face at the mirror. 'There's nothing to tell.'

'Oh puh-lease! The haircut. The fancy eye makeup. The Cinderella-goes-to-the-ball transformation!'

'A dinner party at Windsor is hardly a ball in Prince Charming's palace.'

'Stop trying to divert me, you know it never works.'

'I'm just saying a haircut is no big deal.'

'But look at you, girl, you're ravishing.'

Without the eye makeup, Hanna's face had looked much as it usually did, if a bit shinier. Her hair, however, remained indefinably stunning. 'I do kind of like it.'

'This is what comes of taking my advice.'

'I didn't. I went in for a wash and blow-dry and somehow came out with this.'

'I don't believe you!'

'Look, I didn't mean to be rude about your party. It was fun.'

'That's coming it a bit strong. The Morrisons are tedious and Roger's sweet but his conversation is dire. What did you think of Nicholas?'

'I liked him. You didn't tell me his do-gooding involves books.'

'Does it? I never listen when he talks about it. I was watching him tonight, though, and he seemed very taken with you.'

Nicholas Armstrong had turned out to be a retired business-man whose family had set up a charitable trust to provide books to school libraries in underprivileged areas. Pleased to find that Hanna was a librarian, he'd chatted to her for most of the evening, to the extent that Hanna had feared they might have been im-polite to the other guests. Though, when she'd said so, Amy had giggled. 'God, no, it was as good as a play.'

'Oh, feck off, Amy, and let me sleep. I'm knackered.'

'I'm going. Sweet dreams, Cinderella.'

Having slept late and lazed in the garden with Amy until noon, Hanna declared that today she must find Brian's present. Windsor and Eton were full of shops but London had more to offer, so she decided to brave the train journey, despite the sultry weather. She'd also thought of a quirky addition to the expensive gift of perfume she'd bought for Amy, and the place to buy it was Persephone Books in Bloomsbury. A bookseller and publisher with a shop in Lamb's Conduit Street, Persephone dealt mainly in reprints of books written by women in the years between the world wars, and back in her days as a Londoner, Hanna had been a frequent customer. *Miss Pettigrew Lives for a Day*, writ-ten in the 1930s by an English author called Winifred Watson, had been Persephone's first big word-of-mouth bestseller and remained a firm favourite with Lissbeg Library readers. It was a Cinderella story with a twist: the heroine, a middle-aged, lonely, ineffectual governess, is sent to the wrong address by an employment agency, where her life is turned upside down when she meets a nightclub singer. Given a makeover by the singer and a beautician, she goes from rags to riches in twenty-four hours, enthralled by what's happening yet awake enough to make shrewd comments on her new-found friends' louche, glamorous lifestyles. Knowing that Amy would appreciate the joke, Hanna had decided that *Miss Pettigrew* would complement her gift of perfume, particularly after last night's Cinderella gibe.

Determined to be comfortable and unencumbered, she wore jeans, a T-shirt, and the previous evening's flats and, dispensing with a bag, tucked her credit card and some cash into her pocket. Bloomsbury was one of her favourite parts of London, low on chain stores and high on bookshops, Georgian squares, public gardens, and Victorian terraces backed by mews, which, by the 1930s when *Miss Pettigrew* was written, were famously home to raffish bohemians. Though, as Hanna reflected as she cut through a mews to Lamb's Conduit Street, you'd have to be pretty well-heeled to live there these days.

Entering the little shop, Hanna was charmed, as always, by its shelves and stacks of paperbacks uniformly bound in silver-grey. The books' setting was equally attractive. There were bentwood chairs and wooden tables, and framed posters on the walls, and, towards the back, a woman worked at a computer while another gift-wrapped orders in pink paper and grey ribbon. Though the books were almost identical on the outside, each title had its own endpapers and bookmark, printed with designs taken from fabrics chosen to match the date and mood of the work. Hanna found *Miss Pettigrew* easily, recognising the 1930s furnishing-fabric design, a repeat pattern of a hand holding poppies and stalks of grain, printed in soft yellow and red on a pale linen background. Unable to resist the lure of the other titles, she continued to browse for a further twenty minutes, selecting a book for Louisa in the process. Then, telling herself she must move on and look for Brian's present, she paid for her purchases and left, enjoying the sound of the tinkling bell that rang when the door was opened.

Outside there was a box containing copies of Persephone's catalogue and, pausing to take one, Hanna heard her name called from the opposite pavement. She turned, wondering if someone she used to know was passing. Instead, it was Nicholas Armstrong in a quiet charcoal-striped suit. He waved and, as he crossed the road to join her, Hanna had a feeling that if he'd been wearing a hat he'd have raised it politely. This, she supposed, was the result of spending time among works written in the interwar years by popular woman novelists.

Nicholas smiled. 'This is a surprise. How nice to see you again!'

'I've been buying books.' Hanna indicated the shop behind her.

'I've been talking books at a trustees' meeting round the corner. We have an office off Guilford Street.'

'How extraordinary. I mean, London's huge and we only met for the first time last night.'

'Well, I suppose Bloomsbury is dreadfully bookish. Anyway, it's a delightful coincidence.' He glanced back across the road to where there was a café. 'You don't fancy tea and a bun, do you? I'm parched.'

Despite his commanding presence, he looked wistful, so Hanna said she'd love to and they crossed the road together. Nicholas's idea of tea and a bun turned out to be lapsang souchong and chocolate éclairs, and his description of the meeting he'd attended was absorbing. It was half an hour before Hanna glanced at her watch and said she must go. Looking guilty, he stood up and drew out her chair. 'I'm sorry. Of course. I'm doing it again – I've been monopolising you.'

'No, not at all. The trust sounds really impressive.'

'Well, we do our best, and we've got a good team. Look, I don't know if . . .' He paused, then shook his head. 'I expect you're busy this evening.'

'Not specially.'

'The thing is, if you were free, well, we generally go to a show after a meeting. Kind of a chance to get together and not talk books. Anyway, tonight we've a box for the ballet at Covent Garden. It's *Sleeping Beauty* and there's a spare seat if you'd care to come along.'

The invitation was totally unexpected and Hanna was astonished to hear herself accept. It wasn't until they'd said goodbye, having fixed to meet for a drink before the performance, that she realised that, once again, she'd failed to factor in time and distances. Here she was, in jeans and a T-shirt, with only a few hours to return to Windsor, change, and catch a train back to Waterloo. After which, she'd have to make her way to Covent Garden. It couldn't be done. Nicholas had disappeared in a passing taxi, and she had no means of getting in touch to apologise and cancel. All she could do was call Amy and ask her for his number, a course sure to produce a shower of questions. Groaning, Hanna turned her head and saw her reflection in the café's plate-glass window. Dammit, her hair looked good. It was now nearly four o'clock and she'd fixed to meet Nicholas in a wine bar at seven. Surely three hours would provide enough time to buy herself something to wear and find a hotel loo in which to make herself tidy. Anything was better than inviting more of Amy's un-subtle teasing, and a night at the ballet in Covent Garden was too tempting to miss.

She was about to make for Oxford Street, to find a large depart-ment store, when she noticed a narrow shopfront a few doors away from the bookshop. There was an elegantly hand-lettered sign out-side saying 'POP-UP BOUTIQUE' and through the window she could see clothes hanging on rails in a plain white space. Each rail featured a different palette of subtle colours and, intrigued, Hanna crossed the road to peer through the door. Another notice, on a stand inside, explained that the clothes were the work of a young designer and were on sale there for one day only. Stepping in, Hanna smiled at a girl who was reading a book on a bench at the back of the shop. 'May I look around?'

The girl smiled back shyly. 'Of course. Please ask if you have any questions.'

It took no more than a minute to find the right dress, and the price was so reasonable that Hanna had to check it was correct. She stepped behind a curtain that had been rigged up in a cor-ner and, having slipped the dress on, emerged to view herself in a long mirror. It was a calf-length, oyster-coloured satin slip, with a long-sleeved overdress of crêpe-de-Chine in the palest possible shade of misty grey. It felt slightly vintage, but the simplicity of the single-strand beading around the neck, hem, and cuffs of the overdress was unmistakably modern. Worn with her black ballet flats, it looked absolutely right – dressy enough for the evening, because of the tiny crystal beads, but plain enough to be something she might have chosen to wear for a sunny day's shopping in London. She had bought a cream and grey book bag in Persephone, for her purchases, and now, swinging it onto her shoulder, she saw that it added exactly the right touch. In fact, if someone had had to design an outfit that screamed assured, well-dressed, middle-aged woman librarian, they could hardly have come up with anything more apt.

Having solved the first part of her problem in less than twenty minutes, Hanna continued to saunter around Bloomsbury, swinging the carrier bag into which the shop assistant had folded her dress. After about an hour, she made her way to Russell Square and ate a salad in the gleaming bar of the huge terracotta-clad hotel there. The sumptuous building seemed like a good place to begin the evening, and the ladies' room off the marble atrium provided plenty of space for her to brush-up and change. Emerging like a butterfly from a chrysalis, with her T-shirt and jeans shoved to the bottom of her book bag, she strolled back into the bar, met the barman's surprised gaze blandly, and ordered a glass of tonic with a twist of lime. Then, with fifteen minutes to spare, she caught the tube to Covent Garden and found Nicholas and his fellow trustees in the wine bar.

The evening continued exactly as it had begun. The four trustees were friendly from the start, and one, who turned out to be Nicholas's sister, crowed with delight when she saw Hanna's bag. 'I know book talk is supposed to be banned, but have you read *Miss Pettigrew*?'

'Of course. And I seem to check it out to a borrower every other weekend.'

'Do you? Tell me about your library.'

The conversation continued as they made their way to the Royal Opera House, where Hanna hadn't been for so long that her breath caught in her throat. The crimson and gold auditorium was as beautiful as ever. The orchestra was tuning up, the box gave a perfect view of the stage, and as she settled onto her velvet chair, she heaved a deep sigh of contentment.

Nicholas sat beside her. 'I'm glad you could come.'

'It was good of you to invite me. I can't believe how much I've missed evenings like this.'

'The downside of an idyllic rural life?'

'I suppose so.'

As the lights went down and the curtain rose, Hanna relaxed to the sound of the familiar music. She had seen the production years ago, with Jazz and Malcolm, and, briefly, the memories flooded back and shimmered between her eyes and the floating figures on the stage. Then the story of *Sleeping Beauty* took over and she was wrapped in the fairy tale.

At the second interval, Nicholas disappeared and returned with a waiter carrying a tray of drinks. Glad that she'd had the sense to eat beforehand, Hanna accepted a glass and chatted easily with Pen, Nicholas's sister. Part of the trustees' meeting had been about choosing a read-aloud *Mother Goose* to add to their library selection. 'Nicholas thinks we ought to forget fairy tales and nursery rhymes, but I think every child should be exposed to them.'

Nicholas shook his head at Pen. 'I don't think we should forget them. It's simply a case of a finite budget and many wonderful children's titles to choose from.'

'That's because you think kids pick up fairy tales automatically. They don't. In my view, they're important, Nick, and if children come from poor backgrounds, how are they to access them?'

'You won your argument earlier, let's not rehash it.'

It was such an easy, cheerful exchange that Hanna wasn't the least bit troubled when Pen turned and demanded her support. 'Hanna agrees with me, don't you?'

'I do. Though I think it's easy to project one's sensibilities onto children. I bought my daughter a copy of Grimms' *Household Tales* once. It had the Mervyn Peake illustrations, which I thought were stunning. It was years before I discovered they'd scared the life out of her.'

The others, who'd been listening in, joined in the laughter, and as the lights went down again, Hanna remembered Jazz's face in the spill of light from the stage at the matinée they'd attended with Malcolm. Jazz had been twelve or so, too old for books of fairy tales, and her main interest in the ballet had been practical, so on their way to the performance she had bombarded them with questions. How long did the dancers have to rehearse? Could they eat what they liked, or did they just live on yoghurt? How many instruments were there in an orchestra? Had anyone ever been killed by a piece of falling scenery? But then, in the last act, when Puss-in-Boots, the White Cat, and the other storybook characters attend Sleeping Beauty's wedding, she'd fallen for the soaring Bluebird in the *pas de deux*. Half asleep on their way home, with her head against Malcolm's arm, she'd announced that she wanted to dance the Bluebird role.

Malcolm had hugged her. 'It's not the ballerina's part. You could be the princess he's in love with.'

'Not interested. Why do people always have to make things be about love?'

'Because it's the most important thing in the world.'

'No, it's not. Not that mushy romantic stuff, anyway. It's just a way to stop you doing all kinds of other things. Who'd want to settle down and live happily ever after? That's boring. I want to fly for ever on massive feathery wings.'

Chapter Thirty-One

It was late afternoon, and when Fury came in, Brian was lying full-length on the sofa. He looked up and swung his feet to the floor. 'What's the story?'

'I'm going to have to shift that old bit of roof soon and do Jo out of a bed.'

'Can it wait till Hanna gets back?'

Fury settled his bony behind against the table. 'How's she doing over there?'

'I spoke to her this morning. She'd been to the ballet.'

'Now, that's a thing I've never gone to myself.'

'I used to be a bit of a fan.' Brian went to the window seat and pulled Jo's ears. 'Haven't seen one for years, though. Nor had Hanna, apparently.'

Fury picked his teeth with his fingernail. 'I suppose she's been reacquainting herself with all sorts of things she'd forgotten.'

It was evident that Brian was supposed to rise to this, but he refused to. 'Can the roof wait till she's back?'

'Up to yourself, I'm not the one whose car needs a garage.'

'Well, leave it, then. Jo's missing Hanna enough without us adding to her trouble.'

'Fair enough.' Fury glanced round the room, which was still piled with Mike's possessions. 'Your lad's still here, I see.'

'Well, in residence. Not here, though. He borrowed a bike from the farm below a few days ago. I think he said he was off to Carrick today.'

'You might say he's settled in, so.'

'And God knows what Hanna's going to say when she comes back and sees the state of this place. You know, I never said so out loud because it seemed heartless, but sometimes I used to think Hanna made a meal of things about Jazz. Wallowing in guilt because of how she'd left her husband, and over-compensating if Jazz looked glum. And look at me now, unable to tell my son to pick his socks up.'

It was bizarre how Fury drew things out of you, usually by giving the impression of having no interest. Having begun to confide in him, Brian found himself eager to explain. 'He's not being deliberately childish, and it doesn't mean anything. It's just how he is. Yet the fact remains that I'm stuck, like a fool, somewhere between Mine Host and Angry Dad.'

'I suppose a kick up the arse is out of the question?'

'His or mine?'

'Might be a case of two kicks needed.'

Brian looked rueful. 'I wish I could say you were wrong. Mike's a good guy, you know, Fury. Perhaps we've had enough of each other's company for a while, but I'm genuinely glad I've got to know him a bit better.' Staring out of the window, he gently tugged Jo's ear. 'I don't think I know anymore who Sandra was. I don't know that I ever did, really, but I do hope she'd be proud of our son. I think he's honest and hardworking, and if he's a bit socially inept, that's not the worst of faults.'

Along the road that led up from the farmhouse below, starlings had gathered on telephone wires, chattering in the bright autumnal air. Fury looked down the glen and gave a noncommittal sniff. 'Life is long, isn't it? And, shur, you never know what's going to happen next.'

Brian looked at him sharply. 'Are you up to something?'

'Holy God, man, all I'm doing is making conversation. Do you not know how it works? When you say something and I come back with an anodyne truism, you're supposed to tell me I'm right and then we both give a bit of a sigh. Conversation. What normal people do.' Shaking his head, Fury hitched his rump off the table. 'And you call your poor son socially inept!'

*

The bicycle Mike had borrowed was old but serviceable. After a day of photography, he bowled up to Maggie's place and was sitting on the doorstep when Jazz arrived home. She stopped at the gable end of the house when she saw him. 'You just put the heart crossways in me!'

'That's a great expression.'

'Thank you. I picked it up from my nan.'

'The one from Kent?'

'Don't be an idiot.'

Mike stood up to allow her to get at the door, and Jazz came and unlocked it. 'And you're here because?'

'I just thought we might hang out.'

'Does hanging out involve you cooking more burgers?'

'Could do.'

'Step right in.'

She led the way and he sat by the hearth while she went into the bedroom to change out of her office clothes. When she came back, he glanced up from a book he'd taken from a shelf. 'I wouldn't have put you down as someone who read detective stories.'

'You'd be right. Most of the books there were either my mum's or her great-aunt Maggie's. Apparently Maggie was a crime-fiction fiend.'

'I read a thing called *Beautiful Liars* once.'

'Nothing before or since?'

Mike chuckled. 'Not a lot. Films, though. Can't get enough of them.'

'I'm too busy for either. Lots of reading when I was a kid, but I'm focused on work now.' She went to the fridge. 'Beer or coffee?'

They sat drinking beer on either side of the fireplace with the half-door open and the humming of bees in the garden sliced by the shrieking of gulls. Mike leaned back and crooked his knee over the arm of his chair. 'I can't imagine working nine to five.'

'I couldn't either. My first job was with an airline and I did shifts. Cabin crew. For a while I had a flat-share in France. It was a really cool lifestyle. Then I totalled my mum's car one night, when I was here on a stopover. Ended up in hospital. Came out and was in a "really bad place".' Not wanting to seem over-dramatic, Jazz made air quotes round the words. 'That was around the time you and I met.'

'And then your other gran came to the rescue.'

'A lot of people see it like that.'

'Sorry, was I being rude?'

'Not really. I just hate the thought that I might have needed rescuing. I suppose it's true, though. Mum tries to make it sound better by saying I was rootless.'

'And that's bad?'

'It's bad when it's a euphemism for rolling round like tumble-weed. So, yeah, you could say my gran came to the rescue.' Jazz got up and returned with a packet of peanuts. 'Anyway, she set up the business and gave me a job, and my mum rents me this place, and you know what, you're absolutely right, I have a cushy life.'

'I didn't say that.'

'I quite like nine to five, though I suppose it's different when it's a family business.' She threw him a defensive glance. 'I do know how lucky I am.'

Mike leaned forward with his elbows on his knees, and the beer can between his hands. 'Seriously, I don't see why it matters. What's wrong with accepting help?'

She flipped a peanut into the air and caught it in her mouth. 'There's nothing wrong with accepting help. That's one thing being in a really bad place taught me. I've had plenty of people say I'm living in clover, though.' She missed a second peanut and groped for it as it rolled away between the legs of her chair. 'Well, it isn't often said out loud. It's what they think. Mostly I don't give a damn, but sometimes it gets to me.' Finding the peanut, she sat up and threw it into the fireplace. 'Incidentally, who says I have to answer all these questions?'

'You don't have to. You could tell me to mind my own business.'

'Or you could be less brash.'

Mike laughed. 'Apparently, brash is my default setting. I really should work on that.'

'If you ask me, you're proud of it.'

'Well, it makes for a simple life.'

'And we're back to what you said before, that life is only complex if people allow it to be.'

'The other day you told me that that's what I said to you about families. Not life.'

The stone-tiled floor was beginning to redden in the light of the evening sun. Jazz took a swig of beer and savoured the experience of having a house to which she could welcome a friend. Though her relationship with Mike didn't really warrant the term 'friendship'. In fact, she wasn't sure how to define it. When they'd first met, she'd half thought he fancied her. It was back in the days when she'd lurched from one love affair to another and, having recently been dumped, she might well have fallen into bed with him. But he'd simplified things for them both. 'How about I cut the crap and just say this? You're lovely but I'm not looking for a holiday romance, and if I were I wouldn't be targeting someone who's just broken up with her boyfriend.' Coming from someone else, that might have been devastating but, despite her fragile state, it had made Jazz laugh. Looking at him from under her eyelashes, she wondered if he remembered it. Mike caught her eye and grinned. 'I don't suppose there's any chance that you and I might pick up where we left off?'

'And where was that?'

'The timing was wrong but I guess you could say we were interested in each other.'

He was handsome in an understated way and undeniably attractive, so Jazz was surprised by her own unequivocal reaction. 'No.'

'Well, that's me told. Anything to do with my failing to follow up on those marathon plans?'

'Don't flatter yourself.' Jazz laughed. 'It's nothing personal. It just happens that, right now, I'm the one not looking for romance.'

'Totally focused on work.'

'And loving being single.' It was the first time Jazz had said this aloud and, with a huge surge of confidence, she realised that, for the time being, it was absolutely true.

'Oh, well, it was worth a try. Anyway, I suppose we're practically related, now that your mum's moved in with my dad.'

She held out the packet of peanuts and shook some into his hand. 'Yeah, you and your dad. What's that all about?'

'Who's being brash now?'

'You could tell me to mind my own business.'

'True. But there's nothing to tell.'

Jazz repeated the question she'd asked Hanna, to which she felt she hadn't had a satisfactory reply. 'How come you ended up being raised in London by your aunt?'

'My mum died. Dad couldn't take care of me. My aunt stepped in and became my mum. Literally. She and my dad – my uncle, I mean – adopted me.'

'And you were okay with that?'

'I was a couple of months old so I didn't have a say in the matter.'

'But wasn't it weird with Brian as you grew up?'

'No, because I didn't know he was my dad. Not till I left school.'

'Blimey.'

Mike went to the fridge and got more beer. 'It was no big

thing. I'd seen him as an uncle or something. He wasn't around much.'

Jazz thought of her own reaction on discovering the truth about her parents' marriage. For years she'd been tormented by the fact that her father's long-term affair had begun before she was conceived. Having grown up the only child of parents who adored her, the emergence of his duplicity had seemed to undermine everything, beginning with her belief in him and seeping out to poison her sense of self. Yet Mike's family had brought him up in equally false circumstances, and it didn't seem to bother him at all. 'Didn't you hate your dad for living a kind of double life?'

'Of course not. They'd decided it was for the best.'

'So was it?'

'The question doesn't compute. Like, who can tell? I had a fantastic childhood, if that's what you mean.'

'And you didn't know who your mum was either?'

Mike shrugged. 'Still don't, really. Well, I know who she was but nothing much about her. I think Brian's been eager to tell me all this week but, so far, he's bottled it. I'm kind of glad.'

Two cans of beer would normally be one too many for Jazz, yet she went to the fridge and opened a second. 'But if he wants to tell you? I mean, maybe he feels bad about their decision.'

'I dunno why he should. They wanted to protect me. Anyway, I can't give him absolution, can I? People have to find their own redemption. He's nice, though. A good guy to hang out with.'

'And that's it?'

Mike grinned. 'Families don't have to be complex, not if you don't allow them to be.'

Remembering the question that had crossed her mind the day they'd gone swimming, Jazz decided that he probably took that view of all his relationships, so it was just as well that they hadn't got involved when she was in her bad place. There was nothing unkind or dishonest about his worldview but this level of pragmatism was too much for her to take. Perhaps, although she saw herself as cool-headed, like her father, she was actually a romantic, like her mum. The thought made her giggle and Mike raised his eyebrows. 'Have I said something funny?'

'Not at all. Different families are different, though. You don't have to deal with a fruitcake like my nan.'

'Is she batty?'

Jazz twiddled her beer can, trying to refract a ray of evening sunlight. She wished she hadn't said that about her nan. It felt disrespectful, especially when said to someone like Mike, who didn't do nuance. The usual terms for Mary were 'a character', or 'strong-minded', or even 'difficult', but any of those could equally be expressed as 'a tower of strength'. Taking a slug of beer, Jazz frowned. It was her nan, more than her mum, who'd helped her cope with her parents' divorce. Most of Mary's efforts had been annoying. Having been raised on croissants and organic orange juice, Jazz had been horrified by the huge breakfasts Mary had risen at dawn to cook for her, and infuriated to find her laundry done without consultation, and hot-water bottles in furry covers tucked into her bed. But, though she'd gagged at the sight of runny eggs and black and white pudding, and muttered about locking her bedroom door, Mary's intrusive affection had made her feel loved, and wrapped in security, at a time when Hanna's watchful anxiety had simply added to her stress.

'Nope, not batty. She's getting older, though, and she's high-maintenance.'

'Bed pans and stuff?'

'Of course not!' Jazz shied away from the thought. 'You saw her at the birthday party, swanning around like a star. I said getting old, not ancient. She's just . . . demanding. I know it gets to my mum.'

'That's exactly what I mean. People shouldn't let people get to them.'

Though his tone was partly teasing, Jazz could tell that this wasn't an act. He genuinely didn't see life as complicated. She supposed it was possible that he was in what people called denial, but no doubt he'd dismiss that, too, if she suggested it. So she changed the subject. 'What were you doing in Carrick?'

'Photographing the castle walls. They're spectacular, aren't they? I wanted to see inside but it said "Private". A coach went in, though.'

'Some cruise line has it on its shore itinerary.'

'Interesting. Maybe I could flog them a piece of video for their website.'

'Fury O'Shea would know their name. He's always up at the castle.'

Mike grinned and took a handful of peanuts. 'I get the impression that Fury's always everywhere.'

'You've met him?'

'He's doing some work up at the Hag's Glen. A beaky-nosed guy with a little snappy dog.'

'That's Fury.'

'I bumped into him when I arrived. He gave me a pretty penetrating look.'

'That means you're on his radar.'

'Woah – sounds ominous.'

Jazz flipped another peanut deftly into her mouth. 'Don't worry. If Fury ever decides he's going to make use of you, he'll do it with such finesse that you won't even notice.'

Chapter Thirty-Two

There was a lushness about the farm garden where it seemed to Aideen that everything glittered and gleamed. Paddy had spread nets over the summer gooseberry bushes, as protection from hungry birds. The green globes grew thickly clustered on long, prickly branches, and each sharp spine, like each hair on the fuzzy green berries, was hung with sparkling points of light when the sun shone after rain. Swelling apples sometimes split on the trees, revealing shining flesh beneath their polished scarlet skin, a juicy magnet for bees and burrowing insects. As the light changed with the changing seasons, new points of focus emerged. At dawn and dusk the grass trembled with dewfall, and mist spread a crystal film over the nets that covered the loganberries. Now, as the days grew imperceptibly shorter, honey bees circled the plum trees and buzzed among early blackberries, which already gleamed darkly in the hedge.

Among the spreading fruit bushes was a damson tree, low-growing and resistant to the peninsula's autumn gales. Orla had told Aideen it came from stock that predated the orchard. 'There were fields back here when Conor's granny first came to the farm.

She said wild damsons grew in the old hedgerows, and damsons propagate from their own fallen stones.' The idea had delighted Aideen, who'd never tasted damsons before arriving at the farm. She'd looked them up in a book and found that, because they come true from seed, the little violet-coloured fruits taste exactly the same today as they did when they first arrived in Europe from Damascus. Now, standing under the tree, she remembered sitting up in bed and reading that aloud to Conor. She'd never been good at school and, distressed by her aunt's unexpected death, had done badly in the Leaving Cert, but Conor's job at the library had given her new interest in, and access to, books. 'The fruit came from Italy into France in the middle ages, and got called Damascene because of Damascus. And, wow, look, it's the same as the word for "damask". You know, the fabric. And, here, look, damask roses – they're supposed to have come from the Middle East too.'

'Yeah?' Conor had taken the book out of her hand and kissed her. 'You smell like a rose.'

'Conditioner. I got a two-pack in the EuroStore in Sheep Street.' Though it wasn't terribly funny, they'd got the giggles, which killed the mood a bit and, because he'd been tired, the sex they'd had that night had been unspectacular. But she hadn't minded. Afterwards, when he'd fallen asleep with his arm thrown around her, she'd looked at the contrast between his skin and the whiteness of her breasts. The room had been full of moonlight. His arm was golden brown. It had almost invisible hairs that were soft if you rubbed your cheek against them. They'd shone in the moonlight like damson leaves in late autumn, which turn from green to gold on the tree before drifting down to make pools on the sodden grass.

Aideen's eyes filled with tears. It seemed as if she'd done nothing but cry lately. Bríd still wouldn't say a word to her and, since the disaster, she and Conor had hardly spoken either. She knew he hadn't meant to make trouble but, having done so, he'd got stubborn and wouldn't apologise. It was partly guilt, partly tiredness, and a lot to do with it all having come out in front of his parents, with Dermot there as an embarrassed witness. She blamed herself. If she hadn't got hysterical and needed Orla to soothe her, she might have talked reasonably to Conor, up in their bedroom or out in the garden. Showing him up as an eejit in the kitchen had been awful, and shouting at him through her tears had made things worse. No wonder Bríd treated her like a baby. Given the way she'd been acting, it was no more than she deserved.

Today was one of her deli days but she hadn't gone to work. She knew she couldn't keep this up for ever, or continue to avoid Conor during the daytime and pretend to be asleep when he came upstairs to bed. Sooner or later she'd have to face Bríd, deal with things, and, probably, apologise to Dan. It was all very well getting upset about being dragged into Bríd and Dan's business, but she and Conor had been selfish. What about Dan, who'd now been dragged unwillingly into theirs? And what about Bríd, who, Aideen knew, was in bits about the breakup and really wanted to get back together with Dan?

Devastated, Aideen sat down under the damson tree. It was mid-morning on another sunny day, and the grass was warm. At the far side of the orchard, the hens were scratching in their run, making clucking noises and little dashes whenever they spied a movement in the grass. Since she'd come to live at the farm she'd felt wrapped in a blanket of loving concern, which had made her feel she'd never again be lonely. Yet today she felt more alone than she ever had in her life. She knew Orla would offer comfort if she asked for it, but it seemed pathetic to run to her instead of finding Conor and setting things straight. Sooner or later, one of them would have to act like a grown-up but, as well as feeling weepy, Aideen felt exhausted. Anyway, she thought wanly, the chances of talking to Conor were pretty low. He wouldn't thank her for turning up in the library, or when he was working with Dermot, and most nights she felt so tired that she really was asleep when he came upstairs.

The damsons above her were still unripe. Orla had said they were brilliant in pies and crumbles, and stewed with honey. She pickled them, too, which Aideen had never tried, and made something she called damson cheese, to go with cold meat. Aideen had never heard of that either, and she'd meant to talk to Bríd about it. It was a thick conserve, which Orla said had a deep, intense flavour, and went best with lamb and game or really strong cheese. It sounded like something that ought to sell well round Christmastime in the deli. In springtime this year the tree had been white with blossom, and so much fruit had set that it was weighed down. Looking up, Aideen considered the thick purple clusters. You could make dozens of pots of conserve for Christmas and still have plenty of fruit to freeze to make cheesecakes right up to Easter.

Sadly, she remembered the planning meetings they'd had about growing things on the farm for the deli. It had all seemed so achievable before she'd begun to worry that change would make Paddy's depression worse. Going through government forms and setting up spreadsheets with Bríd and Conor had made the two halves of her life feel integrated. But Paddy's health was only part of the problem. Beneath the shared enthusiasm there had been the matter of Bríd's breakup with Dan; and Aideen knew that part of Bríd's present anger came from a fear that the others had been discussing her with Dan all along. Which was so unfair, she thought, because they hadn't. Conor and Dan seemed to communicate solely by buying each other pints and talking football. And Conor barely had time to discuss his own marriage, for God's sake. Besides, back when Aideen had told him about the breakup, he'd been dismissive. 'Sure the pair of them never stop locking horns.'

'She wants Dan's business to do well. She wants to be supportive.'

'She has a queer way of showing it.'

'You know how unbusinesslike Dan is. She could give him good advice.'

Conor's response had been to snort and Aideen couldn't blame him. Anyone could see that someone like Dan would resent Bríd's bossy advice. She didn't even know why she'd tried defending Bríd to Conor, except that she knew how much Bríd missed Dan. Conor was right, though. Bríd and Dan would probably keep fighting and making up for the rest of their lives.

Conor and I aren't much better, thought Aideen, sadly. I say too little and he does too much and we end up upsetting everyone. And, okay, we've been busy and under pressure, but that's just life. Why can't I deal with it sanely, like anyone else?

She heard the kitchen door slam in the distance, and Paddy came down from the yard to the garden, with water for the hens. He tipped it into a battered pan inside the hen run, hooked the door back into place, and came towards Aideen. 'How's my girl?'

'I'm okay. How's yourself?'

'Ah, sure, I have good days and bad days. This one could be worse.' Paddy sat down beside her and looked up into the damson tree. 'Grand crop we've got this year. What're you doing sitting here?'

'Avoiding everyone.'

'I know. There's times you'd want to get off on your own.'

'You have to come back eventually, though, haven't you?'

'Maybe you'd get your head straightened out first.'

'I doubt I will. There's so many things confusing me and I seem to have no energy. My mind's like a black hole.'

Paddy looked across at her. 'Are you still not talking to Conor?'

'It's not that I'm not talking to him.'

'It's just that you're not talking.'

Aideen grinned. 'I suppose you could put it that way. Look, I've been wanting to tell you I'm sorry.'

'Why so?'

'I shouldn't have thrown that scene the other day. I know it upset you.'

'You were the one upset, and you had a right to be. Conor can be a thick bugger at times.'

'He's not thick! Well, yes, he can be, but that's not the point. The point is that he and me both handled it badly. You shouldn't have been troubled.'

Paddy looked at her thoughtfully. 'You know this depression the doctor says I've got? That's like a black hole sometimes. I'm tired, and I can't get on top of things, and everything feels frightening. Like there's no proper edges to my world, and I might slip off. Some days I feel so hopeless I can't see why anyone would put up with me.'

'Fuss and upheaval and changes are disorienting.'

'No, it's not that, it comes out of nowhere for no reason, that's the awful part. I actually feel I might lose my grip and disappear into the black hole. But you know what keeps me anchored? You do.'

'Me?'

'You and Conor and Orla, and ordinary life going on. Seeds planted and crops growing and lambs being born and kept warm by the side of the range.'

'But they die, don't they? The lambs. We raise sheep to kill them. I was thinking about that the other day and it actually made me feel sick.'

'Everything dies, girl. Lambs and flowers and grain that's cut down to make bread. Whatever lives dies eventually. That's Nature's way.'

Aideen wasn't sure that that fully addressed what she felt about animals driven away to an abattoir, but what he'd said had distracted her. 'So you're saying you like change?'

'If you're talking about the change of the seasons, yes. Or if you mean am I glad you and Conor got married and you came to live here, that's a yes too.'

'But I caused so much trouble. Disappearing off to Florence after wasting everyone's time with all that stupid double-wedding stuff.'

'Didn't it come right in the end, though?'

Aideen frowned. 'Why were you iffy when Conor suggested we might grow stuff for the deli?'

Paddy looked apologetic. 'The good days and bad days aren't all down to depression. Some of it might be natural bloody-mindedness.'

'Don't you like the idea?'

'Maybe I didn't like the fact that it wasn't me who thought of it.'

'So it's not the upheaval? We wouldn't be making you feel worse by changing things?'

'Didn't I tell you before that you can't stagnate in farming? It never makes sense.'

'You were against chasing new-fangled notions, too, though.'

'Ah, there's nothing new about growing crops to sell, girl, and I've nothing against the organic notion, either. I wouldn't say there was a chemical put on this land before my granddad's time. Not before the nineteen sixties, anyway.'

'Then you think it's a good idea?'

'I never said I didn't.'

And Conor hadn't said he had either. It was she who'd got worried and asked Orla and, now she came to think of it, all Orla had said was that they shouldn't rush their fences.

'Edge of the World Essentials are looking for growers. Maybe we might produce for them as well as for the deli?'

'That's for Conor and you to decide between you. You're the farmer and his wife now, girl. Me and Orla are the old folks by the fire.'

'You'd better not let her hear you say that. She'd skin you!'

'True enough, but you know what I mean. You're the next turn of the wheel.'

Aideen stared across the garden to where the hens were clucking around their water dish. She couldn't understand the way she'd been reacting to things lately. Maybe, like Paddy, she'd developed some kind of depression. She frowned. 'You know that black-hole feeling? Do you get mood swings?'

'I do.'

'And I'm tired all the time, I've got no energy. People get on my nerves, too, like the way I fell out with Bríd. And I can't believe how I shouted at poor Conor.'

'Come here to me, love, tell me this, did you say you felt sick?'

'Sometimes, yeah. Are you that way too? Is it a symptom of depression?' Aideen screwed up her face anxiously. 'Do you think I should see a doctor?'

Paddy looked thoughtful again. 'Well, speaking as a farmer, I wouldn't go spending money on a doctor. Not yet awhile. I'd get yourself into the chemist, though, and pick up a pregnancy test.'

Chapter Thirty-Three

Jazz arrived a few minutes late for her first meeting of the morning. The staff was gathered around a table in the largest of their offices in the Old Convent Centre to review the images in their finalised 'Meet Our Growers' campaign. Laminated and printed on heavy cardboard, life-sized copies of the photos Jazz had shown the girls in the deli were displayed against the wall and, as Jazz slipped into her seat, Louisa was speaking. 'I think the whole team is to be congratulated for the work we've done on this – those of you who made suggestions for participants, the creative effort that went into styling, the original brainstorming when we hit on the idea. My central vision for this company was to develop and market organic cosmetics with small producers through real, practical teamwork, and I'm proud to see it coming through in this kind of project.' She indicated one of the photos, in which a handsome, muscular young man, with an armful of flowering comfrey, narrowed his eyes against dazzling sunlight. He was standing with his back to a barn door on which the blistered paint showed layers of different colours, and he wore a faded, frayed plaid shirt.

'Incidentally, Nabil, who looks quite as impressive as the pro-fessional model we used for the focus groups, is gardening for Eoghan, one of our producers. It was you who found Nabil, wasn't it, Jazz?'

'What? No, it was Eoghan who suggested him. That really is Nabil's work shirt, we didn't need to style him. He was totally up for it.'

Louisa smiled. 'I understand Johnny Hennessy brought his own selection of tweed caps.'

The photographer, who'd been invited to the meeting, laughed. 'One better than the next. But, really, the styling was almost all about props. The people looked fabulous because – well, like you said, it was real.'

Louisa looked down at her notes. 'So, we're on track to get these out to retailers, they'll feature on our website, and the orig-inals will come with us to expos and fairs. Let's look at the expo list now and we can run through matters arising.'

When the meeting broke up, Louisa walked Jazz to her desk. 'Is everything all right?'

'Yes. Sorry I was late.'

'We'd only just started. It's not like you, though.'

Jazz sat at her desk and pulled a face. 'I had a long phone call with Mum. She called first thing.'

'Is something the matter?'

'Well, you know Mum. She gets wound up but she's not one to complain.'

Louisa pulled a chair over to the desk. 'So, what's happened?'

'Well, before she called me she'd been on the phone for ages with Nan.'

'Ah. It wasn't about a woman called Pauline Murphy by any chance, was it?'

'Yes. How did you know?'

'Mary mentioned her to me some time ago and she raised the subject again after her birthday party. I don't know Mrs Murphy from Adam, though apparently I should because she does her shopping at Aldi.'

'That sounds so like Nan.'

'Why did she ring Hanna?'

'Apparently, she happened to meet this Pauline Murphy in Carrick and didn't like something she said or didn't say about Brian. Anyway, Nan rang Mum full of dire warnings and ended up starting World War Three. And Mum rang me – I think more because she wanted to vent than anything – and I ended up being late for work.'

'Did Mary actually say "happened to meet"?'

'That's what Mum said she said.' Jazz looked at Louisa sharply. 'Why? Who's this Pauline person?'

Louisa looked troubled. 'I don't know if Mary expected our conversation to be confidential. And I'd hoped that, if she wasn't encouraged to dwell on it, she'd move on.'

'Oh, for heaven's sake, Granny Lou!' Mystified, Jazz had reverted to her childhood name for Louisa. 'Move on from what? What's this about? Mum made no sense, and you're being just as bad.'

'That's because none of it makes sense, darling. Your nan has decided that this Murphy woman is making a play for Brian.'

'What?'

'She told me some time ago and I tried to make light of it, and then she informed Hanna at the party. Which, incidentally, was why it broke up abruptly.'

Jazz groaned. 'And she's been sending a stream of texts while Mum's been in London.'

'To Mrs Murphy?'

'God, I hope not. I think it's just been to Mum. Wait, are you saying you think Nan deliberately cornered this Pauline Murphy in Carrick?'

'Well, I did wonder. Poor Mary.'

Jazz stood up, looking furious. 'Poor Mary? That is such crap! I've never understood why she's had to be treated as if she's mentally defective.'

'Darling, of course not, but she is getting older.'

'She's no older than you are. Besides, you don't know her, not really. I've known her my whole life and she's always been indulged. And now look what it's led to.' Snatching her bag from the back of the chair, Jazz made for the door. 'There's nothing wrong with her! She's just behaving disgracefully and I'm going to put a stop to it.'

*

Half an hour later, as Jazz threw open the bungalow gate, Johnny Hennessy was weeding in his garden next door. Straightening up, he pushed his tweed cap to the back of his head. 'Your nan's round the back, love. I saw her taking in washing.'

It was evident that he was ready to chat but Jazz was on a trajectory, so she gave him a wave and called across the fence. 'I need to get back to work. We were talking about you this morning – that was a great photo. You're a star.' His gratified look added to Jazz's irritation with Mary. Here was a man in his late seventies, cheerful, productive, and prepared to involve himself in a start-up business. She ought to be chatting and making him feel thanked and appreciated, instead of which she was throwing him a line over her shoulder because, once again, Mary Casey had taken centre stage.

She found her nan in the kitchen, folding laundry. Mary's face brightened as she came in. 'Well, this is a nice surprise.'

'Don't bet on it.' Jazz dumped her bag on the table. 'What have you been up to?'

Mary took a step backwards, a sheet in her hands and her face closing in folds of mulishness. 'I don't know what you mean.'

'You damn well do.'

'Don't come in here and use that kind of language in my house, please.'

'Don't try that line on me. It won't get you anywhere. You and I are going to have this out here and now.'

'So Hanna's been complaining about me, has she?'

'What do you think you're at, coming out with that stuff about Brian? You know it's nonsense, so what are you trying to do?'

Mary slammed the sheet onto the table and surged into attack mode. 'I'll tell you what I'm trying to do. I'm trying to protect my daughter. And God alone knows why because, in her whole life, she's never given her mother a word of thanks. All I've ever tried to do is the right thing for my family. I knew she was a fool the first time she went off to England, and would she listen to me? No, she wouldn't. And, I swear to God, her going away hastened her father's death.' Mary's jaw clenched. 'And when she married that father of yours, look at the grief she got, but back she came here and I opened my door and took you in.'

'You said we were welcome!'

'I did, and you were, would you not be such a gawm! I was more than glad to have you, you know that. The point is that I know damn well Hanna never wanted to be here. She couldn't wait to get the hell out and move into Maggie's shed.'

'Oh, stop it, Nan. It's not a shed, it's lovely, and she restored it on a shoestring. She just wanted a place of her own. Can you not see that?'

'She wanted to show the world that she had no need of me. And I suppose you're here to tell me the same thing.' Mary's face crumpled and she sat down at the table. 'Right so. Message understood. I won't say another word.' She shut her mouth with an air of resolution and immediately struck the sheet with the flat of her hand. 'And if Brian goes off with that Pauline Murphy, your mother will have no one to blame but herself. I told her to get a ring on her finger before she moved in with him.'

Jazz sat down opposite her and tried to gather her thoughts. Slightly scared by Mary's flushed face and trembling voice, she spoke gently. 'Mum said that you happened to meet Pauline Murphy in Carrick yesterday. Was it really by chance?'

'Is it my fault that Aldi is doing an offer on crocus bulbs?'

'Were you stalking her, Nan?'

'Jesus Christ, what do you take me for? An undercover agent?'

'You've never planted a crocus in your life.'

'Oh, I know. It was Tom's garden always, and the whole parish looked at me sideways the day I had the new lawn laid. It'll be the same with the crocuses. But, as you'll know if ever you have the misfortune to be a widow, you can't just sit and weep among the ruins. You must spit on your hands and take hold and build something new.'

There was a pause in which Jazz met Mary's eyes and saw

a flicker of shiftiness. Having almost been fooled, she pounced with more aggression than she intended. 'So you *did* go to Aldi on purpose to corner this Pauline.'

Mary tossed her head crossly. 'All right, I did. I wanted to see how she'd respond if I happened to mention Brian.'

'And?'

'And the first thing out of her mouth was a comment on Hanna being away.'

'Well, it's no great secret. How does that prove she wants to steal Brian?'

'All right, it wasn't positive proof, but I thought Hanna ought to be told.'

Jazz controlled herself with an effort. 'Nan, you don't even know this woman – Louisa told me you'd just been to school with her mum. I bet the first thing she actually said was "Who are you?"'

Anger and misery warred on Mary's face. 'I know the seed, breed, and generation of her! But if you and Hanna and Louisa want to pretend that I've nothing useful to bring to the table, that's your loss. Like I said, I know when I'm not needed.'

Jazz tried not to sound patronising. 'Nobody wants you to feel that you're not needed.'

'It's not about feeling, is it? It's about facts.'

'Look, we needed you, me and Mum, when we turned up on your doorstep. If it wasn't for you, I don't know how I'd have coped with the divorce. And we still need you. If you hadn't opened your home to Louisa she might not have chosen to come and live in Finfarran, and if it wasn't for Edge of the World Essentials I wouldn't have a job.'

'Louisa would have found someplace to stay in Finfarran without me.'

'But she didn't have to, did she? Because you opened your door.' Jazz reached for Mary's hand and chose her words carefully. 'You know what Mum needs from you? She needs you to be happy. To get a life.' She paused to see the effect and, as Mary bristled ominously, her voice became sharper. 'Stop thinking about how to prove that I'm wrong and you're right. I know exactly how your mind works. Actually, it's scarily like the way my dad thinks, so you can't fool me and you needn't bother to try.' Mary tried to withdraw her hand but Jazz grasped it more firmly. 'No, Nan, listen. Your family doesn't exist to make you feel good about yourself. Not Mum, not me, not Louisa, who, let's face it, is only an out-law. We've got our own lives, and if they don't focus entirely on yours that's your problem.'

There was a long pause in which Mary looked boot-faced. Then she spoke. 'Well?'

'What?'

'Have you done with your sermon?'

'No, I haven't. That was the diagnosis. Here's the remedy. Why don't you find yourself something to do? Somewhere you really are needed, where you can make a difference.'

'Who'd want me?'

'Oh, Nan, don't be such an ass! You've got energy. You've got two hands and, God knows, you've a tongue in your head. Find yourself somewhere to volunteer and be useful.'

'I can't go grubbing around in the nuns' garden, if that's what you mean. Not with my knees.'

'Well, of course not. You have to play to your strengths, don't you? Think of your style. You've a great eye for clothes – you could work in a charity shop. There's two in Lissbeg and they always have signs up looking for volunteers.'

Mary pushed her lower lip out. 'How would I get myself into Lissbeg every day?'

'It wouldn't have to be every day, it could be a few days a week. Between Mum and me and Louisa, we could organise lifts. I bet Johnny would help.'

'I'm not going to start making demands on the Hennessys.'

There had never been a time when Mary hadn't made endless demands on her long-suffering neighbours but, deciding not to go there, Jazz stuck to her guns. 'We'd work things out and, if you had to, you could always take a taxi.'

'What? Do a job for free and pay out for the privilege?'

'Nan, you've got plenty of money. Taking a taxi in an emergency won't break you.'

'Stop talking as if it's all cut and dried.'

'I haven't got time for any more talking. I have to get back to work.' Jazz stood up and they squared off, one as recalcitrant as the other. 'Look, it's up to yourself. If you want to behave as if you're going gaga, feel free. But it's a bloody dangerous route to go down. Do you want to be seen as a weird old bat that stalks people round Aldi?'

'I didn't stalk her.'

'Oh, call it what you like, you and I know the truth. You were so determined to claim Mum's attention that you lost the run of yourself. What would the next step have been? A visit to Brian? A text to Pauline herself?'

'Of course not!'

'Really? I hope you're sure of that because I'm not. Look, whatever weird stuff has always gone on between you and Mum is your own business. But I can tell you this, she's worried about you. And so am I, Nan, so I wish you'd stop being so damn selfish.'

Mary got up and went to look out of the window. 'I never thought your granddad would die and I'd be left here without him.'

'And what do you think he'd think about how you've been behaving?'

Tom's evening primroses were growing tall in the pots that stood on the patio. As dusk edged towards night, the flowers would expand and release their gentle fragrance, but now they were tightly curled, like a child's closed fist. Mary stared hard into the garden, seeking the strength to turn round, but before she'd found it, the kitchen door had slammed and Jazz was gone.

Chapter Thirty-Four

Fury came in with The Divil at his heels and heaved a lugubrious sigh. 'This one's going to cost you.'

Charles, who was sitting in the book room, looked up mildly from his crossword. 'What is?'

'The latest with the boiler. You've a part banjaxed and there's no chance I'll be able to find a replacement. The firm that made that yoke closed its doors in nineteen-oh-eight.'

'I hadn't noticed a problem.'

'What did you call me for, then?'

'What's wrong with the boiler?'

'I told you. I went down as soon as I got here. Sure I could hear the poor thing kicking as soon as I turned into the yard. I've shut her down. She could have blown up if I'd left her.' Fury sniffed dubiously. 'I suppose I could take the part out and bring it down to Cork. There's a fella there owes me a favour. He might make a replacement.'

'That's good.'

'You'll pay through the nose for it, mind. Getting a part made up these days can cost an arm and a leg.'

'Well, do what you can, will you?'

Charles's mind was clearly elsewhere, and Fury's eyes narrowed. 'Right, what's the story? If it wasn't about the boiler you called, I don't suppose it was just to ask me to tea.'

The Divil, who'd rolled over at Charles's feet, sat up and looked expectant. Charles asked fondly after his health. 'I've been thinking of buying a collar for him in the Finfarran county colours. He could wear it to the match. Actually, that reminds me. What's the news on your spat with the GAA?'

Fury had had an argument in a pub with a GAA committee chair, who'd assured him the County Board wouldn't stand for dogs in the stadium. Despite his aggressive announcements, his plan had always been to smuggle The Divil into the match hidden under his coat and, having blown his cover, he now feared that, as he approached the turnstile, he'd be identified, searched, and ignominiously turned away. It wasn't a subject he cared to discuss, any more than Charles appeared to want to explain why he'd been summoned to the castle. So he went on the attack. 'Never mind The Divil and the GAA, what's happened here?'

There was a brief stand-off over who would answer which question, during which The Divil lost interest and fell asleep. Then Charles's mahogany office chair creaked as he turned the laptop on his desk to show Fury an image on the screen. It was of a small book bound in calf and stamped with a gilded crest. 'Look what I found for sale this morning on eBay.'

'Are you going in for book-buying now, or what?'

'Look at it.'

Charles enlarged the image and Fury blinked at the crest. 'That's the de Lancy mark.'

'And the de Lancy binding.' Swivelling his chair, Charles

indicated the bookshelves all around him. 'Beige leather boards, wine-coloured spines, gilded crest on the front. Isobel's family was granted a coat of arms in the middle ages and the crest is one of the squiggly bits from that. The binding's Victorian. One of her ancestors had it put on every damn book in the place. Something tells me he wasn't much of a reader, more of a *Horse & Hound* guy. I guess he liked his literature to look neat, though.'

Fury put on a pair of glasses and peered at the screen. 'When did this go up on eBay?'

'In the last twenty-four hours, as far as I can tell.'

'And why did you go looking for it?'

'I didn't. I was doing some background research on those visitors' books. Stuck the de Lancy name into Google and this was one thing that came up. You can see why.'

The book, dated 1753, was called *The country gentleman's pocket companion to Irish architecture, compleat with measurements, designs etc taken from historic seats including Castle Lancy in the western province of Munster.*

Fury drew his breath in through his teeth. 'That's worth money.'

'Damn right it is.'

'You're thinking of the lad who broke away from the tour group and went wandering.'

'He crossed my mind.'

Though this was vindication of Fury's position, he shook his head with the air of one determined to be fair. 'Ah, but this book could have been sold, or borrowed, or stolen years ago. The fact that it's up on eBay now doesn't prove when it left the castle. Are you sure it was here when that lad's tour group came in?'

Charles thumped the desk. 'That's the point, man! I can't be sure of anything because I don't know what-all I've got. From which it follows that I can't tell if somebody's taken something. This place was Isobel's project, not mine, so I never paid it much attention. Never thought I'd need to. But it's groaning with books and artefacts, some of them probably rubbish and others that could be worth a king's ransom. And, God, yes, you were right when you called the Carrick Psalter a huge responsibility. I didn't know it was here till I opened the blasted drawer I found it in, and afterwards it kept me awake nights. Gifting it to the library was a big weight off my mind.'

'And now you're fretting about the rest of the stuff.'

'Sure. Because it's all my responsibility. Hell, Fury, I hate to admit it, but letting the public into the castle without knowing exactly what's here was plain dumb.'

'So you're going to stop the tours?'

'Not at all. I'm enjoying them. I just need to pull back and do some spadework. What we need is an inventory. Won't be difficult – there's lots of lists and records scattered about the place. Okay, maybe we need a bit more security during the tours as well, but that's not where we start. First we bring the extant lists together, add in what's not there, and make ourselves a comprehensive catalogue.'

'We?'

'Don't start that again, it's boring. Look at this place, it's an Aladdin's cave. Who knows what we might find? Get with the programme, Fury, this is really going to be fun.'

*

In the nuns' garden, Aideen and Bríd were sitting by the fountain eating ice-creams. 'So you really didn't know?'

'Hadn't a clue. It never crossed my mind. We've been really careful.'

'Not careful enough, obviously.'

'Tell me something I don't know.' Aideen made a face at Bríd. 'Are you really pleased?'

'Of course I am. I think it's gorgeous. So long as you and Conor do.'

'I was so unsure. I mean, I couldn't have been happier myself when I saw the test result. But I didn't know about him – and we weren't talking. Him and me. To each other.' Aideen looked anxious, not wanting to drag up the row again. It had been so great when she'd sent the text telling Bríd she was pregnant and had a gif of dancing giraffes within minutes.

Bríd grinned. 'Yesterday's story, don't worry. But hadn't you missed your period?'

'I suppose so. But mine are always all over the place, and I'd been stressed, and that always affects them.'

'How did you break the news to Conor?'

Aideen had worried about how to do that from the moment she'd seen the test result. Deciding she couldn't trust the first, she'd waited a day and tried testing again, sitting on the floor of the bathroom early in the morning, with her chin on her knees and her eyes on the little window in the plastic stick. There'd been something in the leaflet in the packet about an evaporation line, where if you waited too long to check it you might read the result wrong. But the second result had been the same as the first and, dazed and excited, she'd stood up, wanting to run and tell Conor.

'But he's got lungworm.'

Bríd stared, her ice-cream halfway to her mouth, and Aideen

302 / Felicity Hayes-McCoy

giggled. 'I mean the cows have. Well, some of them. They've been coughing, and he'd dosed them for parasites, and he'd got up early that morning to see how they were.'

'How can you even bear to know about gross stuff like that?'

'It's actually kind of interesting. There's a circular process where cows ingest the larvae, which migrate to the lungs, get coughed up, are swallowed and go to the stomach, and then they're passed in faeces, get into the grass, and go round again.'

'Okay, la-la-la, I'm not listening. Just tell me how you broke the news to Conor.'

She'd gone downstairs and found Orla in the kitchen, where the bread was baking and the cats were curled on the doorstep drinking milk. The room was warm and Orla was at the table peeling apples, a mug of tea beside her and the radio turned on. No one had yet gone up to let the hens out, so Aideen had taken their pan of food and walked up through the yard and into the orchard. Even the chicken wire had been sparkling, where the morning sun fell on the hanging drops of last night's rain. Going into the run, she'd unbolted the shed door. The hens had heard her approach and come tumbling out, bronze feathers fluffing and pink scaly feet mincing neatly across the dew-spangled grass. As she'd bent to feed them, she'd heard the sound of voices below in the yard and seen Dermot and Conor climb down from the tractor, then walk towards the cattle shed. Straightening up, she'd stared at Conor, willing him to turn round and look at her. And, to her amazement, he had. He'd turned, as if he'd heard her voice calling him, and, with a word to Dermot, crossed the yard and walked up the orchard to the hen run. The look on his face had made her knees go weak. Neither of them had apologised for the row: they'd just hugged each other. And then he'd kissed her for so long she hadn't been able to stop herself pulling away. Because she couldn't wait to tell him.

Looking expectant, Bríd licked ice-cream off her fingers. 'Aideen! Stop going all moony. Tell me how you told him.'

Aideen realised she'd just been sitting there remembering. 'Oh, I just said it, and he was delighted. Really, he's so pleased.'

He'd broken down and started to cry and held her as if he'd never let go, and it had seemed to Aideen that every tree in the orchard had shouted in triumph. Then he'd swept her down to the house. Almost the best bit had been how Orla and Paddy had taken the news, though, for Aideen, the joyful exclamations and hugs had been bittersweet. Somewhere at the back of her mind had been a cry for her own unmarried teenage mum, whose discovery of her pregnancy must have been so very different, and whose death giving birth had meant that her daughter had never known her love.

She looked at Bríd. 'You're really glad for me?'

'Of course I am, you dork. Can I be godmother?'

'I'd say there'd be no problem there, but I'd need to ask Conor.' Aideen stood up. 'I said I'd meet him after his shift in the library, and you ought to be getting back to the deli. Poor old Bartck's stuck there on his own.'

'He'll be grand.' Bríd stood up and hugged her. 'Give my congrats to Conor.'

Aideen took a deep breath. 'Don't bite my head off but, you know what it is, I wish you'd make up with Dan.'

Bríd shrugged. 'Oh, I dare say I will sometime. You know us.'

'Okay. Talk soon.'

*

Bríd watched Aideen cross the nuns' garden, a spring in her step and the sunlight glinting on her red-gold hair. This, she thought, is how it is. Aideen has moved on and I haven't. Thoughtfully, Bríd sat down and considered the matter. It didn't lessen their affection for each other, it was simply a fact. Regardless of how close they remained, she still couldn't take her little cousin's advice about her boyfriend, and Aideen, who'd always confided in her, would never fully share the shining moment she'd had in the orchard with Conor.

As Aideen disappeared through the gate to the courtyard, Bríd's train of thought was interrupted by The Divil, who came bounding across the herb beds with Fury striding behind him.

'Pay him no heed, he's only looking for ice-cream.'

'He's missed the boat, I've just finished a ninety-nine.'

'You see, that's life. All about timing.' Fury sat down on the rim of the fountain, clearly disposed to chat. 'Come here to me, did you tell me you hadn't managed to get tickets for the big match?'

'The County Final? No, they were all sold out.'

'Was it one seat you wanted?'

'Yeah.'

'Oh, right. I have two going begging.'

'Have you? Wow. They're like gold dust.'

'True enough, but it's bad for a dog if you don't train him right. That fellow there, now, he knows the meaning of the word "consistent".' Bríd looked at The Divil, who was slobbering gently. Fury fixed him with a piercing eye. 'Oh, yes, he knows what the story is. I told him there'd be no County Final for him if he didn't meet his target. That was the deal, and he understood the consequences, but he still went round making up to the likes of

Charles Aukin, begging behind my back for custard creams and Portuguese tarts.'

'He looks like he's lost some weight, though.'

'Ay, maybe. But he hasn't met his target and he has only himself to blame.' The Divil rolled over and looked up adoringly at Fury, who arranged his face in a mask of judicial severity. 'So, there's nothing for it now but to give them two match tickets away.'

It took Bríd a minute to realise what he was saying. 'Are you offering them to me?'

'Well, I would, but there's no point, is there, if you only need one, not two?'

'Well, but –'

Fury gazed into the distance. 'Unless you and Dan Cafferky are back together?'

'No.' Bríd looked at the two tickets, which had appeared in Fury's hand. 'Though, actually, I was about to ring him.'

'You were?'

'Yes. And I could see if he was free to come along. Look, maybe we could buy the tickets from you.'

'That wouldn't do at all. Your man there needs to recognise that failure impacts on more than just the fella who lets himself down.'

Bríd didn't pause to unravel that. 'Well, if you really don't want them . . .'

'It's not a matter of want, girl, it's a matter of sticking to my word.' Taking her hand, he folded it over the tickets. 'What respect would The Divil have for me in the future if I took him along to that match now?'

Chapter Thirty-Five

Woken by the absence of the sound of raindrops, which, all night long, had been hurled against his window by the wind, Brian got up and found the glen bathed in pearly light. Tugging on a sweatshirt and tracksuit bottoms, he went downstairs in his socks and put on his hiking boots, lacing them as he sat at the kitchen table with the kettle boiling in the background and a slice of last night's pizza between his teeth. The sun was barely up and, although he planned to tidy Mike's clutter in preparation for Hanna's arrival that evening, he decided to go for a walk to the waterfall first. There was plenty of time. Hanna wasn't due until late, and Mike, who was still in bed, ought to be consulted before his scattered belongings were touched.

When Brian opened the front door he shivered. The rising sun had stained the sky with streaks of pink and gold but, at this early hour, the glen was still chilly. Shrugging himself into a quilted jacket, he took a last gulp of tea, set the mug on the table, and went out. Crossing the stretch of rough land between the house and the river, he turned before walking upstream and looked back at his creation. Just as he'd envisaged when he'd designed it, the house blended into the landscape, so that the old walls on which Fury was working seemed scarcely more present in the glen than the new building. From where he stood, Brian could see that Fury's work had almost reached roof level, and that the problem he'd flagged the other day had now become acute. The corrugated iron that formed Jo's shelter had sagged from the ridge of the old pitched roof where it met the crumbling chimney, which Fury planned to take down before putting up the new garage roof. So, whether she liked it or not, thought Brian, the time had come to take Jo's bed into the house.

He began to follow the path of the river, moving against the direction of its flow. As always after rain, its peaty colour had changed from amber to brown. The force of the torrent increased as Brian climbed higher, passed the point at which Hanna had found the heart stone, and approached the rocks down which the waterfall streamed. Where the fall became the river, a foaming pool resolved itself into the mass of water that flowed down the glen, bearing leaves and sticks and flecks of cappuccino-coloured spume. To the right was the stiff scramble that led to the upper valley and the walk around the curve of Knockinver's foothills. He and Mike had climbed it the other day, and he retraced his steps gingerly, finding footholds on rocks that had then been dry and now were wet. Knockinver's majestic walks were different from those he'd taken as a boy in Wicklow, where the valleys were wild but the contours of the mountains were gentle. Back then, before he'd gone to school in England, Brian had spent days exploring bog roads on his bike, hiding it under a bush and walking higher into the hills. Hanna had told him she'd done the same as a child. Yet they'd grown up in very different circumstances. Having been raised in a village with

Lissbeg as her nearest town, she could hardly wait to spread her wings for the city, but the empty upland terrain in which Brian's childhood had been spent was so close to Dublin that he'd never lacked access to urban life, and his father's job in the Gulf had made the distance from Dublin to London seem negligible. For Hanna, going to live in London in her early twenties had been like travelling to another world.

Brian and Kate had often been taken to Dublin on shopping trips, frequently ending with a visit to the theatre, and in his teens, he'd spent school holidays with cousins in London and explored the West End. He saw his first ballet at Sadler's Wells at sixteen and, for a while, became a precocious, priggish fan. But by the time he was back in Wicklow, working in his fledgling practice, he hadn't thought about the ballet for years, so the comment he'd made about Sandra's feet being like a ballerina's had surprised him almost as much as it had made Sandra laugh.

Knee-deep in heather as he followed a meandering sheep path, Brian thought of the week he and Mike had spent in each other's company without ever mentioning Sandra's name. More than once, he'd felt he ought to speak of her but, each time, the moment had been lost. Still, as he'd told himself firmly, probing old wounds was pointless, especially if Mike had no inclination to join him. Avoiding the roots and rolling stones he couldn't see because of the thick heather, Brian concluded he'd done the right thing in letting 'the dead Past bury its dead'. How could Mike, in his twenties, be expected to relate to his parents' brief marriage? And what might he think if he knew it had been so unlikely to survive? They'd been an ill-assorted couple, thought Brian, he with his intense focus on work, and Sandra with the attention-span of a butterfly. He'd used that image once and she'd rejected it. 'A fruit-fly maybe, but if you're looking for gauze and flutter, you've come to the wrong shop.' She'd worn her lack of sentimentality like a badge of honour, though her definition of what the term meant was as arbitrary as her moods.

The first time they'd made love, she'd accused him of being a romantic, and he'd laughed. 'Are you saying that love in the afternoon isn't the essence of romance?'

'Let's get out in the sun and go for a drink.' She'd pushed herself up on her elbows and, not wanting to leave the bed, Brian had pulled her back. 'How come you know all about ballerinas' feet?'

'Mum conned me into classes with a book called *Ballet Shoes*.'

'I think my sister got that for some birthday.'

'They did it on telly when I was a kid. Three little girls in a kooky household go to a dance academy. I got fooled by the ribbons and tutus, but it turned out I hated the classes. And then I discovered the truth about *Ballet Shoes*.' Her hair was dark against the lipstick-stained pillow and she'd spoken with naïve malicious glee. 'It wasn't written for children. That happened later, when the first version flopped. To begin with, it was an adult novel about three kids with different mothers and the same caddish father who dumps them on one of his downtrodden mistresses. Definitely no frills and ribbons. The kids get put on the stage because he deserts them and there's no money, and the oldest ends up dancing in a chorus and turning tricks.' When Brian had laughed and accused her of making it up, she'd shaken her head. 'It's true. I thought it was hilarious and my mum freaked out. I told her life's a bitch and then you die, which freaked her more. Anyway, she let me chuck ballet, so my feet are in perfect condition for you to worship at them.'

She'd giggled and stretched her leg in the air again, pointing and flexing her foot, and they'd kissed and felt immortal. Long afterwards, Brian had wondered if the wariness that had come to characterise him had arisen as much from Sandra's worldview as from the fact that she'd died. According to her, nothing could ever be trusted, because everything was fundamentally flawed, and her cancer, so unexpected and insidious, had seemed to prove her point. Now, listening to the cries of sheep high on the slopes of Knockinver, Brian wondered why Longfellow's line about the dead Past burying its dead had occurred to him. Then, trawling through memories of English Lit at school, he remembered another line from the same poem about not trusting the future. Without Hanna, he thought, I'd never have rediscovered optimism and found the courage to build a house of my own.

The path had taken him to a point at which the waterfall was hidden by the shoulder of the mountain, though he could see the river below him, lit like a golden thread by the risen sun. When he'd first heard the story of the sluice box found in Woodenbridge in Wicklow, he'd set off on his bike in search of gold. Fired by the story of Jason and the Golden Fleece, which a teacher had told him might have arisen from the practice of using sheepskins to catch gold washed down by rivers, he'd taken his parents' bedside rug and trailed it for hours in the water of an upland stream. He'd found no gold and the rug was irreparably damaged, but the romance of the idea had never left him, and he'd told Hanna about it when he'd first shown her the glen. 'Imagine a Bronze Age community down there on my doorstep, lifting glittering fleece out of a river running with gold.'

But Hanna's mind had been on the hag. 'How many people died in the Famine in the eighteen hundreds? A million, and a million more emigrated. Can you imagine the glen before that happened? Noise and bustle and kids shouting, and the sweet smell of turf smoke. Ordinary people, living sparse, crowded lives.'

'Sparse and crowded? Isn't that a contradiction in terms?'

'No, because that's how it would have been. Subsistence farming. Life lived really close to the edge, but big families in little communities, all interdependent. One life pressing against another and nobody feeling alone.'

'You can feel alone in a crowd.'

'I know, but that's not what I meant. Think what it must have been like for the hag if she chose to stay behind when the others left.'

'Could be it wasn't a choice. Old people didn't have much hope of surviving the voyage. Maybe she was left behind to give the rest of her family a better chance of making it to America.'

It was then, seeing Hanna's reaction, that he'd made the lame joke about the hag plotting to find gold once the neighbours had left. It hadn't deflected Hanna. Staring down at the glen, she'd shivered. 'I wonder where she's buried.'

'Don't be morbid. She's probably just a figment of Fury's perverse imagination.'

'But it is called the Hag's Glen.'

'And, like I told Fury, the name could be ancient. You get it in other parts of the country too. Maybe this place has always had a female presence. Maybe it's what it needs.' That had been Brian's first, oblique, attempt to ask her if she'd live with him, and he grinned, remembering how much straight talk it had taken to make her agree.

It was seven a.m. and the day was heating up. Having walked

this far, it was time to turn back. When he came to the head of the waterfall, he saw Fury's van parked behind the distant house. Slithering down, with the heels of his boots jammed well in as brakes, Brian reached the floor of the glen and walked back along the riverbank. In the still air he could hear the sound of Fury's stone hammer, a steady beat, which, like the sheep's cries, must have echoed between these mountains through millennia.

Beside the van The Divil was fast asleep. As Brian approached the little building, he saw that scaffolding had been erected against the chimney gable. Irritated, because another day's wait would have made no difference to the work and brought Hanna into the decision-making, he made his way round to the door. This was one of the structures they'd looked down on when he'd shown Hanna the glen from above the waterfall. She'd pointed to it and wondered if the hag might have lived there and, slightly annoyed by her harping on the tale instead of focusing on his plans for the future, he'd answered shortly. 'Someone lived there, probably a family, judging by its size. You could have had up to three generations sharing the one dwelling. Sparse living and crowded accommodation, like you said.'

Stooping under the low stone lintel, he saw Fury peering up the chimney, hunkered down on a broad, flat slab, which, sunk in the earth floor, had once been the hearthstone. The fallen corrugated iron had been cleared away, along with debris from the rafters and the ridge-piece, leaving that end of the house swept clean. Fury stood up and stepped back, sucking air through his teeth. 'I'd say that chimney would have come down in the next winter storm.'

Brian looked around. 'Where's Jo?' The dog's shelter was gone, as if it had never been there, but turning his head, he saw a stiff bundle and recognised the covering. 'Isn't that the old coat she dragged in here to sleep on? Dammit, Fury, I told you to leave her be until Hanna came home.' Then the shape of the bundle and the look on Fury's face made him realise what had happened. 'Ah, shit, Jo's dead, isn't she?'

'That's the way I found her.'

'The poor old thing.'

'Do you want me to bury the body?'

'I suppose so.' The hearth on which Jo had made her bed was blackened by long-dead fires. Brian stooped and passed his hand across it, then straightened, brushing mortar dust from his fingers. 'I'm worried about Hanna. She's going to take this badly.'

'Christ, you two are great ones for fooling yerselves.'

Irritated, Brian glared at him. Fury shrugged. 'It's not the dog's death that has you worrying. You've been fearful ever since Hanna left that she might not come back.'

'What? Of course she will.'

'Well, I know that, but for some reason, you don't.' Fury reached behind his ear for a half-smoked cigarette. 'What's she done to make you doubt her?'

Brian's impulse to argue was brief. There seemed little point. He watched Fury light up and, although he hadn't smoked for years, found himself craving nicotine.

'Go on, then. What's the story?' Fury reversed the stub in his hand and held it out between his finger and thumb. Aware that, by doing so, he'd accepted him in the role of father-confessor, Brian took the cigarette and drew on it. 'It seemed like a good idea at first. I got more time with Mike. She, well, she got less time with him, which was good, because he was getting on her nerves, which I understand. It was a chance for this reunion too. I mean, I'd have no place at that. It was sensible.'

'But?'

'But she's met this man.'

'That was quick.'

Hardly hearing him, Brian frowned, recalling what Hanna had said to him on the phone. 'He's offered her a job. Well, a kind of consultancy. His family has a trust that gets books into school libraries. It's a charity thing. He wants her to mentor the board. Something like that.'

'What – and move over there?'

'I didn't really listen.'

'Didn't you? Why was that?'

The fact was that, as soon as she'd spoken, Brian's brain had gone into freefall, telling him this was the thing that he'd always known was going to happen. The moment when his foot would plunge through a surface he'd thought was solid and thrust him into a world where Hanna, like Sandra, would be gone. Breathing out a long plume of smoke, he realised Fury was right. At the back of his mind, he'd feared this since Hanna had left for London, and Jo's death seemed no more than another thread in a tightly woven, pre-ordained pattern.

Fury took the cigarette back. 'It wasn't Jo that kept Hanna tied to this place, you do know that?'

'Of course.' Brian paused and looked at the rigid bundle on the floor. 'Actually, I'm not sure what I know.'

'Do you know what I think?'

'No, but I'm pretty certain you're going to tell me.'

'I'd say she'd do better hearing about that dog's death over in London. From you. Face to face.'

'You mean fly over and tell her before she comes home to-night?'

'It's only an observation. I could be wrong.'

'It's absurd.'

'Fair enough, it's your call. I'll get on with me chimney.' Fury pinched out the cigarette and flicked it through the door. 'I just thought there might be a few other things you needed to tell her as well.'

Chapter Thirty-Six

The next few hours passed in a blur and at first they mainly consisted of Brian identifying obstacles that Fury blandly dismissed. Hanna's flight was booked for that evening, so Brian would need to arrive before she left Windsor to catch her plane. What if there was no scheduled flight to get him there on time? What if there were no seats left on her return flight? An online search answered both questions and, with Fury looking over his shoulder, he booked with ease and saw his boarding passes pop up on his phone. The timing was tight, though. What if he was delayed parking his car at Cork airport? According to Fury, that presented no problem. He had to go to Cork himself, about a part for Castle Lancy's boiler, so he'd drop Brian right outside Departures. Having committed himself to the trip, Brian panicked. Where did Amy actually live? How would he know where to go when he got to Windsor? Fury led him to the kitchen, where Hanna had left Amy's address attached to the fridge door. Removing the magnet that secured it, he held out the card to Brian, who was stunned.

'How come you knew that was there?'

'How come you didn't? No woman ever leaves home for ten minutes without sticking her contact details on the fridge. They anticipate emergencies.'

'But I have her number in my phone.'

'And she left you the address, too, so stop wasting time.'

'Wait, maybe I should ring her.'

'Holy God Almighty, are you thick as well as stupid? How do you think she's going to react if you ring and say something bad has happened and refuse to reveal what it is?'

'But I wouldn't.'

'So you'd tell her on the phone? In that case, why fly over?'

'Dammit, Fury, because you said I should break it to her gently.'

'And you agreed, and you've booked your flights, so, for God's sake, get in the van.'

'I can't go to London in track pants and boots.'

'Then go and change. By my reckoning, you'll miss the plane if we're not on the road in three minutes.'

*

Brian made the departure gate with a few seconds to spare and passed the flight wondering what on earth he thought he was doing. Later, he could only assume that he'd travelled from Stansted to Windsor on autopilot, because he remembered nothing but emerging at Windsor and Eton Riverside station and giving Amy's address to a taxi driver. When he stepped out of the taxi he was numb with apprehension, and as he approached her gate Amy appeared at the front door, keys in hand and a clutch bag under her arm. He recognised her from Hanna's description and, when she came to the gate, he put out his hand, feeling like an awkward adolescent. 'I'm Brian Morton.'

The appraising look she gave him was disconcerting. 'Were we expecting you?'

'No. I'm sorry to turn up unannounced but, the thing is, something's happened at home. I thought I'd best break the news to Hanna in person.'

'Here? Not at the airport when she flies in tonight?'

That possibility hadn't been one Brian had raised with Fury, simply because it hadn't occurred to him. 'Ah. No . . . Well, I mean, I thought that if I flew over I could take her out to lunch. Er, you too, of course.'

'We've eaten.'

'Right. Okay. Well, in that case I'll just break the news.'

With a gleam in her eye, which Hanna would have recognised, Amy stood back and let him through the gate. 'Go round through the garden and you'll find her in the conservatory. I'm popping out for cigarettes. Hope you'll like the hair.'

She was gone before Brian could ask what she'd meant so, refocusing, he walked around the outside of the house. The conservatory doors were open and Hanna was sitting with her feet on a stool, reading a newspaper. He was so intent on what he ought to say that, at first, her new haircut didn't register. Then, before it could sink in, she looked up and saw him in the doorway. 'Brian! What are you doing here?' Dropping the paper, she scrambled to her feet. 'What's up? What's happened?'

'Nothing. Everything's fine.'

'No, but why are you here? Is it Mam? . . . Jazz?'

This couldn't be worse than breaking the news over the

phone. Mentally cursing Fury, Brian took her hands. 'Everyone's fine. Mary, Jazz, Louisa . . .'

'Conor?'

'Hale and hearty, as far as I know. I haven't seen him.'

'Oh, Brian! It's not Mike?'

'Mike was asleep in bed when I left the glen. Stop doing a roll-call and listen to me.'

Annoyed, because she'd been frightened, Hanna stepped away from him. 'What the hell are you doing here?'

Having reached the point of no return, Brian couldn't think how to begin. 'I – thought I'd take you for lunch. But Amy says you've eaten.'

'What?'

'I met Amy at the gate. Fury said I ought to fly over.'

'To take me to lunch?'

She was looking at him as if he were mad and, distressed though he was, Brian controlled an impulse to laugh. 'No. No, listen, darling, something sad has happened, and I didn't want you to arrive home without knowing.'

Hanna sat down on the rattan chair on which she'd dropped the newspaper. 'What's happened? Tell me quickly.'

'It's Jo.' Brian knelt by the chair. 'Fury found her this morning. She just – went to sleep and didn't wake up.'

'You mean she died?'

Remembering her hatred of euphemism, and ashamed of himself for using it, Brian nodded. 'She was cold when he found her. She was a great age, Hanna, she couldn't have lasted for ever.'

'I know. It's just . . . Poor Jo.' Hanna wiped her eyes with the back of her hand. 'And you came to tell me. Oh, Brian! Thank you.'

'Like I said, it wasn't my idea. It was Fury's.' Brian touched her hair. 'When did this happen?'

Hanna was blowing her nose. 'What? Oh, the haircut. A few days ago. It was kind of an accident.' She saw his reaction and gave him a wobbly smile. 'I know it sounds daft, it's a compli-cated story. Do you like the cut?'

'Well, it's nothing to do with me. It's your hair.'

'Does that mean you hate it?'

'No, I think it's stunning.'

The front door slammed and, a moment later, Amy came through the living room. Brian took Hanna's elbow, sensing her impulse to hide. 'Have you packed? Do you want a hand?'

'Maybe. Yeah. Come upstairs and you can sit on my suitcase.'

Amy looked at them sardonically. 'Hanna, your suitcase would fit in a glove compartment. If he sat on it he'd probably squash it flat.' She flashed her eyebrows at Brian. 'But don't let me keep you two from the bedroom. After all, it's been a whole week.'

Hanna stiffened but Brian spoke before she could. 'I flew over to tell her our dog has died.'

For the first time in her life, Hanna saw Amy nonplussed. 'Oh, hell, I'm sorry. Oh, Hanna! Had you had it for ages?'

'Had her since she was a puppy.' Having unashamedly lied through his teeth, Brian smiled at Amy. 'I think I should take Hanna somewhere quiet before she faces the airport. Perhaps a walk in a park. I'm sure you won't mind. Jo was a family pet and it's hit us hard.'

'Of course I won't mind.'

Almost before Hanna knew it, Brian had piloted her to the stairs. When they reached her room, she sat down on the bed. 'That was outrageous!'

'I bet you're not sorry I said it, though.'

'No, I'm not. Amy could win gold medals for bumptiousness.' Hanna passed her hand over her forehead. 'I'll have to say a civil goodbye to her first, but *could* we go somewhere quiet? Just on our own, till I get my head around this.'

'Let's start for the airport now and stop somewhere on the way.'

As Hanna went to gather things in the bathroom, Brian called to her, 'Something else has happened. Good news. Fury told me on the way to the airport.'

Hanna came back with her toothbrush in her hand. 'Fury drove you to Cork?'

'With The Divil sitting between us, chewing a rubber bone. It was like watching a confirmed smoker vaping. Fury has banned all snacks between meals.'

'What's the news?'

'He's arranged for Mike to move on.'

She gaped at him. 'Fury has? Why?'

'I gather he'd grasped the fact that you'd found Mike a bit too present.'

Hanna looked stricken. 'I never said so! Well, I did but that was because he dragged it out of me. You know Fury.'

'Only too well. Look at me sitting here when all I'd planned for today was a bit of light hoovering.'

'But what did Fury do? Oh, darling, I'm sorry, I wanted you and Mike to have time to bond.'

'We did. Mike and I have had a good week, but he's not the easiest of house guests. I think we've bonded quite as much as we need to for a while.'

'So where's he going?'

'Castle Lancy.' Brian grinned. 'Charles is looking for someone to make a catalogue of his books – well, an inventory of everything in the castle. The job comes with accommodation, which, knowing the size of the rooms there, will be huge. More than enough space for Mike to spread out.'

'Did Charles have any say in the matter?'

'Fury set up a meeting, and they got on like a house on fire.'

'And does Mike actually know how to catalogue?'

'He's done similar work before. Anyway, part of the idea is just to have someone fit and young round the place. I suspect that Fury's been worried about Charles living there on his own.'

'If that's the case, isn't it just a temporary solution? Mike won't stay around for ever. He'll be off running the San Francisco marathon or filming holiday spots in the Serengeti.'

'That's life, though, isn't it? The human condition consists of temporary solutions.'

Hanna reached for her phone. 'Just a minute. You know Fury's theory of the perfect done deal? Working in several dimensions and leaving everyone better off?' She held the phone out to Brian. 'Can you make any sense of these texts?'

Brian looked at the screen.

FURY WILL DRIVE ME TO SAVE THE CHILDREN
IM GOING TO DO HIM A BATTENB ERG ONCE A
WEEK

Brian grinned. 'I think I can. Jazz rang me up last night. Apparently, she read Mary the Riot Act.'

'What about?'

'Being selfish. Inventing stuff about poor Pauline Murphy. Making endless demands on your attention. She told your mum that, if she didn't get out and do something useful, she'd end up turning into a weird stalker. Said she ought to volunteer for work at a charity shop, and Mary made a fuss about how to get there. It sounds like her travel issue has been solved.'

Hanna sat down on the bed. 'Fury is incredible. And Jazz really did that?'

'Unaided. If you ask me, you've raised a force to be reckoned with.'

Tears welled in Hanna's eyes. 'I've been so worried about Mam. Well, that's not wholly true. I've been dreading the moment when I might have to take her in, like she did me.'

Brian sat beside her. 'I know, and I dare say this is just another temporary solution. Things may get worse. It's good for now, though, isn't it?'

'I suppose so – yes, I'm sure it is.' Hanna took her phone back. 'I haven't replied to the texts. I thought I'd cope tomorrow, when real life reclaimed me.'

'Is that how this feels? Like going back to all sorts of stuff you dread?'

'Darling, of course not!'

'Like stagnation?'

'Oh, Brian! Amy said that, not me. And, you know something? In her way, she's just as good at manipulation as Mam. She's rich and lonely and desperate for entertainment. Meddling in my life just gave her something to do besides internet shopping.' Hanna paused. 'No, that's not fair, she really did want this reunion. It was fun too. I'm glad I came. It's wonderful to feel that I've reclaimed London for myself after all these years. But, darling, I'm glad to be coming home as well.'

Fury was right, thought Brian. There's more to be said and

it needs saying here, not back in the glen. 'Let's get on with your packing and find someplace to walk.' He picked up a paper bag from her bedside table. 'Where does this go?'

'Don't just stick it in anywhere. I'll do it when I've changed.'

'You look lovely as you are.'

'I'm more concerned about feeling relaxed on the journey.' She was pulling on the pair of jeans and T-shirt she'd travelled over in and retrieving her comfortable loafers from under the bed. Brian was still hovering over her suitcase and, having found her shoes, Hanna pushed him gently towards a chair. 'Leave that bag alone. It's Louisa's present. There's one for Jazz in there too.' Then, as she put on her hoodie, she paused, looking guilty. 'Oh, lor', I'm sorry, I never found a present for you. I did search, but nothing seemed right.'

'Presents aren't compulsory.'

'I promise I'll find one when I come over to work with the Armstrong Trust.'

Brian felt as if a lift had just descended in his stomach, but he steadied himself and smiled at her. 'Is that the plan? That you'll take a job over here? What will you do? Lodge here with Amy and fly to and fro like Louisa?'

Hanna looked surprised. 'Not like Louisa. She's back and forth every second week. This would be twice or three times a year, tops. I told you on the phone.'

With another lurch, Brian's stomach righted itself and, suddenly, he found words for what he hadn't been able to say to her. 'I wasn't listening properly on the phone – my mind's been all over the place. But listen to me now, Hanna. This is important. You know I said I wanted us to marry so you'd be financially secure? And how, when you wouldn't agree, I wanted to put your name on the deeds of the house? That was nonsense. I mean, I did want to marry you, and I do want you to feel that the house is yours. But I wasn't being honest. It was all about pinning you down. I wanted to make certain of you. Since Sandra died, I've had this feeling that anything good in my life is foredoomed to slip through my fingers. Fury knew how I felt – God knows how – and he made me see it.' Brian's voice shook. 'I don't know why I thought marriage was the answer. It isn't. It didn't stop Sandra dying and, if she hadn't died, it wouldn't have stopped her leaving me.'

'Darling, that's daft.'

'No, it's not. You didn't know Sandra. Anyway, that's not the daft part. You know the first thing that came into my head when I saw Jo's body? That she was the reason you moved to the glen in the first place, and that you wouldn't want to come home to me now she's gone.'

'Darling . . .'

'That's foolish. I know. Fury said so. More to the point, it's insulting.' His voice shook again. 'I don't want to bugger your life up, Hanna, I've told you that. You've done nothing to deserve a mess like me.'

He stopped abruptly, looking dazed, as if he hadn't realised where his speech was leading him and, as Hanna reached out instinctively, he threw up his hand violently, warding her off. Now it was her turn to feel that the ground had suddenly opened beneath her feet. Rooted to Amy's Heal's carpet, she stared at Brian in horror. They were back where they'd started, looking at each other across a gulf filled with past pain. If he really believed that everything good was doomed to slip through his fingers, he might turn his back on her now, as he'd done with his previous life, convincing himself that, like his son, she'd be better off without him. And any move she made could tip the balance. Thrusting her hands into her pockets, she forced herself to wait, praying that the right words would come to her. Brian remained hunched in the chair, an ominous look on his face. Then, as Hanna hesitated, her fingers closed on the heart stone, which had lain in the pocket of her hoodie since the evening they'd walked by the river. This was the answer. Taking her clenched fist out of her pocket, she walked towards him. 'Nobody deserves to be loved, darling. It's just that some people find each other and know they belong together. Like finding the perfect gift.' Kneeling beside him, she held out the stone and placed it in the palm of his hand. He looked into her eyes and his dazed expression faded as she closed his fingers firmly round the stone. 'This is for you. It's my heart. Let's go home.'

Chapter Thirty-Seven

In the end they didn't go for a walk before taking the train to Stansted. They lay on the bed in each other's arms, not making mad, passionate love, as Amy implied when she knocked on the door, but strangely exhausted by the fact that they'd teetered on an unexpected brink.

Brian was almost asleep when Amy's voice alerted them to the time. Hanna shook him gently. 'We need to go or we'll miss the plane.'

His eyes opened and his arms tightened around her. 'I'm really sorry. I don't know where my head has been this past week.'

'Time is passing and Amy's being arch, so let's focus on essentials. Do you love me?'

'Darling. Yes.'

'Right. Passport? Boarding pass? Money to get us to Stansted?'

'All of those.'

'Then help me beat my way through the innuendo and we'll be off.'

*

For all her assumed assurance, Hanna's mind was in a whirl as she sat in the train to the airport. Leaning her forehead against the carriage window, she remembered the dinner she'd had with Jazz at Maggie's place, and her own airy announcement that the trauma of Malcolm's duplicity was behind her. 'I'm living the perfect life,' she'd said. That simply wasn't true. Or perhaps it was just that the truth wasn't quite that simple.

The train was crowded and Brian was sitting at the other side of the aisle, reading a newspaper. It was hard to believe that, only a few hours ago, there'd been a moment when their future had hung in the balance. Hanna remembered the overwhelming urge she'd had at the birthday party to cancel her trip to London and stay at home. It wasn't lethargy or foolishness, she thought. I dreaded leaving Brian because, deep down, I knew things weren't quite right. She turned her face to the window again, where raindrops were streaming backwards across the pane. When they'd argued about the deeds to the Hag's Glen house, she'd spoken to him like a schoolmarm. 'Neither of us will ever have all of the other. Too much has happened in our separate lives for that.' She'd known he'd rejected that, though he hadn't said so, but she'd got her way, and, at the time, that had been enough. I'm my mother's daughter, she thought. I may be careful to hold my tongue when I'm working, but I make too many pronouncements at home, and don't listen enough. Dammit, I don't even listen to myself. If I'd accepted my own logic in that conversation with Brian, I'd have known that I'm not really over Malcolm. What I told Jazz was a whopping great lie. I'm not living the perfect life. It's true that I'm a survivor, and

I can be proud of that, but there's no point in trying to pretend I've come through without any scars. The fact is that I share Brian's irrational sense of foreboding. I was sure Jazz would be irretrievably damaged by the divorce. I've been shrinking from the prospect of having to live with Mam again. I even half believed Amy's nonsense that life in Finfarran would cause me to stagnate. And, Heaven knows, I recognise Brian's conviction that everything good will slip through his fingers. He wanted us to marry so he could be sure of me, and I wouldn't marry him because I feared he might leave me in the end. We share the same idiotic level of apprehension, and neither of us is ever going to put it behind us completely. Better to recognise it, though. That way we can accept it as a weakness, and help each other to cope whenever it strikes.

The flight was uneventful. Their seats were at different ends of the plane so they didn't talk much until they'd cleared security at Arrivals. There was the usual need to concentrate on round-abouts and the ring road, and it wasn't until they were clear of the city that Hanna, who was driving, relaxed and glanced across at Brian. 'We haven't made bad time. We ought to be home before it's too dark.'

'You know something?'

'What?'

'The hair really is stunning.'

'I think so. I'll probably let it grow out again, though. Curl Up & Dye in Carrick would probably struggle to keep it in shape.'

'You can always go back to your salon when you're in London.'

'I wouldn't be surprised to find it had disappeared in a puff of smoke. The whole transformation thing felt like a fairy tale.'

'Sweetheart, are you really glad to be home? You don't feel that your coach has turned into a pumpkin and all your fine feathers will fall to rags?'

'No, I don't. Besides, you've said it yourself, I can fly back and find others.'

'Tell me about this Nicholas Armstrong bloke.'

'Oh, Brian! Tell me about this Pauline Murphy woman.' She glanced at him sideways, saw him grin, and knew that her point had been made. 'Nicholas is nice, I think you'd like him. It's a small board, made up of family members, so I see why he wants to bring in a new voice.'

Amy, of course, had been eager to imply a far more personal interest: 'You must have seen the way he eyed you at dinner.'

'Well, there wasn't a lot of competition, was there? It was me with my killer hairdo or your friend Mrs Morrison in her droopy beige sequins.'

'And what about me? I was looking pretty sharp.'

'Oh, anyone can see that you're going to end up with Roger. Don't try to deny it, you know I'm right. Even if his conversation is dire, he's sweet and kind, and he follows you round like a lapdog.'

'Oh, well, maybe you're right. He's loaded, too, you know.'

'There you are, then. Stick to your own love life and leave mine to me.'

Nevertheless, though she'd never tell Brian, she'd been well aware of Nicholas Armstrong's interest in her when they'd met. Then, over their éclairs and lapsang souchong, he'd told her he was a widower, dropping in the information with elaborate insouciance.

'I'm sorry to hear it. You must miss her.'

'It was a great loss, but I keep myself busy with the trust.'

Knowing precisely what she was doing, Hanna had mentioned Brian. 'He's an architect. You must meet him sometime when I'm in London again.'

She'd seen his slight disappointment, carefully concealed by good manners, before he diplomatically changed the subject back to books. Now, equally diplomatic, she smiled across at Brian. 'I'd like you to meet Nicholas. You'll have to come with me when I fly over for my first session with the trust.'

She had a feeling that he knew exactly what had just passed between them but, at least while they were still tired and bruised, enough had been said.

*

The sun had set by the time they crossed the county border to Finfarran. Hanna let down the window and a cool breeze flowed into the car. 'God, I've missed the fresh air. London's sticky.'

Beyond Carrick, the towering Knockinver mountains were purple against a mother-of-pearl sky. Leaving the town behind them, Hanna sped on down the motorway, filled with an urge to be home again in the glen. Away to the right, across darkening fields, Jazz was pottering contentedly in Maggie's house or sitting on the red bench, high on the cliff, listening to the waves surging against the rocks below. To the left, in the bungalow, Mary and Louisa would be sitting down to martinis with ice and lemon, accompanied by a Belleek bowl of pimento-stuffed olives. The ritual would have begun with a formal invitation to Louisa to watch the news in Mary's sitting room, where the telly would be on and the coal-effect gas fire flickering, while out on the patio Tom's evening primroses bloomed on the edge of night.

Passing the bungalow, content in the knowledge that Louisa

was there and that Mary now had a new source of interest, Hanna drove on down the motorway and, glancing across at Brian, saw the lights of Lissbeg beginning to glow in the west. The library would be in darkness, as would little shops like HabberDashery, where two elderly sisters had once sold ribbons and pins and two young cousins now sold salad pots and sundried tomatoes, but above the shops, and in rows of terraced houses, lights were on, meals were being made, and workers were putting their feet up.

The gentle rhythms of Finfarran life began to draw Hanna in again, and she considered her own working week ahead. Monday Memories, with its rivalries and reminiscences. The book clubs and discussion groups and adult learning classes, the bizarre demands of confused readers, and the delight of wide-eyed children sitting cross-legged at story sessions. And, among all this general enjoyment, her own quiet moments of delight. The surprise of a nervous newcomer finding an unjudgemental welcome, the pleasure of unpacking deliveries of books, and the enthusiasm of readers who'd been waiting for them. The sight of dust motes in sunlight falling through the old assembly hall's new windows, and coffee by the fountain in the sheltered nuns' garden, where the warmth of the sun released the scent of lavender and lemon balm, and birds fluttered around the stone saint's extended hands. Hanna smiled in happy anticipation of returning to work. Conor would have all the news of what had gone on in town, and on the farm, in her absence. With the advent of autumn, more local people would have time to drop into the library. And, locked in the silence of the darkened exhibition space, the psalter, in all its painted glory, lay waiting for her to reach out and turn the next page.

Swinging uphill off the motorway, she began to drive the familiar back roads towards Fury's forest. The shed at the rear of his house was shut up, and a single light showed in his kitchen window. She smiled at Brian. 'Do you suppose Fury and The Divil are sitting at opposite sides of the table, having cocoa?' Before he could answer, she came back to earth with a jolt. It was going to be awful driving up the glen now that Jo was gone. Seeing her thought on her face, Brian stretched out his hand. 'She really was terribly old and tired. And she wouldn't have liked having her bed moved.'

'No. I know. She belonged in that little building. You don't think . . . ?' Hanna shook her head. 'No, I'm being daft.'

'What?'

'Well, it almost feels as if she and the hag were one and the same.'

'What, you mean reincarnation?'

'Of course not.' They had reached the farm at the foot of the glen. Hanna turned the wheel and the car began to climb the last stretch of road between the high fuchsia hedges. 'I suppose I mean something like it, though.'

'You do remember that the hag story was probably Fury's invention?'

'It doesn't matter. She's just an image, isn't she? You said yourself she represents a timeless female presence, the spirit of every woman who's ever come to live in the glen.'

'Oh, darling, I plucked that out of the air when I was trying to persuade you to live with me.'

Hanna's eyes were on the road ahead. 'Jazz says she can feel a benign presence in Maggie's house, as if Maggie were still there.'

'That's not like Jazz.'

'Which is what made it interesting. I told her that places seem to hold the memory of past generations. Everyone who's ever lived and died there.'

'What did she say?'

'She scoffed, which is very like Jazz, so I wasn't surprised. I still think it's true, though. Remember what I said to you when we first looked down on the glen? About what it must have been like here in the past? Big families in little communities, all inter-dependent, one life pressing against another and nobody feeling alone. There would have been dogs among all the noise and bus-tle, the kids shouting, and the sweet smell of turf smoke. Shaggy, wary, loyal creatures, bred to herd sheep and cattle, like Jo. I think she might have remembered that when she made her bed on the hearth between walls that had sheltered families here for centuries.'

As the car turned a corner, the headlights picked up flashes of scarlet fuchsia and golden furze. Brian smiled at Hanna. 'I used fieldstone when I built our house, you know. Fury salvaged some from the fallen buildings, and we excavated more.'

It was nearly dark now, and the road was a silver ribbon between the high banks that enclosed it. When the car emerged from between the hedges, the house ahead seemed part of the steep contours of the glen. Hanna drew up at the front door. 'I'm glad Mike will be living at the castle, even if it's only for a while.'

'Me too. I'm not sure we needed quite so much proximity, but it'll be good to have him in the neighbourhood. You know he's offered to cook a big family meal?'

'It's feeling alone that breeds foreboding, isn't it? Everything being dependent on your decisions, and not knowing what you ought to do for the best. Having family around makes a difference. Even complicated families like ours.'

Brian said nothing but they both recognised that, for the first time, they were speaking as if their two separate families belonged together.

When they got indoors there was no sign of Mike, or his scattered belongings, but his backpack and camera cases stood by the door. Brian set Hanna's suitcase down beside them. 'Are you hungry?'

'No, just tired.'

'Why not go up to bed now, if you feel like it?'

'It's much too early, I'm sure I wouldn't sleep. I tell you what, I'd love to go up on the roof.'

'Okay. I'm peckish, though. I'll find something to eat and follow you up.'

*

Up on the roof the grasses trembled in a breeze that blew from the mountain. Hanna sat down and looked at the glen below. A ragged film of cloud drifted slowly towards the ocean, which gleamed in the distance beyond the forest, where the treetops were silver-tipped. Through gaps in the cloud, and in inky patches between it, stars burned like pinpricks in blue-black velvet. In London, the reflection of the city lights had blotted out the familiar constellations, but here the glen shimmered in grey starlight.

For centuries before the de Lancys had come to rule the peninsula, people had lived here in the Hag's Glen, building, farming, herding sheep and cattle, while skilled hands in the monastery had painted heaven and earth on cream-coloured vellum. For millennia, bone fires had burned here on solstice nights, sending sparks and flames into the starlit sky. And here am I, thought Hanna, still trying to learn that neither foreboding nor optimism matters. What matters is to be content to live each moment as it comes.

A footstep sounded behind her and Brian came onto the roof, a tray in his hands and something over his arm. He set the tray on the low table and she felt the touch of wool around her shoulders. 'I thought you'd be chilly.'

Drawing it around her, Hanna recognised the deep fringe and homespun warmth of her shawl. 'Where did you find this?'

'Folded away. I found Mary's bowls too. Why did you hide them?'

'I didn't. I just thought they didn't suit your design aesthetic.'

'I think they fit perfectly.' Brian turned to the tray. 'I had soup in the fridge, left over from yesterday. Have some, it's hot.'

Hanna took the pottery bowl, feeling the heat of the soup through the clay, the paint, and the worn glaze. 'Don't tell me you've hung one of your sketches somewhere as well?'

'Damn right I haven't. I told you, I'm a mediocre artist. I'm never going to hang those sketches.'

'Well, that's fine by me. I'm enjoying the light and space.'

'Truly?'

'Honestly.' Hanna put down the bowl. 'Brian?'

'What?'

'You know how Conor and Aideen flew off to Florence to get married?'

It was too dark to see his expression but she could feel his consternation as he turned to her. 'Are you saying that's what you want? To marry me after all?'

'Oh, darling, no, I'm not, I'm so sorry.' Hanna reached out and took his hand. 'I thought you said you didn't want to now?'

'I don't.'

She laughed in relief. 'Well, that's all right, then.'

'So what are you saying?'

'I was just thinking we ought to stick that pin in a map sometime soon.'

Acknowledgements

Many different strands come together when I'm thinking about a book and writing it, and each is prompted by places I go and by people I meet. And often, on social media, I meet people from places I've never been to at all – some of them readers and others authors like myself, taking breaks from spinning stories at our desks.

This is particularly true since I've been writing the Finfarran series, because the books, which are commissioned by my lovely editor Ciara Doorley at Hachette Books Ireland, are also published across the world, from the USA and Canada to China, South Korea, Germany, France, and elsewhere. So, while my first thanks go to Ciara, my copy-editor Hazel Orme, Joanna Smyth, Ruth Shern, Elaine Egan, Breda Purdue, and everyone else on her brilliant Hachette team, and to Mark Walsh at Plunkett PR, I'm also grateful to the supportive online writing community, especially my mates in Ireland (you know who you are).

It's wonderful to hear readers' thoughts and feedback, to see photos of your copies of my books, and of local bookshops, libraries, and book clubs. And to know that you love Fury, get cross with Mary, sympathise with Hanna, and recognise their lives and loves, and Finfarran's countryside, communities, and dynamics, from your own lives and experiences.

Some books need very specific, and slightly bizarre, research! When I wrote the chapter in *The Heart of Summer* in which Hanna goes to Persephone Books in London's Bloomsbury for a copy of *Miss Pettigrew Lives for a Day*, I described the book bag she buys there as having pink handles. Then, several weeks later, I woke up one night convinced that I'd got the colour wrong. Fortunately, I was in London at the time, so I took a hasty bus ride and found that, while Persephone's books are gift-wrapped in pink paper, the handles of their book bags are a beautiful silvery grey. I won't forget how kindly the staff put up with my daft attempts to convince myself, and them, that the colour must have changed since the last time I'd been there, or how cheerfully they allowed me to tweet a photo of their charming shop when I calmed down. Indeed, I'm grateful to all the friendly booksellers in Ireland and the UK, who welcome me when I visit, whether it's to sign books or in search of answers to weird questions like that one, and to the librarians who've arranged Finfarran events on both sides of the Atlantic.

I'd also like to thank the medievalists of Twitter whose daily stream of images, along with the British Library and Dublin's Chester Beatty Library's manuscript collections, continue to inspire my fictional Carrick Psalter. And I'm grateful to the staff and volunteers at the Lafcadio Hearn Japanese Gardens, Tramore, Co. Waterford; to Geraldine McGlynn of Golden Ireland, who introduced me to them; and to the hotels that welcome me on my Golden Ireland road trips, photos of which you can check out among my tweets @fhayesmccoy and the posts on my Felicity Hayes-McCoy Author Facebook page.

The fictional entries made by real-life authors in Castle Lancy's visitors' books are the result of a lifetime's obsession with literary biographies, mainly borrowed or bought second-hand: so, by way of thanks, I urge you to support your own local libraries, second-hand, and independent bookshops. They're an essential part of our communities and we all need to use them or we'll lose them.

Finally, my love and thanks go to my husband, Wilf Judd, and, as ever, to my stellar agent Gaia Banks at Sheil Land Associates UK.

About the author

About the book

Insights,
Interviews
& More . . .

Read on

Meet Felicity Hayes-McCoy

I'VE BEEN A professional writer all my working life and a reader for longer than I can remember. Along the way, my projects have included nonfiction titles; children's books; original TV dramas and contributions to series (including *Ballykissangel*, the BBC's smash hit series set in Ireland); radio soap opera, features, documentaries, and plays; screenplays; a couple of opera libretti; and interactive multimedia. But—given that my childhood was spent largely behind sofas, reading stories—I suspect it was inevitable that, sooner or later, I'd come to write a series of books about books, with a protagonist who's a librarian.

I was born in Dublin, Ireland, studied English and Irish language and literature at university, and immigrated to London in my early twenties. I built a successful career there, as an actress and then as a writer: in fact, it was books that led me to the stage in the first place, the wonderful Blue Door Theatre series by the English children's author Pamela Brown. Back in the 1960s Dublin was famous for its musty, quirky secondhand bookshops beside the River Liffey. My father, who was a historian, was unable to pass the stalls that stood outside them without stopping and never came home without a book or two, for himself or one of the family. I still have the Nelson edition of *The Swish of the Curtain* that he bought me in 1963, with the price and the date penciled inside in his careful, elegant handwriting. It cost him ninepence, which I'm not sure he'd have spent so cheerfully if he'd known that his gift was going to make me an actress, not an academic. Still, I like to think he'd have been pleased to know that thirty years later, as a writer in London, I successfully pitched and dramatized the Blue Door Theatre series for BBC Radio.

To a certain extent, my Finfarran Peninsula series has a little of my own story in it. Though Hanna Casey's is a rural background, like me she grew up in Ireland and moved to London, where she married. In 1986, I met and married the English opera director Wilf Judd, then artistic director of the Garden Venture at London's Royal Opera House, Covent Garden. Unlike Hanna and her rat-fink husband, Malcolm, though, Wilf and I met as colleagues, and we continue to work together, sharing our love of literature, theatre, ecology, and design, and dividing our life and work between a flat in inner-city London and a stone house at the western end of Ireland's Dingle Peninsula.

In my memoir *The House on an Irish Hillside*, I write about our Irish home on this real peninsula which, while geographically similar, is culturally quite different from my fictional Finfarran. One of the defining differences is that our West Kerry home is in what is called a Gaeltacht—an area where Irish, not English, is the language of everyday life. *Gaeltacht*, pronounced "Gwale-tockt," comes from the word *Gaeilge*, which is often translated into English as "Gaelic." And "Gaelic," incidentally, is not a word ever used in Ireland for the Irish language!

I first visited the western end of the Dingle Peninsula at age seventeen, not just to further my Irish language studies but because of a growing fascination with folklore. I was seeking something I'd glimpsed in my childhood in Dublin, a city kid curled on my country granny's bed listening to stories. I'd begun to understand it as a student, ploughing through books and exams. And, on that first visit, I began to recognize something that, all my life, I'd taken for granted. The effect of thinking in two languages.

Since then, partly through writing *The Library at the Edge of the World*, I've come to realize more deeply that my earliest experience of storytelling came from my grandmother's Irish-language oral tradition; and that memories of that inheritance, married to my love of Ireland's English-language literary tradition, have shaped me as a writer.

When Wilf and I first decided to divide our life between two ▶

countries, we weren't escaping from an English city to a rural Irish idyll. Life can be stressful anywhere in the world, and human nature is universal. So, for us, living in two places isn't about running from one and escaping to the other. It's about heightening our awareness and appreciation of both.

There's a story about the legendary Irish hero Fionn Mac Cumhaill and his warriors hunting the hills of Ireland. They chase the deer from dawn to dusk and then gather to eat, drink, and make music. As they sit by the fire, between tunes and talk, Fionn puts a question to his companions: "What is the best music in the world?" One man says it's the cry of the cuckoo. Another says it's the ring of a spear on a shield. Someone suggests the baying of a pack of deerhounds, or the laughter of a willing girl. "Nothing wrong with any of them," says Fionn, "but there's better music." So they ask him what it is and he gives them his answer. "The best music in the world," he says, "is the music of what happens."

Each time life and work take me from Ireland to London and back again, there's a brief window—maybe just on the journey from the airport—when everything I see and hear becomes heightened. For an author, that's gold dust. Focus sharpens, bringing with it a new sense of what it is to be alive. As my brain shifts from one language to another, I discover new word patterns, and reappraise those that are familiar. The contrasting rhythms of the two places provide endless entrance points for creativity; and, for me, the universality of human experience, seen against different backgrounds, has always been the music of what happens.

The Story Behind *The Heart of Summer*

WHEN AN AUTHOR imagines a new novel, a strange alchemy sometimes takes place. Whether an idea suddenly occurs or has been germinating for ages, there's a moment when it seems to take off on its own. Links between themes and characters' plotlines effortlessly present themselves and, though months of work lie ahead, you know you're on the right track. This is one reason I always advise students not to treat writing as a challenge. Forcing yourself to keep going just for the sake of it won't always work, and experience has taught me that, in my case, it never does. I can't flog a story into being. I have to allow it to reveal itself.

The Finfarran novels all share a setting—the fictional Finfarran Peninsula on Ireland's west coast—and the stories they tell are about the people who live there. Each is written to be read as a standalone novel, but all are linked thematically by my initial decision to make my central protagonist, Hanna Casey, a librarian. Once that decision was made, I began to think about the books that might be in Hanna's little local library. Sometimes they simply set a scene and provide a backdrop for my stories. Some are setups for jokes: for example, there's a running gag, much loved by librarians, in *The Library at the Edge of the World* about a reader who's systematically working through the shelves in search of a specific book that has a black dog on the cover. Another of those is the moment when a belligerent alpha male demanding Robert Galbraith's *Career of Evil* is outraged to discover that it was written ▶

not only by a woman but by J. K. Rowling. Other books in Hanna's library are chosen as a central driver in a Finfarran plot, as when, in *The Month of Borrowed Dreams*, Hanna sets up a readers' group to discuss books based on films, and my characters' storylines emerge through their varied reactions to Colm Tóibín's *Brooklyn*.

And, usually, each Finfarran novel plays games with a specific book genre, entertaining to me and to bookwormy readers, but not vital to the enjoyment of the story. In *The Transatlantic Book Club*, for example, characters on opposite sides of the Atlantic discuss Golden Age detective novels while old enmities, hidden love affairs, and a case of blackmail come to light on both sides of the ocean. *Summer at the Garden Café* uses the time-honoured device of a confessional diary. And in *The Mistletoe Matchmaker*, set at Christmastime, the plot's central strand turns on memories of a character's childhood copy of Patricia Lynch's children's classic, *The Turf-Cutter's Donkey*.

So Lissbeg Library tends to be central to the Finfarran novels. But when *The Heart of Summer* came into my mind, it presented itself as a book which would take Hanna off on vacation to London, where she once shared an apartment with friends she hasn't seen since her student days. It also arrived in the person of Amy, who walked into my mind fully formed, along with the line she speaks at the end of the book's first chapter. "So, Hanna Casey, this is where you've been hiding yourself all these years!" I didn't set out to write a book about a character who'd been hiding herself away, but, as soon as that line occurred to me, I knew it would take me somewhere interesting. Amy, of course, sees Hanna from her own point of view, and has her own reasons for it, so there was a whole story to explore there too. And, by removing Hanna from her day-to-day setting and bringing her back to a city where she'd faced one of her life's major crossroads, I had the perfect scenario in which to confront her with another life-changing decision.

Meanwhile, back home in Finfarran, there was a whole cast of characters getting on with their lives whose storylines I could weave into a background for Hanna's story, and her partner Brian's. And, by separating these two people who've found new love together after turbulent past relationships, I could place that new relationship in jeopardy and explore Hanna and Brian in isolation from each other.

And, of course, as in all Finfarran novels, there was Fury O'Shea. He's another character who simply presented himself and has developed in directions I never imagined or intended when he first appeared in *The Library at the Edge of the World*. It interests me that, like Amy in *The Heart of Summer*, he arrived speaking a single line that came to dictate the entire direction of the book. And, like Amy, he shakes up Hanna's life while, ultimately, changing it for the better.

Fury and Amy share a kind of arrogance but, as characters, that's where their similarity ends. I'm never sure quite how to describe Fury, but I think he represents the kind of alchemy I'm talking about here. If there's a spark that draws creativity to the surface, Fury embodies that spark. He's the character in the Finfarran books who brings everything into alignment, bides his time until the right moment for action, and recognises that moment when it comes. All my life, I've read and studied folklore, and I grew up listening to folktales. It wasn't until I'd written *The Library at the Edge of the World* that I realised that Fury is a modern version of the Green Man in English folklore, and the Gobán Saor in Irish storytelling. Both those characters emerged from older stories about gods who were smiths and craftsmen spirits of green places, and represent the Earth and what it produces. They're images of the links between communities and the places where their ancestors settled. So, since the peninsula with its towering mountains, deep forest, and high cliffs above the rolling Atlantic is central to all the Finfarran novels, I suppose it's not surprising that Fury presented himself to me.

As I write this, there's another Finfarran novel waiting for its moment to emerge into the light. I won't rush it because I know I don't need to. I just have to wait for the alchemy to occur. ∽

Have You Read?
More by Felicity Hayes-McCoy

THE HOUSE ON AN IRISH HILLSIDE
by Felicity Hayes-McCoy

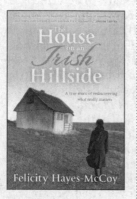

"From the moment I crossed the mountain I fell in love. With the place, which was more beautiful than any place I'd ever seen. With the people I met there. And with a way of looking at life that was deeper, richer and wiser than any I'd known before. When I left I dreamt of clouds on the mountain. I kept going back."

We all lead very busy lives and sometimes it's hard to find the time to be the people we want to be. Twelve years ago Felicity Hayes-McCoy left the hectic pace of the city and returned to Ireland to make a new life in a remarkable house on the stunning Dingle Peninsula. Having chosen to live in a community that, previously, she'd only known as a visitor, she finds herself reengaging with values and experiences and reevaluating a sense of identity that she'd thought she'd left behind.

Beautifully written, this is a life-affirming tale of "a house of music and memory," and of being reminded of the things that really matter.

"Hayes-McCoy is a lovely writer, far superior to the average memoirist. . . . She has a style that's poetic but not showy; finely honed but easy and unforced; descriptive and evocative without seeming to try too hard."

—*The Irish Independent*

"Wise, funny, and blazingly beautiful."
—Joanna Lumley, actor, author, and
television presenter

ENOUGH IS PLENTY
by Felicity Hayes-McCoy

An immigrant to England in the 1970s,
Felicity Hayes-McCoy knew she'd return
to Corca Dhuibhne, Ireland's Dingle
Peninsula, a place she'd fallen in love with
at seventeen. Now she and her English
husband have restored a stone house there,
the focus for this chronicle in response to
reader requests for an illustrated sequel to
her memoir *The House on an Irish Hillside*.

ENOUGH IS PLENTY
THE YEAR ON THE DINGLE PENINSULA

Felicity Hayes-McCoy

The Celts celebrated the cycle of the
seasons as a vibrant expression of eternity,
endlessly turning from darkness to light
and back again. *Enough Is Plenty*, a book
about the ordinary small pleasures in life
that can easily go unnoticed, celebrates
these seasonal rhythms and offers the
reader recipes from the author's kitchen
and information on organic food
production and gardening. It views the
year from a place where a vibrant twenty-
first-century lifestyle is still marked by
Ireland's Celtic past and the ancient
rhythms of Samhain (winter), Imbolc
(spring), Bealtaine (summer), and
Lughnasa (autumn). In this way of life,
health and happiness are rooted in
awareness of nature and the environment,
and nourishment comes from music,
friendship, and storytelling as well as from
good food.

"Magical."
—Alice Taylor, bestselling author of
To School Through the Fields ▶

"A gorgeous book."

—Sunday Independent

**A WOVEN SILENCE: MEMORY, HISTORY &
REMEMBRANCE
by Felicity Hayes-McCoy**

How do we know that what we remember
is the truth? Inspired by the story of
her relative Marion Stokes, one of three
women who raised the tricolor over
Enniscorthy in Easter Week 1916, Felicity
Hayes-McCoy explores the consequences
for all of us when memories are
manipulated or obliterated, intentionally
or by chance. In the power struggle after
Ireland's Easter Rising, involving, among
others, Michael Collins and Eamon
de Valera, the ideals for which Marion and
her companions fought were eroded. As
Felicity maps her own family stories onto
the history of the state, her story moves
from Washerwoman's Hill in Dublin, to
London, and back again; spans two world
wars, a revolution, a civil war, and the
development of a republic; and culminates
in Ireland's 2015 same-sex marriage
referendum.

"A powerful piece of personal and political
history."

—The Sunday Times (Ireland)

"Questions are explored delicately and
deftly."   *—Irish Examiner*

"Writing of high order."
                —Frank McGuinness, author, poet,
                              and playwright

DINGLE AND ITS HINTERLAND: PEOPLE, PLACES AND HERITAGE
by Felicity Hayes-McCoy

The tip of the Dingle Peninsula, at the westernmost edge of Europe, is one of Ireland's most isolated regions. But for millennia, it has also been a hub for foreign visitors: its position made it a medieval center for traders, and the wildness of its remote landscape has been the setting for spiritual pilgrimage. This seeming paradox is what makes Dingle and its western hinterland unique: the ancient, native culture has been preserved, while also being influenced by the world at large. The rich heritage of the area is best understood by chatting with the people who live and work here. But how many visitors get that opportunity?

Working with her husband, Wilf Judd, Felicity Hayes-McCoy takes us on an insiders' tour, illustrated by their own photographs, and interviews locals along the way, ranging from farmers, postmasters, and boatmen to museum curators, radio presenters, and *sean-nós* singers. A resident for the last twenty years, she offers practical information and advice as well as cultural insights that will give any visitor a deeper understanding of this special place.

"For those of us who have long been under the spell of the Dingle Peninsula, and for those who have yet to discover it, this book is a brilliant guide to the land, the culture, the history, and especially its people."
  —Boris Weintraub, former senior writer, *National Geographic* ▶

THE LIBRARY AT THE EDGE OF THE WORLD
by Felicity Hayes-McCoy

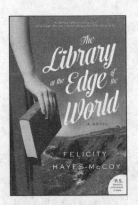

As she drives her mobile library van between little villages on Ireland's west coast, Hanna Casey tries not to think about a lot of things. Like the sophisticated lifestyle she abandoned after finding her English barrister husband in bed with another woman. Or that she's back in Lissbeg, the rural Irish town she walked away from in her teens, living in the back bedroom of her overbearing mother's retirement bungalow. Or, worse yet, her nagging fear that, as the local librarian and a prominent figure in the community, her failed marriage and ignominious return have made her a focus of gossip.

With her teenage daughter, Jazz, off traveling the world and her relationship with her own mother growing increasingly tense, Hanna is determined to reclaim her independence by restoring a derelict cottage left to her by her great-aunt. But when the threatened closure of the Lissbeg Library puts her personal plans in jeopardy, Hanna finds herself leading a battle to restore the heart and soul of the Finfarran Peninsula's fragmented community. And she's about to discover that the neighbours she'd always kept at a distance have come to mean more to her than she ever could have imagined.

Told with heart, wry wit, and charm, *The Library at the Edge of the World* is an empowering story about the meaning of home and the importance of finding a place where you truly belong.

"A delicious feast of a novel. Sink in and feel enveloped by the beautiful world of Felicity Hayes-McCoy."
—Cathy Kelly, bestselling author of *Between Sisters* and *Secrets of a Happy Marriage*

"A charming and heartwarming story."
—Jenny Colgan, *New York Times* bestselling author of *The Café by the Sea*

"Engaging . . . sparkling and joyous."
—*Sunday Times* (UK)

"Much like a cup of tea and a cozy afghan, *The Library at the Edge of the World* is the perfect book to hunker down with. Prepare to be transported."
—LibraryReads

SUMMER AT THE GARDEN CAFÉ
by Felicity Hayes-McCoy

The Garden Café, next to Lissbeg Library, is a place where plans are formed and secrets shared, and where, even in high tourist season, people are never too busy to stop for a sandwich and a cup of tea.

But twenty-one-year-old Jazz—daughter of the town's librarian Hanna Casey—has a secret she can't share. Still recovering from a car accident and reeling from her father's disclosures about his longtime affair, she's taken a job at The Old Forge Guesthouse and begun to develop feelings for a man who's strictly off-limits. Meanwhile, involved in her own new affair with architect Brian Morton, Hanna is unaware of the turmoil in Jazz's life—until her manipulative ex-husband, Malcolm, reappears trying to mend his relationship ▸

with their daughter. Rebuffed at every turn, Malcolm must return to London, but his mother, Louisa, is on the case.

Unbeknown to the rest of the family, she hatches a plan, finding an unlikely ally in Hanna's mother, the opinionated Mary Casey.

Watching Jazz unravel, Hanna begins to wonder if secrets that Malcolm has forced her to keep may have harmed their beloved daughter more than she'd realized. But then, the Casey women are no strangers to secrets, something Hanna realizes when she discovers a journal, long buried in land she inherited from her great-aunt Maggie. Ultimately, it's the painful lessons of the past that offer a way to the future, but it will take the shared experiences of four generations of women to find a way forward for Hanna and her family.

"Felicity Hayes-McCoy's latest novel is a triumph. This is clear-eyed storytelling in a romantic setting, but it's doing far more than weaving a beguiling tale. . . . This book and this journey spill across generations and the result is a deeper meditation on what divides us and what restores us to ourselves and each other."
—*Irish Central*

"The landscape and the cadence of the villagers' language leap off the page. Fans of Debbie Macomber's Blossom series will enjoy this trip to Ireland."
—*Booklist*

THE MISTLETOE MATCHMAKER
by Felicity Hayes-McCoy

The days are turning colder, preparations are under way for the Winter Fest, and everyone is hoping for a little holiday magic on the Finfarran Peninsula. And as Cassie Fitzgerald, fresh from Toronto, is about to discover, there's more to the holidays on the west coast of Ireland than mistletoe and mince pies.

Enchanted by the small town where her dad was born, Cassie makes friends and joins local librarian Hanna Casey's writing group in Lissbeg Library. But the more she's drawn into the festivities leading up to her first Irish Christmas, the more questions she wants to ask.

Why does her sweet-tempered grandmother Pat find it so hard to express her feelings? What's going on between Pat and her miserly husband, Ger? What happened in the past between the Fitzgeralds and Hanna's redoubtable mother, Mary Casey? And what about Shay: handsome, funny, smart, and intent on making Cassie's stay as exciting as he can. Could he be the one for her?

As Christmas Eve approaches, it's Cassie, the outsider, who reminds Lissbeg's locals that love, family, and friendship bring true magic to the season. But will her own fractured family rediscover the joys of coming home?

"The perfect winter heart-warmer."
—Cathy Kelly, bestselling author of *Between Sisters* and *Secrets of a Happy Marriage* ▶

Have You Read *(continued)*

"A delightful read filled with wintry days, cups of tea, and more than a few tidings of comfort and joy, the pages of *The Mistletoe Matchmaker* weave together the lives and secrets of a family—separated by years and distance, but with deep Irish roots, and leaves the reader longing to spend Christmas in Ireland."
     —Nan Rossiter, bestselling author of
More Than You Know

"Engaging . . . full of humour . . . plenty of lively characters to add spice to this charming story."
     —*Books Ireland*

THE TRANSATLANTIC BOOK CLUB
by Felicity Hayes-McCoy

The beloved author of *The Mistletoe Matchmaker* returns with an enchanting new novel, perfect for fans of Jenny Colgan, Nina George, and Nancy Thayer, about residents of Ireland's Finfarran Peninsula who set up a Skype book club with the little US town of Resolve, where generations of Finfarran's emigrants have settled.

Eager to cheer up her recently widowed gran, Cassie Fitzgerald, visiting from Canada, persuades Lissbeg Library to set up a Skype book club, linking readers on Ireland's Finfarran Peninsula with the US town of Resolve, home to generations of Finfarran emigrants.

But when the club decides to read a detective novel, old conflicts on both sides of the ocean are exposed and hidden love affairs come to light. As secrets emerge, Cassie fears she may have done more harm than good. Will the truths she uncovers about her granny Pat's marriage affect her own hopes of finding love? Is Pat, who's still struggling with the death of her husband, about to fall out with her oldest friend, Mary? Or could the book club itself hold the key to a triumphant transatlantic happy ending?

The Transatlantic Book Club continues the stories of the residents of the Finfarran Peninsula and introduces readers to new characters whom they will surely fall in love with.

THE MONTH OF BORROWED DREAMS
by Felicity Hayes-McCoy

On the Finfarran Peninsula on Ireland's west coast, the blue skies and warmer days of summer are almost here. At the Lissbeg Library, Hanna Casey has big plans for the long days ahead. Beginning with the film adaptation of *Brooklyn*, she's starting a cinema club, showing movies based on popular novels her friends and neighbours love. But the drama that soon unfolds in this close-knit seaside village rivals any on the screen.

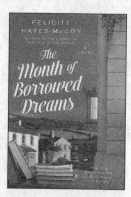

Just when Lissbeg begins to feel like home, an unexpected twist leaves Hanna's daughter, Jazz, reeling and may send her back to London. Aideen worries that her relationship with Conor won't survive the pressures of their planned double wedding with overbearing Eileen and manipulative Joe. Saira Khan throws herself into helping a troubled new arrival to Finfarran. Hanna enjoys getting closer to Brian until her ex-husband, Malcolm, returns, threatening her newfound contentment.

As the club prepares for the first meeting ▶

Have You Read *(continued)*

of the summer, they'll all face difficult choices. But will they get the happy endings they deserve?

"A sparkling, life-affirming novel— sunshine on the page."   —Cathy Kelly

"Heartwarming."
                              —*Irish Independent* ∾

Discover great authors, exclusive offers, and more at hc.com.